A magical miles out in space…

It's supposed to be the happiest place that's not on Earth…

But fifteen-year-old Ronn Evans and his cousins are about to discover that things are not what they seem when they are all but kidnapped by their own government and sent to a mysterious asteroid to find out what has gone terribly wrong because they are the only ones who can get inside.

It's the year 2037 and their eccentric uncle has built his own private land of tomorrow on what is now Earth's second moon. Or is it more like Yesterdayland, where all the time displays stopped nearly forty years ago? It's a small world after all, with surprises waiting at every turn.

Something bad is happening behind the scenes— it may be a long way from the Caribbean, but there are pirates even in space! If Ronn and his cousins want to get back to Earth before disaster strikes, it will take more than wishing on a star, and there isn't a fairy godmother in sight…

A Moon of Their Own

Dwight R. Decker

*V*esper Press

Northlake, Illinois

Vesper Press

Northlake, Illinois

Dedication

For Danielle, Alan, Mark, Ben, and Morgan, who will never have
what the hero of this story has.
A rich uncle.

Contents

Part One

Family Emergency

Chapter One

"**R**onn Evans! Would you *please* pay attention?"

Ronn jerked back in his seat as his English teacher's head emerged from the top of his desk. A gray-haired, middle-aged woman, glowering sternly — the stuff of a high-school sophomore's nightmares.

He knew it was a 3-D image projection and Ms. Crowley was actually at her own desk at the front of the classroom, but the larger-than-life reproduction of her face glaring at him was all too horribly realistic.

His best friend Travis snickered from where he sat at the station next to him.

"I heard that, Travis!" Ms. Crowley exclaimed, though the narrowed eyes of her projection were still seemingly trained on Ronn. "You should pay attention, too!"

As the rest of the class laughed a little nervously, knowing Ms. Crowley might pop out of anybody's desktop next, her head disappeared in a flickering of color, leaving just the virtual page of text on Ronn's display floating in mid-air in front of him.

It was an afternoon like any other, with Ms. Crowley sitting as usual at a control console at the front of the room and trying to convince Ronn and the rest of the class that a poem written in the 19th Century still had something to say in the year 2037. Outside, the springtime weather was warm and clear, and it was hard not to glance out the windows that overlooked the school's front lawn.

Ronn felt a sting of injustice. Looking around, he could see that the fifteen other kids in the room with him were also finding it hard to concentrate on their desk displays and Ms. Crowley's sleep-inducing commentary. So why pick on him? She could have called him privately, her voice audible only inside his own ear canal, and no one would have known

2

she was giving him any heat. But no, she had to do it publicly to make an example out of him...

Up front, Ms. Crowley seemed to be listening to something only she could hear. Then she looked up and out towards the class, focusing on one student in particular. Him.

"Ronn, I just got a call from Dr. Schrader," she said sternly. "You're to report to her office at once."

Everyone in the room turned to stare at him.

Now what? Ronn thought helplessly. Being called out of the middle of class to go see the principal was never good.

In his ear, he heard Ms. Crowley add, "Take your pad. Dr. Schrader didn't tell me what this is about but you probably won't be coming back to class today."

She sounded almost sympathetic, as opposed to her public persona when she told Ronn out loud to go to the office so the rest of the class would know that he had a good reason for suddenly getting up and leaving.

"What did you *do*?" Travis asked in a low voice, sounding impressed that his buddy might have been enterprising enough for once to get into some spectacular trouble.

Ronn was completely at a loss. He had no idea what he even *could* have done. Almost in a daze, he waved off the floating display, grabbed his bookpad, stood up from his desk while ignoring Travis's whispered promise to vid him if the juvenile detention facility allowed him to receive messages, and left the room feeling the stares of fifteen silent classmates on his back.

He walked down the long hall to the school office frantically going over in his mind what this could be about or why anyone in authority would want to see him. As far as he knew, the list of his possible crimes was a short one.

For that matter, he had little to show for his fifteen years on Earth. His grades in school were undistinguished, nor was he anyone who would have attracted attention for his dashing good looks. He was slim, about average height, his brown hair cut short the way most boys these days wore it, and in good enough shape to have played casual sports reasonably well in gym class even if without much enthusiasm or evident talent. He liked to think he wasn't bad looking above the neck, but he hadn't noticed the girls he knew looking adoringly at him when he walked by. While some of the girls counted as at least casual friends, and he'd had his share of crushes, nothing much was happening in the romance department, either.

He was just one more kid in the halls, somebody no one would have looked at twice. Just a kid named Ronn. Actually he was Aaron Nelson Evans, but there had been three other Aarons in his kindergarten class and the nickname had resulted from a desperate teacher referring to him as Ron N. in order to keep them straight.

When he came into the office, the principal was waiting with a middle-aged man in a gray suit and a younger man and woman who had the look of bodyguards in black suits with dark visors over their eyes. Dr. Schrader paced the room looking very displeased. She was also somewhere deep into middle age but had opted for a perpetual thirty-five look in a makeover a few years back.

The entourage stood stolidly by and the man in the gray suit had taken a visitor's chair to wait in comfort. Around Dr. Schrader's desk and control panel floated several projected views of classrooms and the school grounds.

"Er... you wanted to see me?" Ronn asked the principal.

"Actually, Ronn," Dr. Schrader said, "this gentleman did."

The man in the chair was in his fifties and actually looked it. With short gray hair that had receded well up from his forehead and a touch of overweight, he gave the impression of a busy man who had too many important things to do to waste time bothering with even minor and easily corrected signs of aging. A bud in his right ear with a small external antenna, a thin mesh of fine wires over his bare temple, and a data-displaying mini-opticom over his eye were more evidence that he moved in the upper realms and was connected with the great and powerful.

"So you're Aaron AKA Ronn Evans?" The man held a writepad out to him. "Put your thumb on this."

More puzzled than ever, Ronn did.

"All right," the man said, glancing at the pad, then stood up from the chair. "You seem to match what we have on file, so we'll assume it's you. My name is Cosgrove. I'm with the National Security Office and I came to pick you up. Do you need anything from your locker? We're leaving immediately and you won't be coming back for a few days."

"Leaving?" Ronn echoed, now just plain astonished that the NSO was involved — and had an interest in *him*. "For where? Can't I go home and talk to Mom about this first?"

"Believe me," Mr. Cosgrove said, "she knows."

"Wait a moment!" Dr. Schrader interrupted. "I don't like having to do this. You could have at least waited until after school so his parents could decide what to do."

"We're on a tight schedule," said Mr. Cosgrove impatiently. "Waiting is not an option. You might say it's a family emergency, which in a way it is."

Family emergency? Ronn thought in alarm. *Is something wrong at home?*

Before he could ask about it, Dr. Schrader protested. "This whole thing is extremely irregular! How do I know you're really who you say you—"

The principal broke off and touched the bud in her ear. She listened for a few moments, turned a little pale, and muttered a weak "Uh huh. Right. I understand."

She slowly lowered her hand, looking stunned. "That was the school superintendent, my boss. You wouldn't believe who *he* just got a call from. All right, Ronn can go with you. But I want you to sign for him."

"Fine," Mr. Cosgrove said almost through gritted teeth, tracing something with his finger on the writepad the principal held out to him and thumbing it. "Anything to get this show on the road."

Mr. Cosgrove and his companions then hustled Ronn outside, barely giving him enough time on the way to grab his jacket from his locker and stow his bookpad. He was then urged into to a waiting car, probably a rental. It was manually driven by another bodyguard-type in a black suit and shades. Looking out the window and watching the houses and trees in new spring leaf slip past as they drove through Maple Heights, Ronn wondered worriedly what his family had to do with all this and who might be hurt or sick. Mr. Cosgrove waved off his questions with something about it all being explained later.

For the rest of the ride, Mr. Cosgrove was on his com taking care of business, whatever his business as some sort of high-level government official happened to be. Ronn gathered from the one-sided muttering he overheard that Mr. Cosgrove had come out from Washington headed for somewhere else, and had made a slight detour to pick him up.

Somebody considered me important enough to go out of his way to come and get me?

A few minutes later, the car pulled up in the parking lot at the small airport outside of town, barely more than a hangar and a single runway. Ronn was then transferred at a run to a waiting commuter jet with Air Force insignia. At the top of the steps and just inside the door, a stern-looking woman in a blue uniform and a red beret was waiting for him with a small plastic bag.

"Your com, please," she said curtly.

Too intimidated by her aura of authority to object or even ask why, he took his wristcom off and the phonebud out of his ear, and handed them to her. He wondered what they would have done if he'd had an implant. Ripped it out of his head? She put the comgear in the bag, then gave him a small slip of paper.

"Your receipt. When this is over, you can apply to the address on the paper to have your com returned or else submit a request to have the government reimburse you for a new one."

5

"But I can't just replace it!" Ronn protested. "I've got a lot of music and stuff on it and…" Like that recording of the time when he and Travis had compared and contrasted the relative merits and drawbacks of each and every girl in their class. At length. In detail. Let *that* get out and Ronn would have to explain to his parents why they needed to change their names and move to another state.

Showing no sympathy whatsoever, the woman had already turned away, taking the bag with his com with her, and he wondered if he would ever see it again. He suddenly felt very cut off from the world.

Followed by the ever-impatient Mr. Cosgrove, the bodyguards, and some security personnel wearing blue uniforms and red berets, Ronn came into the mostly empty cabin. Though it was a military aircraft, the interior was standard civilian design, with an aisle down the middle between rows of two seats on each side. With a start, he recognized the woman sitting by a window in one of the seats at the rear.

"Mom?" he blurted, starting down the aisle towards her.

She glanced up and saw him, and smiled bleakly as he approached. "They told me they had gone to get you," she said. "It doesn't look like either of us will be eating dinner at home tonight."

Mrs. Evans was just past forty, her long dark hair tied loosely behind her head, and still wearing her casual work-at-home clothes. Despite her attempt at a smile, she did not look happy, and Ronn could guess that she had been sitting at her display console and engrossed in her current project, no doubt thinking she had a couple of hours to work in peace without having to deal directly with demanding clients, when she was abruptly yanked away without even a chance to change.

He sat down next to her and fastened his seat belt. "What's going on? Why are you here? Where are they taking us? And where's Dad? Did they get him, too?"

"He's fine," she assured him as soon as he paused for breath. "He wasn't the one they wanted. I called him at the office when they showed up at the door, and he came home right away to look after the twins while I'm gone. I was right in the middle of a job, too, so I hope he can take over where I had to leave off."

"But what the heck's this all about?"

She sighed. "Well, you knew I have a brother we never talked much about."

"Sure," Ronn said tentatively, not certain where this was going. Of course he knew he had a somewhat mysterious uncle. You couldn't grow up in a family and not overhear things now and then, but he had never gotten the whole story. Some argument with Grandpa many years before, and his uncle had stormed out, never to be heard from again, or something like that. He wasn't even sure of his uncle's name. His mother and aunts had called him Skip or Skippy the few times he had heard them mention him, but that was obviously just a family nickname. Ronn had a feeling that if his family called *him* Skippy, he might storm out, too.

"It's something we never told you," his mother went on, sounding reluctant even to be talking about this. "We thought you'd be better off not knowing, so you could grow up like a normal boy, and not think you didn't have to work because you might get a big inheritance some-day."

Inheritance? Not have to work? *Now* Ronn's interest was piqued. "Yeah...?"

"You'd find out soon enough, we thought," Mrs. Evans said, her voice turning a little sad. "But now... We can't hide it any longer. Your uncle is Jefferson C. Prescott."

Just the name was enough to short-circuit Ronn's brain for a moment. *The richest man in the world! A man so rich he owns his own little moon!*

Since she used it professionally, he had known his mother's birth name was Prescott, but it was a common name and he had never made the connection.

Before he could recover from the shock, Mr. Cosgrove came up to them. "Mrs. Evans, could I speak with you up front?" As she started unbuckling her seat belt, he added to Ronn, "You can sit back and relax. It'll be about three hours."

With a flight of that length from Illinois, Ronn guessed they were going to the West Coast. That did mean he'd be gone for a while. "But you didn't give me a chance to pack!" he exclaimed. "I don't have any clothes or a toothbrush or—"

"Don't worry about it," Mr. Cosgrove interrupted irritably. "You'll be provided with whatever you need when we get there. Now enjoy the trip!"

"We'll talk about this later," his mother promised as she stood up.

Ronn unbuckled and stood up from his seat to let his mother step out into the aisle, then took over the window seat while she went forward to sit with Mr. Cosgrove. That left him to puzzle things out on his own. It was just as well. He needed some time just to absorb the one bit of information he had been given.

As the jet took off, he looked out the window, watching the green fields and treetops fall away below and catching a glimpse of the distant skyline of Chicago to the northeast. Once the jet had leveled off in a westerly direction, he had nothing else to do for the rest of the trip but stare out at blue sky and fluffy white clouds. That and try to think things through.

It wasn't just being the nephew of the richest man in the world. Jefferson C. Prescott was also the most reclusive, perhaps even the most eccentric, billionaire in the world. Ronn didn't know any more about him than what few sensational stories had occasionally filtered through the news and happened to catch his attention, and what he'd picked up in casual reading about the entertainment industry. Since he had never had any reason to care, he had never given Jefferson C. Prescott a whole lot of thought.

What he recalled was that Prescott had come out of nowhere as a young man, making a vast fortune in the media and entertainment business with a revolutionary method of projecting 3-D images in the air without a screen or other medium, and had then proceeded to revolutionize any number of other, unrelated fields with advanced technology that was almost *too* advanced for its time. The barely more than half-believed story was that he had gotten the advanced tech in some sort of trade deal with actual aliens from outer space, and a lot of people thought at first that it was too ridiculous to take seriously. But he did have patents for some extremely advanced inventions that didn't seem to have inventors, and there was that asteroid nobody else could get to.

The more immediately interesting thing that Ronn recalled was that while Prescott had been married several times, no children had resulted. If Prescott was his uncle...

Maybe he died, he suddenly thought. *Maybe that explains all this spyvid stuff.*

If Uncle Jeff had no direct descendants, that might mean his money would be divided among his next of kin. Which, as far as Ronn could figure it, included himself, his younger brother and sister, his mother, two aunts, and some cousins. While life could be about to get a lot more complicated, coming into a few billion dollars he hadn't expected didn't seem to have any down sides he could think of right away. Then he felt a little guilty for trying to calculate the advantage he'd get from the death of his own uncle, but since he hadn't known Jefferson C. Prescott even was his uncle for more than a few minutes, and hadn't known the man at all except as a distant figure occasionally mentioned on the news, it was hard to summon up much genuine grief over his possible passing.

But why would the military be involved, practically kidnapping him and his mother? If there was a question of inheritance, shouldn't it be handled by management types in suits working for the TranStella Company instead of armed soldiers? Wouldn't he simply be invited to a dignified reading of the will in some lawyer's office instead of yanked out of school and flown off somewhere on an Air Force jet?

As he thought about it, he remembered something else. When he was about five, his mother had taken him on a long airplane ride for a mysterious doctor's appointment in a hospital in some city far away, probably Los

Angeles. Some place with palm trees, anyway. All that anyone had told him at the time was that he was having some "tests" done. That had puzzled him, since he wasn't sick, but no one had been inclined to explain why he had to go all the way across the country to be examined when there were lots of hospitals around home. His mother had seemed unhappy about the whole thing herself, as though it wasn't her idea and she was only grudgingly going along with something being forced on her. She had never said anything about it afterwards, either, other than just telling him that he'd understand when he was older.

Besides the various physical examinations like taking a blood sample, somebody shining something in his eyes, and some sort of whole-body scanning, Ronn also remembered a brief meeting with an older man in an office. Ronn had been less introduced and more presented as a specimen to the man, and his mother had exchanged only a few tense words with him. What exactly was said, Ronn had long forgotten. The lingering impression was that the man was extremely important, his mother knew him, and they didn't like each other.

There was one other thing he remembered. When it was all over and they were on their way out of the hospital, Ronn and his mother had encountered Aunt Thalia and her two children coming in. It was another strained meeting, as his mother had never gotten along very well with her older sister, either. Thinking about it now, he realized that it wasn't just him. His cousins must have been there for the same examination he had just been through.

Ronn had never known what to make of the incident, and since no one would tell him what it was all about, he had largely forgotten it as the years passed. Now, though... The nagging question of what important person his mother could possibly know had been answered. So he really had met Jefferson C. Prescott at one point in his life.

But what was the purpose of the medical examination? He could only guess that with a potential inheritance in the multibillion range, Uncle Jeff might have wanted to make sure Ronn really was a relative with DNA testing or something, and not some random kid his parents had adopted in order to make an additional claim on the estate. That way, when the time came to divide the loot, the information would be on file so Ronn wouldn't have any trouble proving who he really was. With billions at stake, even far-fetched schemes like somebody murdering him in order to take his place didn't seem entirely outside the realm of possibility. Since he wouldn't be the sole heir, the same would apply to his cousins.

There were other possibilities, of course. Maybe Uncle Jeff had some rare disease and wanted to see if anybody else in the family had it, too. Or he was looking to see who in the family might be a good organ donor in case he needed a new part, though now he could just grow one. But no matter how much he thought about it, Ronn couldn't come up with any explanations that seemed likely.

One thing was certain. His entire future had just changed.

Not that his future had been any too certain before this. Such talent as he had may have come by way of his father, who was an architect, or his mother, who remodeled houses. He had always done fairly well in his art classes, at least, and seemed to have a knack for playing with his parents' 3-D projection equipment after office hours and designing buildings. His father had been impressed, or so he usually said before proceeding to point out some flaw that would make everything fall down if it was ever actually built. Art was easy — it was structural engineering that would take years of study.

Ronn had even had some idea of making a career out of art, hopefully with somewhat more success than his Aunt Emily, who peddled her odd constructions at weekend craft fairs, but exactly what he would do, or what school he would attend to learn how to do it, not to mention whether anyone would even hire him to do it several years hence in a world in which unemployment was high and entry-level jobs scarce, were problems he hadn't solved yet.

But if his bank account was about to go into ten or even eleven digits, he might not have those problems after all. That happy thought soothed his worries about everything else as he settled into his seat and dozed.

It was early evening by Ronn's body clock when the plane started descending over a bleak and barren landscape, but still mid-afternoon on the West Coast. Out the window, he saw distant mountains and a vast dry and dusty lakebed below. After spending his life to date in the lush, green Midwest, seeing the brown desert was almost a shock.

Ronn realized from the parked aircraft he saw on the ground and the buildings like hangars and control towers that they were landing at a military base. Edwards AFB was his guess. He tried to remember what state it was in. Some old movie he'd seen had referred to it being in California, but that was before the split. So he was probably in Mojave now.

Even as the jet taxied to a stop, a van was waiting for them. As usual, Mr. Cosgrove said nothing about the whys and wherefores, and simply hustled him and his mother out of the plane and into the hot sunlight, and then into the frigid air-conditioned van. He took a seat in front by the driver while Ronn and his mother found seats in the back.

"Did he tell you anything more on the plane about what's going on?" Ronn asked as the van started off.

"Not as much as I'd like," Mrs. Evans replied, watching the desert scenery go by out the window and sounding as though her patience had long worn thin. "He just said they're taking us to a meeting where they'll explain everything, then spent most of the trip asking *me* questions about my brother and our family."

They came into what amounted to a small town within the base, with stores, a theater, housing tracts, and fast-food restaurants. The van stopped in front of a hotel called the High Desert Inn, and Ronn and his mother were taken inside to check in. They were assigned a two-bedroom suite, and some packages of sundries like toothbrushes and toothpaste had already been delivered by the time they came through the door.

Mr. Cosgrove told them they could freshen up after the trip if they felt they needed to, then glanced at the time display in his opticom. "Now I have to see to our other guests. There will be a briefing in an hour that will answer all your questions."

"Other guests?" Ronn asked as Mr. Cosgrove slipped out the door. "I wonder who they are?"

"I think I know," Mrs. Evans replied a little grimly, but didn't elaborate, too busy looking around the living room and the dining area with its attached kitchenette. "All the comforts of home. It's really a small apartment. I hope they aren't planning on keeping us here for a while." She opened the refrigerator door and found several days' worth of food inside. "This does *not* look good..."

An hour later, Mr. Cosgrove showed up with the van again, and they were driven to a small, two-story office building that seemed to be an administration center. Ronn's main impression was of the display out front with two half-scale fighter aircraft models rising on slanting support beams that were supposed to represent jet exhaust.

Mr. Cosgrove and a couple of bodyguards ushered Ronn and his mother inside the building, down a hallway, up some stairs, through a door with more uniformed guards standing on either side, and into — a desert oasis with palm trees under a bright sun in clear, cloudless blue sky? Even Mr. Cosgrove looked a little startled. Despite the sudden dazzling sunlight and arid landscape all around, the temperature was still that of an interior room inside an overly cooled building.

Suddenly, the scene broke up in a blizzard of pixelated color and a second later they were in the Arctic, with vast expanses of snow all around and an igloo nearby.

"How about this one?" asked a boy's voice that Ronn recognized at once. "Better?"

"Theo!" exclaimed an equally familiar woman's voice. "I told you not to mess with the wall settings! Now turn it off and come sit down!"

The scene dissolved again and this time the view reverted to mundane reality as a small, windowless conference room. Mr. Cosgrove exhaled impatiently and led Ronn and his mother on in, leaving the guards outside.

Already sitting at the large table that filled most of the room were two people Ronn knew, while a third, a barely teenage boy, was hastily taking a seat.

"Mom, we've been sitting in this broom closet practically forever!" the boy complained. "I just wanted to make it a little more interesting!"

Relatives. This was turning into a family reunion. Ronn noticed his mother stiffen as she saw who was there.

"Hello, Thalia," she said, her tone several degrees cooler than the already chilly room temperature.

"Hello, Jessie," Aunt Thalia replied in a tone that was even frostier. She was a little older than her sister and impeccably dressed. As far back as Ronn could remember, she usually was. It was as though she went through life expecting an invitation at any moment for a come as you are party and didn't want to be caught wearing anything too shabby. His mother had taken a different path, one that occasionally involved overalls and a hardhat, crowbars instead of couture, and had never shown any signs of regretting her choice, but Ronn did get the idea that Aunt Thalia had always had a way of needling her about it.

With his aunt were his cousins Phaedra and Theo. Phaedra was seventeen and aspired to an acting career, and was accordingly dressed at the outer limit of trendy fashion in a vest that flared at the shoulders and covered the back of her neck with a high collar. She was pretty enough but a little too heavily made up, as though she was trying to pass for older than she was. The sparkles in her lipstick and eye shadow were a bit overdone, Ronn thought. Her otherwise short blonde hair was twisted in a flowing forehead roll that probably took half an hour to shape and strung with a mesh of fine wires and tiny lighting elements that twinkled in faint yellows and oranges to bring out the golden highlights. No missing her in a dark room. Ronn was fairly certain that her hair had been light brown when he had last seen her a couple of years before. She also looked bored, clearly wishing she was somewhere else.

Since he had seldom seen the cousins over the years and barely knew them, he had to think for a moment to remember Theo's age. About fourteen, though he was short and wiry, and looked a year or two younger than the age he had to be.. At least he was taller than he had been at the last family gathering. Unlike his mother and sister, he wasn't dressed at the outermost utmost of style, and just wore casual boys' clothes, jeans and a plain shirt no different from what Ronn had on.

"Hey, Ronn!" Theo called. "I see they got you, too!"

"Please sit down," said Mr. Cosgrove. "We have a great deal to cover."

Following his mother's lead, Ronn sat on the other side of the table from Aunt Thalia and his cousins. While Phaedra and Theo at least acknowledged him with a nod and a crooked grin respectively, since he had gotten along well enough with them in the past even when their mothers were at odds, it was as though battle lines had been drawn down the middle of the table.

Conspicuous by her absence was a third sister, Ronn's Aunt Emily. He wondered if she would be coming soon. His mother got along very well with her. Aunt Emily's son, Ronn's cousin Danny, was about the same age he was and they had been friends and playmates at family reunions almost since they could crawl. If they showed up, it would be nice to see Danny again so he could have someone he could talk to as an equal in all this.

Mr. Cosgrove took the seat at the head of the table. "Now then, let's get started. We are facing a crisis and may not have much time."

"And this has something to do with... us?" Aunt Thalia asked.

"Indeed it does," Mr. Cosgrove replied. "You are all relatives of Jefferson C. Prescott."

"So what has that idiot gone and done now?" Aunt Thalia demanded.

"Disappeared, it would seem."

Aunt Thalia blinked in surprise. "Again?"

Chapter Two

Twenty-some years earlier

Lost in thought, a slim young man walked down a weed-grown, hill-side track that barely qualified as a dirt road, through a forest on a warm day at the height of summer. His clothes were old and worn and not the cleanest, and he had a growth of some days' worth of beard. He was a long way from the handsome businessman in a suit and tie giving PowerPoint presentations to potential backers in elegantly furnished boardrooms that he had been not very long before.

Jefferson C. Prescott's first business venture had been a spectacular failure.

He had taken up a commercial career under pressure from his father, but his heart was never in it. The rest of his family, like his sisters, had definite artistic leanings, and he had emerged from the same gene pool. Perhaps he had spent too much time in college involved in dramatic productions when he should have been studying for his business classes.

In the aftermath, he had rented a cabin in a remote stretch of forest in the Adirondacks beyond the reach of e-mail and telephones to get away from the stress as well as dodge some of the more persistent creditors, not to mention his father and a soon to be ex-wife, and think about what to do next.

Meanwhile, life went on, and he did have to pick up the slight amount of regular mail every now and then even if almost no one other than the discreet forwarding service knew where he was.

That was when some very strange kind of luck blew in his direction.

He came out of the woods where the dirt track met the paved main road, blinked in the sudden bright sunlight, and started to open the battered metal mailbox that stood on a rotting wooden post. Then something caught his eye, a large brownish lump lying in the ditch some distance away.

14

Jefferson first thought it was a deer, or perhaps a bear, if a rather thin one and the wrong color since the native bears were black. Road kill, no doubt, though any vehicle hitting an animal that large would have been damaged itself. Curious, and for the sake of prudence since it would be good to know if there were bears in the neighborhood, he walked over to it for a closer look.

It may have looked like a thin bear from a distance, but up close all the details were wrong. Instead of fur, the softly moaning creature was covered by a dense brown foam that gave it a fuzzy appearance, as though the ancestral scales had compromised somewhere between turning into hairs and tiny feathers. The body shape was roughly humanoid, and probably about six feet tall when it stood upright, with four limbs and a head sprouting from its body in the usual places. All four feet were well-developed hands rather than paws, but each hand had two opposable thumbs as well as three very long fingers. The head and face were even stranger, with enormous dark eyes and a long, sharp, beak that pointed downwards. Jefferson thought of something like the vastly enlarged head of a stork. No bear or bird, however, ever wore a leather-like harness and belt with attached pouches and various small metal tools.

It was not hard for Jefferson to draw the obvious conclusion. This was an intelligent being from somewhere very far away. The creature was also injured, probably struck a glancing blow by a passing car or truck. Out of compassion and simple decency, not even thinking of the money he could make from having a genuine alien in his possession, he carried it back to his cabin. The being was surprisingly light and only semi-conscious, and too weak or dazed to resist.

The alien would have died if Jefferson hadn't tended to its injuries. The friendship that developed over the following days and weeks was genuine as Jefferson helped it recover and they learned each other's languages, but mutual advantage was involved as well.

When they could communicate, the alien told Jefferson his story. He was Prince Skhyylar-ta-Demeskra-ki-Wakhuno, or without the royal title that went on for several more syllables that only a crow could have pronounced correctly, just Skhyylar. His folk, called the Hhakilyaa, had the custom of setting the crown prince down on a random planet without any supplies or support, and letting him fend for himself for about a year. Knowing nothing about the planet in advance, he would have to figure out everything for himself on the fly: what was good to eat, how to get it, how not to attract the attention of hostile natives if any, and so on. If he survived, he was judged worthy to rule. If he didn't survive, there were plenty of other candidates in line right behind him.

In his case, he had been hit by a native vehicle while trying to cross a road within an hour or two of being dropped off on Earth, and badly injured. The driver simply drove on without slowing down, perhaps not even realizing he had hit something. Fortunately, Jefferson had come along a little later, or one of Skhyylar's slightly younger relations would have been up for consideration instead.

The royal candidate was expected to rough it in a howling wilderness and somehow overcome endless dangers he knew nothing about. Going into partnership with a native who would provide food, shelter, and information was unprecedented, but not against the rules, either. As these things went, the prince had an easy time of it for the rest of his stay.

What Jefferson got was the gratitude and friendship of an important member of a technologically advanced alien race. At the end of his allotted time on Earth, Prince Skhyylar went back to his home world far across the Galaxy to resume his participation in court affairs there as a certified worthy aspirant to the throne (or Highmost Nest, to be exact). For his part, Jefferson was appointed the aliens' resident agent for Earth, just then at the far fringe of their expanding area of exploration. His main task was to supply information useful to their scientists, saving them years of field-work. Since the aliens preferred to avoid potentially hostile confrontations with the primitive inhabitants of uncivilized worlds, he also provided cover for their landing parties when they wanted to do on-site research. In return, he was given trade goods that were cheap trinkets for them and technological marvels for us, and they became the basis of his fortune.

Although the senior Mr. Prescott didn't live to see it and died thinking his son was a complete and utter failure, perhaps the old man had sensed a hidden talent in him after all. Perhaps Jefferson really did have a knack for business, and it just took something he genuinely cared about to bring it out. He started a new enterprise called the TranStella Company and reverse-engineered the alien products, astonishing the world with radical advances in a wide variety of different fields. Three-dimensional image projection, replicator technology, and autonomous behavior systems were just a few. Much of the advancement came in the entertainment field, where he often thought his heart truly lay.

As a matter of principle, he stayed out of the offensive weapons business. He explained to his associates that trade goods and trinkets were one thing, but the aliens had some reservations about giving primitive species improved ways to kill each other and would not have been willing to supply him with advanced weaponry even if he had asked for it. Or as he put it, "You don't give an anthill an atomic bomb to drop on an enemy anthill ten feet away." Defensive technology protecting lives and property, such as hardened electronics resistant to electromagnetic pulse attacks and solar flares, was another matter, and the United States came through the EMP

War in better shape than it might have otherwise.

Jefferson changed the world in other ways. Previously little-known raw materials with strange names like praseodymium and dysprosium were vital to alien technology, and became household words as people realized that the national economy suddenly depended on relatively scarce resources not always located in the friendliest of countries. Trying to make policy, politicians stumbled over the difference between yttrium and ytterbium. The United States was fairly well provided with most of the ores from which the key elements were refined, but other countries nearly went to war several times over resources no one could have imagined would be so important a few years before.

Through it all, Jefferson prospered. Almost in spite of himself, some said, but even when he made a poor decision that cost him billions, which happened on occasion since he had little patience for the day-to-day drudgery of running a business, he could copy some new alien artifact and make it all back and then some. Just holding the patents for superconductive transmission of electricity at normal outdoor temperatures when the country embarked on a massive project to replace the national power grid after the EMP War would have made anyone rich without having to do more than sit back and collect the money. And that was just one of Jefferson's numerous ventures.

It may have been a simple act of kindness to what at first glance appeared to be an injured animal, but saving the prince's life had ultimately made Jefferson C. Prescott the richest man on the planet.

Nor had the prince exhausted his feeling of gratitude. When he ascended the throne in due course, he rewarded Jefferson by asking him what he would most like to have, his most cherished dream, his wildest fantasy, the sky's the limit... And Jefferson's dream was almost absurdly easy to make come true. It just so happened that the Royal Navy had a decommissioned fleet base built into a small asteroid that it was about to dispose of by deorbiting it into its local sun. If you can get some use out of it, he was told, just tell us where you want it sent.

Literally overnight, since it shone like a bright star, astronomers realized Earth had a second moon. An asteroid roughly four to five miles in diameter had appeared in orbit some 60,000 miles out. No one had seen it coming. It was just suddenly... *there*.

At first, the astronomers could only assume that it was a large piece of rocky debris from the outer solar system, its orbit around the sun perhaps perturbed by coming too close to, say, Neptune, and sent careening towards the inner planets. Somehow its approach had not been observed, and that it had settled into a stable orbit around Earth instead of colliding with it was thought to be a happy accident.

The newcomer was tiny on a cosmic scale and barely more than a flying mountain, but it was recognized as a moon even so. The precedent was there: Mars' two official and named moons were only about two and three times larger, and both were thought to be captured asteroids as well.

Since the new moon now seemed to be a permanent member of Earth's family, it needed a name. Such things were decided at the triennial General Assembly of the International Astronomical Society, which met that year in Amsterdam. The Working Group for Planetary and System Nomenclature submitted a list of suggestions for the new moon that were then voted on after vigorous debate by the assembled astronomers. Despite strong support for Kaguya, a princess of the Moon in Japanese legend, an ancient Egyptian god associated with the Moon won out in the end, and so the new moon was henceforth to be known as Thoth.

The formal announcement was made in the classic manner as a dignified old astronomer stood at a lectern on a stage in front of an auditorium crowded with astronomers from every country on Earth. Behind the white-haired man of science were several projected 3-D images of astronomical objects, with the animated seething of the double-lobed cloud of lividly glowing reddish dust and gas from the exploding star Eta Carinae particularly spectacular. The professor hadn't gotten any further than "After due consideration, it is our resolution that..." when a man appeared out of nowhere next to him. The faint column of light surrounding the stranger was a telltale sign that he was physically somewhere else and this was a 3-D projection.

The speaker didn't notice the apparition at first, and only an astonished stirring in the audience in front of him alerted him to the fact that something wasn't going as planned. He broke off his prepared remarks, looked around puzzledly, and saw the projected image of the uninvited guest standing to one side. The man appeared solid enough to touch: tall, slender, not quite forty with a neatly trimmed mustache, and wearing a business suit.

"Who are you?" the speaker demanded. "You can't interrupt a meeting in session like this!"

"My name is Jefferson C. Prescott," the man replied, his voice booming from the acoustic fields in the room, "and I have every right to speak. Besides the fact that my company supplied all this" — he gestured to the enormous projected astronomical images behind him — "that moon you're talking about is my property."

With that, the auditorium went silent. The organization's solemn deliberations and orderly procedure had just been turned into high drama, and everyone in the room waited tensely to see what happened next. Most of the audience had probably thought at first that the whole thing was staged, some kind of performance to liven up an otherwise routine affair of assigning a name to an object in space, but it was quickly obvious that the dispute was very real.

"What do you mean, your property?" the old astronomer pressed.

"I own that moon," Jefferson said coolly. "I have the right to name it."

The astronomer snorted contemptuously. "Preposterous. Nobody can own a moon. Not even you."

"Oh?" Jefferson asked. "Why's that?"

The astronomer folded his arms across his chest and assumed a patronizing tone that he had employed in his classroom lectures and which had haunted the uneasy dreams of his students for forty years. "For one thing, there is an international treaty in effect that governs the question of property rights in space. No nation, corporation, or individual can claim any celestial body as private property."

"Isn't that interesting," Jefferson answered with a touch of scorn. "And how can you enforce that treaty? Nobody can get out of low earth orbit anymore. As for my claim on the moon, let's look at a few facts." He assumed a lecturing tone of his own that faintly mocked the professor's. "It was signed over to me by the previous owners. I have a deed validated by the Royal Sovereign of Kharrakhull himself. The asteroid was moved to its present location following my instructions. Not only have I been to it a number of times, I've even established a residence there. Furthermore, I have my defenses, so even if you were to start a crash program to build a troop carrier to send soldiers out to my moon, you couldn't get within several hundred miles of it. Possession is nine points of the law, as they say, and I possess it. So I'm a little annoyed by you characters telling me what I should call my own property."

"All that may be true," the professor conceded grudgingly, then played his trump card, "but you are not a professional astronomer and hence not qualified to take part in this meeting."

"Really? I'm not qualified? I've actually been in space, which is more than most of you have. I've not only met real aliens, I've been doing business with them for years, and you guys haven't even found proof of microbes on other planets yet. I could tell you things I know from my own experience that — oh, wait, I'm not qualified! Well, don't let me spoil your fun. By the way," he added, as he turned to go, "the name of the moon is Vesper. I always thought it was a pretty name. 'Evening star.'"

"But it's a name associated with the planet Venus!" the astronomer exclaimed. "It violates our naming convention! You can't just—"

"I can and I did. Like it or not, it's Vesper, so you might as well learn to love it."

With that, he ignored the imploring shouts from some of the astronomers in the audience to tell them about the aliens and how the problem of travel faster than light had been solved, and how a body the size of an asteroid could be moved so effortlessly across who knew how many light-years, and his image blinked out. That was very nearly Jefferson C. Prescott's last public appearance.

It was also Jefferson's first public admission that he had been dealing with aliens from other worlds. The various agencies of various governments keeping an eye on him and his activities had long known as much, but this was the first time the population at large heard about it. In the firestorm of controversy and wild speculation that followed, Jefferson had to release a statement through his office:

1. Yes, there is intelligent life in outer space. I suspect the aliens' form of life is similar to ours because evolution doesn't have very many choices in making living things. The aliens can eat our food, anyway, though they have to add some trace elements to live on it for very long.

2. There are no star-spanning civilizations anywhere close to us, so we're likely to be on our own for centuries to come. We are at the far edge of a huge territory that the aliens themselves haven't explored very thoroughly. The Galaxy is huge and while Earth-like planets with life on them are common, intelligence seems to be relatively rare.

3. I didn't sell the Earth out to the aliens. We're too remote and too primitive for them to be interested in us except as the object of scientific study. I mostly traded things like cultural artifacts and plant and animal specimens.

4. I don't understand the physics of faster than light travel myself, so please stop asking me about it.

The uproar died down as the public digested the information. The belief that intelligent life probably did exist out in space was already widespread, fed by a century and a half of science-fiction speculation on the subject, so the knowledge that it had been confirmed wasn't too much of a stretch. Since fleets of flying saucers didn't appear in the skies and any teams of alien scientists doing fieldwork on Earth generally kept out of sight, people went on with their daily business as though life out there had nothing to do with life down here, and it all slid into the background.

Once it was known that aliens *had* visited Earth and more or less when, one obvious conclusion was that every reported UFO sighting from the beginning in the late 1940s to early in the 21st Century was either mistaken or a deliberate fabrication. Unless a *second* alien race had been visiting us, which seemed unlikely. With it now common knowledge that aliens did exist but Jefferson frustrating scientists and the public alike by refusing to say much about them, there were some alleged new sightings of mostly dubious accuracy and a couple of outright hoaxes.

A few encounters were thought to be genuine, such as one reported by a highway engineer that involved a group of aliens collecting plant samples in the jungles of Cambodia, and another by a pilot who had been buzzed over central Africa by a flying object that looked like no aircraft ever seen before. Lastly, an Iowa family named Windstaetter claimed to have come across an alien geological research team when they took the wrong back road while on vacation in Wyoming. Showing signs of good nature and even humor, the aliens posed for photos with the Windstaetters before the two groups went their separate ways. It might have been dismissed as a textbook example of a staged UFO hoax, except that it would have been difficult to fake the aliens so convincingly, and Jefferson C. Prescott himself verified that the aliens shown were genuine. The Windstaetters' photos became famous as the only known visual depictions of the aliens and were reproduced all over the world, in scientific reference works as well as in the popular media. Had Mr. and Mrs. Windstaetter realized that would happen, they might not have let their children pose with the aliens making peace signs and funny faces.

There was some outrage for a while in scientific and governmental circles as the full extent of what Jefferson had done with Vesper sank in. Placing an asteroid in orbit around the Earth had to require energy and precision almost beyond imagining by human standards. One small miscalculation and the mountain-sized rock could have smashed into Earth with catastrophic results. Jefferson had not announced his plans in advance or applied for permission from any official agencies. He just did it despite the possible risks, trusting in the abilities of mysterious aliens no one else had ever seen or even heard of before not to accidentally drop the asteroid on top of Washington DC. Jokes were made about giving the term "environmental impact" new meaning, but they didn't seem particularly amusing.

The controversy soon petered out. The asteroid was in place, its orbit seemed stable enough, and what had been done couldn't be easily undone. The eventual feeling was no harm, no foul, although the government did forward a polite request to Jefferson to please not do anything that drastic again as far as rearranging the solar system went.

Some questions remained. For one, what did Jefferson want with a moon of his own in the first place? An eventual if rather out-of-the-way retirement home? A Jeff's Gulch sort of refuge where he and a few friends could sit out the collapse of civilization on Earth, not that civilization seemed in any immediate danger at the moment? What *did* he have up there, anyway? Theories abounded, but if anyone knew for certain, they weren't talking.

Meanwhile, the astronomical community could tolerate a little ambiguity. Earth's first moon was known as both the Moon and Luna, after all. The second one went into the reference works with Thoth as the official name along with an explanation that it was also popularly known as Vesper. An asterisk referred to a note mentioning that the moon was claimed by one J. Prescott, though the claim was disputed and not valid under international law. Presumably his occupation of the moon was not only illegal but temporary, and would end just as soon as the proper authorities could find a way to remove him.

While sending troops to occupy the moon and evict Jefferson may have been out of the question for the time being, he was vulnerable in other ways. Attempts were made to sue him in various courts with the idea of seizing his company's Earthside assets until he renounced all claim to Thoth/Vesper, vacated the asteroid, and turned over the means to get there, but Jefferson had lawyers, too, the best money could buy.

In the end, an American court ruled that Vesper was not a "celestial body" in the accepted sense of the term, but a *space station*, for which private ownership had considerable established precedent, and recognized Jefferson's claim to it. The fact that the aliens had used an existing asteroid as a base, whether for camouflage or just to have something solid to build on, instead of constructing a space station from the blueprints up, may have confused things, but the principle was clear.

Other countries, notably ones where TranStella had major business interests, followed suit. Although some low-level grumbling persisted, the pressure was off. After all, Jefferson had some pretty powerful friends who might not appreciate their gift being taken away from him, and that could have influenced legal thinking as well.

A man with property in space needs a way to reach it and he was well-supplied. The TranStella space fleet came to number five vessels consisting of alien-supplied propulsion systems installed in Earth-built craft. The roster included the *Mirage* and the *Spectre*, two small personal shuttles that resembled executive jets, two larger cargo and supply ships with the unpoetic numbers 01 and 02 instead of names, and a freighter for bulk shipments. Why there were so many ships was puzzling when there couldn't be that much traffic between Earth and Vesper, although one theory speculated that it was for the sake of having spares on hand in case one or more ships were lost and the aliens were no longer willing or even still around to replace them. The ships also seemed to have some never clearly explained limitations on their speeds and ranges that kept them in Earth's vicinity, and there had been no known trips to Mars or even the Moon. Instead, TranStella developed a tidy business putting commercial satellites in orbit for various customers and delivering supplies to space stations when no other spacecraft were available, so there was some justification for the apparently surplus capacity.

Years passed without much obviously happening. Reported sightings of alien spacecraft declined to no more than noise level, and it was generally thought that the aliens had left Earth entirely at some point. Perhaps the asteroid had also been a farewell gift. To the extent anyone could track his movements, Jefferson seemed to be spending more and more time on Vesper and leaving the routine operations of his various enterprises in the hands of his subordinates. He was getting older and perhaps tired of business, and seldom seen publicly.

As the introduction of new inventions slowed to a trickle, finally drying up entirely, no one was certain whether Jefferson had run out of alien technology or simply lost interest. Developing and elaborating on what he had already presented to the world would be enough to occupy scientists and engineers for years to come, but it was only natural to wonder if he had held anything back and what unimagined marvels of alien technology he might have hidden away on his private moon.

There were some occasional hints that Jefferson was working on *something*, even if no one knew exactly what. Somebody was certainly buying huge numbers of trees from nurseries around the country, and there were indications that it was a company with very little physical existence acting on behalf of Jefferson's interests. Some rumors claimed that he had his eye on a location somewhere on the West Coast for a major development project, which might explain the trees although they were Eastern varieties not native to the area. The rumors died down somewhat when it was realized that he would have to be buying a lot of land if he had a planned community or a resort in mind, but there were no signs of any large-scale real estate transactions traceable to him in the entire region.

The rumors had to start somewhere, and their connection with reality was that trucks loaded with mysterious cargos were going north from Los Angeles on I-5 and returning a day or two later completely empty. There was even the story of a state highway patrolman stopping a truck owned by a Prescott company for some minor traffic violation and finding the trailer stuffed with human bodies. As it turned out, they were lifelike robots, but the trooper had a bad moment until he realized what he was looking at.

Just *what* was Jefferson up to?

Whatever it was, he couldn't live forever, and there was talk of a new generation of spacecraft that could go beyond low Earth orbit. In not too many years, the situation might be very different.

Chapter Three

Thursday, April 23 — later that afternoon

Mr. Cosgrove lifted an eyebrow as he regarded Aunt Thalia across the conference table. "Again, you say?"

"It's a habit of his," she replied. "Any time the going gets the least bit tough, he just walks away from it. I remember one time when he—"

Mr. Cosgrove cut her off. "I did read about that little quirk of his in his profile. It's presumably the reason he has his own private moon in the first place, a place to go when he wants to get away from everything. But this is much more serious than going somewhere for a few days to recharge his batteries. He really *has* disappeared."

Aunt Thalia frowned. "Well, we didn't murder him for his money, if that's what you're thinking."

"That is not what we're thinking," Mr. Cosgrove said evenly. "Please allow me to explain. First of all, I apologize for the abrupt way we called you all here, but under the circumstances it was necessary."

"*Called* us here?" Ronn's mother demanded. "You practically kidnapped us!"

"The alternative could have been worse," Mr. Cosgrove said. "Your nephew, Daniel Prescott, the son of your sister Emily Prescott, was abducted this morning. If we had not acted at once, your children might have been next."

"Danny's been kidnapped?" Ronn blurted, recalling in passing that Aunt Emily had never married her children's father, and had kept the Prescott name. He saw that his mother, Phaedra, and Theo all looked shocked, too.

Aunt Thalia was at least startled. "By who?"

Unperturbed, Mr. Cosgrove went on. "We have our suspicions, but never mind that for the moment. We are doing everything we can to find

24

your cousin, of course. Unfortunately, he is probably already out of the country. We don't think he will suffer any physical harm. In fact, hurting him would be the last thing the kidnappers would want to do since they need him alive and healthy. As for the rest of you children, you are in no less danger of being abducted yourselves. Any one of you would do for our opponents' purposes and your cousin Daniel was perhaps merely the easiest one to acquire. However, it would also be in the other side's interest to remove the rest of you from the picture so no one else can make use of your... uhm, privileged position."

It was news to Ronn that he even had a position, let alone a privileged one.

"You're still not making any sense," Aunt Thalia complained. "Why would anyone want our children?"

"Allow me to explain," Mr. Cosgrove said. "What I am about to tell you has not been made public, partly to prevent panic—"

"Not *that* old cliché," Theo muttered.

"—but nonetheless a serious consideration given the circumstances," Mr. Cosgrove retorted, "—and partly to avoid tipping our hand to unfriendly interests. Until the situation is better understood, we are keeping a lid on things. What we do know is that about a month ago, Mr. Prescott went to Vesper with one of his executives and his personal pilot. He told his associates that there was a problem of some sort that he needed to investigate, but did not elaborate further. Always before, he stayed in touch with his people on Earth while he was on Vesper, and continued to conduct his business normally. But this time, something apparently happened. Although the communication systems were still functioning, he no longer answered calls and missed several scheduled conferences. His pilot, who was confined to the docking bay and not allowed to enter the asteroid interior, was forced to return to Earth without him or the executive when his own food supplies ran low. After a week, Prescott's company was in disarray and his subordinates were confused, with infighting on the upper executive levels over how to respond to the crisis."

"I can imagine," said Aunt Thalia, "but I still don't see how it concerns us."

Mr. Cosgrove sighed heavily. "It does unless you have some way of living through the end of the world."

Everybody gasped. "*What?*"

Ronn felt his stomach constrict. Even though neither Aunt Thalia nor his mother looked very convinced by this latest bombshell, he had a feeling that the man wasn't joking.

Mr. Cosgrove raised his hands in an appeal for calm. "Very well, I may be exaggerating. Or maybe not. On two separate occasions since Prescott's disappearance, there was an unexplained change in Vesper's orbit and each time it ended up a few hundred miles closer to Earth. That may not sound like much, but if this keeps happening, and if it comes very much closer, it could conceivably crash into us. An object of that size striking the Earth would result in tidal waves a mile high if it came down in the ocean, or continent-wide devastation if it hit land. The asteroid that killed the dinosaurs was not much larger than Vesper."

Everyone at the table looked at each other in stunned silence. Now Aunt Thalia and Mrs. Evans didn't seem nearly so skeptical.

Mr. Cosgrove continued. "We've concluded that Prescott's lack of communication and Vesper's orbital disruptions are in some way related and that there is indeed some kind of problem. Exactly what, we don't know. Given the possibility of global disaster if that asteroid strikes the Earth, the government decided to act. By Presidential order, the TranStella Company has been temporarily seized for the duration of the crisis, and other governments have done likewise with TranStella's branches and assets in their respective territories. Fortunately, Prescott's employees are cooperating. Whatever happened was unforeseen and unplanned, and they recognize the urgency of the situation just as much as we do. Now we have to get somebody up there to find out what's going on. Although we don't have any deep-space capable vehicles of our own, we do have a personal shuttle and a cargo transport from Prescott's private fleet at our disposal."

"Then that's great," Aunt Thalia broke in. "Your problem's practically solved. But what do our children have to do with it? What good's holding them for ransom if Jeff's dead or if that rock's going to hit the Earth?"

"Our adversaries are playing for much higher stakes than mere ransom," Mr. Cosgrove said. "With any luck, whoever gains control of the asteroid will have access to the master controls, enabling them to fix the problem with its orbit. What probably interests our friends on the other side most is the fact that Vesper must be a treasure trove of highly advanced alien technology that Prescott for some reason chose not to share with the rest of us. They undoubtedly assume that if they can take possession of that, they will rule the world.

"And other forces *are* stirring. Besides the kidnapping, certain hostile elements are reported to be engaging in suspicious activity possibly related to the current crisis. While we have two of Prescott's five spaceships, the other three were being used for routine deliveries to orbit and seem to have been, er, diverted. That includes another cargo transport and a passenger shuttle, as well as the large freighter.

"The missing spacecraft are worrisome because they are the only other ships that can reach Vesper. And that is just the beginning. There is no

26

point in flying to the asteroid if you are unable to get inside once you are there, but since this was originally a facility for servicing an entire fleet of spaceships, there are other docking bays besides the one we occupy, in particular a freight entrance. Whoever has the other ships might have access to another point of entry that the ships we have are not programmed to enter.

"The difficulty is getting inside at all. We can send our people up there on Prescott's ships, but they are unable to go beyond the docking bay. There is an ID recognition system and only specially authorized individuals are allowed into the main part of the complex. We can't just have some soldiers shoot their way inside because of the automatic defenses. A very few people have been granted temporary permission to enter at one time or another, but according to the information we found in Prescott's files, only five persons have permanent access based on their recorded biometric information. Their names are Phoebe and Theodosius Knuppel, Daniel and Julia Prescott, and Aaron Evans. In short, these five children are the only people in the world we can get into the restricted areas. Since Daniel Prescott has already been abducted and his sister is now in high-security protection, that leaves the three present."

As he took that in, Ronn was amused by the look on Phaedra's face. Since her mother was probably convinced that her real name wouldn't excite agents, casting directors, or audiences, she had been going by the stage name of Phaedra Prescott for a couple of years. It must have been a jolt for her to be so bluntly reminded that Phoebe Knuppel was the name on her birth certificate. Theo winced a little, too. Ronn was surprised to find out his name wasn't short for Theodore as he had always assumed and Theo probably hoped everyone else did.

"So *that's* what that 'examination' was for!" Ronn's mother exclaimed. "He told *me* it was to make sure Ronn could be certified as one of his heirs if something happened to him, the liar!"

"He told me the same thing about Phaedra and Theo," Aunt Thalia put in, for a moment sounding surprisingly sympathetic with her sister now that they were in the same boat. "I could tell that wasn't the whole story and he was up to something, but I could never figure out what. Who could have guessed it would be something like *this?*"

The important thing, it dawned on Ronn, was that if only he and his cousins could get into Uncle Jeff's private estate in the sky...

He was about to go on a trip into space.

Never mind what he was supposed to do once he got there. Even though people had been going into space for a long time, this was *big*. There had been commemorations the year before of the 75th anniversary of Yuri Gagarin's pioneering flight, but only a relatively small number of people had been up there in all the years since. Something like two dozen space stations were in orbit close to the Earth now, most dedicated to purposes like science and manufacturing, and the people who went to them had to have the right scientific and technical qualifications. The qualification for going to the stations with tourist facilities was simpler, basically a very large amount of money, but that had been just as much out of the question for Ronn. While he had fantasized about traveling in space like any other kid, maybe teaming up with his buddy Travis to save the universe from some terrible menace, he had never thought it was likely to come true in real life. And certainly not at the age of fifteen.

I can't wait to tell Travis about this!

Something else occurred to him. He wasn't going into space by himself or with Travis.

He would be going with his cousins. That was a depressing thought.

His mother suddenly stood up. "Are you crazy?" she demanded in outrage. "These are *children!* Are you telling us you want to risk their lives by sending them into outer space? There are laws against child endangerment!"

"Easily waived by Presidential order when there is no other way," said Mr. Cosgrove.

Aunt Thalia then pressed him for more details. "Just how dangerous is this likely to be?"

Mr. Cosgrove shrugged. "We assume that if it was very dangerous, Mr. Prescott would not have arranged for his young nephews and nieces to be the only ones granted unconditional access. I promise you that we will do everything we can to ensure your children's safety, though some risks are of course unavoidable in an undertaking such as this. We aren't asking them to be heroes. We just want them to look for their uncle and find out if he is dead or sick or under duress or just being unusually misanthropic. If he can't or won't do anything about the orbital shifts, they will have to figure out some way to deactivate the ID recognition system so we can get some scientists and technicians inside. At that point, their job will be done and they will be sent home immediately."

"Hmm..." Aunt Thalia murmured reflectively.

"Mo-om!" Phaedra exclaimed. "What are you thinking?"

"I'm thinking of your career!" Aunt Thalia answered, sounding as though she was weighing the pros and cons as she spoke. "I don't like any of this and I don't want to risk losing you... but it looks as though we really don't have any choice about it. And as long as you have to go anyway, think of the up side if you pull it off! You'll be famous, maybe you'll even save the world! You can't buy publicity like saving the world!"

"Can't somebody else save the world?" Phaedra asked miserably.

"Yeah!" Theo piped up. "Let me! I'll go!" No one paid any attention to him.

"Listen to me," Aunt Thalia added, addressing Phaedra directly. "I approached your uncle a couple of times about using his influence to get you in the door at the studios, but he had some crazy old-fashioned idea about having you make it on your own and he wouldn't do anything! Your own uncle owned whole entertainment companies and he still expected you to go to cattle calls and audition like everybody else! He was even a little angry because I'd told you that you were related to him, like I was going to keep something like that a secret when it could do so much for you. Well, maybe he wouldn't do anything for you before, but now we can finally get some mileage out of the Prescott family connection. This is a once in a lifetime opportunity! Think about it!"

"I want to think about it, too!" Theo crowed, again with no one listening.

Mrs. Evans had heard enough. "I'd rather take my chances with the kidnappers!" she exclaimed, grabbing Ronn's arm and pulling him out of his chair. "Come on! We're leaving!"

She dragged Ronn to the door and waved her hand at the optical sensor in the wall next to it. Nothing happened. She turned and looked angrily at Mr. Cosgrove, still sitting placidly at the head of the table while the various Prescott relatives bickered.

"Open this door!" she exclaimed. "*Now!*"

"Not until we've resolved matters," Mr. Cosgrove said.

Mrs. Evans actually stamped her foot. "Oh, they're resolved all right. We've resolved that Ronn's not going! If you don't let me out of here, I will find a lawyer as soon as I do get out of here and sue you for kidnapping!"

Mr. Cosgrove remained unruffled. "Mrs. Evans, please understand that there is a state of emergency in effect. You can sue us all you like after this is over, but not until then. The situation is extraordinary, I grant you, but these three children are the only ones who can do what has to be done. We would prefer it if you were to sign the necessary releases, of course. Now please sit down and let me go over a few more things."

Mrs. Evans looked helplessly at the unyielding door, then turned back to the table. "All right, but Ronn's still not going."

After she and Ronn took their seats again. Mr. Cosgrove gestured. The room light dimmed and a glowing 3-D display showing an asteroid in space appeared above the table. It was a somewhat irregular lump of rock like any other asteroid too small for its own gravity to mold it into a sphere. Overall, its shape was about that of a flattened ice-cream cone, rounded on top, somewhat tapered towards the bottom, and scarred by craters large and small everywhere. A few scattered white and red lights shone where surface installations were located. Since unauthorized spacecraft couldn't approach the asteroid within several hundred miles, the imagery must have been obtained from a distance by long-range spycams. The government probably kept the little moonlet under constant surveillance by lurking satellites just in case Prescott or the aliens were cooking something up.

An inset text block indicated that Vesper was some four miles across at the top, and about five from top to bottom. The dimensions were also given in kilometers, but since the United States had still not adopted the metric system for the most part, that was just so much useless information.

"Here is what we know," Mr. Cosgrove said. "Only Prescott's own ships can land on Vesper. According to our interviews with his pilots, they had to stay with the ships so they could leave at a moment's notice, and were not allowed beyond the crew quarters in the immediate area of the docking bay. So we have no detailed information on what else is in the place. We do know that the rock has hollow spaces within and it was formerly used as a base for a space navy, and we would presume there must be things like a power plant, water tanks, storage areas, and service facilities."

"Hey, you're the *government!*" Theo pointed out rather unnecessarily. "Don't you have all kinds of nano-spytech you could slip in?"

Mr. Cosgrove gave him a frosty glare. "Most of our spytech came from *him.* Whatever we have, he has countermeasures we don't. There was also something of a gentlemen's agreement early on. Your uncle's fortune is so vast that he could buy entire countries and certainly influence politics any way he chose in ours. It was somewhat informally understood that he would stay out of politics and we would not unduly annoy him with intensive surveillance. On the other hand, it would be imprudent *not* to keep an eye on someone as powerful as he is, especially someone with friends as powerful as *they* are. He seems to accept some low-level monitoring as part of the usual give and take but keeps his guard up, so our knowledge of his activities is necessarily limited."

Mr. Cosgrove gestured again and the asteroid image turned on its side, showing the upper surface from directly overhead. In the center of the cratered terrain and taking up about half of the available area was a featureless gray disc. "Nor do we know what is under the dome on top since we are unable to see inside. It is covered with a layer of pulverized rock, most likely as shielding against radiation. There is a large open space underneath, but what does he have in there? It is just over two miles in diameter, so there is a great deal of room to fill. We think it might be a nature preserve based on the number of trees his company has been acquiring for unknown purposes, but some amount of construction is known to be going on as well. An eventual private resort in space, perhaps? We can only guess."

He waved, the display flickered out, and the room light came up again.

"Didn't you say he'd had some people up there?" Aunt Thalia asked. "Haven't you talked to them about what they saw?"

"We've tried," Mr. Cosgrove said, sounding as though he was thinking, *As if it wasn't the first thing we thought of, lady!* "A number of Prescott's own employees have been inside and *ought* to know what is going on in the asteroid's interior, such as project managers, designers, and construction supervisors, and we have made an effort to locate them for questioning. Those that we have been able to find are mostly lower-level employees who have voluntarily had selective memory blocks emplaced as a condition of their employment, so they are unable to tell us very much. It certainly takes the concept of 'non-disclosure agreement' to a new level. I just wish *we* were allowed to use something like that... More critically, some high-level TranStella personnel are known to have gone to Vesper recently, and they are also long overdue without any communication."

He touched a control pad and several still 3-D head shots of the missing men and women appeared, followed by vidclips of their worried-looking next of kin made by government investigators.

One fortyish man in an expensive-looking suit was identified by a floating caption as **CALEB LOWTHER, EXECUTIVE VICE-PRESIDENT FOR CORPORATE STRATEGY AND BUSINESS DEVELOPMENT**.

"Oh, I know him!" Phaedra exclaimed.

"Yeah," Theo chimed in. "Unca Cal! What a diff!"

Ronn recognized him, too. The "unca" bit was a joke and a folksy pronunciation of "uncle" that Theo injected with dripping scorn. In a short-lived attempt to make himself the public face of TranStella's entertainment enterprises, "Cal" Lowther had hosted two or three vidshows aimed at kids, not only as a master of ceremonies but also in some implied but not clearly defined way as the true genius behind all the wonderment and fantasy. Forget about the hundreds of writers, artists, animators, designers, and builders on staff actually doing the work — he tried to give the impression of taking a few moments from his busy schedule single-handedly creating all that wonderment and fantasy to share said wonderment and fantasy with his little friends. His affected persona of a kindly storytelling uncle had not disguised the underlying stiff, stuffed-shirt, sucking on a lemon reality, and his vid hosting career came to a quick and merciful end.

"This is the executive who accompanied Prescott on his last visit to Vesper," Mr. Cosgrove said, ignoring the comments. "As I mentioned, he has not been heard from, either."

Ronn had never met any high-ranking business executives personally and couldn't judge whether Lowther was typical for the breed. Instead of trying and failing to look like a kindly kidvid host, here Lowther appeared to be straining to look fierce and determined in the portrait, wearing some of the latest comgear along his temple between his left ear and eye like a confident captain of industry, but he wasn't doing very well at that, either. The expression seemed forced, as though the role he was playing was just a little beyond him.

A vidclip followed, showing Caleb Lowther addressing a conference, and reading from a prepared text displayed somewhere off to the side.

"In our projections for the coming year," he droned, as though going through the motions of something that was expected of him but without any enthusiasm or even any expectation that his audience would be interested enough to be listening very closely, "we anticipate a synergistic blend of new and traditional business models designed to utilize both established and innovative distribution and marketing platforms."

Ronn wasn't sure exactly what he had said, if anything at all.

Lowther's blonde wife, one **NICOLE LOWTHER,** seemed particularly distraught in the next vidclip. She was all but in tears as she wailed, "I'm so worried that something might have happened to Caleb way out there in space!" Then she broke down entirely and buried her face in her hands as she wept in gulping sobs, and Mr. Cosgrove turned her off.

Aunt Thalia's eyes narrowed. "I hope you're keeping an eye on her. That was about the phoniest performance I've ever seen. She knows something."

"Please," Mr. Cosgrove said brusquely. "We checked her out. She has her own career and is not even employed by TranStella. There is no reason to suspect her of anything. Her husband has been gone for weeks without a word, so of course she's upset."

"If you say so..." Aunt Thalia sat back in her chair and crossed her arms, a sure sign that even though she had decided not to push the issue, he still hadn't convinced her.

Mr. Cosgrove leaned forward in his chair, his suddenly very serious and penetrating gaze somehow taking in everyone sitting at the table.

"You can refuse to cooperate with us," he said in a tone strongly hinting that there would be no more arguments, "but we would still have to put you in a protection program as we have Daniel's mother and sister. In the meantime, other countries might get their hands on Prescott's alien technology and attempt to use it against us. We would have no choice but to strike first, and I am not exaggerating when I say there is a threat of outright *war* hanging over the success or failure of this mission. Even worse, the asteroid might hit the Earth and destroy civilization. It is all up to you what you want to do, of course..."

Faced with those alternatives, Ronn's mother swallowed hard. Without saying another word, she and Aunt Thalia signed the releases allowing the government to send their children into who knew what risk and hazard.

The fate of the world now depends on us? Ronn thought queasily, looking at his suddenly subdued cousins. *We're doomed...*

Thanks to the well-stocked fridge and cupboards, Ronn and his mother had an ample dinner back in their hotel suite, but neither was in the mood for saying much. There were guards outside the door and Ronn wasn't even allowed to leave the suite to go to the soft drink machine, though he could call the front desk and have anything he wanted within reason sent over. It all seemed like a bad case of barn doors being locked after the horse was disappearing over a distant hill with a last whinny that sounded a lot like "See ya!"

Someone called and asked for his shirt, pants, and shoe sizes for the extra clothes that were to be supplied. After that, the possibilities for occupying their time for the rest of the evening were few. When she tired of watching the news and entertainment vid channels on the room's 3-D wall display, Ronn's mother went to bed early.

With his own phone in a bag somewhere and outgoing calls and messages on the room com blocked, Ronn couldn't call his father or Travis. Somebody didn't want any information about where he was or what he was doing inadvertently leaked to unfriendly hackers.

Checking around on the Net for the latest news didn't turn up anything about Vesper, Uncle Jefferson, or even Danny's kidnapping. Whatever was going on behind the scenes, the government hadn't released any information to the public as yet. It was more than a little strange to be at the center of something so important that nobody knew about.

Ronn then looked to see what he could find out about the mysterious Jefferson C. Prescott. As famous as Uncle Jeff was, a lot of articles and newsvid features must have been written about his family and early life. How was it that Ronn was only now finding out they were related?

He soon realized why. Once he got past the obviously deranged sites accusing Uncle Jeff of being at the center of some scheme to take over the world — when someone really *was* in league with space aliens, a conspiracy theory had to go some to be outright crazy, but people managed — there simply wasn't much out there about Prescott's family or early life. Most articles about him had titles like "The Last of the Tycoons" and concentrated on his later career. Uncle Jeff seemed to be a recluse by nature with a surprisingly low profile even during his publicly active years well before Ronn was aware of things, and not a lot of personal information had

33

been made available.

Ronn suspected something fishy about it all. Nobody that famous could hide that completely without investigative journalists digging up every last scrap of information, from interviewing old school friends to calling up birth and marriage records. Perhaps Uncle Jeff had cherished his privacy and wanted to keep his family out of the spotlight, and had arranged an informal blackout with the media — most of which he owned anyway — on publishing his personal details, or had launched a data-destroying program to wipe out what was there and keep anything new from being posted. There might have even been a targeted block on Ronn's personal Net access, filtering out most information relating to matters Prescott. If anybody could do something like that, Uncle Jeff was the one.

Then again, he couldn't scrub *everything*. Ronn had a feeling that if he had started to suspect something and had taken the time and trouble to check out Jefferson C. Prescott's life and times in detail, he would have found indirect connections almost at once. The clues were certainly there. Just the name of the town the man was born in or the names of his sisters would have rung bells. But Ronn had never given the reclusive Mr. Prescott much thought, or taken enough interest in him to look things up, while the 90% effective media blackout on his personal life had kept casual showbiz gossip and rumors from reaching an ordinary kid in Maple Heights, and it had all gone right by him until now.

Feeling very much alone and isolated, Ronn ended up spending the rest of the evening watching vids without much interest.

When he finally went to bed, he lay there for a while and mulled over the events of what had been one long and very strange day, not to mention the prospect of going into space tomorrow. Getting up that morning, he certainly hadn't had any idea where he would be that night. He might have thought that he would be too excited to sleep very well, but just sitting down for several hours on a cross-country flight had tired him out more than he realized, and he drifted off before the wonder of it all had really sunk in.

Chapter Four

A knock on his bedroom door early the next morning startled Ronn awake. It opened before he could collect his thoughts enough to mumble a reply.

Mr. Cosgrove came in and dropped several packages on a chair. "Your extra clothes, some basic camping and survival supplies, and a backpack," he announced. "You have fifteen minutes to take a shower and get dressed. When you are ready, the guards outside will take you to the restaurant for breakfast. Your mother is already on her way over. Bring everything in your backpack." He turned and left the room.

Now Ronn remembered what had happened the day before and why he was where he was — and where he was going. He'd had all night for his subconscious mind to absorb it, and he mainly felt a little numb.

I'm not up to this... he thought, but all he could do was take things as they came.

He showered and put on the new jeans and shirt that had been supplied. With a couple of minutes to spare, he used the time to check his mail on the bedroom's vid display.

A message had come in from Ms. Crowley, and he had to watch her oversized recorded image deliver it personally.

"I have been informed that you will be away from school for a few days. While I understand that family emergencies take precedence, I must remind you that exams and the end of the school year are coming up next month. I am certain that you have no desire to fall behind in your studies during your absence, so I am attaching your homework assignments for the next week."

It figures... The fate of the world might be resting on his shoulders, but he was still expected to do homework. As he dissolved the display, he made a rude gesture in Ms. Crowley's direction even though she couldn't see it. Her image was so lifelike that it gave him almost as much satisfaction as if she had actually been there.

More cheeringly, there was also a sympathetic message from a grinning Travis: "All they told us was that you'd been hauled off for some kind of family emergency but we didn't have to worry about it. I hope it isn't too serious. And here I was hoping you'd put sneezing powder in the Teachers' Lounge air purifier or hacked into the final exam answers! Drop me a note from wherever you are when you get a chance and see you soon, buddy-pal!"

What Travis had said gave Ronn something to think about. Besides it being actually true in a way, everybody would accept that "family emergency" cover story at face value since it was in the realm of everyday experience. But when this affair was over and if he lived through it, would the whole story *stay* secret? If it got out that he was a billionaire's nephew, life at school would never be the same again. If he even *could* go back to that school, anyway. Maybe he'd have to stay home with his bodyguards and have private tutors instead. This was a problem that twenty-four hours before he couldn't have imagined ever having to worry about.

Then the guards knocked on the door, so there wasn't any more time for brooding or fooling around on the Net. Oops, he'd forgotten to download his homework assignments...

He slipped his backpack on and the two guards escorted him out of the hotel. Blinking in the sudden bright sunlight, he saw the sky was a cloudless blue and the day was already promising to be a hot one. Not that he would be around long enough to have to worry about the local weather.

After a quick walk from the hotel to the restaurant, which bore the name "Club Muroc" on the sign over its entrance, the guards led him into a small, private dining room and left him. On the walls were blown-up photos, some in 3-D, of various aircraft through history, from biplanes to scramjets. His mother was already there, musing over a cup of coffee as she and Theo sat at a long table, but Aunt Thalia and Phaedra hadn't shown up yet.

A chef in a white uniform stuck his head through the half-open doorway to the kitchen and called to Ronn.

"How do you like your steak?"

"Steak?" Ronn echoed in surprise, then replied, "Medium."

"And your eggs?"

"Uh... over easy, I guess. Couldn't I have pancakes instead?"

"You could," the chef said, "but steak and eggs are the traditional astronauts' breakfast before a mission. Goes back at least to Apollo days."

"Okay, steak and eggs then."

"One medium steak coming right up!" The chef popped back into the kitchen.

"You should hear what's traditional for Russian cosmonauts on the way to the launch pad!" Theo offered.

Mrs. Evans ignored him, probably suspecting it was something she didn't need to know, and turned to Ronn as he took off his backpack and sat down next to her.

"Morning," she said. "I was surprised by the steak, too. After the way we've been treated, I was expecting a bowl of soggy corn flakes at best."

Cousin Phaedra made her entrance, looking drastically different compared with the day before. Instead of something at the extreme of Los Angeles fashion, she wore a plain khaki shirt, shorts, kneesocks, and hiking boots. Her hair was tied behind her head in a loose ponytail and she hadn't bothered with make-up or the illuminated hairnet, though a few stray sparkles still glittered in her eyebrows. She actually looked like a normal human being instead of some holotoon creation. The effect was somewhat offset by the newness of her clothes, which gave her the appearance of modeling them rather than wearing something practical for a real expedition into the unknown.

Phaedra was followed by Aunt Thalia, who was in the middle of an argument with Mr. Cosgrove.

"...Blocking my calls was a violation of my civil rights!" she huffed.

"Maybe so," Mr. Cosgrove said calmly, "but until this situation has been successfully resolved, not one word is leaving this base."

"So what's the harm of telling Phaedra's publicist?" Aunt Thalia demanded. "If she's going into space and saving the world, people ought to know about it! This could make her career! She should at least let her fans know she's all right!"

"All two of them...?" Theo muttered almost inaudibly.

"Mom!" Phaedra protested. "Just drop it, okay? I just want to get this over with! I don't care if—"

"Well, you *should* care," Aunt Thalia snapped. "And if you won't worry about your career, I will. I should be arranging guest spots and public appearances for you already instead of wasting time sitting around some dusty airbase in the middle of nowhere!"

"But I haven't even done anything yet!" Phaedra pointed out.

Aunt Thalia brushed it aside. "Just details. You can't start too early with something like this. Now see here, Mr. Cosgrove. I have other clients, too! I absolutely *insist* that—"

"Please save it for later," he said wearily, then addressed the group as a whole. "Enjoy your breakfast. The van will be here to pick you up in half an hour." With that, he left the dining room.

Aunt Thalia harumphed indignantly as she sat down at the table. "That man continues to infuriate me no end!"

After breakfast, several guards escorted the group outside to the curb where Mr. Cosgrove was waiting with the van.

"I'll accompany your children to the hangar," he told Mrs. Evans and Aunt Thalia. "These ladies will take care of you for the rest of your stay." He indicated a pair of athletic-looking young women waiting nearby. They wore severe dark clothes and shaded visors with built-in com units over their eyes, and Ronn didn't doubt that they had sidearms under their jackets.

Aunt Thalia had a parting embrace with Phaedra, while Theo hung back and waited to get what he clearly regarded as the sappy stuff over with.

Mrs. Evans hugged Ronn, murmuring, "Just come back, all right?"

"I'll try," Ronn assured her. It wasn't exactly something he'd forget to do.

Sentiment was fine, but his mother was also a practical woman. As they drew back from the hug, Mrs. Evans added. "I don't know where you'll end up before it's all over, so I added something to your account."

Ronn took out his wallet and glanced at his cashcard. The display on the back showing his balance and recent transactions did indicate a modest increase in available funds, though his mother seemed to have an optimistic idea that he wouldn't need plane fare from any place further from home than Cleveland.

"We should be able to get the government to reimburse us for any necessary expenses," Mrs. Evans added, "but who knows how long that will take? Just don't go crazy with it!"

"Okay, Mom," Ronn assured her, putting the card back in his wallet, recalling that he had been through this scene once before when he was issued some spending money for a class trip. "I'll only spend what I absolutely have to, if I even can spend it. That moon of Uncle Jeff's doesn't exactly sound like a mall."

"Let's hurry it up, people!" Mr. Cosgrove urged. "We're on a schedule!"

With the fussy official herding them into the van, there was no more time for goodbyes. Ronn got on first, found a seat by the window, slipped out of his backpack and sat down, and waved to his mother standing outside.

Meanwhile Aunt Thalia was still calling last-minute instructions to Phaedra as she got on the van, mostly about keeping Theo out of trouble. Her final "Make me proud!" almost seemed like an afterthought.

As soon as they were all seated, the van started off. On the way, Theo glanced down at his new clothes — the same sort of jeans, shirt, and running shoes Ronn had been issued — and demanded, "How come we didn't get orange flight suits? All the astronauts in the vids do!"

"We didn't have any in your size!" Mr. Cosgrove replied grumpily from his seat by the driver.

They were driven across the base, went through a couple of security checkpoints, and ended up inside an enormous hangar. As they got out of the van, an odor of oil and jet fuel hit their nostrils. Rows of small windows near the arching gridwork of the roof high overhead let in some amount of light. A huge American flag with its thirteen small stars in a circle around one large star was hung up on one wall, all but glowing in red, white, and blue from the sunlight shining through the fabric from the windows behind it. Around them in the vast interior were several aircraft of various types undergoing or awaiting maintenance.

"Wow!" Theo exclaimed, looking at a glossy black fighter that resembled a large arrowhead carved out of obsidian, actually some new heat-resistant ceramic for high-speed flight. "It's a new G-class scramjet!" He noticed a bulky, lumpy gray colossus beyond it. "And that's an FI-30 VTOL troop transport! This is stuff I never thought I'd ever see!"

"Kindly don't brag about it to all your little friends when you get back," Mr. Cosgrove said sourly. "It would be nice if your country could have at least a few secrets."

"Aw, that stuff's all over the Net!" Theo protested.

"That may well be," Mr. Cosgrove replied, "but it's not what we're here for. Come this way."

Inconspicuous and almost lost in the hangar stood what at first glance looked like an ordinary commuter plane, shimmering metallic blue and resting on conventional landing gear with rubber tires. It was about the size of a typical executive jet, and could have been mistaken for one except for the configuration of the swept-back wings and tailfin. Instead of tapering, the stern was a bulbous pod housing the engines. There were no exhaust ports, however. Built into the rear was a large, reflective concave dish with a silvery ball-tipped rod about three feet long protruding from the center. It looked more like a dish antenna than a propulsion system. While there was an oversized windshield in the front, no windows were visible on the sides. On the tailfin was the white TranStella comet-tailed star logo, and the name *Mirage* was painted in small lettering near the nose. For a spaceship, it was absurdly small, and it looked almost ordinary in comparison with all the high-tech marvels parked around it.

It was by far the fastest and most powerful craft in the hangar.

"At least it isn't the *Moonbeamer*!" Theo muttered to Ronn.

The reference was to the spaceship in an old science-fiction vid series called *Starbusters*, a rather mean-spirited comedy that took the view that space travel was a horribly expensive and downright stupid fantasy for little boys. The show had not survived the revelation that the Earth really had been visited by aliens with faster-than-light starships, but its trademark retro-designed spaceship that was always breaking down at the worst possible moment still lingered in the popular mind as a symbol of incompetence and failure.

"Right," Ronn said. "With Uncle Jeff's ship, we might actually get where we're going."

A cargo bay hatch just back of the passenger cabin was open and two men in grease-stained overalls were finishing with stowing boxes — probably rations and other supplies for the team on Vesper — inside. Standing nearby and watching the loading operation was a thin, gangling man of about thirty, with the close-cropped hair typical for people who spent a lot of time with a helmet on. He wore a plain blue flight suit and an electronic display visor over his eyes that had lightened almost to transparency inside the hangar. As Mr. Cosgrove and the others came up, he turned and approached them with a crooked grin.

"May I present Captain Rogowski," Mr. Cosgrove announced. "He'll be the pilot on your flight today."

"Hi, how ya doin'?" Rogowski said, shaking everyone's hands.

"Hey, I've heard of you!" Theo exclaimed. "You landed the *Chesapeake* after that aborted launch last year!"

Ronn remembered the incident since it had been all over the news at the time. It was reassuring to know that the pilot for this mission was someone with a record of being good at his job.

For a moment, Captain Rogowski looked a little embarrassed to be reminded of his place in history. "Yeah, well, it was just as much my hide on the line, so I did what I could. That and saving the government about five billion for a new shuttle—"

"The *Constellation*, right?" Theo asked. "That's the next name on the list for Washington-class second-generation shuttles, isn't it?"

"So they tell me, but I wouldn't have been around to find out."

A tall, slim woman in a similar flight suit and with blonde hair not much longer than Rogowski's then appeared, sparing him from having to deal with any more of Theo's enthusiasms. She also wore a dark visor, which seemed to be standard for pilots whether they needed eye protection in a given circumstance or not.

"This is my co-pilot, Captain Saha," Rogowski said. "She'll take over if I drop dead on the way."

"Hello," she said with a faint nod and a strong projection of *Never*

40

mind the small talk and let's get going.

"And with that," Mr. Cosgrove said, "I believe my job here is done. You'll receive further instructions when you arrive on Vesper. Have a good trip, and I'll see you at the debriefing." He started to turn away.

"You aren't coming?" Theo asked.

Mr. Cosgrove paused, astonished by the mere thought. "Good heavens, no. It's all up to you now, and I intend to go back to the hotel and get some sleep." He walked towards the waiting van, and for one last bleak, hopeless moment, Ronn wished he could go with him.

"It's time we got on board," Rogowski announced, and herded Ronn and the others towards the open doorway on the side of the *Mirage* while Captain Saha followed.

The forward door was hinged on the bottom and had steps built into the inner surface. When opened, it swung down so that what had been the top edge rested on the ground and it could be used as a staircase. It even had railings on both sides.

The interior space of the cabin was about that of a large RV. The floor was plushly carpeted, and along the curving wood-paneled walls were six seats that were more like easy chairs, three in a line along each side of the cabin with a narrow aisle down the middle. In front of each seat was a small table with a pop-up computer display, probably intended as workstations so Prescott and his associates could take care of business while in flight. In back of the seats were a small galley and a couple of doors. Up front was the pilots' compartment, and through the open doorway Ronn could see two seats facing the windshield and a console with complicated-looking controls, glowing indicator lights, and readouts.

Captain Saha sat down in one of the pilot seats and started checking over the displays on the panel in front of her while Rogowski closed and secured the outer door. A second, interior door sealed the cabin.

"Find a seat and strap yourselves in, kids," he told them. "It's a three-hour trip, but there's a can in the back if you need it, along with a galley with drinks and snacks in the fridge. There's even a built-in entertainment system with music and vids, so you can probably find something to keep you occupied."

"Any games?" Theo asked, heading for the rear seats.

"I didn't think to check," Rogowski said. "You'll have to look for yourself."

"Did Uncle Jeff really get this ship from the aliens?" Theo then wondered. "Looks an awful lot like a regular plane."

"Well, it's supposed to," Rogowski replied. "Your uncle had the aliens modify a standard executive jet, maybe so it wouldn't look obviously not from around here on the ground. Even so, the wings and the blue color, which is some kind of anti-friction glazing, pretty much give it away, and there are other mods under the skin we can only guess at. What makes it really obvious is that propulsion unit in the tail. We don't have anything on our own spacecraft that looks the least bit like it. When it lights up, you need eye protection to be anywhere near it, not that it's a good idea to be anywhere near it. If you want to be poetic about it, some people call it 'diamond fire,' because it kind of does look like a glowing diamond from a distance. We just call it the 'torch,' but exactly how it works to push the bird from Point A to Point B, there are some theories but nobody really knows."

Ronn stowed his backpack underneath the front seat on the left side, then sat down and buckled the shoulder strap and seatbelt. Across the aisle from him, Phaedra did the same.

"You kids have no idea what a thrill it is to fly one of these babies," Rogowski went on. "Any of our ships, you mainly ride on top of a booster that could blow up out from under you at any moment if the least little thing goes wrong, as I found out the hard way a few months back, and you're in orbit in a few minutes. As for ever being able to really go somewhere, I didn't have much hope. Nobody's landed on the Moon in over sixty years and it doesn't look like anybody's going back soon. Mars you can forget. Every President comes into office announcing a big program to put somebody on Mars in twenty years, but it's always twenty years from the moment the hand comes off the Bible. Any sooner and they'd have to start paying for it, I guess. So I thought the best I'd ever be able to do would be taxiing between space stations in low Earth orbit, but then the government got its mitts on this, about a thousand years ahead of anything we've got of our own. And it's easy to fly. Simple controls, built-in AI does everything for you. Can you drive, Phaedra? You could probably fly it, too."

"If it's so easy, what's so exciting about it?" Theo demanded. "It sounds like the pilot's just along for the ride."

"Not exactly," Rogowski said. "You link up with the ship. It's like you become a part of it. You aren't just riding in some big machine and nudging it one way or another, you are the bird and you can feel the wind in your feathers. But enough chitchat. I have to get serious now."

He called up a display on his wristcom and read off a list of safety rules and emergency procedures. There weren't many. Because the shuttle was the product of alien technology far in advance of Earth's, it was thought that not much could go wrong. Besides, the technology was so mysterious that there wasn't much anybody could do about it if something did.

"In case of real trouble," Rogowski added, "like sudden loss of cabin pressure, a sensor in your seat will automatically activate a respirafoam bubble. It's like an air bag, only you're inside it. We've reverse-engineered it and we're testing it now for use in our own spacecraft, though I hear it's not real comfortable for very long. It'll keep you alive until somebody can pick you up, and that's the main thing. Let's all just hope we have a nice, safe trip without any incidents. And now it's time for me to start earning my pay."

He went forward and into the cockpit. Through the open doorway, Ronn saw him sit down in the pilot's seat next to Captain Saha.

Several minutes went by while they went through some kind of check-out procedure involving projected 3-D displays, but Ronn couldn't see exactly what they were doing from his angle. Otherwise, nothing much seemed to be happening.

"What's taking so long?" Theo finally complained.

Rogowski was still remarkably patient. "We have to wait for permission to take off," he called back. "This bird is completely invisible to radar so they have to clear airspace for miles around."

Perhaps to avoid having to listen to further gripes from the customers, Rogowski then closed the cockpit door.

They waited for several more minutes. Ronn began to wonder if he should take a look at the entertainment system and see what was available in case this went on for much longer. Then—

"Strap yourselves in if you haven't already, kids!" Rogowski exclaimed over the cabin speaker. "We're clear for takeoff!"

"Shouldn't that be 'go for launch'?" Theo called back.

"Not when you're taking off from a runway!"

The simulated wood wall panels on either side turned transparent, showing a view of the hangar interior around the shuttle. Ronn felt as though he was sitting next to a window three feet high and running the length of the cabin. The high-def view was so clear that if it hadn't been for the lack of grease and aviation fuel smells drifting through, he could have been convinced there wasn't anything solid between him and the outside.

In complete silence, the ship started to move. It taxied out of the hangar into the bright sunlight and on to the nearby runway, where it stood for another couple of minutes to wait for final clearance.

"Here we go!" Rogowski suddenly called out and the shuttle headed down the runway, gathering speed as it went. Ronn was pressed back into his seat. Moments later, the nose lifted, then the rest of the ship. In the viewscreen next to him, he saw the brown desert landscape dropping away beneath them.

It was so much like a regular airplane taking off that it was almost a little disappointing. Rockets should blast off with a deafening roar amid belching fire and billowing smoke, and astronauts should be mashed flat into their seats by crushing G-forces. Doing it this way took all the drama out of going into space, Ronn felt.

The shuttle even flew like a plane. Nothing unusual was obvious at first. But the ship kept going up and up — and up. The flat line of the distant horizon began to curve. Details on the ground far below melted into blurs of brown and occasional green. Even the scattered white clouds were soon far below. The warm blue sky turned to a stark cobalt blue that quickly faded to black, and stars began to appear. Whatever else happened from here on out, Ronn had gotten this far. He was in space.

Somewhere, a list was being kept with the names of all the people who had been in space since Yuri Gagarin's time, now numbering in the thousands. It was nice to think that the name Aaron Nelson Evans would be on that list for all time to come. There had been a Ron Evans that Ronn had once come across in a vid about space travel, one of the Apollo astronauts back in the 1970s, but now this Ron(n) Evans would really be him and not just somebody with a similar name.

Travis would be so jealous when he got back and told him all about his trip (never mind the *if* he got back qualification). But even though having been in space would be good for a lifetime's worth of bragging rights, bragging just wasn't Ronn's style. He wished mainly that Travis could have come along.

He sat back in his seat and looked out the window. Without any reflections from glass or plastic panes and probably with some image enhancement to bring out faint light sources, the view was more vivid than it would have been through an actual window. It was like looking into space with nothing between the stars and his own naked eyeballs. The Earth was somewhere out of sight behind them and the stars shone coldly and steadily, more brilliant than he had ever seen them from the ground. Even the Milky Way was clearly visible, a band of pale light stretching from one end of the sky to the other.

After about twenty minutes of powered flight, Rogowski shut down the engines. "Okay, kids," he announced over the speaker, "we'll be coasting the rest of the way, and you can get up and move around the cabin now. Weightlessness can be tricky if you aren't used to it, so I've got the artificial gravity on. Down is towards the floor, just like on Earth."

"Artificial gravity...?" Ronn started to ask.

The com connection was two-way and Rogowski could hear him. "Something else your uncle got from his alien buddies that he hasn't let anybody in on yet. Nobody knows how it works and the system is sealed so you can't even get a look at it. There's a whole bunch of different theories about that, too, but the one that makes the most sense is that it can't possibly work given what we know about physics, so it's either magic or there's something we don't understand. Lots of alien tech is like that."

Then Captain Saha emerged from the pilots' compartment, pausing in the doorway to tell Rogowski, "Don't wake me up unless you have a heart attack or something." She went on into the cabin and sat down in the empty seat behind Phaedra.

The cabin lights were dimmed so they could sleep if they wanted to, and Phaedra sat back in her seat and closed her eyes. Theo played games instead. He seemed especially fond of something involving the projected images of two old-fashioned metal robots about eight inches high fighting each other like boxers, slugging it out in a pool of light on a tabletop. Ronn recognized the game as a re-imagined classic that dated well into the last century.

He settled back to look out the window some more. He wasn't sleepy despite his early rising and the difference in time zones scrambling his sense of what time it should be, and he felt he should get the most he could out of the unexpected adventure.

After a while, looking at the stars finally wore a little thin and he called up a vidshow from the ship's entertainment directory, projected in front of him and with the sound turned low to keep from bothering everybody else in the cabin. Eventually, he did doze for a bit.

When Ronn came out of his nap, Captain Saha was awake and reading a projected page of text from a bookpad, but Phaedra wasn't in her seat. From the sound of things, she was up front and Rogowski was showing her how to fly the shuttle. Either he thought the more people who knew how to fly the thing, the better, in case something bad happened, or else he was just bored on a long flight without much to do between takeoff and landing, and chatting with a pretty girl, even if she was a little young for him, was his idea of a pleasant way to pass the time. Ronn was a little jealous that he wasn't being shown, too, but he had to admit that Phaedra was cuter than he was.

When she came back a little later, she paused next to Ronn long enough to say, "He was right. This ship is easy to fly. It does everything for you except pack your lunch. I'm not even sure why it needs a pilot at all except to tell it where to go."

She went on past her seat towards the rear of the cabin. Ronn didn't think anything about it until she suddenly screamed. Startled, he turned and looked back.

Phaedra stood in front of a door she had just opened, as though she had jumped about a foot backwards, and she held her hand over her mouth, staring wide-eyed at something.

Ronn started to get up, but Captain Saha was ahead of him. "They were supposed to get rid of that thing," he heard her mutter as he followed her towards the rear.

Phaedra had opened a storage closet door instead of the door she really wanted. Limply hanging from some kind of bracket in the closet was a body: a twenty-something woman with closed eyes. She wore a soft cap like a beret at a jaunty angle on her short blonde hair, and a blue and green uniform consisting of a vest over a blouse, a short skirt and dark tights, and ankle-high bootlets. A script inscription on her vest over her heart read "Ashley."

"Is she... *dead*?" Phaedra choked.

Captain Saha just sounded disgusted. "She was never alive. It's a bot. A robot flight attendant. I'm afraid your uncle had some really tacky taste."

I wouldn't say that... Ronn thought. The bot had the most beautiful face he had ever seen, even if on second thought her features did seem a little too perfectly sculpted to be real. She looked utterly lifelike, as though just sleeping. Ronn knew that one of the Prescott company's pieces of introduced alien technology was the autonomous behavior system that made limited judgment possible for robots, so it figured that Uncle Jeff would have the very best on his private shuttle.

With that explanation, Phaedra recovered quickly. "It's still pretty gruesome. Why is she hung on a rack like that?"

Captain Saha shrugged. "Bots can sag over time if they're stored standing up, I guess. Not my field."

"But what a life," Phaedra said. "You're only awake when you're working, and then you're put into the closet to sleep until you have to go back to work again."

"You're forgetting that the human look is just cosmetic and it isn't really alive," Captain Saha told her. "You wouldn't feel sentimental about an automatic serving cart that had been put away, and that's all this is when you come down to it."

Theo was all interest and curiosity. "Can we start her up?" he asked eagerly.

"Not on this trip," Captain Saha said coldly, closing the door. "I don't think you need somebody to fluff your pillow or mix your drinks. Besides" — she paused to glance at the upper corner of her visor — "we only have another hour to go. It's about noon, so how about some lunch? There are some meal packets in the galley."

Now that was interesting, Ronn thought as he set the tray with a grilled ham and cheese sandwich, some chips, and a Coke on the table in front of him and sat down again. He had never seen a bot that advanced before. The really lifelike models were still fairly new and hadn't made their way to his small town yet, but they had been in the news now and then. As almost completely convincing human robots that could be programmed to perform routine tasks that required some degree of making on-the-spot decisions when unexpected situations were encountered, they were still mostly a theme-park novelty, replacing the walkarounds — real people dressed up as cartoon characters. Despite overblown worries that bots might eventually replace human beings entirely, they were too expensive for most jobs to be practical substitutes for existing robotic machines that didn't have to look at all human, let alone for what little low-paid human labor was left. There was also an instinctive feeling of uneasiness that many people felt about even the most lifelike bots. They weren't lifelike enough in some subtle way, a tiny but crucial gap between living and almost but not quite living that Ronn had heard called "the uncanny valley." The result was a reaction like that of Captain Saha and Phaedra. It was hard to find a commercial use for a product that so many people thought was just plain creepy.

At last, long after the thrill of spaceflight had faded away and it was hardly any different from the cross-country airplane flight the day before, the engines came on again. Ronn felt himself being lightly pressed back in his seat as the ship decelerated — for the braking maneuver, the *Mirage* had been turned around, with the rear thruster pointed forward.

"Vesper, dead ahead!" Rogowski announced over the speaker.

Ronn could have done without the "dead" part.

A projected image appeared in front of Ronn, showing where the *Mirage* was headed. At first, Vesper was just a very bright star. As it slowly grew larger, it took on a definite shape as a ragged sunlit crescent. Within the horns was a black, starless void. Tiny lights appeared in the dark center, marking surface installations of some kind. The object continued to increase in size, taking on a sense of mass and bulk. Soon he could see craters and rugged hills in the lighted portion, and as the landscape expanded to fill the screen, it became a world in itself. It was tiny on the planetary scale, but from the human point of view it was vast and overwhelming. Ronn even heard Phaedra gasp slightly when she saw the sun rising spectacularly over the glowing rim of the mostly silhouetted asteroid. Perhaps she wasn't as blasé as she pretended.

Rogowski brought the ship around the miniature planet, braking as he went, and at last turning the now sufficiently showed ship around to face forward again. Ronn watched the torn and blasted rock pass by out the side window view. Then the *Mirage* angled towards the surface and the rocky wasteland of craters grew even larger in front of them. To Ronn it looked as though they were approaching a rugged gray wall. It was hardly comforting to realize that someone on the asteroid itself would see the *Mirage* coming straight down towards the ground, slowing but still at a fairly high speed.

Just as Ronn was starting to worry whether Rogowski was aware of how close all that hard-looking solid rock was getting, something started opening up ahead, a rectangular entranceway framed by blinking red lights.

The ship shot through the opening and its wheels touched down on the floor of a brightly lit corridor with white metal walls, large enough to accommodate spacecraft even bigger than the *Mirage*.

At that point, the exterior displays went out, leaving Ronn and the others sitting in the suddenly rather confined cabin. All he could tell from the ship's movement was that it had slowed almost to a stop by the time it landed and only rolled a short distance. Some further maneuvering followed, probably taxiing into an airlock, waiting for air to be pumped in, and coming out the other side, then the *Mirage* stopped entirely.

"I think we're here," Theo said in some awe.

Rogowski came out of the cockpit and opened the inner and outer side doors. A slight whoosh followed as the pressurized air inside the shuttle escaped to the somewhat thinner atmosphere outside, and the bottom-hinged door swung down.

"All ashore that's going ashore!" he called out jauntily, and went down the built-in steps.

Ronn unbuckled his seatbelt, stood up, and squirmed into the straps of his backpack, then joined Phaedra and Theo as they lined up at the doorway.

Theo started down the steps and promptly lost his footing. He landed in a sitting position on the bare metal flooring, looking more surprised than hurt. Phaedra stumbled on the steps but managed to keep her balance by hanging on to the railing.

"Careful," Rogowski said from where he stood by the steps. "Gravity's only about 80 percent Earth normal here."

"*Now* he tells us," Theo muttered, getting back to his feet.

Forewarned, Ronn took it easy coming down, and Captain Saha followed. Stepping onto the floor and taking a deep breath, he noticed that the chilly air in the docking bay seemed almost a little too clean and antiseptic, as though whatever filters were recycling the air were a bit too efficient, removing something that on dirty old Earth would have seemed like part of the flavor. The overall lighting was on the dim side, perhaps designed for eyes that had evolved somewhere else and would have found normal sunlight on Earth a little too bright.

They were in a huge open space with white, black-trimmed metal walls and floor, large enough to accommodate the *Mirage* in a parking area in the corner and much more besides. The ceiling was far overhead, almost lost in the gloom.

Several cables and tubes slithered out of the wall and attached themselves to the hull of the *Mirage*, while a couple of self-propelled carts with waving mechanical arms rolled around it.

"What's all that?" Ronn asked Rogowski.

"Some sort of automatic maintenance and recharging for the propulsion unit. Lord knows nobody human could fix anything in that ship if something went wrong. Well, maybe the vid system or the fridge. That's people-type stuff. But the propulsion or the artificial gravity, forget it."

The *Mirage* wasn't the only ship in the docking bay. Nearby was one of the cargo carriers Mr. Cosgrove had mentioned, a bulky and bulbous-looking transport ship with stubby wings. It was at least twice the size of the private shuttle and also sported the TranStella logo.

Several men came into the docking bay from a door leading to a corridor outside. Two wore blue uniforms with combat boots and holstered sidearms as well as the usual dark visors, and with them was a burly officer barely in his thirties. A nametag on the officer's chest read **RAMIREZ**.

After an exchange of salutes with Captains Rogowski and Saha, the officer stepped forward and Rogowski introduced him to Ronn and the others.

"This is Captain Ramirez. He's commanding the military side of the operation."

"Air Force Special Tactics, I bet," Theo spoke up. "You guys must be a Combat Control Team!"

"Something like that," Captain Ramirez said, then addressed the group. "Glad you could make it. Too bad you had to be dragged into this, but when the people running the show figure something out, orders are orders. Certainly the story of *my* life."

While his men set to unloading the boxes of supplies from the *Mirage*'s cargo hold, Ramirez led the new arrivals through a nearby doorway and across a corridor to the crew lounge. The doors looked more like airtight hatches that could be quickly closed in the event of an emergency

In the lounge, not much larger than a typical rec room in the basement of a house on Earth, they found several men and women sitting on the floor. Some were security personnel and others were scientists, some reading and the rest working on laptop displays. They glanced up when Ramirez and the new arrivals came in, and showed some signs of interest as though relieved that something was finally happening after days of boredom.

49

There wasn't much space for so many people, and certainly not enough chairs. Rolled-up sleeping bags and other gear added to the crowding. The adjacent bunkroom and a kitchenette were tiny and hardly eased the situation.

"Why all the security people?" Ronn asked Rogowski in a low voice.

"Well, for security. The scientists were sent up to look the place over and the Special Ops team came along to protect them in case Prescott had guards or if we ran into any players for other teams." Rogowski turned to one of the scientists, sitting on the floor and looking over a projected laptop display that looked like schematic diagrams of the asteroid. "How's it going, Doc?"

"Not well," the scientist complained, then shut off the display and stood up a little stiffly. He was tall and thin, in late middle age and looking it, wearing casual clothes rather than the white lab coat Ronn would have expected, and nearly bald with a gray beard that was in some need of trimming. "This lounge was never meant for more than two or three people at a time, and now we've got over a dozen of us crammed in here with nothing to do because we can't get into the main complex itself. God, what I'd give for a close-up look at the artificial gravity-generating system!" He shook hands with Ronn and the others as the introductions were made. "My name's Kininger, and I'm the lead scientist here. I'll be in charge of your mission."

"So when do we get started?" Theo asked.

Dr. Kininger checked his wristcom. "Let's see… it's about one. I take it you already had lunch on the way up? As soon as possible, then. There's no reason to wait until tomorrow. I'll explain the layout and what we need you to do. Then you can be on your way."

The scientists conferred to finalize what they wanted done and in what order. In the meantime, Ronn, Phaedra, and Theo were advised to practice walking out in the corridor so they could get used to the lesser gravity. One of the security officers came along, occasionally offering some advice on how to move while keeping an eye on them.

Despite his initial spill coming off the shuttle, Theo took to it readily. Before long, he was all but bouncing off the walls as he practiced running and leaping. Phaedra just seemed to regard it as one more inconvenience to be borne with as little patience as possible. Ronn didn't quite go to Theo's hyperactive extent, but he found he liked leaping a bit further than he could have managed on Earth. Since the difference in gravity wasn't extreme, the way it would have been on the Moon with only one-sixth Earth's gravity, all three quickly adapted and could soon walk normally.

"The fun part will be getting used to Earth's gravity again when we go back home," Phaedra said, then added gloomily, "Whenever that is…"

50

After an hour or so, another security officer came out into the corridor to get them. He took them back inside the crew lounge and had them sit down around the small dining table. Dr. Kininger commandeered the remaining chair and the other scientists crowded behind them, while the security people stood in the rear.

Glancing around the room, Ronn had a sudden feeling of just how strange the situation was. All these scientists, all the Air Force personnel guarding them... all of them adults, all of them highly trained specialists in their fields... None of them could do what had to be done but three kids could. Ronn sensed that every adult in the place felt that this was definitely not the way things should be, and he and his cousins were only tolerated out of necessity because Uncle Jeff had stacked the deck that way.

"Just seeing this place from space on the way in made me realize what we're up against," Dr. Kininger began. "The powers that moved this rock through space could swat us like flies if they decided we were getting to be bothersome. I don't think a few guards armed with pistols could do much if the aliens got serious about eliminating us. The politicians are convinced that the aliens are no longer around, though, and Prescott has been on his own for some time. It isn't the aliens we have to worry about now, anyway—"

"Then what are we worried about?" Theo piped up.

"Perhaps 'worry' was a poor choice of words," Dr. Kininger replied with a hint of irritation. "Our problem is that we can't fool the recognition scan in the checkpoint. On Earth, of course, as soon as anyone comes up with a new ID system, like retinal scanning or facial recognition or skin-oil analysis, somebody else figures out a way to get around it. Here, we think Prescott has a system based on dozens of different datapoints derived from the extensive physical examinations you kids had ten years ago, and no imposter could possibly simulate a match with all of them. Maybe someone could if given enough time to analyze the system thoroughly, but we don't have that luxury. That's where you kids come in. Or go in, actually."

"So exactly what is it you want us to do once we get inside?" Phaedra asked.

"We can't give you specific instructions because we don't know what's beyond the checkpoint," Dr. Kininger said. "We'll just have to play it by ear. Your ultimate goal, of course, is to find your uncle. He's probably somewhere in that large domed area on top, but there's a lot of asteroid between here and there that you'll have to make your way through to get to it. Failing that, look for the master control center. Since you're Prescott's duly authorized heirs, you should have the permissions you need to let the rest of us in and then we can take it from there. If you can find any of the missing TranStella employees, they should be able to help you with the control settings. In a nutshell, that's it."

Some of the scientists joined in at that point and a discussion followed about whether to send all three kids in at once or have one stay behind as a reserve in case something happened. While it wasn't guaranteed that the kid going in second would have any better luck than the first two if something bad was lying in wait beyond the checkpoint, the scientists thought they should have a spare handy. Some amount of time was wasted on wrangling over who should go first and test the cheese to see if a trap snapped, and in what combination. In the end, the scientists settled on the Ronn and Phaedra option, justifying it as Phaedra being the oldest and most responsible, with Ronn as the next oldest providing support even if they weren't entirely sure what he was good for.

Theo wasn't happy and nearly threw a tantrum. "I wanna go!"

Phaedra took him aside. "Look, that doesn't even work on Mom anymore and it isn't going to work with these scientists! It's what they've decided, so just live with it, all right?"

Dr. Kininger overheard and added, "You can go in when Ronn and Phaedra signal that it's safe."

Theo quieted down but he still wasn't happy.

A scientist named Dr. Takahashi was the scientific party's engineering and technology specialist, and she fitted Ronn and Phaedra with earbuds and ear-mounted vidcams for staying in touch with the crew lounge. The gear was then tested, taking still more time until the scientists were satisfied that everything was working properly.

"We'll see what you see as you go along," Dr. Takahashi told them. "Then we can decide what you should do based on what you find. It's probably a maze on the lower levels, so don't go too far from the door at first and get lost. We can't send anybody in to look for you. At the first sign of trouble, come back here at once."

"What if we run into the bad guys?" Theo asked.

"I was just going to brief you about that," one of the guards spoke up, a young sergeant with the name **WORDEN** on his chest. "Your best bet is to avoid them entirely, so be on the lookout as you penetrate deeper into the interior. If you do encounter any hostiles, run, hide, whatever you can to avoid capture. Worst case, surrender. We doubt if they would hurt you because you'd be too valuable to them as hostages. To put it bluntly, they could hold you for one very hefty ransom, and they probably wouldn't leave that much easy money on the table. But just to be on the safe side, have any of you had weapons training?"

The cousins looked at each other blankly.

"Ever fired a gun?"

More blank looks.

"I've played a lot of shooting games..." Theo started to say, then trailed off as he saw that it might not be considered applicable experience.

Sgt. Worden sighed. "We don't have time to train you and have you practice, but we can't have you going in completely defenseless, either."

They were all given Stingers, light-weight plastic pistols that fired electrically charged darts intended to leave an opponent lying on the ground and contemplating the error of his ways while he writhed helplessly. Supposedly idiot-proof and ideal for rookies and amateurs who had no experience with regular firearms, Stingers were called wireless tasers by some, "bug zappers" in police slang. A dart's charge could be manually adjusted, since what would just annoy a 250-pound thug might kill a small man or woman, but having the leisure to fiddle with the thing in the heat of a situation gone bad was not always guaranteed. With their short range and sometimes questionable stopping power, about the best that could be said was that a Stinger was better than nothing, but not by much, and the most desirable outcome was not having to use it at all.

After tucking the Stingers into holsters looped on their belts, they were given a quick lecture on how to use them, which amounted mainly to point, shoot, and pray.

Finally, they were issued some meal packets and water-filled canteens, and they were good to go.

"At least we assume that if the system lets you in, it will let you out again," Dr. Kininger said, "but we can't be sure until we try it. In case things don't go as planned, there must be places inside where you can find food and water, like the domed area on top, since Prescott and his people must eat something while they're here, but getting there might be problematic. These will give you a couple of days while we figure something out."

Nice to know... thought Ronn glumly, and Phaedra didn't look any more cheerful about the prospect of being trapped inside.

Since Vesper was on the same time as TranStella's Santa Barbara headquarters, it was now three in the afternoon and at last time to do what they had come to do. Loaded down under their backpacks and canteens, Ronn and Phaedra went with Dr. Kininger and some of the other scientists down the corridor outside the crew quarters to a closed metal door at the end. Still sulking, Theo followed along, carrying his backpack and canteen in case Phaedra and Ronn signaled an all clear right away.

"Then goodbye and good luck," Dr. Kininger said, shaking hands with Ronn and Phaedra.

Well, this is it...

Ronn suddenly felt nervous. After all the excitement of the past two days, it had come down to this. In a few moments, he and Phaedra would be on their way into unknown territory with a job to do that neither of them knew how to do.

I really don't feel up to this, he thought, but home was a long way away and there was no backing out now.

He looked at the door. It seemed dauntingly solid and there was no obvious way to open it. "So how do we get in?"

"That panel to one side," Dr. Kininger said. "Phaedra, you're closest. Put your hand on it."

Phaedra lifted her hand to a square of red plastic about six inches on a side. It lit under her palm, then the door slid sideways into the wall, revealing an entrance into a narrow, bare metal-walled corridor some fifteen feet long, lit by overhead lights. Another closed door was at the other end.

Dr. Kininger blinked. "We couldn't get it to do even that much."

Phaedra paused, looking doubtfully into the corridor.

"Go on in," Dr. Kininger urged. "If it recognizes who you are, it certainly won't hurt you."

Phaedra looked as though she would like to be just a little more convinced of that point, then swallowed and stepped through the open doorway.

Ronn wasn't sure if he should also put his hand on the panel, but the doorway remained open, so he stepped through in turn.

Phaedra was waiting for him, and they started down the corridor towards the far door.

"Hey! Wait up!" somebody behind them shouted,

Hearing the sound of running feet approaching them, Ronn and Phaedra turned.

It was Theo, half leaping in the reduced gravity as he ran to catch up with them. He was struggling to slip his arms through the straps of his backpack as he slipped past the startled scientist and all but threw himself through the doorway.

"Come back here!" Dr. Kininger yelled and started after Theo. Just as he crossed the threshold, Dr. Kininger was caught in a flash and a discharge of crackling energy, and knocked on his back on the floor.

"I don't think so!" Theo shouted back at him. "No way I'm missing this party!"

Ronn glanced at Phaedra. "Should I grab him and send him back?"

She shook her head. "He might as well come along. When he gets like this, you can't tell him no." She raised her voice and called back to Dr. Kininger, who was ruefully rubbing his hindquarters and struggling to his feet, just as the door closed again. "Take my word for it, you're better off if he's with us!"

And so Theo joined the expedition.

They went on through the corridor. Multi-colored lights shone on them, one after another. A female voice from nowhere announced: "Identified: Phaedra Knuppel."

More rainbow beams of light played over Ronn, making his skin tingle, while another, dimmer beam shone directly into his eyes. He guessed that any number of identifying datapoints were being verified, from retinal scans to the DNA in his skin cells, all based on that mysterious examination in California when he was five. He must have passed, since the voice then announced, "Identified: Ronn Evans."

"It tickles!" Theo exclaimed as the voice acknowledged him as well.

When they reached the far-end door, the voice declared, "Identification complete and confirmed."

The door panel slid open, and they stepped on through.

Part Two

The Three-Dimensional Scrapbook

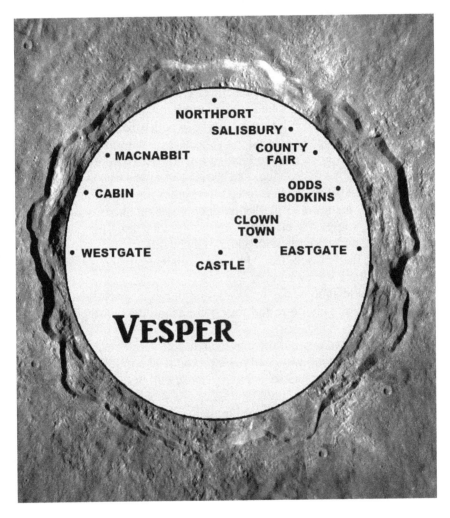

Chapter Five

Whatever Ronn had been expecting, it certainly wasn't this.

They came out into a small waiting room modeled after an airport terminal building of a century before, with wooden benches and a closed ticket window. Brightly colored travel posters on the walls promised fast, comfortable service in antique-looking aircraft with propellers to destinations like New York, London, and Paris. The effect was as though they had just gotten off an airplane after a long cross-country flight.

A man's mature and pleasantly deep voice suddenly spoke without any obvious source. "Welcome to my world, Phaedra, Theo, and Ronn." The voice sounded kindly with a hint of a chuckle.

"I think that's Uncle Jeff!" Phaedra exclaimed, looking around excitedly. "Is he here somewhere?"

Ronn could almost read her mind — if they had found him first thing, their job was already done and they were as good as on their way back home.

"Since you've made it this far," Uncle Jeff's voice went on, "you've certainly come a long way, and perhaps you'd like to relax and sit down to a good meal. A car to take you to my house will be along shortly. Please step outside. Enjoy your stay!" The voice fell silent with a finality hinting strongly that it would not be heard from again.

"I guess it was just a recording," Phaedra said, disappointed. "But it used our names, even got them right…"

"It *was* a little spooky," Theo added. "Almost like it was really him talking to us personally. But then he *invented* that autonomous behavior system stuff, or at least got it from the aliens."

Ronn was starting to feel relieved. Not being machine-gunned or vaporized by a laser beam as soon as they stepped through the door was a good sign, and Uncle Jeff's simulated self had sounded friendly. This mission might go better than he had thought.

They went out the front door as instructed, coming into a starkly bare corridor with white metal walls and floor, about twenty feet wide and ten feet high, with glowing light panels spaced at regular intervals along the ceiling. In one direction, the corridor curved out of sight a short distance away, while in the other it ran straight ahead as far as they could see.

As they watched, an antique car with its cloth top down and driven by a man in a chauffeur's uniform came around the nearby bend and stopped in front of them. The car was evidently British whatever its make, with the steering wheel on the right. Although it was a good century old and should have had a chugging gasoline motor, it made no noise at all. Burning gasoline in the confined spaces of a network of narrow tunnels would have fouled the air in short order, so no doubt the original internal combustion motor had been swapped for something clean.

"You must be Mr. Prescott's niece and nephews," the driver said, tipping his cap. "May I offer you a ride? It's a long walk to the guest house."

Ronn and his cousins exchanged glances. Why not? They had no idea what else to do now that they were here, and this was something. They got in the car, with Phaedra in the front seat next to the driver and Ronn and Theo in the back, and it started off down the corridor.

At least it had been a corridor when Ronn first saw it. Now it was a narrow country road leading through what seemed to be the green English countryside with hedgerows and low hills on a warm summer day, with no sign of walls on either side or a low ceiling. The light was gentle, seemingly coming from a sun far overhead in a bright blue sky.

"It's wide-area 3-D image projection," Phaedra said matter-of-factly. "I've been on shows where they used it. You can see how it's a little fuzzy at the edges."

As they rode along in near-total silence, Phaedra turned to the driver next to her. "Have you seen our Uncle Jeff anywhere?"

"Please direct any enquiries to the staff at the house," the driver replied almost automatically.

Phaedra frowned, then had a sudden thought and glanced back at Ronn. "Have you heard from the scientists?"

Ronn realized that he hadn't. "I just assumed they were listening in. Doc, can you hear me?"

No reply.

Phaedra poked in her ear to tap the bud but she didn't get any response, either. "Well, that's just great. We lost contact. Now what?"

Ronn turned in the seat and looked to the rear. All he saw was simulated English landscape stretching to the simulated horizon. They were already some distance into the complex and it seemed pointless to turn around and go back. "I guess we'll just have to go on and figure something out later. Maybe the vidcams still work," he added, but if something was blocking voice contact with the crew lounge once they were inside, the vidlink was probably broken, too.

Ronn and his cousins looked at each other in dismay. They really were on their own, in the middle of... *what?*

After a drive of perhaps a mile, the driver slowed the car and stopped in front of a country inn with a sign out front that said **WESTGATE**. The road seemed to stretch on for endless miles into the rural landscape, but this was as far as they were going.

The driver got out of the car and opened the passenger doors for them. "Shall I help you with your bags?" he inquired.

Ronn pointed to his backpack as he clambered out. "Er... we don't have any bags. Just these."

"Very well, sir. Off you go, then. When you wish to return, ring for me." The driver got into the car again and drove on. Even though the projected road seemed to extend into the far distance, both the car and driver disappeared almost at once in a flurry of video interference, as though passing through a curtain.

"That effect needs some work," Theo remarked.

"Now what are we supposed to do?" Phaedra asked.

Ronn looked uncertainly at the inn. "I guess we go in here."

Inside, they found what might have been the front lobby of a small English hotel, with a reservation counter (unattended but a sign next to a chrome-plated, hand-operated bell read **PLEASE RING FOR ASSISTANCE**). In the back was a door to an elevator, which opened moments after they came in. A short, roundish, gray-haired woman in later middle age stepped out, wearing a gray dress with a white apron.

"We've been expecting you!" she exclaimed as warmly as though they were her own grandchildren. "I'm Mrs. Flynn, the housekeeper. You must be tired and hungry after your long trip, so please follow me."

She led them inside the elevator, and here the attempt at a quaint atmosphere from days long ago came to an end. Instead of a cube or a cage lifted by cables, the elevator cab was a cylindrical capsule barely large enough for the four of them. They went up for a considerable distance in silence while the glowing numbers above the door changed to mark the passing levels.

When the cab stopped and the door opened, they emerged into a lounge with dark wood paneling, paintings of woodland scenes on the walls, thick carpeting, and comfortable-looking chairs and sofas. Waiting for them was the staff.

Uncle Jeff had followed all the clichés with the tall, dignified butler in an elegant old suit, a couple of chefs in white uniforms with tall paper hats, and three pretty young women who looked enough alike to be triplets in black maids' uniforms with frilly white caps and aprons. Despite what Captain Saha had said about Uncle Jeff's tacky taste, the maids wore knee-length skirts, their uniforms more practical than revealing or flashy.

Do these people live here all the time? Ronn had to wonder. How much did you have to pay people to get them to spend months or years at a stretch 60,000 miles from Earth? Well, it was probably an easy job. Weeks without much to do might go by between the short periods when there were guests in the house.

"Welcome to Westgate Manor," the butler announced with a stately bow. "I am Wilfred."

He introduced the rest of the staff, each bowing or curtsying as appropriate, and whose names Ronn immediately forgot. They then dispersed while Wilfred remained.

"Dinner will be served at six," he added. "I am sure that you would like to freshen up after your trip, so I will show you to your rooms."

Phaedra had been glancing around. "Is Uncle Jeff here?" she asked eagerly.

Wilfred shook his head. "Mr. Prescott is not currently in residence. In his absence, however, we shall endeavor to make your stay as pleasant as possible."

"Then where is he?" Phaedra pressed.

"I am sorry," Wilfred replied with almost maddening indifference, "but I do not have that information."

"I guess we're back to Square One," Ronn said.

"I'd like to *get* to Square One!" Theo exclaimed. "That'd be getting *somewhere!* This is more like we're stuck at Square Zero."

"Now, please come with me," Wilfred said.

Resigned to not getting any answers just yet, Ronn and the others followed him out of the room and down a hallway. They seemed to be in a large, luxuriously furnished mansion. Through the doorways they passed, Ronn caught glimpses of a dining room with a table large enough to seat a dozen or more people, and several rooms of indeterminate purpose that could have served as study, living room, parlor, sitting room, or salon, with old-fashioned chairs and couches. Table lamps were lit in each room, but there was a sense from the curtained windows that it was daylight outside. It all seemed a little too formal and impersonal to be a private residence and struck Ronn as more like a guest house or a bed and breakfast.

From there, Wilfred took them up a wide staircase to the second floor. Several doors on either side of a hall running the length of the house led to a dozen guest bedrooms. Wilfred assigned Ronn and his cousins each to a separate room and left them.

An overhead chandelier lit up as soon as Ronn entered his room. He took off his backpack and the now useless earcam, dropped them on a handy chair, and looked around. At first glance, it could have been a very expensive hotel room, complete with adjoining bathroom. The furniture looked old, yet had a feeling of being newly made. Antiques had to have been new once, of course, but even the carpet on the floor showed no signs of human feet having ever stepped on it. A projected time display and nightlight by the lamp on the nightstand next to the bed indicated 3:35.

The bathroom was about what might be expected in a high-class but old-fashioned hotel. The plumbing worked, and hot water was instantly available with a twist of a faucet. Even the basic amenities were on hand, like a bar of soap, shampoo, a toothbrush and toothpaste, a small shaving kit for gentlemen guests, and fluffy towels and washcloths. None of it was here automatically, Ronn realized, and every item had to be brought from 60,000 miles away. Somebody had put a lot of thought into this.

After that, what interested Ronn most were the large curtained windows and a door that led outside. He opened the door and stepped through to a balcony that looked out over a warm country afternoon in apparent mid-summer under a clear blue sky. The slight breeze was fresh and clean, even pine-scented, unlike the rather canned-tasting air belowdecks. The air was about room temperature, Ronn thought. *A very large room.*

Though it was a convincing simulation of the open sky with no sign of metal gridwork, he knew from the schematic projection of the asteroid he had been shown that he had to be standing in a rough circle about two miles in diameter with a domed roof vaulting overhead. The sun, if there was one, was somewhere above and behind him.

Immediately around the house was a broad green lawn that sloped gently downwards and came to an abrupt end at the edge of some very dense woods. A paved walk or bike path ran down the slope from the house and through the lawn, and was lost between the trees. Ronn should have had a good view from where he stood on the second-floor balcony, but whatever lay beyond the trees was lost in a thick, low-hanging haze that blotted everything out a short distance away. It probably wasn't a natural fog, as in water droplets suspended in the air, but more likely an artificial distortion intended to obscure the view.

Just what does Uncle Jeff have out there?

With no obvious answer to that question for the moment, Ronn turned and went back into the room. It was edging on towards four, and if dinner wasn't until six… Even though he'd napped on the *Mirage*, he kicked off his shoes and stretched out on the bed.

He woke up a couple of hours later. Now it was time to think seriously about dinner, and he decided to take a shower. He had already taken one that morning, but after the trip another couldn't hurt.

When Ronn came out of the bathroom, he found some clothes laid out on the bed, apparently with the expectation that he wear them at the table.

He took a look at them and did a double-take.

He was expected to wear a *tie*? Ties were for men four times his age. Ronn didn't even know how to tie one. The white shirt and the navy-blue jacket he could live with, but he'd have to draw the line at the useless neckwear.

They must have gotten his sizes when he was scanned for ID, and he wasn't even surprised to find that the clothes fit. If anything was eyebrow-raising, it was how fast the clothes had been made.

After dressing, Ronn went downstairs and was the first to come into the elegant dining room. The long table had been set for just three at one end. Large windows along the wall were covered by floor-length draperies and a chandelier shone from the ceiling overhead. Generic landscape paintings hung on the walls, above a couple of heavy wooden sideboards displaying antique dishes set on edge.

Soft music played from somewhere, pleasant but barely noticeable. To the extent Ronn could recognize any of the tunes, they were instrumental versions of the hits of forty years before performed by a string orchestra that wasn't trying very hard to sound enthusiastic about what it was doing.

The rear wall was almost entirely taken up with the glass face of a large water-filled aquarium. There were no fish inside, however, or much of anything else. Why there was a tank of water in the dining room puzzled Ronn unless Uncle Jefferson simply hadn't gotten around to stocking it with fish yet. Taking a closer look, he noticed a small button to one side, labeled **DISPLAY**. He pressed it and the water instantly swarmed with fish above a graveled bottom with seaweed and rocks. The foreground was dramatically lit by lights above and below, and the background seemingly stretched forever into darkness even though it was obvious from the outside that the tank was only about two feet wide.

Theo came into the room just then, also wearing a blue sport coat. Like Ronn, he hadn't bothered with a tie.

"Oh, I know what this is," he said, standing next to Ronn. "When they first came out with 3-D projection, they still had some problems with open-air displays because images were semi-transparent. But projections in water looked great because water's a lot denser than air. So to take advantage of that and bring some cash in to keep going while they were working the bugs out of the open-air system they were really after, they came up with these virtual aquariums for places like doctors' offices that just want 'em for relaxing displays in the waiting room. Perfectly lifelike fish that you don't have to feed. They can even mix fresh and saltwater fish, like goldfish and clownfish you could never put in the same tank." He pointed to a particularly striking orange and white striped fish. "This must be one of the deluxe models, though they sold some really huge ones to the big aquariums like the Shedd in Chicago and Sea World so they could get in whales and stuff."

Ronn was impressed in spite of himself. "You really know a lot about this."

"While you were snoozing on the way here, I found an introductory vid of the company's history for new employees."

Trying not to admire the kid's resourcefulness, Ronn kicked himself for not realizing the possibilities of the *Mirage's* on-board vid catalog,

"There's a label for 'Special Effects,'" Theo said, pointing to it. "I wonder what 'Ghost Fish' is?"

He touched the button and the light in the water changed to an ethereal blue. The fish were still there and swimming around, but now they were spectral outlines and silvery highlights.

Theo whistled in appreciation. "I don't know why anybody would want it, but it's a great effect."

That seemed to be the virtual aquarium's only trick, and Theo set it back to its normal display mode. As they turned towards the table, Ronn noticed a framed printed newspaper clipping hanging on another wall, yellowed and several decades old.

MAGRUDER MANSION BURNS

"I think that's *this* place!" Theo exclaimed, pointing to the accompanying grainy black and white 2-D picture showing the Colonial-style mansion before the fire, with its elegant pillars and a cupola on the roof.

Having grown up with parents who designed and remodeled houses, Ronn had some sense of how the inside of a house matched the outside, and he shared Theo's suspicion that the photo was of the house around them.

"Well, it's a copy, anyway," Ronn said. "I'll bet when Uncle Jeff was a kid, that was the fanciest house in town, and maybe he always wanted to live there. Maybe he even told himself, 'Someday I'll get rich and buy that house!' But it burned down before he had the chance, total loss it sounds like, so it was probably never rebuilt. He still had that dream, though, and he eventually had it reconstructed here."

Then Phaedra made her appearance, wearing a rather frilly blue dress that went all the way to her ankles.

"That's a new look for you," Theo observed, not sounding as though he thought it was a particularly good one and she might as well have been wearing a bonnet and a shawl.

"It's what they gave me," Phaedra said, looking dubiously down at herself, "and I didn't feel like arguing about it. But it's like something Mom might have worn to her senior prom. Somebody forgot to tell Uncle Jeff what decade this is." She stuck her matching blue-shod foot out from under the hem. "What's really scary is that the shoes actually fit. They must have scanned me down to my atoms!"

Wilfred the butler briefly appeared in the doorway. "Please be seated. Dinner will be served momentarily."

As they sat down in the chairs at the table, Ronn remembered a similar occasion. "I don't think the three of us have eaten together since that last family reunion just before Grandma died."

"Yeah," Theo said. "They put us all at the kids' table even though Phaedra griped about not getting to eat with the grown-ups, and Danny and Julia were there, too. We were just fine but the grown-ups started arguing about something we weren't supposed to hear. Let's face it. Our moms just don't get along. What was it all about, anyway? I forget."

Ronn had forgotten, too, but it was all too typical. As he shook his head, he noticed Phaedra looking at him as though there was something on her mind and she needed to tell him about it, but wasn't quite sure where to start. After a moment she overcame her hesitation and launched into it.

"I just want to say that whatever it is with our mothers, it doesn't have anything to do with us. We're stuck here with a job to do whether we like it or not, and if we work together, the quicker we can do it and the sooner we can go home."

"Fine with me," Ronn said with a shrug to show that he hadn't even thought of the old family feud, and Phaedra seemed satisfied.

Wilfred reappeared just then, carrying a tray with three bowls of tossed salad on it. As he placed the bowls in front of them, he announced, "Our menu tonight features prime rib *au jus*. How would you like yours?"

"Wow!" Theo exclaimed. "Steak for breakfast and prime rib for dinner! We're really eating high on the hog on this trip!"

Phaedra frowned. "I don't think that's quite the right animal."

"Medium for me," Theo told Wilfred, then leaned over to him and added in a low voice, "You can just get more bunny food for Phaedra. She's a vegetarian."

"I am not!" she insisted. "That was *last* month!" Then she turned to Wilfred, and affecting the pose of quite the sophisticated young lady, inquired, "Do you have wine?"

"Certainly," the butler replied. "We pride ourselves on our well-stocked cellar."

"Excellent. I'd like a nice red wine, say a Cabernet Sauvignon—"

"I'm sorry," Wilfred said with utter regret in his voice, "but I believe that you have not yet attained the age of eighteen. May I suggest a selection from our assortment of soft drinks instead?"

Phaedra sputtered and Theo snickered. Sixty thousand miles from home and they still couldn't get away from at least *some* adult supervision...

Somewhat later, when Ronn was finishing his salad, he realized his cousins were arguing with each other and he had been too occupied with his own thoughts to hear the beginning. Wilfred had left the dining room, so they were alone and waiting for the main course to be served, and something was bothering Theo.

"I think they're all bots!"

"I'm not so sure," Phaedra answered. "Wilfred and Mrs. Flynn seem too lifelike! Why wouldn't Uncle Jeff have a staff of real people?"

"So he wouldn't have to feed 'em!" Theo shot back. "I think they're bots and I'll prove it. Just wait."

Before long, Wilfred entered the dining room pushing a cart with the main course and side dishes on top. He took the salad bowls away and passed out the plates with prime rib and the small chrome *jus* containers. Theo was the last to be served, and just as Wilfred set the plate down in front of him—

Theo grabbed his fork and stabbed the back of Wilfred's hand. Hard. The tines went in deep.

Instead of screaming in pain, Wilfred merely looked at Theo in mild surprise. "I beg your pardon, sir. It would appear my hand was in your way." He withdrew the fork. "I shall bring you a clean utensil."

There was no blood. If anything, the puncture wounds in his hand were rapidly closing. Wilfred turned and left the dining room, pushing the empty cart in front of him.

"What did you do that for?" Phaedra demanded, horrified.

"I knew it!" Theo exclaimed in something like triumph. "He's a bot! They're probably *all* bots!"

"Let's just hope that Wilfred isn't so lifelike that he holds grudges," Ronn said lightly, and started cutting up his prime rib. Inwardly, he felt uneasy. Wilfred had been utterly convincing. Maybe a little stereotypical as a butler, but Ronn hadn't had any reason to doubt that he was alive. Theo was probably right, too. If Wilfred was a bot, so were the chauffeur, Mrs. Flynn, the chefs, and even the pretty maids all in a row. Was there anybody *human* around they could talk to?

As he ate, Ronn found that the food was excellent, but Uncle Jeff could certainly afford the best for his guests.

When everyone was finished with the main course, Wilfred reappeared to clear the table and serve dessert. He said nothing about the incident with the fork. For that matter, his hand didn't show any signs of injury at all.

Perhaps reflecting Uncle Jeff's own rather simple tastes, the dessert was warm apple pie topped with vanilla ice cream. Even that was superb, almost too rich for palates used to commercial ice cream back home.

After scraping every last drop of melting ice cream off the plate with his spoon, Theo leaned back in his chair and patted his stomach. "Now that was a dinner worth coming 60,000 miles for! I'll bet it was a lot better than those rations the scientists stuck us with. Hmm... wonder what *they're* eating right now?"

"They're probably worrying about why they lost contact with us," Phaedra said. "As far as they know, something awful happened to us the moment we stepped inside the place."

With a slight twinge of guilt, Ronn remembered that they were here for a reason, not just to enjoy fine dining. "Yeah, we'll have to figure out some way of letting them know we're all right. Maybe one of us should go back to the docking bay tomorrow..."

Theo looked too stuffed to want to do much of anything. "Oh, let 'em stew. We're doing just fine and they can guess Uncle Jeff wouldn't let us inside just to kill us."

Now that the meal was over, Wilfred escorted them to a room down the hall. "This is the den," he said. "Here you will find various opportunities for amusement until it is time to retire. If you require any further service, please ring." He then left them on their own, disappearing who knew where.

The room was furnished with comfortable chairs and a couch, along with game controls, a wall-sized vid display system, a mini-fridge with soft drinks and snacks, and even shelves with old books. At one end was an open fireplace with a crackling fire. While it gave off enough heat to be cozy for curling up on the floor in front of it, there was no smell of burning wood, so the fire was probably virtual.

"Are we supposed to just watch vids until bedtime?" Phaedra asked.

"I think that's the general idea, yeah," Ronn answered. "This place was designed to be a guest house for weekend getaways. But that isn't why we're here. I think we should explore the house. Maybe we'll find some clues about what happened to Uncle Jeff."

"Good idea," Theo said. "Sounds like it'd be more interesting than sitting around here watching vids I could see in my room back home."

Neither Wilfred nor Mrs. Flynn appeared to shoo them back into the den as they roamed the house. The entire staff seemed to have vanished for the night.

While Theo and Phaedra looked around on the first floor, Ronn went up to the second. All he found were bedrooms along the long hallway. At the end of the hall was a large master bedroom where Uncle Jeff might have slept when he was in residence. The room showed no signs of occupancy, however, without even any shirts hanging in the closet or socks tucked away in the dresser drawers. Ronn would have expected some personalization in a bedroom in which someone actually spent a large part of his life, but it was about as personal as a hotel room. He suspected that Uncle Jeff had never once slept here and his actual residence was somewhere else. He was even beginning to wonder if any guests had *ever* stayed in this house before, or if he and his cousins were the first.

Going back downstairs, Ronn looked for Phaedra and Theo so he could report his lack of success, and found them in the library. At least it was a room with shelves along the walls filled with more old-fashioned paper books than Ronn had ever seen in one place before. A couple of tables with lamps on them and some comfortable-looking armchairs were also on hand for the ease of any guests who might care to peruse a book while they were here. An English country estate might have had a room like this a hundred years before. Phaedra was poking through the shelves without much interest while Theo sat at one of the tables looking at a book that might have been 80 or 90 years old.

"Hey, look what I found!" he exclaimed as Ronn came in, and held the book up.

Ronn looked. *"Tom Swift, Jr. and His 3-D Telejector...?* Looks like Uncle Jeff's idea of 3-D image projection has been around for a while."

"The company vid for newbies explained it had been practically a cliché in sci-fi for decades," Theo said. "The problem was actually making it work in real life without some kind of screen for display. Even then Uncle Jeff had to get the tech ready-made from the aliens and figure it out from there. It works partly by changing the reflectivity of air molecules. But air's pretty thin, so it's tough to get images that look like solid objects. That's why it works even better in water and doesn't work at all in a vacuum. What's interesting is that nature beat everybody to it with mirages, but that has to do with different layers of hot and cold air."

As far as Ronn could tell from a quick glance at the titles on the spines, this was just a general collection of old books for the diversion of any guests inclined to read, and not some sort of official archive that would have plans and maps of the asteroid or anything else that they really needed to know right then. Neither Theo nor Phaedra had found anything useful, either. The library was just another dead end, and they went back out into the hall to look further.

At the far end, they found a back door that led out onto an open-air deck with a large swimming pool filled with water.

"And I didn't even bring my swimsuit," Phaedra sighed longingly. "If only I'd known this was here..."

"It wasn't like we thought the place would turn out to be Club Jeff," Theo said.

They reluctantly turned away from the pool and went back into the house to finish the inspection.

One door was fairly mysterious as to where it might lead. Ronn wasn't sure what he expected to find when he opened it. A master control room, perhaps, with Uncle Jeff sprawled dead over the instrument console? Or more likely, just a supply closet with mops and buckets.

Instead of either, the door opened on a narrow stairwell leading down beneath the main part of the house, beneath the ground itself.

"Now this looks interesting," Theo said. "Wonder where it goes?"

Ronn started down the steps. "We might as well find out."

At the foot of the stairs was a fairly ordinary garage with a wide door that gave access to the outside. If the house stood on top of a low hill, the garage had a ground-level entrance at the bottom. It also served as a workshop for maintenance workers, with tools like hammers and saws hanging on the wall over a bench and table. Sitting quietly in their bays were a blue jeep and a couple of scooters probably meant for inspection. Like everything else in the place, nothing showed signs of ever being used.

Those scooters looked interesting. While Ronn didn't have a license for four-wheeled vehicles as yet, the scooters were the same model he'd spent a family vacation riding around a resort the summer before.

"I used to have an electric jeep when I was little that looked just like that," Phaedra said, "only smaller and it was red. Or at least I had one until somebody *wrecked* it," she added, glaring at Theo.

Theo shrugged. "I just wanted to see what that baby could do..."

"No big surprises here, it looks like," Ronn said to change the subject. "Not what we wanted, though."

"But it's nice to know this stuff's down here," Theo pointed out. "Might come in handy for getting around."

They went back upstairs to look somewhere else. Phaedra took off with Theo down the hall, but Ronn headed in a different direction and found himself in a part of the mansion he hadn't expected. While it might have been intended as a guest house for weekend retreats, business would still have to go on. One wing of the house had been set aside for that regrettable necessity, with a small auditorium for presentations and a conference room with chairs around a large table.

Next to it was a smaller room that looked like a home office, in the style of fifty or more years before. The walls were lined with bookcases while a large wooden desk stood in front of a window with closed drapes. The office seemed ready to move into, but as far as Ronn could tell, no actual business had been conducted in it as yet.

A desk would be a likely place to find some clues, but there weren't any papers on top and all the drawers were empty. Besides a blotter and a small lamp, all that was on top of the desk was an old-fashioned telephone with an actual rotary dial and a receiver resting in a cradle, connected by a wire to an outlet in the floor. It was a pure museum piece, and most likely a non-functional display.

Except... Uncle Jeff would have needed a way to call his pilot in the docking bay to tell him when he wanted to return to Earth and to get the shuttle ready. And that phone was physically connected to something.

Ronn picked up the handset and put what he guessed to be the speaker end to his ear. He heard dial tone, then a click, then a female voice: "Number, please."

Has to be a bot. But this was a place built by a man who made and sold autonomous behavior systems, so maybe he could talk to the voice.

"Can you connect me with Mr. Jefferson Prescott?"

"I am sorry, but I do not have that information."

Well, why don't *you?* Contact information for the master of the domain ought to be listed *somewhere*, but there probably wasn't any point in arguing about it with a bot. Then he realized that it might be a good idea to put the minds of some no doubt very worried scientists at ease. "Is there a phone in the docking bay?"

"I am sorry, but I do not have that information."

Maybe Uncle Jeff always just called the pilot's own phone when he wanted to tell him to get the shuttle ready for a flight home? Suddenly Ronn had a crazy idea. Uncle Jeff would have to stay in touch with his enterprises on Earth even when he was here, and from the look of things he was anticipating guests who would be businesspeople who couldn't be cut off from their own affairs for very long, either. It was a long shot, but if it worked...

He rattled off his father's number, figuring his mother was probably still without a com.

"I am sorry, but that is not a Vesper number."

"It's an Earth number," Ronn explained, suspecting that the experiment was about to come to an end right about here. Only it didn't.

"Very well, sir," said the voice. "One moment, please."

Another click was followed by silence for a few seconds. Incredibly, a humming started at the other end, and someone answered.

"Hello?" It was his father.

"Dad!" Ronn exclaimed, astonished that the call had gone through.

"It's me!"

There was a slight delay. At a distance of about 60,000 miles, a signal traveling at the speed of light needed a third of a second to reach Earth, and at least another third of a second was required for a reply to come back.

"Ronn? Where are you? I thought you'd be on that moon by this time!"

"I am! We made it!" Apparently his father had been briefed on what was going on. That would save a few explanations. "I'm fine, and so are Phaedra and Theo. Thing is, we were given comlinks when we went in a few hours ago so we could keep in touch with the scientists, but we lost contact as soon as we were on the other side of the checkpoint. Can you pass the word along that we're all right and we're looking around the place just as we planned?"

"That's good to hear," Mr. Evans said, sounding a little more cheerful, then he realized something. "You mean you've been missing and out of touch for hours and they don't know what happened to you? They haven't told *me* a thing about it yet. I wonder how much longer they were planning to wait before saying anything? The government people will probably want to talk to you themselves, so we'll have to arrange something. Where exactly are you calling *from*?"

"You'll never believe it. From a phone on Uncle Jeff's desk in his house here!" Ronn told him a little more about what he had seen and done so far, then asked, "Have you heard from Mom?"

"You've probably talked to her more recently than I have, but they tell me she's fine. Not very happy, though. At least I could stay home. They've got guards watching the house so the twins and I are safe. From exactly who or what, they won't tell us, but it doesn't look like we'll be going anywhere for a while."

There was something Ronn had to ask. "Dad, how much did you *know?* About Uncle Jeff, I mean?"

A pause followed, then an uncomfortable-sounding sigh, as though Mr. Evans found it a difficult subject to talk about. "Everything, I suppose," he finally said. "I did marry the sister of the richest man in the world, after all. That isn't something you can hide very well. And even despite the family feud that I never did fully understand, your Uncle Jeff sent some work our way right when the firm was going through a rough patch a few years ago. Some of that house you're staying in might be our design. It was actually at his request that we didn't tell you before this. I didn't like keeping secrets, but your mother thought it was a good idea and you'd be better off growing up normally like any other kid. Like I told her at the time, though, it was bound to come out anyway, and probably at the worst possible moment. And here we are."

And here I *am, you mean.* Ronn wasn't sure how to reply. It had been *Uncle Jeff's* idea to keep the family relationship a secret from him?

He heard a shuffle and glanced up. Phaedra and Theo were standing in the doorway and looking in at him in surprise.

"Okay, I have to go. The cousins will want to call their dad and after that we'll probably head for bed."

"Just be careful up there, will you?"

"Doing my best." Ronn said goodbye and hung up.

"Who was *that*?" Theo demanded.

"My dad. Uncle Larry to you, I guess."

"The phone *works*?" Phaedra almost screamed.

"Seems to. Just ask for an Earth connection and give the number."

As he left the room, he saw Phaedra trying to figure out which end of the handset was which. It occurred to him that he might have tried calling Travis while he was at it, just to let him know that he was all right, but decided that it would have just gotten him in trouble with the government people who wanted to keep the whole thing a secret. He'd better wait until he was back on Earth, whenever that was.

A little later, they all gathered in the den again to compare notes. Not surprisingly, Aunt Thalia was still offline. There had also been a complication in that Phaedra and Theo had then called their father, only to find out that no one had told him what was going on. Mr. Cosgrove would probably not be very happy about the accidental breach of security, but neither Theo nor Phaedra was sure their father had really believed their explanation of where they were anyway. On the other hand, their step-father and mother's current husband turned out to have been duly informed when they called him, though only to the limited extent that Ronn's father had been. Phaedra then had the idea of calling her friends, but had decided against it for about the same reason Ronn had. Being between boyfriends at the moment further reduced temptation since there wasn't anyone she absolutely had to call. Ronn reflected gloomily that he was still short the first girlfriend necessary to be between any.

As for further exploration of the house, they couldn't think of any place they hadn't looked yet. Since they hadn't been able to find anything in the house that could tell them what had happened to Uncle Jeff, all they could do was go to bed, get some sleep, and look some more in the morning.

And it had been a long day. "I just flew in from Earth and boy, are my arms tired," Theo said, yawning.

"Just your arms?" Phaedra asked. "I'm tired all over."

Theo choked on his yawn. "That joke's so old it's practically got whiskers! And you say you're in show business..."

When Ronn went up to his room, he found a new swimsuit in exactly his size on the bed.

Either it was a coincidence or they had somehow been overheard even though the staff was out of sight. Phaedra's expressed regret that she hadn't brought a swimsuit had been noted and the need filled.

You could call them bots and explain it by mumbling something about "autonomous behavior systems," but it was a little disturbing just the same.

Before going to bed, Ronn decided to see what the view outside was like at night. He opened the door to the balcony and stepped out into a warm country evening, with stars twinkling in the darkness overhead. In the distance, Ronn could see some scattered lights, dim and misty.

Except for the almost eerie silence, it could have been a summer evening on Earth. It was hard to believe he was actually in a simulated environment on an asteroid 60,000 miles out in space. Lights shone through several of the windows in the house behind him, but he couldn't see much more of the immediate area than an expanse of grassy lawn out front. As far as he could tell, no other buildings were nearby.

He wondered once more what Uncle Jeff had out there, but the answers would have to wait until morning.

Chapter Six

When Ronn woke up, sunlight was filtering through the curtains.

At first he couldn't place where he was. This wasn't his room at home. As his mind cleared, he realized why he was waking up for the second day in a row in some place other than his own bedroom.

Almost tripping over himself until he remembered to allow for the lesser gravity, Ronn got up and went into the bathroom to brush his teeth and take a shower. When he came out, he found his freshly laundered regular clothes laid out on the now made bed. The more formal clothes from last night had disappeared, which was a relief since it meant he wasn't expected to get fancy for breakfast as well. He dressed, then went downstairs.

Phaedra was already sitting at the table in the dining room, wearing her safari outfit and boredly drumming her fingers. Theo hadn't shown up yet, and it looked as though breakfast wouldn't be served until he did.

"About time you got down here," she said. "I called my stepfather a little bit ago and got transferred to Mr. Cosgrove. It sounds like the scientists are getting kind of antsy back in the docking bay and want us to hurry up and find some way to let them in."

Ronn sat down at the table across from her. "I can't blame them. Things looked a little crowded in there."

"Well, they can just wait. I told Mr. C. that even if we did find the control center, we'd have to figure out how things worked. I don't know about you, but I don't want to start pushing buttons until I have some idea what'll happen."

"I hope you told Theo that."

"Don't worry, I can handle him. I've had years of practice."

Ronn hadn't seen much evidence of that so far but let it pass. "So what are we going to do today?"

"I decided we'll just ad lib it the first day. As long as we're inside, we might as well look around. We can figure out what to do next once we have some idea of what's here—"

Phaedra was interrupted by the arrival of Theo, in t-shirt and shorts. "Just took a little dip out back," he said, toweling his wet hair.

Phaedra looked appalled. "You went swimming by yourself? Without any lifeguards?"

"Didn't need any," Theo replied casually. "There's a notice posted on the door out to the pool explaining how there's all kinds of sensors and stuff, so if you get into trouble, something will pull you out of the water. Makes me want to fake drowning just so I can see how it does it…"

Now Phaedra looked horrified. "Are you crazy? Uncle Jeff might not have gotten around to installing the system yet!"

With everyone there, it was Wilfred's cue to make an appearance and inquire as to their dining preferences.

After breakfast, Ronn and his cousins went outside the house to look around the grounds. As far as anyone could tell by their senses alone, it was a warm day in early summer.

Overhead arched a bright blue sky with a few clouds. There was even a sun that was well up, or at least a light source opposite the house and presumably on the other side of the dome. The sun was oddly fuzzy, as though partially hidden by mist. While it wasn't too bright to look at, Ronn found it difficult to make out its size or exact shape. Since he never looked directly at the sun even on Earth, the difference was hardly disturbing.

The trees blocking their view of anything very far away and the grass on the lawn seemed perfectly real, and equally real-looking flowers bloomed in beds along the sides of the house. Perhaps robot grounds-keepers tended to all that.

As they had seen the day before, the house was on top of a low, grassy hill, with forest all around on flatter ground. A narrow paved road emerged from the forest on the south side of the house, disappeared into a tunnel at the bottom of the hill, and came out on the north side. Another road came out of the woods to the east and intersected the north-south road just past the house. A driveway branched off from the east-west road and looped around in front of the house.

Steps led up to a porch spanning the length of the house, and pillars supported the balcony above. A "colonnaded portico," Ronn remembered from a description of a house his mother had recently remodeled. Several chairs stood waiting on the veranda for any guests who wanted to enjoy the morning breezes.

A short distance behind the house rose a nearly perpendicular rocky wall like the side of a very steep cliff face about a hundred feet high, stretching as far as anyone could see in either direction.

Putting together what he had been told and what he saw around him, along with the fact that the entrance to the house in the tunnel below had been called "Westgate," Ronn guessed that they were at the nine o'clock point of a roughly circular crater some two miles in diameter, with a more or less flat floor enclosed by sheer rock walls a hundred feet high, and covered by a dome. It was a lot of real estate to fill and they could see almost none of it from where they now stood.

"What *is* this place?" Theo asked no one in particular as they stood on the grass of the front lawn and surveyed the edge of the forest a little way down the hillside in front of them. "Some kind of private estate?"

"There must be more to it than that," Ronn said. "I saw lights in the distance last night from my window. Maybe it's a something like a housing development in space."

"Maybe..." Theo replied doubtfully, "but would anybody really want to *live* all the way out here? It might be more like a vacation resort."

"I suppose we should do some exploring and see what's around here," Ronn said, glancing at the footpath that led into the woods.

Phaedra spoke up. "If we're going to take the grand tour, we should at least plan this. I'm not about to walk around for hours. And I don't see why we should even walk. Not with that jeep we found in the garage."

Planning was mostly a matter of realizing that they would probably be gone most of the day in unknown territory. They went back inside and found Wilfred, and Phaedra asked if it was possible to have some sandwiches made.

"Certainly," he replied. "If you would advise me as to what you require, I will attend to the matter for you."

Wilfred didn't write anything down when they told him in some detail what they wanted, merely nodding and then disappearing somewhere within the house. Within minutes he reappeared carrying a tray with bulbs of water and packed lunches, prepared exactly as they had asked.

Amply supplied for a long day, they went down to the garage below the house. As Ronn expected, the garage door opened onto the road that ran along the tunnel cutting through the hill beneath the house. Between vehicles to ride and roads to run them on, all they needed was a map of the crater, but in their search of the house they hadn't come across one.

With only two scooters and having to stay together, it seemed best to take a vehicle they could all ride in. Since the jeep was a basic model and manually instead of self-driven, and since Phaedra was the only one of the three who could drive a manual, a simple process of elimination put her in the seat behind the wheel. ("It isn't enough being their babysitter," she muttered, "I have to be their chauffeur, too!") Ronn sat in the front passenger seat next to her while Theo sprawled across the back seat.

Phaedra pushed a button on the dashboard and the jeep started. She gingerly eased it out of the garage and into the tunnel, seeing how it responded to the controls. Seconds later they emerged into daylight. Without a map, all they could do was head in the handiest direction and see what turned up. So far, they hadn't seen any signs of bad guys, but that didn't mean there weren't any out in the further reaches of the crater. They would just have to keep a lookout and hope they never crossed paths, or they might find out how pathetically inadequate their Stingers really were.

The jeep didn't make any noise other than the swish of tires on the pavement, and they could have heard the sounds of the world around them, if there had been any. There were no bird calls, no insect noises, no human voices, not even the rumble of distant machinery. A heavy, brooding silence lay over everything. The air was fresh, so there had to be some large-scale ventilation system, but Ronn couldn't shake off the feeling of an oppressive deadness around him.

If the house was on the west side of the crater, they were going north along the curving rim towards the twelve o'clock point. Much of the time, the road ran directly along the sheer cliff face of the crater wall to their left, but occasionally there were thick stands of trees between the cliff and the road, while on the right was the edge of a forest too dense to see very far into. Ronn wondered if the crater was maintained in a state of perpetual summer, or if a simulated fall and winter had to be designed into the program for trees like maples to shed their leaves once in a while.

Once they even passed a waterfall, pouring down the cliff face into a pool at the bottom. With several streams of water cascading over artfully placed rock ledges, it had to be a designed scenic effect rather than simply a broken pipe somewhere.

Glancing back, Ronn could see the cliffs rearing high over the treetops against the blue sky and stretching into the distance behind them. Occasionally, when they veered close to the crater wall, they saw free-standing columns spaced at regular intervals, supporting a continuous horizontal beam or rail on top. Ronn guessed it was an elevated monorail track, but he never saw a train actually running on it.

The crater floor had been landscaped so that it was relatively flat from one side to the other, but with some rolling terrain and even low hills. While the road more or less followed the outer edge of the crater, it also wound somewhat. No doubt the intent had been to prevent a clear and unobstructed view very far in any direction at any point along the road.

Nothing of much interest appeared until the road turned into the woods and they came to a clearing on the right where an old cabin stood among the trees. Phaedra parked the jeep at the side of the road and they got out for a closer look. The cabin was far from newly built and any paint that had ever been on the boards had long peeled or flaked away to gray wood, but it seemed solid and the shingles on the roof looked to be in good repair. From the outside, the cabin looked to be ready for a hermit or mountaineer to move in immediately.

"What's *that* doing here?" Phaedra asked.

"Maybe it's a replica of the cabin Uncle Jeff was living in when he met that alien," Theo suggested. "It'd probably have a lot of sentimental value for him."

"I wouldn't be so sure it's a replica," Ronn said slowly. "I mean, who would miss an old cabin out in the woods somewhere? And this is Uncle Jeff we're talking about. I bet it's the real thing and he had it moved here."

The door was unlocked and they looked inside. Something was wrong. A wooden chair lay on its side while the rustic table in the center of the one room looked as though it had been pushed away from where it should have been, spilling some books and other odds and ends to the floor, including a smashed dinner plate.

Besides that, though… If this was the cabin in which Uncle Jeff had hid out for a year, he had been more comfortable than it might have appeared from the outside. The bed, table, and one wooden chair were all of decent quality, the walls were lined with shelves filled with old printed books, and there was even a serviceable if very basic kitchen area. The bed was made, with a plain, well-worn old blanket and a simple pillow on top.

"Is it supposed to be like this?" Phaedra wondered.

"Maybe there was a fight!" Theo exclaimed, sounding as though he was mainly sorry that he had missed seeing the action.

"Between *who?*" Ronn asked him, but got only a shrug in reply.

There was no sign of Uncle Jeff here, however, now or at any time in the recent past. All they could do was go back to the jeep and drive on down the road.

Soon they came to another little house in a somewhat larger clearing between the road and the edge of the woods, with a rail fence separating the road from the front yard and a large garden. The wooden, white-painted house resembled a 19th Century farmhouse, except that it was con-siderably smaller, to the point of being impractical for someone of normal size to actually live in it, and the proportions were off. From the founda-tion, the walls slanted outwards as they rose to the roof. The windows and doors weren't even rectangles but a little skewed, wider at the top than at the bottom, while the shutters were too small for the windows they were supposed to cover. The colors were improbably bright as well, ranging from the brilliant red of the shutters to the all but radiant green of the roof.

"I've seen houses like that in theme parks…" Theo said a little uncertainly.

"Is it a prop?" Phaedra asked. "A stage-set kind of thing? Nobody can possibly live in it, can they?"

Yet as they drove a little past it, they saw a man hoeing in the side garden.

Only it wasn't a man. He was proportioned like a man with a body that was more or less human except for outsized feet, but the head was that of a cartoon rabbit brought to life. To be exact, he was a cartoon-rabbit caricature of an old man wearing bib overalls.

"This *is* a theme park!" Theo exclaimed.

"Let's stop here," Ronn said to Phaedra. "I want to get a look at this."

The rabbit broke off hoeing as the jeep pulled up by the fence. "Dagnab it!" he shouted hoarsely in an exaggerated old man's voice, shaking a fist at them. "You kids git outta here! Ain't nobody gonna come messin' in *my* carrot patch, dagnab it!" He went back to hoeing and seemed to forget the kids were there.

Now Ronn knew who it was. "It's MacNabbit the Rabbit!" He had to stop himself before he added, "Dagnab it!"

"Why that character?" Phaedra wondered. "Did Uncle Jeff have a beloved childhood memory of sleeping with a stuffed animal doll of MacNabbit that said 'Dagnab it!' every time he squeezed it?"

"This isn't Uncle Jeff's childhood here — the character isn't that old," Ronn said as he put some scattered pieces of knowledge together in his mind. He had watched a lot of cartoons when he was younger and his mother would be amazed if she knew the junk she had thought was rotting his mind then was now turning out to be actually useful. "This must be from when he was getting 3-D projection off the ground. MacNabbit was a character they used in some of the first holotoons."

"Hand over your carrots if you know what's good for you!" an unnaturally gravelly voice snarled.

The jeep was suddenly surrounded by several buck-toothed humanoid gophers about three feet tall, wearing striped t-shirts and clichéd burglar masks that made them look more like raccoons, and brandishing toy pistols. At least Ronn hoped they were toys.

He recognized them as the Gopher Gang. To be a star, a cartoon character needed a supporting cast, or better yet, antagonists to give him some opposition, and the Gopher Gang filled that role for MacNabbit. They were single-mindedly obsessed with trying to steal his carrots and always contriving impractical schemes that failed either because they were too absurdly elaborate or because MacNabbit realized what the Gophers were up to and came after them with Ol' Thunder, his shotgun. Since they never succeeded in making off with any carrots, what they ate in the meantime was a mystery.

For some reason, the Gopher Gang had decided to rob them instead of MacNabbit. In a real theme park, it would have been part of the tour to give the guests a little thrill, but had Uncle Jeff had ever intended anyone but himself to see the place? Were the Gopherbots acting on their own? For that matter, did those pistols actually work? They never fired them in the cartoons, but there weren't any restrictions here on violence in entertainment intended for children.

How seriously should I take this? "Sorry, we don't have any carrots," Ronn told the gang leader.

"Well, let's see what you *do* have," the Gopher retorted. "Search the car, boys!"

Just when Ronn was starting to wonder if Stingers worked on bots, MacNabbit looked up from his hoeing and saw the Gopher Gang about to swarm into the jeep.

"I thought I told you pests to git!" he shouted, brandishing a shotgun that Ronn could have sworn hadn't been anywhere in sight a couple of minutes before.

"We'd better scram!" the Gopher leader yelled to his minions in near-panic. "I think the old coot means it this time!"

The Gophers took off running into the woods as MacNabbit came through the gate in the fence in front of the house. Waving the shotgun wildly, he chased after them but never fired. The odd thing was that the sound of thrashing through the underbrush in the woods stopped as soon as everyone had disappeared from view, as though they had all frozen in place.

Phaedra watched them go in amazement. "That was strange..."

Then it got even stranger. A human-sized, anthropomorphic cartoon fox walking upright on two legs came up to the jeep, although it wasn't clear where he had come *from*. He carried a bulky sample case and wore a garish checked suit that might have been a stereotype for a cheap salesman a hundred years before,

"Greetings and salutations!" the fox announced in an oily voice. "Allow me to introduce myself. My name is Mountebank J. Fox and by profession I am a commercial traveler."

"A commercial... *what*?" Phaedra asked blankly.

"In the vernacular, I believe the term is salesman. Can I interest you in our special for today?" The fox opened his sample case, displaying an ill-assorted collection of gleaming small metal gadgets. "No self-respecting household in this modern day and age can be without a left-handed corkscrew!'"

Phaedra looked at Ronn in complete bafflement. "What's going on?"

"It's been a long time since I've seen any of the MacNabbit cartoons," Ronn said, "but he basically wants to be left alone. Instead, he's constantly being bothered by crooks trying to steal his carrots or salesmen trying to sell him worthless junk."

"My good fellow," declared the fox pompously but with a hint of wounded pride, "'worthless junk' is entirely in the eye of the beholder. Someday you will be caught in the dark somewhere with a screw in need of tightening and you will regret not having purchased an all-purpose electric screwdriver with a built-in flashlight, whistle, and crossword-puzzle dictionary when you had the chance!"

"Sounds great!" Theo exclaimed. "How much?"

The fox looked startled, as though he had not anticipated making a sale so easily. "Well, that is to say... I am willing to entertain an offer."

"Five bucks?"

The fox seemed completely at a loss. The situation had apparently evolved well beyond his decision-making capability. He probably would have been happiest if he had been allowed to leave at that point without selling anything, but now Theo was the insistent one.

"Very well," the fox said after a moment. "I must admit, however, that I exaggerated slightly in representing the product. There is no built-in crossword-puzzle dictionary included with the current model. However, if you should require one, I can obtain it for you by special order—"

"Fine," Theo said. "I don't need a dictionary anyway."

The fox in turn rummaged through the gadgets in the sample case until he found the screwdriver and gave it to Theo. "Now, as to the matter of payment...?" he said expectantly.

Theo fished a card out of his pocket and handed it to the fox. "Just take five bucks off."

The fox looked dumbfoundedly at the card. "Exactly *what* is this supposed to be?"

"It's money, what else?" Theo said, surprised that there would even be a problem.

"Have you no legal tender in the form of banknotes, in particular portraits of deceased political notables? I will also consider coins, cheques made out to cash, money orders, or any other negotiable instruments you may care to provide."

"Afraid that's all I've got," Theo admitted.

The fox held the card close to one eye and squinted, turned it upside down and backwards, and even put it in his mouth and bit on it, then finally gave it disgustedly back to Theo and snatched the screwdriver out of his hand.

"I believe I shall conduct my trade elsewhere," he said, sounding anxious to be done with the whole affair.

He tossed the screwdriver in his case and snapped it shut, then turned and strode away with injured dignity, disappearing into the woods across the road.

"How about that?" Theo exclaimed. "He was programmed to sell stuff but never for what to do in case he actually did sell something."

Either that, Ronn thought, or like a lot of cartoon characters, the fox was based on old clichés that survived in cartoons long after they were obsolete in the real world, like rich men wearing top hats, and dated from an era when physical coins and bills were still commonly used to buy things. The fox really should have been set up to process cashcards, though. It would be a good way to sell souvenirs to visitors. If Uncle Jeff ever really expected to have any visitors, anyway.

"Wanna buy some cookies, Mister?"

Ronn turned. Standing by the jeep on his side were several little girls with squirrel faces and ears and bushy tails in back, wearing matching green uniforms and berets, and each carrying several small boxes.

"Spinach Crème is new this year!" one added in a squeaky voice.

"What, no garlic and prune?" Ronn asked, remembering the cartoons. Another running gag was the Squirrel Scouts, who were always knocking on MacNabbit's door and trying to sell him weird varieties of cookies.

"Right here!" the troop leader exclaimed cheerfully, pointing to one of the boxes she was carrying. "How many boxes can we put you down for?"

As if the Gopher Gang hadn't been bad enough... Ronn shot a glance at Phaedra. "I think it's time we moved on."

"I was just thinking the same thing." Phaedra hit the **START** button and sent the jeep speeding down the road.

"Wait!" the Squirrel Scout leader called after them. "Don't you want your cookies?"

Then they rounded a bend in the woods and the holotoon characters were out of sight.

"That was kind of an old joke," Phaedra remarked as she drove. "The real scouts don't even sell cookies any more. Too much like junk food, somebody decided."

"Yeah," Theo added, "they got all good-for-you, so now they sell fruit bars and veggie rolls. Sales went way down, I heard. Even Phaedra couldn't move the goods when she was in Scouts."

Phaedra turned in her seat to glare back at Theo. "Don't remind me," she stared to say with cold deadliness—

—Just as they went over a slight rise, and the jeep suddenly hit the brakes with a screech of skidding tires on pavement and veered off to the side of the road, coming to a stop in a flurry of dirt and gravel.

A little stunned and shaken up, they looked around to see what had happened. The jeep may have been intended to be manually driven by maintenance crews who had to decide on the spot where to go and when to start and stop, but it did have some automatic safety features. If the forward scan hadn't detected a line of obstacles in the near distance and automatically triggered the brakes, the jeep would have plowed into a marching band.

A teddy bear marching band.

Apparently unaware of the near disaster, a procession of marching teddy bears, each about two feet high and wearing red and gold-trimmed band jackets and hats, was crossing the road, from the forest on one side to the forest on the other, playing a jaunty and slightly silly tune on the scaled-down instruments they carried. One particularly fat teddy bear was playing a tuba.

As Ronn and the others watched, the teddy bears went on their way until the last of them was lost in the forest on the far side and the music faded away.

"Well, that certainly added to the weird count," Theo finally said. "I can't think of any vidshows or toons with a teddy bear band in them, though."

"Maybe Uncle Jeff created it especially for this place?" Ronn suggested as Phaedra turned the jeep back onto the road.

But if their uncle had some purpose in mind behind the marching band or was just being whimsical, no one could say.

Chapter Seven

Soon the forest came to an abrupt end and they found themselves at the edge of a town.

It was a reconstruction of a New England coastal village with a stretch of sandy beach and a simulated view of the seemingly endless Atlantic. Phaedra parked the jeep and they took a walk around for a closer look. The only sounds in the empty silence were their own footsteps.

They stood on the boardwalk along the edge of the beach and looked out at the ocean while projected seagulls silently wheeled overhead. Even though they knew they were in a crater and should have been looking at a rock wall, the feeling of being on the shore of an ocean stretching to the horizon was almost convincing. All that was needed was the smell of salt air and rotting seaweed. That and the sound of the lapping waves. The ocean swelled like a real ocean, but it was like watching a vid of an ocean with the sound off.

When they walked along the town's one main street, there was an overwhelming impression that it wasn't quite finished yet, even though the shops had glass in the windows and merchandise on display. Nothing moved along the deserted street and sidewalks. No cars, no people.

The details of the buildings struck Ronn as too specific for it to be just some generic town meant only to add background to a theme park. *I wonder what this place is supposed to be?*

The answer to that came when they saw a large Victorian house with turrets ahead, just past the row of shops.

"I know that house!" Phaedra exclaimed. "I've seen it in some of Mom's old photos. It's our great-grandparents' house in Northport!"

Now the pieces were coming together. Northport, Massachusetts was the town where Uncle Jeff's grandparents had lived. He had probably visited it as a boy, maybe even spent a summer or two there. He apparently remembered it happily enough to reconstruct it.

84

They went up on the porch and found that the front door wasn't locked. Looking around inside, Phaedra said the old-fashioned furniture in the living room matched what she remembered from the pictures. The other rooms were either empty or only half-finished, as though work had stopped until the supplies or furnishings necessary to continue the project could be brought in. The house reminded Ronn of one of his mother's remodeling jobs in progress.

There wasn't anything more to see here, they decided, and went back to the jeep.

After leaving Northport, they drove through more forest, then found themselves in another small town.

"It's Salisbury!" Phaedra blurted, but Ronn and Theo recognized it in the same instant since they had also been to the real place on family visits.

It was the New York State town where their grandparents had lived and their mothers and Uncle Jeff had grown up. Within the projection zone, the streets and buildings seemingly extended as far as might be expected in a town of that size, with the Catskill Mountains in the distance, but only a couple of blocks downtown had been physically re-created.

Unlike the Northport set, Salisbury was populated and gave every impression of being a town that had some life to it. The people on the streets were dressed in the clothes of forty or more years before, and walked past Ronn and his cousins without any sign of noticing them. Since they were just extras on the stage, the nearer figures were bots with a narrow range of functions, while the ones in the background were more likely projections. Even Uncle Jeff must have had some budget limits, and probably only used bots in crowd scenes where necessary for individuals who were seen close-up or had to interact with the surroundings in variable ways.

The cars parked along the street were in the forty-plus year range, but looked amazingly new. Too new, Ronn thought, and knocked on the hood of one to see if his hunch was correct. It was. The sound was that of plastic instead of metal. They were replicas rather than originals, full-sized plastic models. And why not? Uncle Jeff would have had machines that could scan large objects and mold 3-D color copies out of plastic.

Ronn's guess was that the building fronts he saw around him had been produced exactly that way, probably by flying a drone through the real Salisbury with a 360-degree scanner. Then, with the help of old photos, the scans had been edited so that when assembled, the molded components reflected the town as it had been in the Nineties rather than as it was now.

The toy store caught Ronn's eye. Its window display was noticeably more detailed than those of neighboring shops. Feeling that this had to be more than mere background, he tried the doors. They opened and he went inside. With nothing better to do, his cousins followed.

Something was in fact very odd about the toy store. It was much larger inside than it appeared from outside, probably taking up the entire block of stores while the adjacent storefronts were just dummy facades. The toys were old-fashioned, what a store might have sold nearly half a century before — but *what* toys. The model airplanes hanging from the ceiling far overhead looked almost large enough to ride on, and the dolls and teddy bears on the shelves were twice the size they should have been. That classic fashion-model doll Ronn's little sister played with even today, not knowing it was an electronically enhanced version of a design that dated back to the 1950s, was about two feet tall here. Probably no real toy store on Earth fifty years ago had ever had such a rich selection of wonderful toys, all brightly colored and shining, but why was everything so *big*? Even the display counters were unnaturally high.

After a few moments, Phaedra suddenly exclaimed, "Now I get it! This is what a toy store looks like when you're about five!"

Ronn looked around again with that in mind and saw that she was probably right. He had a few memories of his own of toy stores he had been in when he was much younger and shorter, and it seemed to fit. This must have been a re-creation of how Uncle Jeff remembered things.

In the back of the store was an operating electric train layout on a tabletop, just about eye-level for Ronn and Phaedra while Theo had to stand on a box to see it. It was enormous on this scale with engines and cars each a couple of feet long. Strangely, the track had three rails.

Since it was a display in a toy store, it was designed to showcase a maximum of trains and accessories. The layout itself was little more than a huge oval of track on which a freight train pulled by a model of a chugging steam locomotive made an endless circuit through a flat landscape of city and countryside that represented the world of about 1950, a world long gone even by the time of Uncle Jeff's early childhood, but perhaps a classic period for toy trains.

Ronn had a feeling that just watching a train go around in a circle would get old fast, and he wasn't convinced that a train set would be much fun for very long. Maybe that was the point of the add-on accessories on display like working crossing gates and automatic barrel loaders, to freshen things up. There was even a cattle car parked on a siding with plastic cows being unloaded and loaded back on the same car in a continuous if futile-seeming loop through a plastic stockpen. The real oddities were novelty cars like an aquarium car with swimming fish visible through the transparent sides and the circus car with a bobbing giraffe's neck and head protruding from a hole in the roof.

"It's a toy world in a toy world…" was all Ronn could think of to say.

"It doesn't stop there," Theo said. "Look at this."

Near the edge of one corner of the layout were the buildings of a model town. Since they were fairly crude and toy-like and since replicator technology allowed copies to be any size, Ronn could guess that they were scans of plastic buildings made for train layouts decades before, and twice the size of the originals. Theo pointed to a store with a sign reading "HOBBY SHOP." Through its windows, Ronn could see a toy train display inside, a miniature version of the large display the store itself was a part of. And there were tiny trains moving on the tracks. Ronn wondered if there was a hobby shop on the tiny layout, with an even smaller train layout inside that. *How far down does it go?*

After leaving the toy store, they started back down the street, and the scene around them changed again. They were no longer in the commercial district of a small town but in a residential neighborhood, standing in front of a one-story brick building with large windows. A freestanding sign out front by the sidewalk read **SALISBURY ELEMENTARY SCHOOL**.

"That's not a background projection," Phaedra said. "That's a real building."

"So it's probably the school he went to," Theo concluded. "I'm starting to get an idea of how Uncle Jeff thought. If something's here, it was important to him."

"Maybe this place is kind of like Greenfield Village," Phaedra suggested, sounding as though she had actually been there.

Ronn had been there, too. "At least Henry Ford collected historic buildings that were important to other people. This is like Uncle Jeff's private 3-D scrapbook."

"Can we go in?" Theo wondered.

They looked at each other uncertainly, reluctant to go inside the school.

Then Ronn realized what was bothering them and he laughed. "We're acting like it's a real school with real teachers who'll kick us out if they see us. But this isn't real. We're in a theme park. We're *supposed* to go inside and look at it!"

They went into the building and started down the central hallway, opening doors on either side as they walked along, ready to bolt at the first sign of trouble. The first few rooms were empty, however, without even any blackboards on the walls. Just when they were about to give up and go somewhere else, they came to a Fifth Grade classroom that was both furnished and occupied. As they somewhat hesitantly came in, they found a room full of kids in decades-old clothes sitting at desks so old-fashioned that they probably didn't have built-in 3-D display systems.

Like the ten-year-olds, the plump, middle-aged teacher paid no attention to the newcomers at the door. She continued her lecture in Geography, standing at the front of the room and pointing to a pull-down map of South America. "As you can see, Chile is a long and thin country that runs down the west coast. It shares a border along the Andes Mountains with Argentina and..." She even wore glasses, something just this side of extinct by the time Ronn became aware of the world around him. People did still wear sunglasses of a sort, but they were lightweight visors. *How could people stand to have those clunky things sitting on their noses all day?* He wouldn't have been surprised to see her use an ear trumpet like he'd seen in old pictures, too.

The teacher and her students were solid and not projections, and Ronn had a sudden thought. *She looks like somebody!* Not anyone he knew, of course, though there was some generic similarity with a few teachers he'd had, in particular Ms. Crowley. But this teacher's face had enough specific individuality that she must have been modeled after a real person, probably Uncle Jeff's actual Fifth Grade teacher. If that teacher had been in her 50s some forty or more years ago, she would most likely be gone by now, but here her memory lived on.

"Bots," Theo said. "Not even particularly bright ones, it looks like. I don't think they know we're here."

They went further into the room, encouraged by the fact that none of the boys and girls turned to look at them. A closer look showed that each one was individually characterized, too.

"If we could find Uncle Jeff's Fifth Grade class picture," Ronn said, "I bet we'd see all these kids in it. And if he'd tagged their faces with their names, we'd even know who these bots are modeled after."

"This is getting creepy," Phaedra murmured.

"Getting?" Theo echoed. "This place blew the top off the Creep-o-Meter back there with the rabbit. Let's get out of here!"

Ronn had a sudden thought. "Wait! If this is Uncle Jeff's Fifth Grade class, *he* must be here, too!"

"You mean a boy bot that looks like he did then?" Phaedra asked. "I know what he looks like now, so maybe I can pick out his younger self."

They went up and down the rows of desks completely unnoticed while the class continued around them, but none of the boys fit the description. There was, however, one empty desk, in the row by the windows and halfway back. Figuring that Uncle Jeff would include the entire class on an ideal day when no one was out sick, and that it wasn't likely there would be a spare desk left empty in the middle of the room, they decided it had to be his.

"Does he come here now and then and sit in on the class to relive old memories?" Phaedra wondered.

Ronn grimaced. The thought of a grown man sitting unnoticed in the middle of a class of Fifth Graders seemed... strange. Then he realized that the desk wasn't any different from the others.

"Look at the desk! It's sized for a Fifth Grader! A grown man wouldn't fit into it."

It was a mystery, and at least for now impossible to solve. They left the room and the eternal Geography Class just as the teacher was cycling into a repetition of the lecture that had been in progress when they came in. "As you can see, Chile is a long and thin country..."

"I don't know about Uncle Jeff," Theo said once they were back in the hall, "but I tried to forget about Fifth Grade as soon as I was out of it."

Outside the school, they walked down the street a little further to see if the neighborhood extended as far as it appeared. Just past the chain link fence marking the edge of the playground and school property, their surroundings changed yet again.

In front of them was a church, with organ music coming from inside. Wedding music.

Phaedra had also caught on to how the place worked. "That wouldn't be here if there wasn't a reason for it. I wonder whose wedding this is supposed to be?"

"Whose do you think?" Theo asked. "Remember where we are?"

They went up the steps, opened the seemingly massive wooden front doors, which were actually a light plastic and swung freely, and stepped inside. All the pews were filled with people dressed in what were considered the best clothes of maybe a quarter of a century before. Ronn had never seen so many men and boys wearing ties in one place outside of an old movie, or people wearing glasses, for that matter. All were facing towards the altar, where a minister was conducting a marriage ceremony. It was a repeat of the Fifth Grade classroom. No one took any notice of the intruders, and somebody was missing. The bride was there, long white dress and all, and so were the best man and the maid of honor, but there was only empty space where the groom should have been standing, and no one seemed to be aware that someone rather important for the occasion was lacking. The minister continued to pronounce the ritual words, oblivious to the problem.

"Look!" Phaedra pointed at the people in the front pew. "That's Mom! And Grandma!"

Even in their younger forms, Ronn recognized his grandparents and teenaged mother and aunts. As far as he could tell, everyone else in the church was individually characterized, and probably based on the real people who had actually been present at the wedding the scene recreated.

It was strange to be walking and talking through the middle of a wedding with no one paying them the slightest attention, perhaps a little too strange. They didn't stay long.

"That was even weirder than the classroom," Theo remarked as they came down the church steps.

"I guess that was Uncle Jeff's first marriage," Phaedra said. "I remember Mom saying it was to his college girlfriend, before he got rich, and it didn't last. He had his fourth wedding in a hotel that he owned in L.A., and nobody in the family went to that one."

Which means there's another Jeffbot missing.

A little further on, they found themselves on a quiet street in a residential neighborhood of stately old houses and big maple trees. As they faced one large white wood-frame house in particular, no one had to state the obvious. All three immediately recognized it as their grandparents' house. Since it was Uncle Jeff's boyhood home, of course it had to be here. In real life, it was much further from downtown Salisbury, but even a two-mile-wide crater didn't have quite that much room to play with.

"The real house is still in Salisbury," Ronn said. "He really outdid himself making this replica."

"More than that, it's what it looked like about forty years ago! Look at the garage!" Phaedra pointed to a white wooden shed to the side that looked as old as the house. "I've only seen it in photos. It was torn down before we were born—" She broke off when she saw her brother marching up the sidewalk towards the porch. "Theo! What are you doing?"

"Seeing if anybody's home!" Theo went up on the porch and knocked on the front door.

Ronn glanced at Phaedra. "I'm not sure I want to know." She didn't look any too comfortable, either.

Somebody *was* home. After a few moments, the door opened from inside and a woman in her mid-thirties appeared.

"It's Grandma!" Phaedra said lowly to Ronn. "I've seen her pictures from when she was young."

Ronn recognized the woman as well. She was younger than his mother was now, and like seemingly most people in that bygone age, she wore glasses. Now this *was* getting into disturbing territory, since Grandma was someone he had actually known. He also knew she was dead and had seen her body in the casket at her funeral. Yet here she was, seemingly alive again. Since he had only known her when she was old, seeing her as she was when she was much younger and not as he remembered her wasn't so much of an emotional shock.

"Oh, you must be here to see Jeff," Grandma said pleasantly, as though she knew them as maybe the nice neighbor kids from across the street.

"Come on in."

Ronn and Phaedra followed after Theo through the door. It was a house all three were thoroughly familiar with, but as it was long before they first remembered seeing it, with different living room furniture.

"He's in his room right now, so you can go on up." Grandma gestured to the staircase leading to the second floor, apparently trusting them completely, and went into the kitchen.

"Should we?" Phaedra asked uncertainly.

"Oh, why not?" Theo demanded and started for the stairs.

"This must be when he was a still a kid," Ronn said to Phaedra, "before that wedding we saw. We seem to be doing his life out of order."

"I just wonder if he'll be missing here, too," Phaedra replied, and followed Theo up the stairs.

Walking along the upstairs hall, Phaedra opened one of the doors as they passed it. "This was Mom's room," she started to say, then gasped. The room was empty except for curtains on the windows, evidently to make the house look occupied from the outside. "What a selfish jerk! He didn't even bother re-creating her room!"

"Well, maybe he was concentrating on what was important to him," Ronn said. "Anything else was just sketched in no more than it had to be for a background."

"It's like my mother — his own sister! — didn't count for anything in his mind," Phaedra said bitterly. "She isn't even an extra in the story of his life. He cut her out of the script completely in the rewrite."

Ronn looked into another room. It was also just bare walls and floor with only curtains on the windows. "Your mother wasn't the only one he left out. Mine, too, it looks like, if she was born by this time. There's about an eleven-year age difference."

"Lots of love in this family, I'm telling you," Theo muttered.

That left a room at the end of the hall. In their time, it had been a guest bedroom completely purged of all signs that it had ever belonged to a member of the family no one spoke of. Uncle Jeff wasn't the only one who had rewritten the family history.

As they came in, they saw it was now a boy's bedroom from just before the turn of the century. Unlike the other rooms, it was completely furnished with an obsessive attention to detail. The first thing that caught their notice was the bed, neatly made despite being in a boy's room. An orange and white striped cat lay curled up on top of it. It stirred, opened its eyes and raised its head to look at the people coming in, then lowered its head and seemingly went back to sleep. There were even catbots...?

Compared to Ronn's room at home, it was all terribly old-fashioned, but as he looked around, he felt a twinge of appreciation. Even though

Ronn and the boy his uncle had been were separated in time by nearly forty years, this was a room he might have liked for himself if he had lived back then.

Posters on the walls showed long-forgotten rock groups and advertised 2-D movies that were popular then but now too archaic to be shown much anymore. There were also shelves with old printed books, while other shelves were crammed full with plastic models of old airplanes and cars. Somehow it wasn't surprising that building models had been one of his hobbies. Judging by what was outside, it still was.

Against the wall next to the head of the bed and in an aisle between the far edge of the bed and the side wall, a video console was running an ancient game with primitive 2-D graphics on a boxy vid display unit.

Theo was curious about what game it was, and they came around the bed for a closer look—

On the floor, a boy of about twelve lay sprawled on his stomach. The back of his head was gone. Still clutched in his hands was a controller unit connected by a wire to the console.

Phaedra started to scream and Theo looked as though he was ready to be very sick, but Ronn had gotten a better look at what was spilling out of the head. Instead of blood and brain tissue, it was just a puffy mass of something like purple steel wool. Torn ends of fine wires dangled at the edges of the wound.

"Wait!" Ronn exclaimed. "It's a bot!"

Theo looked a little better. "Well, now we know why he wasn't in school today..."

"I don't think that's it," Ronn said. "This bot looks older than Fifth Grade, like about twelve or thirteen."

Phaedra had also gotten most of her composure back. "And his mother doesn't even know?" she asked, her voice still a little unsteady.

"I keep telling you, these are bots!" Theo exclaimed testily. "She isn't programmed for anything like this. She'll just go on doing what she's been doing all along. Like the catbot over there," he added, pointing to the sleeping feline on the bed. "Something bad happened right in front of it and Jeff's body has been lying here ever since — and it isn't the least bit fazed."

"We could ask Grandma if she's seen anybody come into the house lately," Ronn said. "She might be up to that much."

"Your point is?" Theo asked.

"We're here to find Uncle Jeff," Ronn reminded him. "Not only is *he* missing, but a bot showing him at ten isn't where it ought to be and there should have been a bot of him at the wedding. There might have even been one at his old cabin — *something* was obviously taken out of it that didn't want to leave, and a Jeffbot seems pretty likely. Now a bot of him at twelve is torn up. I think there's a pattern and it's part of the mystery we have to solve."

Downstairs, Grandma Prescott turned up again to usher them out of the house.

"I hope you had a nice visit with Jeff," she said. "He doesn't have many friends, so I'm always glad when somebody comes to see him."

One friend wasn't so nice. "Er... are we the only ones who've come by to see him lately?"

Grandma looked a little blank. "Pardon?"

"I mean, has anybody else come to visit him in the last few days? Do you remember what they looked like?"

Grandma smiled. "I hope you had a nice visit with Jeff. He doesn't have many friends, so I'm always glad when somebody comes to see him."

"Just short-term memory, it looks like," Theo said. "I don't think we'll be getting anything useful here."

They left the house, still shaken by what they had seen upstairs, while Grandma went back to doing whatever a bot did when no one was looking. It shouldn't have been any more tragic than seeing a teddy bear with its stuffings torn out, though that would have been sad in its own way, but these bots looked so human that it was hard *not* to regard even the more limited ones as human in most respects.

More troubling was the realization that they might not be alone. It may have been Uncle Jefferson's private paradise, but there was a snake in it.

Outside, they found that the projection zone ended just past the house, and there was only the edge of the forest beyond. They had now seen everything in the Salisbury section and it was time to move on.

Chapter Eight

They heard the merry-go-round music even before they rounded the turn through the surrounding forest.

Along the right side of the road was a fence and an open gateway with a sign over it reading **COUNTY FAIR**. In front of it stood a life-sized, lifelike plastic cow statue labeled "Gertrude," apparently the fair's official mascot. Inside the fence, they could see old-fashioned tents, booths, and rides.

"Hey!" Theo exclaimed. "That looks like fun! Let's stop!"

With nothing better to do... why not?

A real county fair would have had a large parking lot, but this one just had an open space barely big enough for two jeeps by the ticket booth at the front entrance. Phaedra pulled the jeep up and they got out.

The man inside the ticket booth waved them on through without even asking for money. While perhaps not exactly authentic, it was just as well. After their experience with the fox, Ronn doubted if their cashcards would have gotten them in.

As fairs went, it was probably considerably condensed, more a suggestion of a fair than a complete reconstruction. Just past the gate was a short midway with snack stands and game booths, and beyond them a few basic carnival rides like a merry-go-round, a Tilt-a-Whirl, and a Ferris wheel. At least those were real. The other rides, the livestock sheds, and the grandstand and racetrack in the further distance were probably projected background. The Ferris wheel was relatively small, about sixty or so feet tall, with open seats rather than enclosed cars, but Ronn was impressed that Uncle Jeff had gotten something so large and cumbersome all the way to Vesper.

A few people moved among the booths, ranging in apparent age from toddlers to seniors, but none seemed to be doing anything *except* walk around. Just more minimally programmed bots, it looked like. There were so few fair-goers that it would have been a very slow afternoon at a real fair, but Uncle Jeff probably hadn't wanted any more foreground bots than he absolutely needed to suggest that the place wasn't completely deserted.

It also looked as though the kids riding the merry-go-round would be riding it forever. While it stopped at intervals and then started up again, no one ever got off the carved wooden horses and none of the kids waiting with their parents by the ticket stand ever got on. The blaring carousel music would probably get tiresome before very long...

A pretty girl of about sixteen came up to them. Her light brunette hair was long and she was casually dressed for a summer day at the fair in blouse, shorts, and tennis shoes. "Have you seen Jeff?" she asked.

"Uh... no, we haven't," Ronn said truthfully.

"What's keeping him?" the girl demanded, sounding disappointed. "He was supposed to take me on the Ferris wheel."

"I think we walked into another chapter of Uncle Jeff's life story," Ronn said in a low voice.

"I hope it was a happy memory," Phaedra said. "He sure went to a lot of trouble to recreate it."

They started to turn away, leaving the sad bot to wait for someone who would probably never come. But the girl suddenly grabbed Ronn's arm. "How about if I hang with you guys until Jeff shows up? I might as well have some fun instead of just standing around waiting for him."

Phaedra stared at the girl for a moment, then glanced at Theo. "You don't happen to have a fork on you, do you? I'm suddenly not so sure about this one."

The girl looked at her and Theo quizzically. "Are you two dating?"

"Are you kidding?" Phaedra demanded in a tone that was equal parts indignation and astonished realization that *I'm arguing with a bot like it's real*. "He's my little brother!"

"Babysitting, huh?" the girl said with a grin.

Phaedra shot her a poisonous glance.

"I thought he looked a little young for you," the girl went on, then sized Ronn up. "How about you, big guy? You don't have a girlfriend around here, do you?"

"Er... no," Ronn gulped.

"Great. Then we're both footloose and fancy free, as my Dad likes to say. My name's Bonnie, by the way. Let's do the fair!"

This was *strange*. Bonnie had to be a bot, but this was a degree of initiative far beyond anything Ronn had ever heard of before. In theory, a truly self-aware and independently thinking bot would be no different from a living being, and there would be trouble over issues like slavery and legal rights, but as far as Ronn knew, artificial intelligence had not yet been developed to that point. With Earthly technology, anyway.

Ronn had an uncomfortable feeling that advanced alien tech was at work here, and Bonnie was a lot closer to self-awareness than would have normally been possible on Earth. Worse, she was trapped in a never-ending county fair scenario and even seemed dimly aware of it. Did Uncle Jeff occasionally come by to enjoy a recreation of a long-ago day at the fair, a middle-aged man that the Bonnie-bot was programmed to see as his sixteen-year-old self?

She was also astoundingly real-looking, indistinguishable from a living human being. Her lips moved convincingly as she spoke, revealing teeth as well as an occasional glimpse of a tongue behind them. She even blinked at a normal rate. Maybe her complexion was just a shade too perfect, but otherwise... If Ronn hadn't already known she was a bot, he never would have guessed it.

He went with her on the Tilt-a-Whirl, then they tried their luck at the shooting gallery, where he won a little stuffed bear for her. She was delighted and carried the bear with her everywhere they went from then on. Ronn was a little bothered because he knew that she wasn't real, she was a bot, and what would she do with the bear later? She "lived" here at this fair and would never leave.

Ronn was starting to feel thirsty, but discovered that the snack stands weren't real. The cotton candy was simulated, as were the popcorn and the hot dogs. In fact, he realized, the one thing this fair lacked that a real one would have was food odors. It made sense, since there was no point in having large quantities of real and perishable food on hand for just one human visitor who came by only occasionally. Ronn did find a vending machine that dispensed free bulbs of water, however, something that would store well. Since the water of thirty-five years ago was packaged in bottles. Uncle Jeff apparently allowed himself an occasional anachronism.

Ronn took a drink, then noticed Bonnie looking at him a little oddly.

"Er... want some?" he asked, not sure of the protocol. Bots obviously wouldn't need to drink anything — couldn't, really — but maybe they had to be humored for the sake of appearances by at least offering them a drink.

"No..." she said slowly, "and that's what's so funny. I can't remember when I last drank something, so I should be thirsty, but I'm not. I can't figure it out."

This was getting awkward. "Well, maybe later," he said quickly as his cousin came up.

Phaedra had an annoyed expression, as though she was tired of watching Ronn and the bot having a better time than she and Theo were, and probably about to suggest that they get out of there.

Before she could say anything, Bonnie suddenly forgot all about her lack of thirst and exclaimed, "Let's go on the Ferris wheel!"

"Uh... I don't do heights very well," Phaedra said.

"I think I'll take another crack at the old-time vid games in the arcade," Theo added a little quickly.

Bonnie shrugged. "You're no fun," she said, then took Ronn's arm and led him to the Ferris wheel. The fact that they went right by the ticket booth without paying and no one objected didn't seem to register on her as anything unusual. They climbed into the bottommost seat, and when an unspeaking, expressionless attendant locked the bar across their laps, the Ferris wheel started automatically.

If nothing else, it might be a chance to get an overview of the area from a height. But no — as the wheel turned and the seat rose, he could only see the "real" part of the fair below. The convincing background projection of other parts of the fair seemed to be effective only at ground level. Fog obscured everything else any distance away. Overhead, the sky was still bright blue with a hazy sun now well past noon.

Bonnie, at least, seemed to be enjoying herself, looking eagerly around. Was she really able to see more than he could, or was she only programmed to act that way?

When their seat reached the top, the wheel stopped turning and they paused. Then Ronn felt Bonnie's hand take his.

Holding hands with a girl was not something he had much experience with. It did seem that Bonnie's hand was a little too smooth, almost a pliable plastic in texture, but he could have just imagined that since that was how he would have expected a bot's hand to feel. Surprisingly, it had a natural warmth to it.

So here he was, holding hands with a bot. Since it would have made things unpleasant to jerk his hand away and it seemed to be what Bonnie wanted, he went with the moment.

"It's been really fun today," she murmured, looking off into the distance.

She didn't elaborate, but Ronn wondered if she might have remembered other days when it wasn't so fun.

The Ferris wheel started back down and she let go of his hand to grab the bar with both of her hands, talking about something that had happened at school a month or two earlier by her time, maybe thirty-five years earlier by Ronn's. *Somebody did way too good a job on this bot.* Even for the sake of characterization and plausible personality modeling, a bot shouldn't have that detailed a memory of a life it had never lived.

After that, they had seen everything there was at the fair, and Phaedra and Theo both seemed anxious to leave as soon as possible.

Bonnie walked with them to the entrance, clinging to Ronn's arm while holding the stuffed bear, and obviously unhappy that he was leaving. "Do you have to go so soon? I was just starting to have a good time! We've got the whole afternoon and we haven't even seen half the fair!"

Actually, we've seen all of it. All that's real, anyway. The rest is just a projection.

"I've never even been to the other part of the fair," Bonnie added, "so I was hoping that at least once I could..."

She trailed off, catching herself with what looked like a faint hint of realizing something she had never realized before, something horrible.

Ronn stared at her. Phaedra and Theo stared at her, too.

By this time, they had reached the front gate. Bonnie suddenly stopped, stiffened, and stood there rigidly for a moment. Then she looked at Ronn and his cousins as though she was seeing them for the first time.

"Have you seen Jeff?" she asked.

She just reset! "Er... no," Ronn said.

"What's keeping him?" the girl demanded. "He was supposed to take me on the Ferris wheel."

"Well, if we see him," Phaedra said quickly, "we'll tell him you're looking for him. Now we have to go!"

They hurried through the gate, got in the waiting jeep, and took off down the road.

Ronn glanced back, just before the curve of the road through the trees cut off the view.

Holding the stuffed bear, Bonnie still stood at the gate to the fair, still waiting for someone who would probably never come.

Chapter Nine

"Sorry to break up your summer romance," Phaedra said, sounding annoyed as she drove past the endless trees on either side, "but that was getting just a bit too weird back there!"

"Yeah," Theo added from the back seat. "Maybe you didn't notice, but she was a *bot*!"

"I realize that!" Ronn exclaimed, more vehemently than he intended. He actually felt a little sick about what had just happened. "But she was way more lifelike than a bot should be!"

Theo shrugged. "Or maybe Uncle Jeff just knows how to make his bots act like real people. And if she was modeled after a real person, she'd be able to do more stuff than one of those guys in the background that just walk around."

Ronn decided to let it drop rather than go on arguing, but he still wasn't as convinced as Theo was that Bonnie was just the product of some unusually advanced engineering.

A little further along, they came upon a quaint English village on the right side of the road, seemingly dating back several centuries with beam and plaster houses.

Now Phaedra was curious. "What is it — the set for *Brigadoon*?" she wondered as she parked the jeep.

Ronn and Theo were hardly as interested as she was but went with her into the deserted village anyway. When they came into an open market square with a central fountain, it was suddenly filled with dancing townspeople in period English villagers' costumes, singing as music was played by an unseen orchestra somewhere. The villagers went through a verse or two, then vanished and the square was silent and empty again.

"Now I know!" Phaedra exclaimed. "The song's 'To Thine Own Self Be True' — it's a set from *Odds Bodkins*!"

Ronn tried to remember. "Oh, right... I was kind of little but the songs were all over the place that summer and that one sounds familiar…"

"It was about ten years ago," Phaedra said. "Big old-style Broadway musical. It gets revived now and then. Mom pushed me to try out for it in a community theater production last year. It's set in the early 1600s and it's about a touring company that comes to a small English village during a fair and puts on some Shakespeare plays, so you get a show reenacting several famous scenes with new songs." She launched into one of the show's more famous songs, though the lyrics were anything but new: *"Shall I compare thee to a summer's day…"* She trailed off when she came to the end of words she remembered.

"Interesting," Ronn murmured for lack of anything better to say, "but what does it have to do with Uncle Jeff?"

Theo jumped in with that explanation. "His company did a 3-D recorded version of the Broadway stage show that could play in different cities. It was like a live performance except the actors weren't really there."

"Don't they call shows like that… movies?" Ronn asked.

"Not exactly," Theo said, warming to the subject. "They were trying to make it look like an actual live show, but it didn't go over. If people wanted to see a movie, they'd watch a vid, while people who like live shows want to see live actors. It also cost a lot to put on because it needed a whole bunch of projectors that had to be arranged just right."

As they walked back to the jeep, the phantom villagers put in another brief appearance with a snatch of music and song, then dissolved into limbo for good and all.

"Our revels now are ended," Phaedra murmured. *"These our actors, as I foretold you, were all spirits and are melted into air, into thin air…"*

"I wonder where they got that title?" Ronn said half to himself, pausing at the jeep to look back at the town. *"Odds… whatkins?"*

Phaedra actually knew, probably because she had studied up on the show when she auditioned for it. "It's a cleaned-up way of saying 'God's body,' which was considered disrespectful swearing in those days, like how 'Jiminy Cricket' stood in for 'Jesus Christ.' The funny thing is, and I think the people who wrote the show knew it, 'odds bodkins' might sound Shakespearish, but it only goes back as far as the 1700s. Shakespeare actually used the expression 'God's body' in one of his plays without any whiffling around about it. But 'odds bodkins' seemed to fit for the musical, so…"

They got back in the jeep and drove on.

After the little detour into synthetic Shakespeare, they soon came to a parking space on the left side of the road. Beyond it, the treeline curved inwards, leaving a small, open grassy area. At the far edge stood a huge mushroom that served as an overhanging sunshade, with a flat-topped mushroom below that was meant as a table, and four small mushrooms around it that could be used as seats. Another large mushroom at the back of the clearing had a door in the stem, marked with a crescent moon emblem.

"Hey, a rest stop!" Theo exclaimed. "We could eat our lunch here. It must be way past noon and I'm hungry!"

"That's because somebody wanted to spend the whole day at that fair," Phaedra grumped, and pulled the jeep in to the parking space.

Just then, some sort of mystery van drove by with four toon human characters and a dog inside, in theory on their way to solve a baffling crime. It was the first traffic they had seen on the road other than themselves.

"It won't be a real ghost anyway!" Theo called after the van as it rounded a curve just down the road and disappeared behind the trees. "Just some guy faking it so he can scare people away and collect the inheritance — oh, never mind."

Over the tabletop, Phaedra spread a cloth that had been packed with the lunch, and laid out the sandwiches, bags of chips, and drink bulbs.

The mushrooms were plastic and the seats were soft. Maybe it was something triggered by pressure on the mushrooms, but when they sat down, the background suddenly changed around them.

What had been a line of normal-sized trees was now a dense green wall of gigantic stalks of grass several feet high, and the scattered trees were monolithic trunks rearing far into the sky overhead.

As they looked around in astonishment, an ant at least two feet long came out of the grass. It paused to wave its antennae at them, then retreated back into the greenery.

Theo started singing something about "robot ants" to the tune of "This Old Man," but Phaedra cut him off.

"I think I know what vidshow this is from! You know, the toons where a little girl has a mouse for a friend and she can shrink down to his size when she says some magic words?"

"I remember them," Ronn said. "Back-ups for the *Super-Rabbit* show a few years ago, right?"

Phaedra nodded, eyeing the grass intently to see if the characters she had mentioned would show up, but they never did. Perhaps the bots weren't finished yet.

"Why are all these outside characters even here?" Ronn wondered. "Uncle Jeff certainly doesn't own *them* like he does MacNabbit the Rabbit. He's pulling stuff in from all over."

Nobody had an answer for that, and they ate their sandwiches without

101

saying much. The silence all around them made things a little less than cheerful.

On the way back to the jeep, Ronn heard horses whinnying and neighing from a distance and from above. He looked up. High in the sky, five winged horses with girls wearing gleaming armor riding them passed overhead, and were quickly lost from view when they went beyond the treetops. Ronn briefly wondered if they were bots, but even in 80% gravity they looked too heavy to actually fly with those relatively small and slowly beating wings. Besides, while the middle three seemed stable enough, the horses and riders on either end were blurry and shot through with color interference, as though there were problems with the 3-D projection.

"*Team Valkyrie,*" Phaedra remarked. "God, I loved that show! I wanted so much to be in it, but I was only about five."

"I've heard of it," Ronn said, "but it was a little before my time."

"Some Japanese thing," Theo added. "Usual five teenage girls with super-powers form a team and fight monsters."

Phaedra sounded miffed. "Oh, come on! There was more to it than that! The characters had real personalities, and the plots were more involved, and…"

"And a real dumb idea, too," Theo went on, ignoring her. "Sending teenagers out on a mission to save the world? Like that'll ever work!"

It took Ronn a moment to work out the convolutions of Theo's sarcasm. "Oh, right… At least *we* don't have to save the world *every* week."

The overall silence closed in on them once more and Ronn was actually glad when they were back on the road.

On the left side of the road stood what looked like it would be the monorail station once the monorail was in service, a 1950s conception of "futuristic" with a lot of glass and sweeping cantilever roofs overhanging platforms on an upper level where non-existent travelers could wait to board non-existent trains. A large sign out front read "**EASTGATE**." Since the guest house had been at Westgate, they must have been directly across the crater from it, or halfway around the circle. If Vesper was ever opened to the public, this might be the main entrance.

On the other side, towards the crater interior, they saw a large open area with cranes, forklift trucks, and other equipment among stacks of crates and piles of prefabricated building walls. Laid out flat near the road were several large sheets of red plastic that were actually complete walls of simulated brick with the white-framed windows already in place. Ronn's guess, remembering pictures he had seen in his North American History class, was that it amounted to an enormous model kit that would assemble into a full-sized replica of Independence Hall. He almost expected to see a giant tube of glue next to it.

A fleet of self-propelled moving equipment, like forklift trucks but with grappling arms, stood motionless as though in a parking lot, connected to charging cables, and waiting for the call to start work. They didn't have any obvious operator cabs or controls, and must have been either remote-controlled or programmed for autonomous operation. Nearby, several rows of trees from saplings to full-grown awaited transplanting, with automatic sprinkling equipment on hand to keep everything watered.

Phaedra parked the jeep and they looked around for a while, but didn't find anything that looked like an office or anybody who could answer questions. No workers were in sight, alien or human, and nothing moved in the silence. It reminded Ronn of one of his father's building projects, a large construction site on a Sunday. The workers had gone home the Friday before with every intention of coming back on Monday to resume work where they had left off. Only here, days — or weeks? — had gone by since then and they had never come back.

Further back were several large circular platforms set in the crater floor, a couple flush with the surface and loaded with stacks of crates, a couple of others lowered to the next level below, which seemed to be a huge warehouse. Elevators, apparently.

"All this must just be the freight entrance," Ronn decided, "and the central headquarters is somewhere else."

"I've been wondering how they got all the big stuff up here," Theo said. "I didn't think they could've brought it through that little corridor we came in."

They got back in the jeep and Phaedra drove on. From there it was just more forest. Ronn idly watched the trees on his right go by until—

He spotted an irregular mass of metal and plastic just inside the woods as they passed, and yelled, "Stop!"

Phaedra hit the brake, lurching forward in her seat as the jeep screeched to a halt. "Don't scare me like that!" she exclaimed.

Theo had been knocked into the seatbacks in front of him. "Don't worry about the kid in the back," he muttered. "I'm getting used to it and bruises heal quick."

"Sorry," Ronn said, "but I saw something that didn't look like it should be there. We ought to take a look."

Still complaining, Phaedra and Theo got out of the jeep and followed Ronn into the woods. There they found a wrecked spacecraft about the size of a fighter jet. It was mostly intact but crumpled where it had hit the ground hard, plowed a short ditch, and knocked several trees over. Beneath the craft were some ruptured pipe ends, possibly from an underground irrigation system although no water was gushing out of them just now, and a smooth, solid rock flooring that showed through in places. The cockpit canopy had shattered and Ronn could see two bots in helmets and flight suits sitting inside, moving feebly, going through the motions of manipulating the control panel. Since they had been jarred out of alignment, their hands were no longer connecting with the controls. Apparently they weren't equipped with autonomous behavior systems and were just programmed to repeat an automatic behavioral sequence without any capability of adapting to new circumstances. Their movements were not only senseless but slow, as though their internal power was running down.

"This isn't a display," Ronn said uncomfortably. "This really is some kind of accident."

Theo took a closer look at the wreck. "And it isn't just any spaceship. That's a KX Fighter from the *Galactattack* game."

"I don't remember that game," Ronn admitted. "What's so special about it?"

"First practical 3-D projection game on the market," Theo explained. "Really crude compared to what came later, but it was the first game you could play outside of a box and shoot down spaceships flying around your room. The company history vid talked about it quite a bit because it came out just in time for Christmas that year when Uncle Jeff's company was overextended and he couldn't get credit anywhere, He sold a squillion of the things right when he needed a lot of cash fast. Saved his bacon."

"So it would have some sentimental value for him," Phaedra concluded. "But what's it doing *here,* and why is it all smashed up?"

"Something went wrong somewhere," Ronn said slowly, speculating as he spoke. "There's probably some area with a *Galactattack* display, with full-scale replicas of the fighters, some even working, and this one went out of control, maybe strayed too far and lost the control signal in the area where it was supposed to be, and ended up crashing here."

"I'd love to see where this thing came from," Theo added. "If Uncle Jeff has full-sized displays of his company's old games somewhere, he's probably got one for *Third Star Action Brigade*. Now *there* was a bunch you'd want backing you up if you were ever pinned down in a firefight with Quintorians."

They went on their way, but there was little to see after that except more of the seemingly never-ending forest. Much of the southern half of the crater looked to be undeveloped and Ronn wondered if it was intended as a sort of wilderness preserve.

The crater wall at the six o'clock point was not a sheer cliff face, but more of a shallow upwards slope. There didn't seem to be a Southgate, and instead a setting resembling the American West was in the works with buttes and other eroded reddish sandstone landforms straight out of Monument Valley as well as the occasional cactus. It still had a raw, unfinished look to it. They passed the beginnings of a Western town, not much more than a few building frameworks and some stacks of prefab plastic walls colored brown and gray to resemble weather-beaten wood.

Unless the crater was actually teardrop-shaped rather than circular, the southern slope went on for much further than it should have. Ronn suspected that some game was being played with forced perspective. The tepees in the far-off Apache village might have really been only about three feet high and the mountains beyond barely more than sculpted hills. To top it off, six American Presidents looked down on them from the seeming distance. Uncle Jeff had even duplicated Mount Rushmore, adding a couple of his favorites who weren't in the original back on Earth.

Now they were coming up the southwest side. They passed more side roads but other than for what looked like the watchtowers of a frontier fort rising above the treetops somewhere well off the main road, they saw nothing of further interest until the manor house came into view.

Since the afternoon was well advanced and the simulated sun was edging into the west, knocking off exploration for the day was as good an idea as any. Phaedra found the entrance to the garage and parked the jeep, and they went up into the house.

A dip in the pool seemed like the perfect way to relax after one very strange day. It should have been a good opportunity to think things through and try to make sense of what he had seen that day, but Ronn's thoughts kept going back to that bot at the fair. He tried to tell himself that she was just a robot, a mechanical thing, but he couldn't shake the feeling that there had been more to it than that.

After the swim, it was time to call Earth. They found an old-fashioned voice-only speakerphone on the conference room table and used it to call the number Phaedra had been given that morning. A high-level meeting was in progress, and it sounded as though some very important people had been waiting for their call. Ronn and his cousins were allowed to talk only briefly to their mothers, just enough to reassure them that they were all doing fine, then Mr. Cosgrove took over as the official in charge. Dr. Kininger down in the docking bay was patched in as well, which was an extra complication since the connection wasn't direct and had to be relayed back from Earth. With 120,000 miles from Dr. Kininger's mouth to Ronn's ear, transmission each way took two-thirds of a second, so the slight delays were noticeable.

"You kids gave us a real scare when your com system failed right after you went inside," Dr. Kininger said. "We thought we'd lost you for several hours there." Then, not succeeding very well in hiding the eagerness in his voice, he asked, "Did you find a control center so you can let us in?"

Ronn admitted that they hadn't, and Dr. Kininger's disappointment was obvious. Well, he *was* stuck in that cramped little crew quarters with all those other people.

They told the listeners what they had seen since leaving the docking bay, and the reaction was general astonishment.

"*That's* what Prescott's got up there?" a woman in the background was heard to say — and Ronn could have sworn she sounded like the President. Was *she* listening in on them? "His own private theme park?"

"That's pretty much what it looks like," Ronn told Mr. Cosgrove when he came back on. "By the way, do you know anything about Uncle Jeff's old girlfriends from back when he was about sixteen? We ran across a really lifelike bot of one and I was kind of curious."

Mr. Cosgrove seemed to think it was a trivial question, but there was a pause in the conference just then as some officials argued with other officials about how to proceed in response to what they had heard, so he spared a moment to bring Aunt Thalia in again. As the oldest sister, she was the closest to Uncle Jeff's age and would have known who his friends were.

"Bonnie?" Aunt Thalia said when Ronn described the bot. "Of course I knew her."

"I hope she didn't die young and tragically," Phaedra put in, "and this was Uncle Jeff's memorial to the girl he once loved..."

"Not exactly," Aunt Thalia said. "The real Bonnie's still alive. She was living up in Santa Barbara the last I heard, not far from TranStella headquarters. I think she owns a piece of the company. Diamonds may be forever, but stock options are the gift that keeps on giving. She wasn't just his high-school girlfriend, she was his third wife. About the best of the bunch, I always thought."

"So maybe it's like a recreation of their first date," Phaedra suggested. "He never forgot her. It's a little creepy, but kind of sweet."

"Not if you knew *him*," Aunt Thalia replied somewhat sourly. "It's probably more about the occasion than about the girl. I don't think he was pining over a lost love when he built it. He was just reconstructing an important event in his life and Bonnie just happened to be the girl who was there at the time."

"All right," Mr. Cosgrove interrupted. "Enough of the family reunion. Let's get back to business."

After some more back and forth and asking questions about details that Ronn and his cousins were a little hard-pressed to answer since they hadn't thought to take notes, Mr. Cosgrove finally decided to bring the session to a close.

"So what do you want us to do tomorrow?" Ronn asked.

"Or are we done?" Phaedra broke in hopefully. "Can we come home now?"

"Not quite yet, I'm afraid," Mr. Cosgrove replied. Phaedra's groan could be heard 60,000 miles away but he ignored it. "As long as nothing's happening, stay where you are tomorrow. We need some time to sort out what you've told us so far. You should be safe in the house and it doesn't sound as though any hostile forces have shown up as yet. Besides, you've probably seen everything important in the crater itself and we don't know how dangerous it might be if you go down into the lower levels. By this time tomorrow evening, we may have a better idea of what we need to have you do."

"Well, that sounds boring," Theo griped.

"Never satisfied, are you?" Mr. Cosgrove said. "If you really want something to occupy your idle hours, you might search the house again and see if you missed the control center the first time. It must surely be *somewhere*."

"I think I'd rather be bored..." Theo muttered.

Mr. Cosgrove then let their mothers come on for some final love yous and admonishments to be careful.

After the call was over, they went back to the den and lay on the floor by the virtual fireplace to talk for a bit before dinner.

"You can tell what's on their minds," Theo said. "Once we find a way to disable the ID scan, they'll come running in and that'll be the end of our usefulness. It'll be back to Earth for us."

"What's wrong with that?" Phaedra asked. "At least we'd be out of here and back home. Maybe *you* want to stay here but I certainly don't."

"I'd just like to explore the place some more," Theo replied. "We just went around the outer edge and there's an awful lot we haven't seen yet. Who knows what he's got in the middle?"

Ronn found himself agreeing with him. Now that they were here and seemingly not in any immediate danger, and as long as the food held out, he wouldn't mind a few extra days of exploring. Especially when the alternative was going back to Ms. Crowley's class.

His musings were interrupted by Wilfred's sudden appearance. "Dinner will be served momentarily. I have taken the liberty of laying out the appropriate attire in your respective bedrooms, so you may now go upstairs and change."

"Aw, come on!" Theo exclaimed testily. "What's wrong with the clothes I've got on? What'll happen if I don't change into your monkey suit?"

"Dinner will *not* be served," Wilfred declared. "I am merely abiding by the instructions specified by Mr. Prescott," he added a little less sternly, then turned and left the room.

"There's no arguing with the boss," Ronn said, "especially when he isn't even here."

After changing clothes, they assembled in the dining room again, but to Ronn's surprise the table had not been set. Instead, Wilfred came in and opened the doors that led from the dining room to the veranda.

"Since it is such a pleasant evening outside, I thought you might enjoy dining *al fresco*."

Ronn glanced at the equally surprised Phaedra and Theo, but everyone just shrugged and followed Wilfred outside. A table had been set up on the veranda near the railing, with a view of the lawn and the surrounding trees. The sky glowed in gorgeous simulated sunset colors of orange and red directly overhead, fading to gathering darkness in the east, above the other side of the crater. A cool breeze blew gently from somewhere, but all around was nothing but utter silence. After gallantly seating Phaedra, Wilfred went back into the house and Ronn and Theo sat down.

"It may be nice out," Phaedra said, "but it's also just too quiet. Just listen! It's like a graveyard out there. No bugs, no birds, no traffic, *nothing*. It's like we're the only living things in the whole place."

"Which we *are*," Ronn reminded her.

"Don't forget the trees and the grass," Theo pointed out. "Maybe there are live worms in the dirt, too, but it's not like they make a whole lot of noise…"

Suddenly, an owl hooted from the trees. Then some birds chirped. Then an insect buzzed. Then there was a whispering swish of the wind.

"I guess somebody heard us," Ronn said.

"Now the question is where the **NIGHT SOUNDS** button is and who pressed it," Theo added, but when Wilfred reappeared to serve the soup and he asked him about it, the butler simply declared that he did not have that information.

Something occurred to Ronn as he sampled a spoonful. Beef barley and not half-bad. "I just realized there's one thing you'd expect in a place like this that it doesn't have. Or at least I didn't see any signs of it."

"Oh? What's that?" Theo asked between slurps of his soup.

"A zoo," Ronn replied. "We didn't see any animals at all out there. Real ones, I mean. Those toon bots don't count. The plants like the trees and the grass seem to be real, but nothing else is. Even the seagulls we saw at Northport were projections."

"I'm not exactly surprised," Theo said. "Animals have to be fed.

There'd be birds flying around and nesting all over the place, making messes on everything that would have to be cleaned up... Then again," he added thoughtfully, "the company vid mentioned that Uncle Jeff is a big sponsor of the mammoth cloning project, and he even supplied alien tech to help out in reconstructing really old and damaged DNA. They've already made baby mammoths and woolly rhinos, and they're working on other things. It does seem a little strange he doesn't have any of them up here."

Ronn nodded. "It isn't like he doesn't have a lot of room he hasn't done anything with yet, so maybe a zoo is down the road. Or maybe not. Like you said, live animals would need a lot of upkeep, and I get the idea he wants this place to run itself as much as it can."

As they ate, they talked about the day's events. Ronn still felt more than a little bothered by what had happened with the Bonnie-bot at the county fair display, but realizing that Phaedra didn't want to discuss the subject, he decided not to mention it. The real mystery was why some Jeff-bots weren't where they should have been and one had been outright murdered, if the word even applied to bots, but after hashing over any number of theories, they didn't come to any new conclusions as to what it all meant.

"I have to admit that I did find out a lot more about Uncle Jeff than I really wanted to know," Phaedra said about halfway through dessert.

Ronn and Theo agreed that summed things up about as well as anything. After dinner, there wasn't much else to do but watch some vids in the den until time for bed.

As Ronn lay waiting for sleep to come, he thought about the things he had seen that day. Some of them had been little short of disturbing, but the one thing he couldn't get out of his mind was a sad little bot trapped in a county fair that would never end.

Chapter Ten

Sunday, April 26

After breakfast the next morning, they called Earth to find out if there was any news or if the officials in charge had come up with something for them to do today after all. Mr. Cosgrove replied that there was nothing to report and probably wouldn't be until that evening, when they were to call back.

With an entire day of leisure stretching out before them, Phaedra went up to her room with a book she had found in the library while Theo retired to the den to watch vids and play games. Ronn took a walk outside the house, but the footpath into the forest only led to a clearing with picnic tables and a gazebo, in case the high-powered businesspeople staying at the guest house were in the mood for an open-air barbecue. A nagging thought was on his mind and he finally decided to do something about it.

He didn't tell the others exactly where he was going. All he said at lunch was that he wanted to do a little exploring on his own that afternoon.

Phaedra was not happy. "Are you out of your mind? They told us to stay here today. And going off by yourself without us? What if something happens to you? We should stick together."

"Maybe it's a bad idea," Ronn said a little hesitantly, knowing she would think the idea he really had was downright terrible, "but I'm getting bored hanging around here. I'll stay on the main road, same route we took yesterday without anything bad happening to us, so I should be all right." Retracing the same route was hardly exploring, but no one picked up on the contradiction.

Since the three were on their own and there weren't any adults here to enforce good sense, Phaedra couldn't have stopped him even if she had really wanted to. He was a big boy now and her main worry was keeping

110

her own brother from doing something crazy. Fortunately, Theo was feeling lazy, maybe a little tired after the last couple of days, and more interested in lounging around the house than going anywhere. If something happened to her cousin because he was an idiot, well, it wouldn't be her fault.

Ronn went down to the garage after lunch, picked out one of the scooters, and set out down the road. Since it was the same model as the scooter he'd learned to ride at the summer resort, he could handle it well enough. He probably could have figured out the jeep with a little practice, but he didn't want to have to learn how to steer and brake while trying to go somewhere. Best to stick with something he knew.

The warm air against his face as he rode through the forest felt pleasant, and he could almost enjoy the ride in the bright simulated sunlight. Except... it was just so *quiet* around him. That point was especially obvious since Theo wasn't along to keep up a stream of chatter.

A road cutting across the crater would have been a more direct route, but Ronn had no idea how the interior was laid out and didn't think it would be a good idea to venture into parts unknown by himself. Instead, he followed the road around the north rim of the crater. He sped up as he approached MacNabbit the Rabbit's house, not wanting to get caught up in a repeat of yesterday's complications. MacNabbit was still out hoeing in his garden and didn't even look up as he zipped by, and Ronn was through the section before any of the supporting characters had a chance to react to his presence.

It was the same county fair, where nothing had changed or ever would change, with the same bot extras milling around or riding the merry-go-round, the same blaring carousel music.

Right on cue, a pretty girl of about sixteen came up to him. "Have you seen Jeff?" Bonnie asked. She was no longer carrying the teddy bear.

"Uh... no, I haven't," Ronn said.

"What's keeping him?" Bonnie demanded. "He was supposed to take me on the Ferris wheel."

She was about to turn away, but a puzzled expression appeared on her face and she looked back at Ronn. "You look familiar. Do I know you?"

"I was just here yesterday," Ronn said. "You and I went on the Ferris wheel and everything. I even won a teddy bear for you at the shooting gallery."

"Oh... that," Bonnie said, as though it took an effort to remember. "I was wondering where it came from. I wasn't sure what to do with it, so I put it down somewhere..." Now her expression was less puzzled and more anguished. "What's going *on*, anyway? It's like I've been at this fair forever and I can't go home, and Jeff's supposed to come but he never does..."

"Bonnie," Ronn said, "would you like to leave the fair? Would you like to come with me?"

"Is that *allowed?*"

"I don't know, but who's going to stop you?"

"I... well..." Bonnie paused, not seeming to have an answer.

Ronn had a feeling that if he could just get her beyond the reach of whatever controlled her, something interesting might happen. He didn't know where it would lead, but he was convinced that she was more self-aware than a bot normally was and she was trapped in some kind of endless loop here. "Just come with me. Nobody will hurt you."

Bonnie was still uncertain, fighting an internal battle between what she wanted to do and what her programming was telling her to do. By this time, they had reached the front gate. As before, Bonnie suddenly stopped, stiffened, and stood there rigidly for a moment. Then she looked at Ronn as though she was seeing him for the first time.

"Have you seen Jeff?" she asked.

She just reset again! Maybe this is hopeless...

"What's keeping him?" Bonnie repeated. "He was supposed to take me on the Ferris wheel."

"Not again!" Ronn exclaimed, losing his patience. He took Bonnie by the arm and gently pulled her along.

She staggered and stumbled, but went along with him through the gate.

On the other side, they stopped by the plastic statue of Gertrude the Cow and Bonnie glanced around. "I... I'm outside!" she exclaimed in wonder. "I wasn't sure it was... *possible!*" She looked at Ronn. "I remember you! That's right... you were here before! And we went on the Ferris wheel and... then you left..."

"You remember now?"

Her hand flew to her mouth and her eyes went very wide. "Oh God! What's happened to me? Where *am* I?"

I'm going to have to be the one to tell her. Well, no need to hit her with it all at once. Ronn motioned to the scooter. "Just come with me. Maybe we'll find some answers."

The seat on the scooter was long enough that Bonnie could ride behind him. She held on tightly to him, maybe more tightly than she needed to. Ronn doubted that bots were as fragile as human beings, and she would probably come out of an accident better than he would.

He went back around the northern rim of the crater. Bonnie said fairly little along the way, too occupied with watching the strange scenery go by. She had lived, if that was the right word, in this crater for several years, but she probably had no memory of being brought here and had never been away from the county fair set since then. All she knew was that she wasn't in Salisbury anymore.

She spoke up when they approached the guest house. "Oh, what a pretty house! It looks just like the Magruder Mansion!"

"The one that burned down?" Ronn called back, remembering the framed newspaper clipping on the wall.

Bonnie's memory of it seemed fuzzy. "Oh... I guess it did. Too bad. It was a nice place. I always wanted to live there."

You must not have been the only one.

Ronn parked the scooter in the garage below the house and took Bonnie upstairs.

Phaedra was by herself in the den, curled up on the couch with a book and listening to music as Ronn and Bonnie came in. "Oh, you're back. Did you find anything new—?" She was a little slow looking up, but when she did, she saw Bonnie.

"You went all the way over to the other side of the crater to bring back that... that *bot*?" It sounded as though she had intended to say "thing" up until the last fraction of a second.

Ronn shrugged, trying to make it seem as though it wasn't that big a deal. "I just thought she might be able to help us."

"Help us *what?*" Phaedra all but choked.

"Look," he said firmly, "let me handle this. I have some ideas. If they don't work out, we can always take her back to the fairground."

"*You* can!" Phaedra exclaimed. "I don't want any part of this!" She jumped up from the couch and stormed out, heading to her room upstairs.

Bonnie looked uncomfortable. "I'm sorry if I've caused you any trouble."

"She'll get over it," Ronn said, hoping his optimism wasn't misplaced. It was that uncanny valley again.

He waved the music off and had Bonnie sit down on the couch, then sat next to her so he could turn and face her. "I'd just like you to answer a few questions."

"If I can..." she said uncertainly. "Sometimes I have trouble remembering. It's like there's something out there that would explain everything if I could just reach it, but I can't."

Ronn could hardly believe what he was hearing. This was far beyond any imaginable programmed behavior. "All right, let me ask a question and see where it goes from there. Back at the fair, you said you were waiting for Jeff Prescott. Had he ever been there before?"

Bonnie thought for a moment. "Er... sometimes, but not always."

Ronn guessed that she had been programmed to wait for Uncle Jeff as though they had agreed to meet at the fair, just as their real-life models had done some thirty-five years before. In normal human behavior, events were not repeated endlessly, but even a bot with an autonomous behavior system would not be aware that it was going through the same cycle over and over. Bonnie, though...

"Yes!" she suddenly exclaimed. "I remember! And then one day he didn't come and I haven't seen him since. And then you came... oh, it's all so mixed up!"

"How old was Jeff when you saw him?" Ronn asked.

"What do you mean?" Bonnie asked, puzzled. "He was just... Jeff."

"Was he a teenager like us or a man around fifty?"

Bonnie laughed. "Are you kidding? Why would I want to see the fair with an old guy? Jeff's a boy in my class at school, same age as me."

That didn't mean Bonnie wasn't programmed to see Uncle Jeff as something other than he actually was, as the boy she had known instead of a middle-aged man reliving a happy day of his youth.

"But there was always something funny about it," Bonnie went on. "We always did the same things, Jeff always said the same things... it never changed. It was kind of weird and I didn't understand it, and every time it seemed like I almost had it figured out, it would slip away again. But now that you mention it... I saw an old guy in the crowd once or twice, but most days he wasn't there. The times he was, he seemed to be watching Jeff and me really close. Kind of creepy in a way. But I haven't seen him lately..."

Ronn gave a start. *How could I be so stupid? Bonnie wasn't waiting for the real Uncle Jeff at all — there was a bot of him at that age! That means another Jeffbot is missing!*

But the old man she mentioned... that *would* have been the real Uncle Jeff. At least that was one definite sighting of him, although at some point well in the past, and Bonnie's blurred perception of passing time wasn't enough to pinpoint exactly when he was last seen. Not a lot of help.

More out of curiosity than for the sake of the job he was supposed to be doing, Ronn asked Bonnie a few more questions.

"What's your full name and where do you live?"

"Bonnie Hutchinson and I live in Salisbury, New York."

"How old are you?"

"Sixteen."

"What year is this?"

"This is getting kind of boring. Can't you go look at a calendar?"

A bot with feelings and opinions? She hadn't just been modeled after the original Bonnie Hutchinson, most of the original Bonnie's memories had come along in the process.

"Okay," she suddenly said, "how about I ask you a few questions?"

"All right," Ronn said uneasily, not sure how she'd handle the answers.

"What's *your* name and who exactly are you?"

"Ronn Evans. I'm Jeff Prescott's nephew. The other two you met are my cousins Phaedra and Theo."

"It's funny Jeff would have nieces and nephews the same age he is... Unless... What year *is* this?"

"2037."

Bonnie's eyes widened. "That would make me an old lady! And where are we? I mean, where is this whole place?"

"It's basically a private theme park on an asteroid in space 60,000 miles from Earth, about a quarter of the way to the Moon. Uncle Jeff got really rich in the years since you knew him in school, and he seems to have built the place partly to recreate scenes from his life."

After taking that in for a moment, Bonnie said, a little sadly, "I'm not a real person, am I?"

"Well... Strictly speaking, you seem to be a robot with all the flesh and blood Bonnie Hutchinson's memories. I'm sorry to have to tell you this... But you seem pretty real in your own way," he added quickly.

She took it remarkably well, shaking her head in amazement. "I remember when I was a little girl playing with my Barbies... who knew I'd end up *being* one?"

Ronn wasn't sure what his own reaction would be if he woke up one day and found himself in the body of a robot, but he doubted if he would be very calm about it.

"It's almost a relief to find out for sure," Bonnie added. "I was starting to wonder if I'd died and gone to Hell. I didn't think I'd been *that* bad... All I knew was that I never got thirsty or had to eat anything, and I kept having to do the same things over and over..."

"You were *aware* of this?" Ronn asked.

"Sometimes. It was like a dream I couldn't wake up from. Mostly I'd just go along with it and not think about it, but now and then I'd start to wake up, and I'd almost have the answer... but then it was like I'd go back to sleep for a while and dream some more. Now that I'm away from the fair, I feel like I'm finally really awake."

"Were there others like you? Robots that could think and feel, I mean?"

Bonnie considered. "I don't think so. Nobody else at the fair seemed like they were awake at all. Except... Jeff. The Jeff at the fair. I guess he would have been a robot like me, if you say the real Jeff is around fifty now. I was starting to think he knew something about what was going on. He wasn't just going through the motions. I was slow to wake up myself, though, and one day he was gone before I could start asking things, and after that I was alone."

She paused and shook her head, as though to clear the bad memories out of her mind. "And this is all Jeff's doing? I should have known! He always did love his cool toys. But if I'm a robot... how can I think and feel and remember like this? I don't know much about robots except from movies and TV, but should I be this... human?"

"It's a mystery to me, too," Ronn admitted. "Most of the bots we've seen are just that, bots with limited programming. A few, like the staff here, seem almost human, but even they have limits if you push them far enough. You, though... I can't explain it. Maybe it was some accident from modeling you after a real person using alien technology, stuff Uncle Jeff got from beings from space, and he didn't realize himself how exact the copy was. That it could start thinking on its own, I mean, with the memories of the original. I don't think it was planned that way."

"Beings from space? Really? This just gets weirder all the time. But why would he want to make a copy of *me?*"

"We think he wanted to recreate his first date. He was later married for a while to the original Bonnie, so maybe that has something to do with it."

"I married him?" Bonnie reflected a little dreamily, confusing the original with the copy. "Well, I can sort of see me falling for him. There was something about him... he wasn't like the other boys. He had, I don't know... more imagination maybe. When he was enthusiastic about something, he could pull you in and make you excited about it, too, even if you weren't really interested at first. From the way you put it, though, it doesn't sound like it lasted. I can see that, too. He could be pretty intense, probably kind of hard to live with."

Then she turned serious. "So what do you plan to do with me? I don't want to go back to the fair. I was stuck in that place too long!"

"We're stuck here ourselves," Ronn said, "or at least until we can figure out what's going on. I guess you can just hang with us and come along back to Earth if you want."

"Thanks. It's not like I have much choice. But are you sure it'll be all right with your cousins? I don't think that girl likes me."

"Phaedra? Sure, she can be a little prickly, but give her a chance and she'll warm up to you." *I hope.*

"Ronn," said Mrs. Flynn, coming to the den doorway and looking in, "if you wish to have your clothes washed, I—"

If a bot could show an utterly baffled expression, Mrs. Flynn did when she saw Bonnie. "I'm not sure I know you..." she said as though trying to think with something she didn't have. "We weren't told anything about a fourth member of the party."

"This is Bonnie," Ronn said. "She just joined us." He waited a little worriedly for the response, wondering if Mrs. Flynn might react badly to the new development, recognizing Bonnie as a fellow bot.

But no, the housekeeper still looked puzzled. She apparently wasn't advanced enough to distinguish between bot and human.

"Very well," she said after a moment, as though accepting the situation without any question. "I shall inform the staff that we have an additional guest."

"Er... no need to set an extra place at dinner," Ronn added. "Bonnie's made other arrangements."

"Right, then," Mrs. Flynn said and left the room.

Ronn turned back to Bonnie. "If you're going to be staying here, you should have your own room. There are some vacant ones upstairs."

"Good idea," Bonnie said. "Uhm... do you have any books I could read so I don't get too bored? And so I can catch up on the news for the past few decades?"

She can read, too? How much of the real Bonnie's memory got copied into her, anyway? "Well, books like what you're probably thinking of pretty much aren't being made anymore, and I haven't seen any bookpads around the house, but I know where there's a lot of old books. Some might be recent enough to help you."

He showed her the library, where she picked out a few likely looking volumes, then took her upstairs.

They had just come into the hallway when Theo emerged from his room. He saw Ronn with Bonnie and looked a little startled, though not disturbed by it like his sister had been.

"My other cousin, Theo," Ronn explained. "I don't know if you remember him, but you met him the other day."

"He does look kind of familiar," Bonnie said, extending her hand to Theo as he came up to them. "Hi, I'm Bonnie."

"Yeah, we've met," Theo said. He shook her hand, then glanced at Ronn. "Say, if we get back to Earth, can I borrow her? I have to do a science fair project next term and..."

"You'll have to ask *her*," Ronn said, though her expression already answered that with a look of *Not in a million years, kid*. He took Bonnie on down the hall to show her to an empty room.

After leaving her there to settle in, he came back out into the hall and found Theo waiting for him.

"You do realize that's our *aunt*, don't you?" Theo asked. "One of them, anyway. Sort of."

"I think it's more like our aunt's very identical twin sister," Ronn said.

117

"Besides, she's mentally about thirty-five years younger than the real Bonnie and she never married Uncle Jeff."

They went downstairs and Ronn told Theo what he had found out from Bonnie's answers to his questions. Since Theo was of a techie turn of mind, Ronn hoped he might have some insight, but he seemed even more amazed by Bonnie's near-humanness than Ronn was. Perhaps it was because Theo understood the limitations of bots better than Ronn did, and to him Bonnie was only too clearly something that should not be.

A little before dinner, they went for a swim in the pool.

Ronn was hanging on to the side, debating whether to get out of the pleasantly warm water. Theo sat in a plastic chair by a table with a thoroughly unnecessary umbrella overhead and puzzled over an old book that had caught his attention, and Phaedra was across from him and drying off with a towel.

They heard the door to the house open, and looked up to see Bonnie come out. She was wearing a two-piece swimsuit, modest by the standards of 2037 but probably stylish in Uncle Jeff's youth, and flip-flops.

"Hi," she said as she came up. "One of the maids dropped off some clothes for me, and I found this. How do I look?"

Perfect, Ronn thought, startled. *A little* too *perfect*. The even, lightly tanned complexion showed no scars, blemishes, moles, birthmarks, or pimples anywhere. Her overall proportions were probably some ideal for a sixteen-year-old girl of her height, maybe close to impossible to maintain in real life without a lot of diet and exercise in her time, or expensive body enhancement now. Her original body might not have looked that good. Other than for its inhuman perfection, though, her robot body was utterly lifelike in nearly every detail. She even had a belly button, which was perhaps taking things a little too far. The really telling point was the fact that the maid had supplied Bonnie with extra clothes as a matter of course without even a formal request for them. Bonnie was so far advanced that the other bots had accepted her as human.

"Are you sure going swimming is a good idea?" Ronn asked. "We don't know how waterproof you are."

"I can just lounge by the pool, can't I?" Bonnie said. "I don't have to get wet—"

Theo scrutinized her closely as she passed him, then exclaimed, "Whoa!"

Phaedra looked disgusted. "Theo! You're too young — and she's a *bot!*"

"That's just the point!" Theo retorted. "She's got some kind of access panel on her side!"

Hearing that, Ronn scrambled out of the water and came up on the pool deck. The thought of Theo opening Bonnie up and poking around inside without responsible supervision was more than a little alarming.

As Ronn quickly dried himself off, Theo was already examining Bonnie, who only reluctantly stood still for him. Just under her ribcage and to the left of her stomach was the faint outline of a rectangle about three inches by four, marked by a very thin and shallow groove.

"Can I take a closer look?" Theo asked her.

"Well... all right," Bonnie replied hesitantly, clearly not comfortable with being inspected like she was just so much machinery.

"Hold still, please," Theo said and touched his right index finger to the panel outlined on her side, and started tracing along it.

"Do you *mind?*" Bonnie yelped.

"Sorry, just trying to figure out how to open it..." Theo muttered, then thought of something. "You can feel this? You've got a sense of touch? Am I tickling you?"

"It's not that... More like you're getting a little personal there, Junior. But, yeah... I can feel things. Pressure, anyway. I don't think I can feel pain, though."

"Makes sense," Theo said. "Even a bot has to have some kind of feedback from its surroundings. You want to be able to pick something up without breaking it by squeezing too hard. You'd also have to have a sense of your body just to walk around. But pain... who needs it? Wilfred hardly even twitched when I stuck a fork in him."

"You aren't sticking any forks in me!"

Then the panel unexpectedly snapped open, swinging on hidden hinges on the left side.

"Geeze!" Theo blurted. "Look at that!"

"Just don't touch anything, all right?" Bonnie insisted worriedly.

This may have been *really* advanced alien tech. It was hard for Ronn to say for sure just what they were looking at. All he could see was masses of fine wiring like silver clouds framing a small panel with some empty jacks and several read-outs with glowing red numbers, but Ronn had no idea what sort of information was being displayed.

Theo shrugged, closed the panel, and let Bonnie go on about her business. Which was to sit on the edge of the pool and dangle her feet in the water. With no openings in her lower extremities, it seemed safe enough. She said she could feel the water on her skin and had some idea of what temperature it was, but there was no real sense of pleasure other than a memory of what doing something like it on other occasions had felt like. Ronn's guess was that it gave her something familiar to do while she enjoyed the company of people who could talk, even if Phaedra ignored her. She *had* been stuck at that county fair for a long time.

Although Bonnie was up in her room and out of sight, Phaedra was still annoyed with Ronn, and dinner that evening was rather low-key.

Afterwards, they sat around the table in the conference room and called Earth from the speakerphone. This time, the people on the other end were much better prepared. Their mothers were again only allowed to speak briefly to reassure themselves that their children were all right, then Mr. Cosgrove took over.

What followed was a long and tiresome discussion that didn't accomplish very much. Some officials wanted Ronn and his cousins to start systematically exploring the interior of the crater in the hope of finding Prescott's control center. Others, losing patience with the idea of depending on mere children to accomplish anything worthwhile, preferred for them to return to the docking bay first thing in the morning so the scientists could experiment with smuggling unauthorized personnel through the ID recognition system with them. If that didn't work, the kids would be hustled home and the security personnel left behind would try to blast their way in, never mind any defenses.

"It sounds like things are getting a little desperate down there," Theo said to Ronn out of the speakerphone's range.

Ronn had the same impression. He wasn't even sure he wanted to leave so soon. He was actually starting to feel comfortable in the house, and as long as the food supplies held out, he could stand a few days of exploring the crater. Phaedra, of course, was delighted by the prospect that the nightmare might be over sooner than she had dared hope.

In the end, nothing was really decided. "We should have something worked out for you to do when you call in the morning," Mr. Cosgrove said. "Oh, and one last thing. Based on what you told us, we've been making a few inquiries. It seems the Vesper project was a fairly blatant case of hiding something in plain sight. Prescott has a company that designs and builds attractions for theme parks. He also announced plans several years ago for building a theme park of his own that would have included many of the attractions you described, though officially it never seems to have gotten out of the design stage. Most people in that particular business have long assumed the project was either dead or on indefinite hold even though design work and prototype construction have continued all along. Apparently all that was a cover for what he was doing on Vesper. As nearly as we can determine, he was having sets and props made in the Los Angeles area where the free-lance designers and contract shops are located, and shipping them in prefab sections to an old private airport he owns up north around Ojai. There, the trucks were unloaded in one of the hangars. Then he would load everything on that freighter of his and send it to Vesper. He had the whole airport masked under wide-area image projection so nobody ever saw what was going on. A great many people knew one piece or another of the story but only a relative few were in on all of it. Even we didn't put the pieces together until now."

"But why would he want to keep it a secret?" Ronn asked. "It all seems perfectly legal."

He could almost hear Mr. Cosgrove's shrug. "You tell us. You're the ones up there. From what you've said, it sounds as though it was something personal for your uncle. Perhaps he simply considered it no one else's business."

After the call was over, they had nothing but time, so they retired to the den to watch a vid or two.

Bonnie was waiting for Ronn when he reached the top of the stairs on the way to his room, as though she had heard him coming.

"Can we talk?" she asked.

They went for a walk outside. Between the starlight and the lights from the house, there was enough light to see by, and they strolled down the path and into the woods.

"Ever since I left the fair," Bonnie said along the way, "it's like I can feel my brain changing. I'm remembering more and more... all kinds of things. I've been trapped for so long... I just need to talk to somebody."

They ended up in the picnic clearing and sat down on one of the benches along the edge of the woods. The stars shining above the silhouetted treetops all around were completely convincing, though perhaps brighter and more plentiful than in a night sky on Earth. The one wrong note was the silence. Since no one had pushed the **NIGHT SOUNDS** button that evening, there were no insect or bird noises, and no wind rustling through the trees. It reminded Ronn of the sky show at the Adler Planetarium in Chicago, and just needed a recorded lecturer, background music, and special effects.

"I'm not sure I'm complete yet," Bonnie went on. "I mean, there are some things I'm just not feeling. I should be a lot more upset about being a robot. I can't eat, I'll never be able to have babies, I don't know how long this body will last... One part of me thinks I ought to be running around screaming, but the rest of me thinks, 'That's cool,' and I'm really just kind of numb about it. I can't even imagine what my future will be or what kind of life I can have."

"Just take one day at a time," Ronn suggested. "We'll figure things out as we come to them."

It probably wasn't the greatest advice ever, but at least Bonnie seemed to find it reassuring.

They had started sitting somewhat apart on the bench, but after a while, Bonnie leaned against him, as though finding some comfort in simple human contact, and putting his arm over her shoulders seemed like the appropriate response. She snuggled even more closely.

Am I going to end up with a robot girlfriend? Ronn wondered. *I like her, and if we'd met thirty-five years ago, Uncle Jeff might have been in for some competition, but... She isn't just a bot, she's also my aunt, or maybe my cousin... It's kind of confusing.*

Maybe she was just clinging to him because he was the only support she had here and she might feel differently once she was safe and secure somewhere. In any event, it was something that could wait until they got back to Earth to resolve.

Well, at least she'd be a cheap date, he thought ruefully, looking down at the girl under his arm staring bleakly off into the darkness. *I wouldn't have to buy her dinner...*

As though wanting to lighten things up before they became too depressing, Bonnie asked about life on Earth in what must have seemed like the impossibly distant future for her. She also wanted to know more about Ronn, where he lived, the life he led at home, the school he went to, even what his teachers were like. He told her as best he could.

"I had a couple of teachers like your Ms. Crowley," Bonnie then said with a wry smile. "I guess some things never change."

She also liked the fact that Ronn's school day was a couple of hours shorter than hers.

"We make up for it with a lot more homework," he explained, "so it's probably about the same either way."

"But if you can sit at home and do all your work on the computer, it's not like you need to spend a whole lot of time at school except for band practice." Then she turned a little more serious. "I'm remembering so much now that I feel like I was in school at good old Salisbury High just a few weeks ago. Guess I won't be going back there any time soon..."

She talked about herself and the life she had lived, decades before, and even some of the history she had witnessed. For Ronn, the disputed Presidential election of 2000 was just a section in the history unit and back there somewhere with the disputed Presidential election of 1876, but for Bonnie it was something she had seen on the news every night and heard her parents talk about at dinner.

"If you ever want to know anything about hanging chads," she told Ronn, "just ask me!"

"Er... I'll keep that in mind... Uhm... shall we call it a night?"

It was getting late by this time and Ronn was starting to feel sleepy.

For her part, Bonnie didn't exactly sleep, but she did need some down time for diagnostics and internal maintenance, and her mind was so close to human that she had to dream now and then.

So a night they called it and they went back to the house.

Part Three

The Ivory Castle

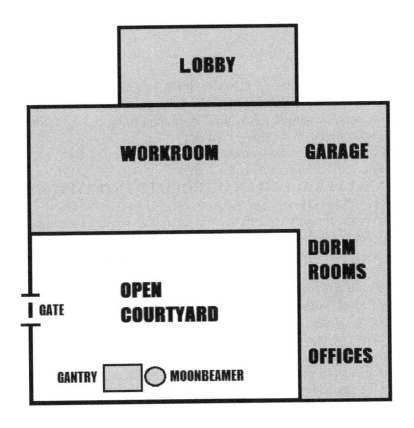

Chapter Eleven

Monday, April 27

Early the next morning, a sudden lurch knocked Ronn out of some murky dream. As he sat up in bed in the dark room and tried to remember where he was, he sensed a low-level rumbling, more felt as a vibration than actually heard, that quickly died away.

Distant sirens howled somewhere outside, followed by a booming masculine voice echoing across the crater:

"INTRUDER ALERT! UNAUTHORIZED ENTRY! INTRUDER ALERT! UNAUTH—"

The voice abruptly cut off, leaving an almost painful silence behind. Ronn got out of bed, felt his way to the balcony doors, and looked out. The crater was black emptiness with no lights anywhere, not even simulated stars.

It sounds like we've got company...

A pale light with no obvious source came on near the bedroom ceiling. Emergency lighting, evidently. Ronn heard stirring out in the hall. He went to the door and opened it. The faint emergency lighting was on here, as well, and Ronn saw the others coming out of their rooms. Pajamas and slippers had been provided for everyone, and Phaedra was pulling on a robe as she came into the hallway. Even Bonnie appeared, though wearing her regular clothes of shorts and blouse.

"What happened?" Phaedra asked worriedly.

"Somebody must have forced their way through the ID system," Ronn replied.

"*That's* obvious," Theo snorted, "but is it our guys? They were talking about breaking in last night, remember?"

"Yeah," Ronn said, "but they were just talking about it. They didn't sound like they were this close to actually *doing* it. And would they do it in the middle of the night? They're on the same time we are."

Phaedra turned and started for the stairs. "We'd better call them and find out."

As they came down to the front hall, they encountered Wilfred, ghostly in the dim light.

"Please return to your rooms," he said mildly. "Breakfast will not be served for another two hours."

"But what's going on out there?" Theo demanded.

"I do not know the specific cause of the irregularity," Wilfred replied, "but there is no reason for alarm."

Feeling that the entire asteroid going into some kind of emergency mode was an excellent reason for alarm, Ronn and the others left Wilfred standing where he was in bemused puzzlement, if a bot could be said to be puzzled or even bemused about anything, and raced to the phone in the conference room.

As it happened, the scientists in the docking bay had already called Earth, and a crisis meeting by conference call was even now in session.

"Vesper shifted its orbit again," Mr. Cosgrove told them. "The scientists are estimating that it will be another couple of hundred miles or so closer to Earth on average. That's still a long way out, but of course this can't be allowed to continue. Whether it has anything to do with the break-in, we don't know. We have had reports that Prescott's freighter, one of the three ships that went missing, took off last night from somewhere in Europe. It would have arrived early this morning, probably at a different docking bay on the other side of the asteroid. Our guess is that the ship's crew immediately tried to breach the security barriers by force. We were prepared to do that ourselves as a last resort, but since we didn't want to trigger a hostile response, we decided to try non-violent means first by sending you inside to turn the barriers off if you could. Our friends were probably too impatient and just charged in, with results they should have been intelligent enough to foresee."

Dr. Kininger suddenly came on with near-panic in his voice. "We've just been given an ultimatum! There was an announcement telling us we have ten minutes to clear out. They said they'll evacuate the air in the docking bay and crew lounge if we don't."

"'*They*'?" Mr. Cosgrove queried. "Who are 'they'? Is there someone alive in charge of this?"

"We don't think so," Dr. Kininger said, forcing himself to calm down. "It's hard to tell with autonomous behavior systems, but it sounds like some automatic procedure, maybe in response to the break-in. Captain Ramirez has decided our only option is for all of us to return to Earth at once and let the higher-ups decide on the next move."

"What about *us*?" Phaedra all but screamed.

"I hate to have to say this," the scientist replied, "but you're two miles away and several levels up. We have to be gone in ten minutes — you'll never get here in time, and you don't want to be caught in one of the corridors if they start draining the air."

"I am sorry this had to happen while you were there." Mr. Cosgrove sounded genuinely regretful for a moment. "We never expected anything like this."

"But what can we *do*?" Phaedra asked.

"Your best option," Mr. Cosgrove said, "is to find the control room and adjust things so a shuttle can dock again to pick you up. If not... All I can tell you is to hold tight until we can work out a way to rescue you. It sounds as though you're safe and well supplied with everything you need where you are, so do all you can to avoid contact with any hostile forces and —"

He was interrupted by a familiar voice. "Listen, kids," Captain Rogowski said. "It turns out we're going to have to cram everybody into the cargo carrier for the ride home and leave the *Mirage* here. It's in the middle of some kind of automatic maintenance and recharging process we can't control or stop, and it won't be ready to fly again for another three days. So if you can manage to get down here sometime on Thursday, I'm sure Phaedra can fly it after what I showed her on the way up."

"*Me?*" Phaedra gulped. "Fly that thing...?"

"Sure you can, kid," Rogowski said reassuringly. "Easy as driving a car. Even the landing procedure's mostly automatic." ("*Mostly*, he says..." Phaedra murmured to herself.) "If I could've camped out in the *Mirage* for the next few days so I could fly you home myself, I would have, but not with that maintenance routine going on and all the doors open. We'll be clearing out in a few minutes, so good luck—"

His voice was lost in a burst of static, then the phone was so much inert plastic.

"So that's where we are," Phaedra said grimly.

They tried the telephone in the office, but that had gone dead as well, perhaps the result of the lockdown. They were now completely cut off from Earth. Still, as Mr. Cosgrove had told them, they were safe enough where they were, at least for the moment. All they could do was go back to their rooms and try to get a little more sleep if possible.

Dawn had been cancelled. When Ronn woke up a couple of hours later, it was still dark outside even though the artificial sun should have been well up by this time. What time it exactly was, he didn't know since the projected time display above his nightstand just showed glowing dots instead of numerals. The emergency lighting had been turned off, and when he got up and looked outside, the stars shone overhead, and there were distant lights out in the haze just as there had been the night before. The crater was evidently still in some sort of lockdown condition, but the lights in the house now worked normally, which made the situation a little easier to deal with.

They ate breakfast without saying much. Things had gotten too serious for bickering or complaining or making smart remarks, which pretty much left Phaedra and Theo without anything to say. Bonnie sat quietly in one of the parlors, apparently reading, and far enough from the dining room to be out of Phaedra's sight though she could hear what was being said.

"They've probably taken off by now," Theo said after a while. "We're by ourselves up here." That was a depressing thought.

"Except for whoever's trying to break in," Phaedra added. That was even more depressing.

Meanwhile, Ronn tried to think things through as he ate.

They were in a "guest house." It was called that because that was what it was. A house for *guests*. If there was a master control center, it certainly wasn't here.

Nor was there any sign of a permanent presence by Uncle Jeff. Clearly, he stayed somewhere else when he was in residence on Vesper. Which meant there was a second house somewhere.

Which was probably where Uncle Jeff was right now.

They had made a complete circuit of the entire crater without seeing any obvious places where he might be living. Ronn doubted if Uncle Jeff was staying in MacNabbit the Rabbit's toon house. The reconstructed houses depicting scenes from his boyhood had not shown any signs of being lived in, either, at least not by anybody of a biological nature. Though it might have been the real thing and not a reconstruction, even the Adirondack cabin had looked more like an exhibit than a current residence.

With the artificial fogs and projected backgrounds, as well as the side roads to who knew where, it was hard to tell just how much they had seen compared to what they hadn't, but it began to dawn on Ronn that there was one very obvious place they had missed so far. Since they had only gone around the edge of the crater, they hadn't been in the interior. Specifically, the exact center.

"I'll bet that's where it is!" Ronn suddenly exclaimed.

Startled, Phaedra and Theo looked at him.

"What'sh where?" Theo asked thickly through the piece of toast in his mouth.

"Okay, guys," Ronn said, "I think I've figured it out."

He explained his reasoning as to where Uncle Jeff's real house would probably be. It made almost too much sense. The center of the crater was an obvious and dramatic choice for the master of the domain. It wasn't even all that far away. It would be just a mile from the guest house, a straight line to the east.

"I think we should go over there right now and try to find Uncle Jeff," he finished.

"When somebody's breaking into the crater?" Phaedra asked, seemingly thinking Ronn had come up with an idea somewhere on the shady side of crazy. Even Theo looked doubtful.

"I don't think there's a better time," Ronn said. "They might not know the layout of the crater any better than we did when we first got here, so it'll be a while before they figure out where Uncle Jeff's HQ is. Meanwhile, we can get there first."

Phaedra still wasn't completely convinced it was a good idea, but at least Theo finally agreed to go along with it.

As for how to get there, a paved road led through the woods in that direction.

"But it's still night out there!" Phaedra exclaimed.

"The scooters have headlights," Ronn said. "It's either that or we sit around here and wait for something to happen."

Phaedra still wasn't happy about it, but finally agreed. "Oh, all right…"

Bonnie came into the dining room. "I want to go, too," she announced.

"Sure," Ronn said. "This involves you as much as the rest of us."

Phaedra wasn't happy about Bonnie joining the party, either, but didn't argue about it.

They grabbed their Stingers from their rooms, just in case something might be waiting for them out in the night, then went downstairs to the garage. With Phaedra on one of the scooters and Theo riding on the seat behind her, and Ronn and Bonnie on the other, they started out.

Headlights on, silent darkness all around, they rode through the forest along the road that led to the center of the crater, passing occasional distant lights visible between the trees. In the dark and unable to see beyond the range of their headlights, they came out of the forest without any warning, and braked to an abrupt stop.

They stood there and looked up in awe at a gleaming white castle shining in the glare of spotlights, on the opposite side of a small lake of blackly shimmering water. A bridge stretched from the shore across the lake to the front of the castle.

Ronn recognized the castle as a replica, perhaps somewhat reduced in size, of a famous Los Angeles hotel. It was nicknamed the Ivory Castle because its white façade and somewhat Gothic design gave it a fairy-talish look, though it was more an abstract sketch of a castle than literal Mad King Ludwig. It might have been the hotel where Uncle Jeff married his fourth wife.

"Don't tell me he lives *there!*" Phaedra exclaimed.

"It's not exactly what I expected," Ronn admitted. "I was thinking of something more like the guest house, maybe a bit bigger..."

"Well, you got that right," Theo said. "This is a *lot* bigger."

Ronn turned his scooter towards the causeway. "As long as we're here, we might as well take a closer look and see what turns up. A place like this has to be important somehow."

They rode along the wide lane across the bridge to the front of the castle. There, instead of a drawbridge or a portcullis, they found the main entrance of a luxury hotel. They parked their scooters out of sight in the shadows of some shrubbery by an empty stretch of wall, and walked towards the doors.

As they came up, they found an animated routine in progress. A black limousine stopped in front every couple of minutes, a uniformed doorman opened the car door, two or three well-dressed people got out, and the limo drove off, probably to some hidden staging area in the darkness to wait for the next circuit.

A grating in the sidewalk to one side of the entrance seemed to be there for no other purpose than for a beautiful young woman with unnaturally bleached blonde hair to step on it and have her dress lifted up by blowing air. Theo wanted to take a closer look — to see how it was done, he said — but Phaedra pulled him along.

They were met at the doors by a very overweight doorman with a little black mustache and wearing a gaudy uniform with a lot of braid and brass buttons, and a thin man in something like an English riding costume and a top hat. It took Ronn a moment to shake off the shock of seeing someone so rotund, since people just didn't *get* fat like that anymore, and another moment to recognize the doormen. Laurel & Hardy were still icons in Ronn's time, so he knew who they were, but why weren't they wearing their trademark suits and derbies here?

With big smiles, as though the four teenagers were the most important guests who had ever come to this hotel, Mr. Laurel and Mr. Hardy grandly opened the doors for them and they went on through. Inside, they were immediately met by a babble of voices and the barely audible strains of bland music playing somewhere. The lobby was filled with a milling crowd of well-dressed bots representing different entertainment eras. Ronn recognized some of them, all those dateless pizza and movie nights he had spent watching vids with Travis and their buddies finally paying off, and Phaedra could identify many more.

It was an impossible assemblage of celebrities stretching well over a century, ranging from the earliest silent stars to the current 3-D performers, from Charlie Chaplin to Connor Callahan. Stuffed into tuxedos, action stars like John Wayne and Errol Flynn mingled effortlessly with Arnold Schwarzenegger and Jackie Chan, while an elegantly gowned Mary Pickford seemed to be swapping gossip with Meryl Streep and Miriam Ferreira. It wasn't so astonishing to see Diana Ross meet Diana Rigg, since they had been contemporaries and *could* have met in their respective primes, but for two old 2-D TV stars from very different eras like Lucy and Urkel to cross paths bordered on surreal.

The selection was recent enough to include the stars of *Snow Patrol*, a vidshow Ronn remembered from a few years past. Standing there with no fixed purpose but to hold drinks in their hands were two ex-Army buddies trained in mountain rescue, who put their skills to work in civilian life as guides and ski instructors. Since that by itself would make for a boring show, every episode they did a little search and rescue for lost skiers and stranded hikers who had unaccountably lost the tracking beacons they were supposed to carry with them, not to mention occasional airplanes that were always crashing in blizzards. The buddies were a long way away from the snow-covered slopes but wore their red ski jackets anyway. With them was their mascot, a lovable but lazy St. Bernard named Monty. The huge dog sat placidly by with a red survival pack strapped to his back. At least with dogbots, there was no worry about whether they were housebroken.

Bonnie gazed in un-botlike fascination at the spectacle as they passed through. "It's like a wax museum come to life," Ronn heard her murmur to herself. Calling it "life" was stretching the definition since they were just moving bots, but that was the same thing *she* was.

None paid Ronn and his cousins the slightest attention as they endlessly executed their programmed behavioral sequences. He didn't have time to watch them closely, but he suspected that the people who had gotten out of the cars out front circulated through the crowd, then disappeared into a hidden exit, met up with the limos outside somewhere, and began the cycle all over again.

Suddenly Phaedra shrieked.

The bots failed to react, continuing to follow their programming, but Ronn and Theo whirled to see what was wrong.

Phaedra stood staring in horror at a bot that looked just like her. It had apparently been made when she was a couple of years younger and a little shorter, but it was definitely her. The contrast between the real thing, in a safari outfit and a casual ponytail, and the imitation, with styled hair and wearing a formal dress, was striking. The bot wasn't doing anything more than holding a half-filled glass of probably simulated cola as she stood off to the side of a small group of current celebrities, and looked on with an expression of awe and envy as though wishing she had the courage to join the conversation.

Phaedra thought of something hideous and shot a worried glance at Bonnie. "She — *it* — isn't like *you*, is she? Thinking, kind of half-alive, I mean?"

"That's about the nicest thing you've said to me since we met," Bonnie said with ill-concealed sarcasm. She stepped over to the Phaedra-bot and tried to get its attention. "Hi, how's it going? Great party, huh?"

The Phaedra-bot smiled vaguely but barely seemed to notice Bonnie. She turned away without saying anything and began another behavior cycle of looking on in awe.

Bonnie shrugged and turned to real-Phaedra. "Nope, she's all gizmos as far as I can tell. I don't get a feeling of anything more."

"That's a relief," Phaedra said. "I'd hate to think there was a copy of my mind somewhere. But when did he make that, and *why*? What a weird moment to show me in... Besides, I'm not *that* googly-eyed star-struck!"

"The heck she isn't," Theo muttered to Ronn. "I have to say Uncle Jeff got her just about right."

"Maybe Uncle Jeff took more interest in your career than you thought?" Ronn suggested to the still fairly well horrified Phaedra.

Theo took a closer look at the Phaedra-bot, which completely ignored him as he hovered over it. "It's not *that* exact a copy," he said to his real sister. "It's what you'd get making a bot based on pics and vidclips. Hey, it isn't just a hotel lobby, it's a Hollywood party like maybe an awards show. You should be glad Uncle Jeff thought you belonged here. It's not like you've been to a lot of real ones, you know."

Phaedra glanced at Ronn. "Of all the little brothers in the world, I had to get that one."

Ronn wondered uneasily if there was a Ronn-bot somewhere, though he couldn't imagine where one might fit the way Phaedra's did in a gathering of Hollywood celebrities. There just wasn't that much interesting about him.

"Anyway, guys," he said, "now that we've got that little mystery solved about as well as it's going to be, we should be moving on."

"Move on where?" Phaedra asked. "You dragged us all the way over here, but it still isn't telling us a whole lot."

"Yeah," Theo added. "It's just another stage set with a bunch of bots."

Ronn looked around the lobby for some clue that would tell them where to go next, and something caught his eye. Just beyond the reception counter, where a couple of clerks waited for guests who would never check in, was a door in the back wall that seemed somehow out of place, as though it didn't fit in with the rest of the hotel lobby decor.

"Then again, maybe not," Ronn said. "I think I just spotted something..." For lack of any better ideas, the others followed him through the crowd towards the rear of the lobby.

Too distracted by what he saw around him to quite watch where he was going, Theo nearly stumbled into the classic Three Stooges with Curly. They just stood there poking and slapping each other, doomed to go on poking and slapping endlessly until their power cells finally ran down, and Theo only managed to dodge them at the last second. Following in turn, Phaedra just seemed unconvinced that this little detour would be any more productive than anything else they had done so far.

When they reached the door, Ronn opened it and looked inside. "*Now* we're getting somewhere!" he exclaimed as he saw what lay beyond. There really was more to the hotel than just another and very strange stage set.

Through the doorway was a large, shadowy workroom considerably out of place in a Los Angeles hotel and at least the size of the gym back at Ronn's school. The main lights were off but some small lamps were on here and there on various long tables covered with workstations, models, and large sheets of paper with architectural drawings. While none were on at the moment, Ronn recognized some of the 3-D display units and virtual manipulators as the same sort of equipment his father used in his office. Other devices looked as though they were far more advanced than anything available on the commercial market on Earth, and some were completely inscrutable as to what they did.

In the center of the room was a huge circular table standing in a pool of light from an overhead spot and probably more than thirty feet in diameter. On it was a model layout Ronn immediately recognized even though the buildings were tiny. "It's this place!" The scale looked to be about one to 300 or so, but even reduced to that extreme, a circle more than two miles across was enormous. On other, smaller tables nearby were models of completed individual structures in larger scales.

"I guess this is the central construction office," Ronn said. "When they get the prefab parts up here, they still have to assemble them."

"This must show how the whole thing's supposed to look when it's finished," Theo added, looking in fascination at the center table.

At a glance, Ronn could see that future plans included somewhat scaled-down replicas of the Statue of Liberty and the Empire State Building (was that a tiny monkey climbing up the side?) in the interior regions. Either that or they were already there and simply out of sight from the road, or else fogged over. There was so much fine detail in the huge model, too tiny for the most part to be recognizable, that it was hard to get an overall picture of what was there and how it all fit together.

Theo wanted to take his time looking it over. "I wonder what's up those side roads we drove by the other day?"

"That's not what we're here for," Phaedra reminded him and hustled him onwards. "We need to find Uncle Jeff's private office. He's got to have one *somewhere*, and this does look like it's the place it has to be. Maybe then we'll get some answers."

They passed a work table on which several dismembered human arms and legs were spread, apparently a repair and test bench for malfunctioning bots. By it, next to the aisle, stood a chest-high cabinet, and on top at eye-level was a life-sized clown's head, connected to an external power source by a wire emerging from its neck. As Ronn went by, the clown's eyes followed him. He hoped it was just some automatic response and that somebody wasn't really *in* there.

Bots and aliens may have done most of the heavy lifting in construction, but there had been a staff of human beings overseeing at least some of the work. A few people had known what Jefferson was ultimately up to, like high-level designers and TranStella executives who had spent time on Vesper. Beyond the workroom, a corridor led past a row of small offices, though apparently for the staff and none of them Uncle Jeff's own.

After the offices was a block of bedrooms for maybe a dozen people and a rather industrial-looking commissary and dining room. Everything was spotlessly clean as though meticulously maintained every day by a crew of bots even though nobody was currently staying here. Unlike the guest house, there was also a sense of *use*. People had been here in the recent past. Some small personal items had been left behind, a jacket in a closet, a half-used packet of deodorant strips on a bathroom shelf... There was even still food in the commissary storeroom and Theo snagged a bulb of Pepsi from a refrigerator. Wherever Uncle Jeff actually *lived*, though, it didn't seem to be here, either.

The corridor ended at a side door that opened on a large, half-lit courtyard taking up most of the entire interior space of the rear half of the hotel. The back and west walls were blank façades enclosing the area, while on the east side was a wing of the building with windows looking out from real rooms. Along the walls were stacks of plastic crates, various odds and ends of equipment like a forklift truck, and some general construction-site clutter, but the real eyecatcher towered over the rear wall.

A rocket resembling an oversized 1950s jet plane stood on end, poised vertically on its tail fins, a slender, pointed spindle about fifty feet high with rakishly swept-back wings. Next to it was an open metal framework with several flights of steps zigzagging up to a platform at the top on a level with the rocket's forward crew compartment. It was a retro fantasy design, like no actual spacecraft ever built, and bore the name *Moonbeamer* on its gleaming chrome hull.

"What's the ship from *Starbusters* doing *here*?" Ronn wondered, recalling that he had once heard the ship compared to a hood ornament, whatever that exactly was. The show was long gone but the preposterously aerodynamic *Moonbeamer* and its absurdly dauntless crew were still remembered as a parody of what space travel was supposed to be like. The ship itself had become ironically iconic as a symbol of the dream that had never quite died, and had been duplicated here as a theme-park attraction that had outlived the show that originally inspired it.

"I saw it at Great American Funland," Theo said. "Uncle Jeff's company probably made the rocket for the park, and this is just a second copy of it."

It was also much smaller than the version shown in the vids, a model perhaps a third of its hypothetical actual size. Ronn noted the transparent aircraft canopy near the tip of the pointed nose, and estimated that maybe only one or two people could fit inside at most, compared to the show's crew of half a dozen wacky characters.

As Theo explained it, the pretense in the ride's original conception on Earth was that the guests would ride in the rocket itself, but what was on display was really just a mock-up that never left the ground. Rather than actually boarding the rocket, the customers were diverted into a small auditorium nearby where they experienced a light show that convincingly simulated a trip into space on the non-existent full-sized spaceship.

Even if the rocket did have something to do with Uncle Jeff's career, why was it standing by itself in an otherwise empty courtyard, instead of in some appropriate display?

"Maybe it's just stashed here until they get around to moving it to wherever it's really supposed to go?" Theo suggested. How it could be moved from inside a walled enclosure was another question.

"This is all *really* interesting," Phaedra spoke up, "but are we getting anywhere? As far as I can tell, all we've found out is that Uncle Jeff's still missing."

"Not only that," Theo added, "he's even more missing than when we started, because he should be here if he's anywhere, and he isn't here, either."

For a moment, Ronn thought he almost understood Theo's logic. But the kid was right. The mystery had only gotten deeper. There should be some answer somewhere that he just hadn't come across yet, but he was running out of places to look. Maybe it was time to find some way down to the lower levels and see what was there—

A horn blared. It was loud in the all-pervading silence and not all that far away, and sounded like a truck. Nearby, Ronn heard a slight rattling, and saw a large panel in the west side wall starting to slide upwards like a garage door. It was slow at first, then exposed a sudden gleam of headlights from a vehicle waiting outside.

"Quick! Hide!" Ronn exclaimed, looking hurriedly around for cover. He spotted a stack of plastic crates in a shadowy corner of the courtyard, and led the others in a dash along the wall towards it.

"Exactly what are we hiding from?" Phaedra demanded between gasps for breath as they settled in behind the crates. "I haven't seen anything but bots since we got here—"

"Isn't it obvious?" Ronn replied. "Bots wouldn't be driving a truck and blowing a horn, especially away from the stage-set areas. I don't think we're alone anymore, and until we see who it is…"

"Shh!" Theo hissed urgently. "Somebody's coming!"

On the other side of the courtyard, they saw a lone man walking along the far wall, past some crates and piles of equipment. He must have emerged from some other door than the one they came out of. Ronn had a sense that the man was not a bot or a projection. He seemed too purposeful and motivated, and there just wasn't a *reason* for a bot or a projection to be here. He was the first real person they had seen since leaving the docking bay.

"Is it Uncle Jeff?" Phaedra whispered.

"No," Bonnie replied in a low voice. "I can see him clearly. It's not the Jeff I knew or the older guy I sometimes saw at the fair. This guy kind of looks like the manager at the place where Dad bought his last car, about forty, I think—"

"That leaves Uncle Jeff out," Theo said. "He's ten years older."

"Quiet!" Ronn urged. "He's coming this way!"

The man passed them some yards away and was briefly well-lit in a pool of light. He went on across the courtyard towards the side wall where the panel had now risen.

"He looks familiar," Phaedra whispered, trying to keep her voice down despite her sudden excitement. "Wait, now I recognize him! It's Cal Lowther, the worst vidshow host ever! He's that missing company V.P. Mr. Cosgrove showed us! Mom sure got that right when she said she thought there was something suspicious about his wife in the vid. Mr. Cosgrove wouldn't listen to her, but he should have. If there's one thing Mom's good at, it's spotting bad acting."

It was probably a miracle that Lowther hadn't heard them. Meanwhile, now that the door in the wall was high enough for it to clear, the truck rolled silently into the open area in the center of the courtyard. It was a flatbed, perhaps intended for hauling supplies and building components around the crater construction sites, only now it was loaded with about a dozen soldiers. As the truck came to a stop and the driver turned its head-lights and engine off, the men in the back immediately jumped to the ground. They wore camouflage-striped fatigues and caps, along with side-arms in holsters on their belts, and carried duffel bags.

Ronn glanced at Phaedra to make sure she wasn't about to run out from behind the crates and up to the men in the hope of being taken back to Earth straightaway, but she had caught on to the general foulness of the situation just as much as he had.

"I don't think they're our guys," she murmured.

"Can't tell who they are," Theo muttered. "I bet they're mercs."

"Mer— huh?" Phaedra wondered.

"Mercenaries," Theo explained with a distinct lack of patience.

Meanwhile, the driver and a woman who had been sitting in the front seat next to him got out of the truck and the man Phaedra had recognized as Caleb Lowther approached them. They spoke loudly enough that their voices carried across the courtyard and Ronn could hear every word.

"You *idiot!*" the woman all but screamed at him, looking as though she wanted to tear into him on the spot. "You were supposed to have the bioscanners deactivated!"

This wasn't quite the welcome Lowther had apparently expected. He stopped and fell back a step.

"They *were!*" he exclaimed, sounding self-defensive and even peev-ish. "Somehow you set off the alarms anyway! I've spent the last couple of hours trying to reset everything while I was waiting for you to get here. Forcing your way in didn't help. You almost triggered a shift and then we *really* would have been stuck."

"We couldn't wait a week for you to figure out how to let us in!" the woman retorted. "We had to come up the hard way, and that took a while."

From her tone, Ronn guessed that there wasn't a whole lot of love between the two. They didn't even shake hands, but just stood facing each other.

The woman wore metallically sparkling slacks, half-boots that reached just above her ankles, and a blouse with a high-collared vest over it; she would have blended in perfectly on any Main Street in America. It was hard to see her face clearly at that distance and in the scant light, but Ronn could tell that she had medium-length dark hair and her voice at times had a harsh ring.

"I know her, too!" Phaedra whispered in surprise. "It's our Aunt Vanessa!"

"Ex-aunt, you mean," Theo said under his breath, then added helpfully to Ronn. "Fourth and last wife. So far."

Ronn nudged Theo's ribs with his elbow. "Quiet!"

While he wished the others wouldn't talk with so much chance of being overhead, what they had just said could be classified as Good to Know. He now had a name to work with for figuring things out. But of all people, what was an ex-wife doing here?

Meanwhile, Vanessa was still complaining to Lowther. "I don't have the permissions to come inside anymore, remember? Jeff cancelled everything as soon as I told him we were through. We had to fight our way through the automatic defenses, and it's a maze down there. Not only that, some of the men were hurt in the electric curtain. They weren't killed, thank God, and the medic was able to stabilize them. We put them up in the East Bay crew quarters, but we'll have to send them back to Earth for treatment."

"Wonderful..." Lowther muttered. "Isn't *anything* going to go right with this show? Well, the main thing is that you're here and now we can get moving."

"I hope you haven't been sitting on your hands waiting for me," Vanessa grumbled.

Lowther looked stung by the implied accusation. "Not at all. We've just been a little short-handed, but everything's in place and ready for you."

"So you found it?" she demanded.

"'It?' Oh, you mean... er, no. At least not exactly. Prescott's notes were scattered and hard to follow—"

"I am so sorry to interrupt this happy reunion," the truck's driver broke in, his accent distinctly French. He also wore camouflage fatigues as well as a jaunty beret. His face was hard to make out, but otherwise he was a lean and wiry man of about average height. A very large and hulking man at least a head taller than he was stood next to him. "I am sure you must have much to discuss, but what should my men and I be doing at this moment while you are exchanging greetings? They are tired and hungry from the long journey." He gestured sweepingly to the men waiting behind him, standing there with their gear.

"This is Commandant Rafale," Vanessa said to Lowther. "He's the leader of our contract force."

Lowther nodded to him. "Not your real name, I take it?"

"Of course not," Commandant Rafale replied. "It is strictly a *nom de guerre* in the most literal sense. In my profession, one learns to hide one's past." He indicated the burly man next to him. "And this is Enzo, my comrade in many battles and second in command."

Enzo just grunted. The Frenchman's henchman evidently wasn't one for conversation.

Lowther turned to Vanessa. "Why all the security personnel, anyway?" he asked, hardly sounding pleased. "I explicitly asked for some laborers and more engineers."

"That's what I requested," Vanessa replied uneasily, "but our sponsors thought we might run into the feds, and we'd need armed back-up. The men will double as laborers, so we're covered."

"I still don't like it," Lowther groused. "The feds are gone, so it's just us. Who do they expect to shoot?"

"One cannot be too careful, can one?" Commandant Rafale asked. "Consider me your insurance policy in case we are not as alone as we think."

"As long as we're introducing ourselves," Lowther went on, "I'm Caleb Lowther, TranStella's Executive Vice-President for Corporate Strategy and Business Development."

"A most impressive title," Rafale remarked, "although once word of this operation spreads, you will have it not for much longer. Now what is it you wish me to do?"

"Wait a moment and I'll take you inside so you can get your men settled in the rooms," Lowther said. "I've been keeping about some of Prescott's people locked in the handball court, and before we do anything else, we should get them out of here. They're mostly designers and construction supervisors, people Prescott hired to help build the place. Now that there are a lot more of us, they'd just be eating up food supplies we're going to need. We'll bring them up, load them on the truck, and take them to the East entrance. Then we can fly them back and let our Earthside people take care of them until the operation is complete and we're out of here."

Rafale nodded. "Understood."

"In that case," Vanessa said, "I'd better duck out of sight while you're putting them on the truck. It wouldn't be a good idea if they knew I was involved in this at all, let alone even here. It'll probably come out soon enough, but at least if they talk when they get back to Earth, they won't mention me right off the bat. You, though..."

"Right, I'm thoroughly compromised," Lowther replied. "After I kept them locked up downstairs for days on end and cut off their communications with Earth... well, they don't have any reason to like me very much. A couple offered to join me for a share of the profits, but we don't really need them since we have our own people for figuring out what's worth taking around here, and I didn't want to run the risk of somebody pretending to join me just so they could get to a com. Anything else?"

"The feds in the North docking bay might cause some trouble," Vanessa answered.

"They're gone," Lowther said, sounding rather pleased with himself. "Cleared out a little while ago. My threat to drain their air got rid of them. If they try to come back in force in a few days, it'll be too late."

"You did know about the kids, didn't you?" Vanessa asked.

Ronn stiffened at that, and he could feel the others next to him strain even harder to hear what was being said.

"Kids?" Lowther echoed blankly. "What kids?"

"I guess you didn't know," Vanessa said. "The feds brought up Jefferson's niece and two other nephews, hoping the kids could get the rest of them inside. Judging from what little com traffic our ground station was able to intercept, the kids got in but the feds didn't. The last we heard, the kids managed to make it up to the park and they're holed up in the Westgate guest house."

"Should we be concerned about them?" Lowther asked. "Maybe we should pick them up and bring them here so we can keep an eye on them, or send them back to Earth with the staff."

Vanessa shook her head. "Not worth the trouble. They're just kids, babes in their uncle's toyland. What can they do to stop us or even slow us down? They don't even know what's going on, and they're completely on their own. They shouldn't cause any trouble where they are, and we may need them later for opening things that Jeff coded for their biometrics."

"I don't see why," Lowther said. "We've already got the one, right?"

Danny!

"The others might be useful just the same after the trouble we had getting in," Vanessa replied, "and a little extra insurance is always good. I'll pop over to the guest house later today when we've got the situation here more organized, just to introduce myself and have a nice friendly little chat to explain to the brats how things are going to be. Some sweet talk mixed with a subtle threat or two should keep them in line."

"I'll leave it to you," Lowther said, and turned to the Commandant. "Bring your men. It's time to collect the prisoners and move them out of here."

"Very well," Rafale answered with a casual salute that seemed more mocking than respectful, though Lowther didn't seem to pick up on it.

Lowther, Rafale, and Enzo left the courtyard with most of the mercenaries, while Vanessa and the two remaining mercs stood waiting idly by the truck. Unable to come out from behind the crates without being seen, Ronn and the others could only wait tensely where they were for events to play out.

"I think they're coming back now," Bonnie said after a few minutes, "and boy, somebody sure isn't happy."

"I don't hear a thing," Phaedra replied, as though she thought Bonnie was making it all up.

Bonnie's hearing must have been better than the human norm. A minute or so later, some protesting voices could be heard coming into the courtyard. Vanessa stepped back into the nearby shadows, then Lowther and several mercenaries led about half a dozen men and women in casual civilian dress into the light. They all looked disheveled, and the men had scruffy beards.

"You aren't going to kill us, are you?" one of the male prisoners asked nervously.

That question seemed to bother Lowther, as though some slight tinge of guilt remained about what he was doing. "No, and I'm a little insulted that you think I would. I'm actually doing you a favor, sending you back to Earth. You might have to wait another couple of weeks before they let you go, but at least you'll be that much closer to home."

"You really are a first-class jerk, Lowther," another man said.

"But I'll be a rich one," Lowther retorted. "You were idiots, buying into his toys and fantasies when there was all this advanced alien tech around worth billions. I saw the potential, you didn't, end of story."

A woman spoke up. "It doesn't matter! I keep telling you why your little scheme won't work the way you think and you won't listen! You're so blinded by the thought of all that money that you don't even realize—"

"We've been through all that!" Lowther interrupted. "We have a team of engineers to figure it out, so it won't be a problem."

"That's what *you* think," the woman said darkly.

Lowther waved her off. "Just get on the truck and be happy we're sending you home. This operation is too far along to stop it even if I wanted to."

"Did your wife put you up to this?" another man demanded. Lowther winced but ignored the crack and walked away.

The Commandant's men had the prisoners climb onto the back of the truck, and a couple of mercenaries joined them as guards. Another merc got into the cab, started the engine and turned on the headlights, and backed the truck out of the courtyard.

As soon as it was gone and the gate had lowered again, Vanessa came out of the shadows and Lowther turned to her and Rafale.

"Let's go to Prescott's office," he said. "I want to show you what we're dealing with here."

Along with the remaining mercenaries, they walked to a door at the other end of the courtyard and went inside the building.

"Maybe it's just as well we didn't find Uncle Jeff's office after all," Theo murmured. "We would've walked right in on that rat Lowther."

"I think we're done here," Ronn said in the lowest voice possible. "We'd better get out before somebody comes back, and it might be a good idea to be sitting around looking sweet and innocent at the guest house when Aunt Vanessa shows up."

The others agreed with mute nods, and keeping to the shadows along the walls, they slipped out of the now-deserted courtyard and back into the building. From there, they retraced their steps to the front. After pushing through the Hollywood party that was still going on, they found their scooters and headed back across the bridge. They didn't turn their headlights on until they were well inside the forest.

Peering into the darkness ahead, Ronn thought about what they had seen. His overall feeling was that it was more fun to watch adventure vids than to be living in one. For one thing, a happy ending wasn't guaranteed in real life. Even in total-immersion games, players who met tragic ends could get up and go see if there was anything left in the fridge. Here... There was nothing virtual about this reality.

And they *still* had no idea where Uncle Jeff was.

As they came out of the woods and saw the lights of the guest house ahead, the first faint pink hints of dawn were showing in the east behind them.

"Looks like they got the sun working again," Theo said.

Chapter Twelve

"At least we now know more than we did," Ronn said as he rolled the scooter into its parking space in the garage.

"Mainly that we didn't know the half of how bad things really are," Theo replied, getting off the back of Phaedra's scooter. "I liked it better when we didn't know that."

Phaedra dismounted in turn. "And we still don't know what happened to Uncle Jeff."

"Well, wherever he is," Ronn said, "he certainly isn't running things anymore. Sounds like his own people were plotting against him."

Phaedra nodded. "I've heard Mom say he was devoting less and less time to his business and letting his executives run it. He must have trusted the wrong people."

"We also know that we owe a lot of the mess we're in to Uncle Jeff's really bad judgment in picking wives," Theo added.

"Hey!" Bonnie exclaimed.

Phaedra rolled her eyes. "Are you still here?"

Ronn broke in to head off a fight. "I think we really need to talk about what we've just seen so we can decide what to do next. Shouldn't we go upstairs so we can sit down?"

Theo shook his head. "We're probably better off talking right where we are. The walls have acoustic-field ears upstairs."

"That's right," Phaedra said. "I found that swimsuit on my bed after I'd mentioned not having one."

Ronn glanced around. "The walls might have ears down here, too, but then Uncle Jeff could have the whole crater bugged and we wouldn't be safe from being overheard anywhere. The real question is whether they're listening to what we're saying back at Bad Guy Central, and I kind of doubt it. Lowther didn't even know we were here, don't forget. I think it's more likely that what we say in the house isn't passed on anywhere and the monitoring upstairs is just something for finding out what the guests might want or need, not for spying on them."

"We're probably as safe here as anywhere." Theo sat down on the bench by the work table, glancing up at the hammers, saws, and wrenches hanging on the wall above him. "This garage looks like it's just for maintenance techs, so it probably wouldn't be bugged even if the rest of the house is."

It looked as though this was where the conference was going to be held and they were going to be here for a while. Ronn leaned back against the bare wall by the end of the bench and Phaedra sat down next to her brother. Bonnie, who wouldn't get tired standing, remained where she was, just outside the circle of the other three.

"So what do we say when Auntie Gruesome gets here?" Theo asked.

"*You're* not going to say anything," Phaedra replied firmly. "Let me do the talking if she asks any questions."

"Er... why?" Theo wondered.

"I've met this woman." Phaedra grimaced, as though it had not been one of her happier experiences. "Mom took me to see her when Uncle Jeff wouldn't do anything for me in getting my career off the ground. Vanessa was something like Vice-President of Marketing for the TranStella Company when she married Uncle Jeff and Mom thought she could pull some strings to get around him."

"Didn't work, did it?" Theo put in.

"No," Phaedra admitted, "but you could tell how she got to be where she was in Marketing. A lot of pretty words, a lot of ifs and maybes and let's keep in touch, and you feel so positive about how well the meeting is going that you almost don't realize she's really saying no way, not now and not ever, and probably wondering why she's even wasting her time talking to you. But get this. You know how Mom can be pretty calculating and cold-blooded when she's in business mode?"

"Kind, sweet lady, Mom is," Theo said to Ronn, who could only assume his cousin was looking at her through the eyes of love, "but don't ever play cards with her."

"Well, when we came out of that interview," Phaedra went on, "I heard Mom say, 'God, she's good!'"

"Not a compliment, I take it?" Ronn asked.

"More like she'd met her match and then some," Phaedra said. "I'm just saying Vanessa and I have already met, so I have some idea of what we're up against. She'll probably expect to talk mostly to me anyway since she knows me. All you have to do is pretend you've never seen her before and not say anything. Remember, she thinks we're just dumb brats, and we have to let her go on thinking that."

They then talked about the other things they had seen and heard. They now knew that there had been some sort of corporate mutiny within the ranks of the TranStella Company itself, aided by some foreign country, but Uncle Jeff's whereabouts were still a mystery. The one piece of good news, very relatively speaking, was that their cousin Danny was on Vesper and presumably alive and well, not that they could do anything for him. The not so good news was that the bad guys knew they were here in the house and there was probably no hope of a rescue from Earth very soon. All in all, their position was somewhere between precarious and dangerous. The only thing they could do was wait for Aunt Vanessa to show up and hear what she had to say.

"We should basically sound her out on what she wants and not say much or admit anything ourselves," Phaedra told the others in conclusion. "We shouldn't even let her know what we saw and heard back at the castle. The less they think we know, the better off we'll be. That way, they won't be so tempted to get rid of the witnesses."

With that dismal thought in mind, they trooped back upstairs.

About noon, adjusted time, Bonnie was up in her room and the three cousins were having a light lunch on the veranda. Ronn happened to glance up from his hot dog and saw a blue jeep coming up the lane from the woods. Vanessa was sitting in the back and two mercenaries were in front. The jeep stopped in front of the house and she got out. She was dressed casually but stylishly for a week of looting in slacks, blouse, and ankle-boots, but the first thing that caught Ronn's attention was the holster she wore at her belt.

"Battle stations, everybody!" he said lowly to Phaedra and Theo. "Enemy in sight."

"Like I told you," Phaedra replied, glancing at Theo while continuing to munch on her salad, "let me do the talking."

Leaving the mercs to wait in the jeep, Vanessa went up the front steps and into the house without bothering to knock or ring the bell. Wilfred must have intercepted her, and he appeared in the doorway to the dining room a minute or so later.

"It would appear that you have a visitor," he announced stiffly. "She claims to be your Aunt Vanessa and wishes to speak with you in one of the parlors."

"I guess we were about done anyway," Phaedra said resignedly, putting the rest of her salad aside.

They got up from the table and followed Wilfred through the dining room and into an elegantly furnished sitting room, then the butler took his leave.

Vanessa was waiting, trying very hard to look sweet and happy to see them. Seen up close and in a good light, it was clear she'd had the full range of body enhancement in her thirties. She was in Marketing, after all, and looking almost too good would have been a professional necessity even more than a personal one. She must have been forty-something trying to look like a permanent twenty-five, and there was an offputtingly artificial look to her features, the nose a little too sculpted and the cheekbones a little too prominent, not a single gray hair on her head, and her eyebrows just a little too thin. She was beautiful in a hard sort of way, but Bonnie looked more natural than she did.

Everyone just stood there for a moment looking at each other but not saying anything. Ronn realized that Vanessa had to be wondering about their lack of surprise at seeing her. When they planned this, it had seemed best to go with being silent and sullen rather than trying to fake a reaction.

"Hello," she said with a not very convincing smile when the silence had gone on a little too long. "I'll bet you thought you were all alone up here with no way to get back home. Well, this is your lucky day. I'm here and so are some other people. We can have you home in a few days."

She paused with an even wider smile, no doubt waiting for whoops of delight. When none were forthcoming and the kids just looked at her with indifference bordering on hostility, she went on quickly. "So you're Jefferson's niece and nephews. I'm your Aunt Vanessa. Well, I used to be, but I hope you'll still think of me as family."

"We've met," Phaedra said a little coldly.

"Oh yes, your mother brought you around that time to see if I could do something for you. I'm sure you have a lot of questions, so let's all sit down and we can discuss things comfortably.

"Now, I'm probably the last person you expected to show up on your doorstep," Vanessa continued as she took a couch and the others found chairs, "and you must be wondering what's going on—"

Bonnie came into the room just then, wearing a black, white lace-trimmed maid's outfit with apron and cap. "Excuse me," she said, trying to sound mechanical.

Vanessa, looked up, startled. "Who the… who's that?" she demanded suspiciously. "I thought there were just three of you — oh, it's a bot."

Phaedra and Theo were too surprised to say anything and Ronn jumped into the breach. "Came with the house." *What the heck is she up to?* If he needed any last little smidgeon of convincing that Bonnie had a mind of her own, he had it now.

"I am sorry to interrupt you," Bonnie said in a flat, toneless voice, backing out of the living room. "I will wait until you are finished before I clean in here."

She withdrew into the adjacent room and sat down in a chair, then went rigid, as though going into some dormant phase or standby mode. She was perfectly positioned to observe and hear everything that went on in the room she had just left.

Vanessa watched Bonnie go, her eyes narrowed as though she sensed that something wasn't what it should be but she wasn't sure what. "Must be one of the earlier releases. We had bots able to talk a lot more convincingly than that."

"That one's a little peculiar anyway," Phaedra said and changed the subject. "Before we talk about anything else, where's Uncle Jeff?"

Vanessa looked irritated for an instant, obviously not liking Phaedra's tone, then quickly changed to an expression of woeful sadness. "I'm so sorry, but he's, well... he had an accident. He's injured. We're taking care of him, of course," she added with a forced smile.

"What kind of accident?" Phaedra asked. "What happened to him?"

"Something... exploded," Vanessa said hesitantly, as though she didn't want to discuss it and didn't even have her story straight. "It's serious but not life-threatening, so you don't have to worry about him."

"Can we see him?" Phaedra pressed.

A hint of something not very pleasant crossed Vanessa's face but she left it at shaking her head. "I'm sorry, but he's in intensive care so he can't see anybody. We're sending him back to Earth so he can get proper treatment. I'm sure he'll be much better by the time you return home."

Ronn could tell from Phaedra's expression that she wasn't buying any of this. He exchanged a quick glance with Theo, who just rolled his eyes.

Phaedra continued her offensive. "And what about our cousin Danny? He's here, too, isn't he?"

Vanessa gave a slight start, as though she hadn't expected them to know that. "He's fine," she answered almost a little too quickly. "He'll be with us for a little while yet, but you don't have to worry about him."

She made an effort to smile again, but as she looked around, from Phaedra to Ronn and then to Theo, she only saw expressions ranging from cold disbelief to outright hostility. She gave up all pretense of trying to be warmly reassuring.

"I see I'm not getting much cooperation here. All right, have it your way. It's too bad you kids had to be dragged into this, but it happened and we'll just have to get along as best we can."

"And exactly *what* did we get dragged into?" Phaedra asked.

Vanessa sat back on the couch and folded her arms across her chest. "Believe me, I'd be doing you a big favor by not telling you. But since you insist... Basically, your uncle has been getting advanced technology from aliens for years. Any time he needs a little extra money, he has something from the aliens reverse-engineered so it can be made on Earth, then patents it and licenses it out. He's made billions doing that. It's hard to think of a field that hasn't been influenced by Prescott technology one way or another in the last twenty years." She launched into a singsong recital that sounded like a memorized corporate sales pitch, and given what her job had been, it probably was. "Autonomous behavior systems, 3-D projection, desalinization of seawater, molecular layer manufacturing, multi-scan replicators, superconducting power transmission, cold lighting systems, DNA decoding, limb-regeneration, accelerated-growth cloning... the list goes on. But you probably know all that."

"Pretty much," Phaedra said. "It sounds like our uncle has done a lot of good things for the human race. So what are *you* doing here?"

"Your uncle didn't give the human race even a tenth of what he could have!" Vanessa burst out. "The odds and ends of alien tech he shared with the rest of us were nothing compared to the really amazing things he held back. Artificial gravity, faster than light travel... why don't we have starships ourselves now? We can't even build regular spaceships like Jeff's private fleet with that white-light propulsion system nobody understands. And so much more. I was married to him, remember, and I saw some really incredible things that he refused to let the human race have. We could be living in a golden age of peace and plenty for all humankind if he hadn't been so selfish. That's why my associates and I came to Vesper... to make sure that all these wonderful things don't stay locked away just because one man didn't care enough to share them. We just want to let the rest of humanity enjoy the benefits, too."

Phaedra looked at her as though she couldn't believe what she had just heard. "So you're saying that you're here to steal everything for the benefit of humanity and not yourselves?"

Vanessa frowned and her voice turned chillier. "That's an unfortunate way of putting it, but yes, my associates and I do consider ourselves entitled to appropriate compensation for our efforts. In comparison with how much the human race stands to gain, I'm sure that hardly anyone will begrudge us our modest share. So here's how it's going to be. I can't promise we'll be friends, but if you'll just follow a few rules and be patient, we'll all come out of this safe and sound. You'll be back home before you know it."

Phaedra raised an eyebrow. "Rules?"

"Just a few little things for your own safety, really," Vanessa replied. "The park isn't anywhere close to being finished, and many areas are still under construction and might not be safe. I don't want to have to worry about you getting hurt, so please stay here at the house for the time being. You can go outside and get a little exercise, of course, but don't leave the grounds. It would be a shame if I had to post a guard or two here to keep an eye on you, or confine you somewhere for your own protection, but I'll do it if I have to, and it won't be nearly as pleasant as being on your own in this big house."

"Anything else?" Phaedra asked.

Vanessa didn't even have to think about the answer to that. "We may need you to help us out with a few things. Your uncle did have your biometrics recorded for identification purposes, and you may be able to get into places where the rest of us are blocked. Please be available at all times for any such calls. Nobody will get hurt, I promise you. Oh, do you have any means of communicating with Earth?"

Phaedra shook her head. "No, we've been cut off for a while."

Ronn wasn't sure if that was a good thing for Phaedra to admit so readily. Maybe it would encourage Vanessa and Lowther to be on their best behavior if they thought everything was being reported back to Earth. Or maybe not. It might make them lock the kids up somewhere to keep them from blabbing. Those two would probably see through a bluff sooner or later anyway.

Vanessa looked relieved but forced an expression of sympathy for their plight. "That's a shame. Something to do with the lockdown after the forced entry we had to make, I suspect. Your mothers must be worried."

A long pause followed. "Any questions?" she finally asked.

Even though Phaedra had insisted on doing all the talking, Ronn spoke up. "I have one."

Phaedra frowned at him for breaking protocol but let him continue.

"What are these lurches we've felt? The people who sent us here were worried that Vesper might end up falling out of its orbit and crashing into the Earth."

The question seemed to catch Vanessa off guard, and she had to take a moment to think of a suitable reply. "Just routine adjustments in Vesper's orbit," she assured him. "To keep it stable or something like that. Our engineers have it under control. It's nothing you or anybody else has to worry about. Any other questions?"

Nobody said anything, and she stood up. "Now that we understand each other, I'll be going."

She started for the foyer, then stopped and turned back towards the others. "One more thing. You're 60,000 miles from home. It's a long way from any police, and I'm the only friend you have here. Some of the people I'm working with aren't as nice as I am. With so much at stake, they won't take kindly to you getting in their way even if you are just kids. Don't do anything to remind them that you're even here."

"In other words," Phaedra said, "don't do anything stupid."

Vanessa nodded. "Exactly. I knew you were bright kids. I think that about covers everything. If anything else comes up, I'll let you know. Just stay put and enjoy the amenities." With that, she left.

As soon as Vanessa was out the door, Bonnie came into the room. "You mean to say Jeff dumped me for *her?*"

"We don't know," Ronn said. "You might have dumped *him*. But what's that outfit all about?"

Bonnie did a pirouette. "You like it? I borrowed it from one of the maids. Cute, huh? I wouldn't want to have to wear it *all* the time, but—"

Phaedra glared at Bonnie. "And what do you think you're *doing*? I had it all worked out until you swiveled in and nearly blew the whole thing!"

Bonnie was startled by Phaedra's vehemence. "I wanted to listen in on what this Vanessa person had to say without her knowing who I am."

"I'm not even sure *what* you are!" Phaedra snapped.

Bonnie shrugged. "Well, whatever I am, I'm mixed up in this, too."

"Bonnie's right," Ronn said. "Let's *please* try to get along."

Phaedra took a moment to regain her composure. "All right, fine," she then grumbled. "But she must have known the real Bonnie. What if she had recognized you? I thought I saw some wheels turning even if she didn't make the connection."

"And so what if she did know me? Jeff could have made a robot of me at sixteen — and come to think of it, he *did!*"

"Never mind all that," Theo broke in. "So, what about our 'aunt'? What do you guys think of what she said?"

"She lost me at robbing Uncle Jeff for the benefit of humanity," Ronn replied. "We may be just dumb brats to her, but how stupid does she think we really are?"

"I don't think she told us everything about the lurches, either," Theo said. "For your information, Cuz," he added to Ronn, "you can't just 'fall' out of orbit. Once you're in an orbit, you don't have to keep 'stabilizing' it. Nobody has to stabilize the Moon's orbit every now and then. Maybe if you're really close in and there's still some air molecules to slow you down and make you lose altitude over time, but not this far out. So what's really going on?"

"Whatever it is, she didn't sound particularly concerned about it," Ronn answered. "It'd be awfully hard to spend their loot if the Earth was wrecked, which would make what they're doing here pretty pointless. These guys certainly aren't acting like they expect some sort of worldwide disaster. So I tend to believe her, at least that it's nothing we should worry about. We can't do anything about it anyway."

"What about all that bleth about Uncle Jeff being hurt?" Theo snorted. "She expected us to believe it?"

"There must be some reason why they *can't* let us see him if she had to feed us that," Ronn said. "My guess is that they've got him locked up somewhere... or else he's dead."

Everyone gave a start. He had just put into words a possibility they had been trying not to think about.

After a moment, Phaedra shook her head. "No, I don't think that's it. She was too definite that he's still alive somewhere, and I didn't get a sense that she was lying. What she meant by 'an accident,' though... I'll bet if there was an accident, it wasn't accidental."

"They could just kill *us* and be done with it..." Theo said bleakly.

"Which Vanessa just about came out and said they could if we got to be the least bit in their way," Ronn reminded him. "Why don't they do it? Lowther and Vanessa look a little too squeamish for something like that, but it wouldn't bother those hired goons one bit. She did say they might need us, but maybe they really don't want to be charged with any murders when they get back to Earth since somebody's bound to talk if things go bad."

"They're looking at billions if they succeed," Phaedra said, "and it sounds like they already burned a lot of bridges just getting here. There isn't much that's going to stop them now."

"So," Ronn concluded, "if we're going to do anything stupid, we should plan it very carefully."

"We probably shouldn't do anything," Theo said. "I vote we sit tight and wait it out."

"Sit here and do nothing?" Ronn asked. "Why?"

"Remember what Rogowski said about the *Mirage*?" Theo answered. "It's recharging or something and it'll take two or three days before it's ready to fly again? I bet Vanessa and Lowther don't even know it's there. I think we should just wait a couple of days, then make a run for it. We could be out of here and on our way back to Earth before they know we're gone."

Phaedra was horrified by the idea. "That means I'd have to fly the thing! Even though I don't trust her," she added hesitantly, as though desperately grasping at a straw, "Vanessa did promise to take us back to Earth—"

"Like we *want* to go with her?" Theo demanded. "Even if she means it and they don't plan to hurt us, we'd still probably be locked away somewhere for weeks like they did those other people we saw. *We know too much!* They won't want us spilling the beans to the government, at least not until they're out of reach somewhere back on Earth. If we can get out of here on our own, we can tell the FBI or somebody what we know right away, and maybe pull the rug out from under this bunch."

"And if we go back with them, we'll basically be hostages," Ronn said. "I don't really want to put myself under their thumb for who knows how long. No thanks."

Phaedra still didn't look happy about the prospect of being a pilot, but Ronn and Theo's arguments pointing out the problems of the alternative seemed to have their effect. "All right, if I have to, I guess I'll have to..." she finally conceded.

After lunch, the afternoon stretched out in front of Ronn, and he was starting to feel a little bored sitting around the house. Phaedra seemed perfectly content to lounge by the pool and read, while a good stock of games meant Theo could be happily occupied for hours. Ronn, however, wanted to do some more exploring, and maybe see what the intruders over at the Ivory Castle were up to. Unfortunately, the risk of getting caught somewhere he wasn't supposed to be, or not being at the house where he *was* supposed to be, might upset the good thing he and his cousins had going. Bored or not, Ronn would just have to stay where he was.

The problem of how to occupy his time that afternoon was solved when Vanessa came back a little later. Only one mercenary was with her this time, as though she had decided the kids weren't enough of a threat to be worth two. She did have somebody else with her, though.

With Vanessa leading the way, the merc helped Ronn's cousin Danny stagger up the steps to the porch and through the door. He was a thin, lanky boy about Ronn's age, though a little taller, and probably hadn't had a change of clothes since he was kidnapped several days before. He was pale and occasionally shivered even though the temperature was fairly balmy. He didn't seem to have a cold or the flu, though.

It's more like he had some kind of shock, Ronn thought, appalled to see the cousin he had known for so many years like this.

Vanessa had Danny sit down on the couch, where he promptly sagged to one side, too weak to sit up straight. He seemed too dizzy or nauseated to talk, as though he would throw up if he even tried to say something.

Vanessa then turned to the astonished Phaedra. "You should put him to bed right away. Our medic checked him out and said he should be all right in a day or two with some rest. In the meantime, here's a list of medicines that might be helpful. The house should have them in stock. The butler will probably know."

"But you said he was fine!" Phaedra exclaimed.

"I thought he'd snap out of this a lot faster," Vanessa retorted. "Things change. Get used to it." She pointed to Ronn. "You there. Come with me."

There goes the afternoon...

"What about us?" Phaedra asked.

"Yeah, what about us?" Theo added.

"Just stay here," Vanessa said curtly. "He'll be back in a couple of hours."

Out the corner of his eye, Ronn saw Bonnie standing in the dining room doorway, where Vanessa couldn't see her. She looked unhappy about the prospect of his leaving, but he shot her a glance that he hoped she would interpret as telling her not to say anything or insist on coming along.

Assuming nothing bad happened, this could actually be a good thing. He might find out more about what was going on, maybe even something about Uncle Jeff. He would have to wait until he got back to hear Danny's story.

Phaedra didn't look very happy, either, probably because she didn't like the idea of Vanessa splitting them up and working on them individually. There wasn't any arguing with Vanessa about it, however, and they would just have to go along with it.

At least they didn't have to worry about Danny anymore. Even in the shape he was in, having him with them was an improvement over Lowther and the others holding him somewhere. Ronn hoped he would have recovered enough in a couple of days to make the dash to the docking bay.

"Mind telling me what this is all about?" Ronn asked as Vanessa and the merc led him out of the house and to the jeep.

"Oh, just a little job," Vanessa answered with affected casualness. "Shouldn't take too long—"

A couple of distant gunshots echoed somewhere to the north. In the utter silence of the crater, sounds that weren't confined to blocked-off areas carried a long way.

Startled, Vanessa tapped her earbud a couple of times. "Damn, they still don't have the com working in this place yet. Get in," she said to Ronn, indicating the back seat. As she got in the front passenger seat, she added to the driver, "We'd better check that out. Fortunately, it's right on our way. There's a road in back of the hill. That'll take us where we need to go."

Ronn leaned back in the seat while the jeep started off. He could have tried asking Vanessa for more information, but she didn't seem to know much more about what had happened than he did, even if she had been inclined to chat, which he doubted. But who had been shooting, and what was there to shoot *at?*

Chapter Thirteen

They drove through the now familiar territory around the northwest arc, passing the cabin in the clearing, and came to MacNabbit the Rabbit's house. Another jeep was parked by the fence at the side of the road and a couple of mercenaries were picking up some small objects that had been scattered on the pavement. MacNabbit was nowhere in sight but on the ground were two small bodies. As Vanessa told her driver to stop the jeep, Ronn saw that the bodies were oversized rodents wearing cartoon criminal costumes.

Vanessa jumped out and went up to the mercenaries by the other jeep. "What happened, Sergeant? I heard shots—" Then she saw the Gopher Gang members on the ground and recoiled.

"Weirdest damn thing," the sergeant drawled. "We were just taking a load back to the Castle when we saw this big rabbit hoeing a garden, so we stopped to take a closer look. Then we got jumped by all these goofy bots that looked like big cartoon rats or something dressed like crooks. When they pointed guns at us and started grabbing stuff out of the jeep, we shot a couple and the rest scattered, so that's what you heard."

Ronn felt uneasy. The Gopher Gang was annoying but harmless. Even if they were bots, it was too much like killing something alive and conscious. He was glad that the Squirrel Scouts had apparently decided it might not be a good idea to try selling cookies just then. And that MacNabbit had chosen to disappear instead of pulling out Ol' Thunder, which Ronn doubted was at all functional. The "load" that the sergeant had mentioned, in the back of the jeep and strewn on the road, looked like small pieces of machinery, mostly coils wrapped around rods and maybe alien tech that had been torn out from somewhere.

"Say," the sergeant went on, "the boys have been wondering if they could use bots for target practice. Kind of a waste of ammo, but it isn't like there's much of a threat here anyway, so I thought why not, but I told 'em I'd check with you first to make sure—"

Vanessa interrupted with almost a scream. "Are you out of your mind? Do you know how much it costs to build a really good bot? Even if we can't get anything else out of this crazy theme park, we could sell these bots for *millions* on Earth. Leave the bots alone, understand?"

The mercenary stiffened, obviously not caring for being yelled at. If he was about to object, however, he thought better of it and left things at mild self-justification. "Yeah, well, but it's not like there's a shortage of bots around here—"

"Don't even think about it!" Vanessa snapped. "You've caused enough damage just shooting these two. Take them back to the Castle and let Justin have a look at them. Maybe they can be fixed and repurposed so we can get something for them, I don't know... but don't shoot any more!"

Vanessa got back in the jeep, leaving the two mercenaries to sort out the mess they had made.

While Vanessa seethed in silence, they went on to the Salisbury set and Uncle Jeff's old neighborhood. At first Ronn thought they were going to do something in the Prescott family home, but Vanessa had the driver pull up in front of a house down the street where a scooter was already parked. It was an ordinary two-story, wood-frame house under spreading maples like all the other houses up and down the street and not much different from Uncle Jeff's.

"Wait here until we get back," she told the driver as she and Ronn got out of the jeep. "Don't worry if it's an hour or two. You're getting paid the same regardless."

She turned away and didn't see it, but Ronn noticed a scowl on the driver's face, as though he felt he wasn't being paid nearly enough to take orders from her.

Vanessa led Ronn along the sidewalk towards the porch of the neighbors' house. "All right," she said on the way, "here's what you need to know. We found some notes in your uncle's files that mentioned this house. It seems to be sitting on top of an elevator leading down to a lower level where there's something very special. Exactly what, the notes didn't say, but wouldn't it be wonderful if it was a hangar with a working faster-than-light spaceship?"

Ronn wasn't sure how that would be so wonderful for him if she and Lowther got their hands on it, but just asked as they went up the steps to the porch, "And I come into it where?"

"We need you to open a door, basically. And then we can see what we have."

Coming through the front door and into the living room, Ronn saw that the house had a furnished interior, turn of the century judging by the box-like television set in a corner. Whether it was an accurate reproduction of the actual living room in one of Uncle Jeff's neighbors' houses or just something generic for the circa 2000 time period, he couldn't say. Vanessa hustled him on through the house and down some stairs into a basement that had been finished as a rec room.

The overhead lights were on and Ronn saw a model railroad. Not a display like in the toy store, but something a new hobbyist graduating from a train track on the living room rug and getting more serious would have built with store-bought models. It stood along the basement wall and was about five feet by nine, probably built on an old ping-pong table. On top was a miniature world of eighty or ninety years before, with an intricate track plan winding and looping around and through a landscape of city and countryside, with miniature buildings, trees, roads, cars, even tiny human figures. The ground was utterly flat, with no difference in elevation from one end to the other, adding to the effect of a world on a ping-pong table. It was somewhat reminiscent of the enormous electric train layout Ronn had seen at the toy store, but the trains and scenery were much smaller and far more could be packed in. Since it was a lot of world condensed in a relatively small space and not as spread out as it would be in reality, the detail was almost overwhelming at first glance. Ronn had some toy cars at home that would have fit in perfectly, and he recalled that they were labeled as being one-87th actual size, or what was termed HO scale.

Mounted along the long side against the wall was a printed scenic background with forested hills and mountains, city skylines, and hazy blue skies to suggest that the miniature world extended into the distance.

Ronn stepped closer to take a better look. About halfway along the long open side opposite the wall was a control box, where the old man would have stood, overlooking his domain from a lofty, even god-like height while running the trains,

It was all terribly old-fashioned, but it looked like it would be a lot of fun to play with. He could understand the appeal it must have had to the old man and then to his uncle. It was like looking down from above on your own little world—

"Come on!" Vanessa snapped and grabbed him by the arm to drag him over to the wall at the other end of the basement.

A world of your own was one thing, but the real world has a way of intruding. Ronn saw a hot water heater, a washing machine, and a dryer, probably there for added authenticity rather than actually working. All perfectly normal, except there was also a blank-looking metal door that didn't fit the rest of the basement's period decor.

Vanessa opened it and urged Ronn into a small elevator cab, a capsule like the one back at the guest house. She closed the door behind them, a

157

light came on, and the cab started down.

She lightened a bit during the descent, apparently deciding it might help to explain things a little more. "What you saw up on top was where a lot of this all started. A retired man down the street had a model railroad in his basement when Jeff was a boy. Jeff was fascinated by it the few times he was allowed to see it, but he wasn't that much interested in model trains for their own sake. They were getting to be pretty much an old man's hobby by then, and he didn't take them up himself. It was that idea of a miniature world that stuck with him."

"Was that the neighbor's actual train set up there or a reproduction?" Ronn asked.

"It's the real thing. Jeff wasn't that old when he got rich, and he started early with collecting things that had been important to him. When the neighbor died, Jeff bought the train layout from his widow, who I heard was more than glad to get rid of it, and put it in storage until he could do something with it. Who knew it would end up *here*? That much we could understand, but why was this elevator installed in the basement? I doubt very much if the original house in Salisbury had one."

After a ride that went on and on, the elevator finally came to a stop and the door opened. As Ronn stepped out of the cab, he noticed gravity was stronger here, that much closer to the artificial gravity-generating grid deep inside Vesper, and he was probably back to about his normal weight. He found himself in a small, featureless room about ten feet by ten, with a single overhead light. A table had been shoved into a corner, and on it were some pieces of portable test equipment.

Someone was already there, a tall, thin black man of about thirty in overalls. He was examining a door in the wall with a scanning device mounted on a visor over his eyes, and running hand-held sensors over the door frame. He turned towards Vanessa and Ronn as they came into the room, raising the visor to his forehead.

"Well?" Vanessa asked him.

The man shook his head. "Still nothing. We're going to need the boy. Somebody with the permissions has to open it, but after that there aren't any restrictions on who can go through."

"This is Dave Kiefer, one of our engineers," Vanessa told Ronn. "He's here to evaluate alien tech for us." She gestured for the man to move away from the door. "All right, stand back and let him try opening it." She glanced at Ronn. "Let's see if you have any better luck with the thing than we've had so far."

"You aren't expecting to find the Grail in there, are you?" Kiefer asked Vanessa.

"Never mind about that!" Vanessa snapped, cutting him off as though she thought Kiefer was about to say too much.

The Grail? Ronn wondered, but suspected he wouldn't get any answers asking Vanessa about it.

"I don't have any idea what could be here, really," she added. "A huge storage room filled with all the alien tech Jefferson kept hidden away would be a good outcome. His notes were awfully vague, though. *He* thought this place was important somehow, so we might as well follow his lead and see what we find. Ronn, would you please get *on* with it?"

"Uh... could you tell me what this is all about?" Ronn asked.

Vanessa exhaled impatiently, but Kiefer jumped in to explain. "See that red square next to the door? It's some kind of ID sensor. To open the door, somebody with the right permissions has to press it. There are a lot of these red plates next to doors we can't open. We think the plates were left over from the previous owners since their location doesn't seem to follow any logical order, and most of them may just open up on empty rooms the aliens cleared out. Going by some notes Mr. Prescott left, he did use at least a few blocked rooms for unspecified purposes, which was why the plates were reprogrammed so that only you or his other heirs could activate them."

Now Ronn understood. They had planned to use Danny to get them into places that only someone with registered biometrics could access. But with Danny too sick to be much good, they had drafted Ronn in his place. Suddenly feeling taken advantage of, he considered refusing for a second or two. But this was hardly the time or place to assert his independence. Not crammed into a small room far beneath the upper surface with two adults, one of them armed. Now that things had come this far, there wasn't much more harm opening the door could cause anyway. Besides, he was curious himself about what was on the other side, and he stepped up to the door.

He placed his palm on a red plastic plate by the door frame. The plastic surface glowed warmly for a moment. A female voice from nowhere announced: "Identified: Ronn Evans. Access granted."

The door slid into the wall to one side, opening onto a vast open space. Light streamed in from harsh fluorescent lights somewhere high overhead. The air was fresh and cool, if a bit dry, but it was filled with an almost choking smell of... *plastic?*

They came out on what seemed to be a concrete railroad station platform perhaps dating back to the 1950s. On either side were gray passenger cars with logos for the long-extinct New York Central Railroad. Several people were standing on the platform as though waiting for trains, like a woman with a baby carriage, a porter with suitcases, and a couple of hat-wearing businessmen with briefcases, but they weren't lifelike, high-tech bots. Instead, they were strange, inert plastic dummies, crudely detailed with the barest suggestion of faces, and their exposed skin and molded-on, long out-of-fashion clothes colored with about as much precision as with a paint roller. A couple were standing in hard, transparent puddles.

Ronn looked back and saw that the world ended just behind him. The door they had just come out of was the only feature in a vast gray wall that extended dizzily upwards and where the train tracks and everything else came to an abrupt stop.

"What the fratz *is* this place?" Vanessa demanded.

It was hard to see very much with the railroad cars on either side, but an open shelter, a roof supported by posts to protect waiting passengers from the rain, not that there would ever be any rain here, ran along the middle of the platform a little ways ahead. To get a better overall view, Ronn started to shinny up the end post, which felt like smooth plastic rather than metal, but slid back down. He had forgotten to take into account his now increased weight. He tried again, gripping the post more tightly with his hands and legs, and actually got somewhere. Since the post was at the end of the shelter, he could climb onto the roof and stand up.

With his head above the tops of the passenger cars, he looked around. A short distance down the track was the roof of a train station, and beyond that he saw the buildings of a nearby town, houses, and trees, all unnaturally crowded together. The buildings had an odd glossy plastic sheen to them, while the trees looked like green fuzzy lumps rather than leaves sprouting from spreading branches. To his left, the gray wall behind him stretched into the middle distance, where it suddenly stopped, seemingly meeting blue sky and a distant, mountainous horizon at a right angle. The sky and horizon were unconvincing, like an enormous printed backdrop mounted on a long wall. To the right was yet another long wall, but it was a featureless black, as though the world also came to a sudden end not very far away in that direction. The lights high above were enormous glowing tubes set in a kind of white ceiling instead of a blue sky.

For one crazy, delirious moment, Ronn wondered if he had been shrunk to less than an inch tall and this was the model train layout he had seen in the basement spreading out before him.

No, that can't be right... Even if he had been shrunk, he would have also had to be moved sideways back across the room to the layout. Instead, he had definitely been in an elevator cab that had gone straight down for a considerable distance.

Besides, there were some things that had to be impossible even for alien tech, like shrinking people to HO scale. What became of the other 86/87ths of your mass? Could you breathe air molecules 87 times bigger than your lungs were made for? Or even see with pupils 1/87th their normal size?

Now Ronn thought he understood. It was probably every model railroader's favorite fantasy to be able to shrink himself to scale size and wander around his layout. Since shrinking himself was impossible, Uncle Jeff had done the next best thing. He had enlarged the model railroad. Once the original layout had been scanned, it could be reproduced exactly at any desired size as long as there was enough raw plastic and coloring.

The world around him, then, was a duplicate of the model railroad in the house above, enlarged to human size. Even the human figures, what Ronn had thought were dummies, were actually copies of tiny figures with crude detailing and painting, enlarged to 87 times their original size, and including an inadvertent simulation of the glue used to stick them in place.

If the original layout was five by nine feet... Ronn did a quick calculation in his head, rounding the scale to 90 to make it easier. As best he could figure it, the enlarged version would be in the 450 feet by 800 range, a cramped little area in real-world terms but relatively huge here.

It was a strange whim on Uncle Jeff's part, but there was so much sheer *room* in the asteroid that he could indulge it. Perhaps this had been a huge empty space formerly housing a hangar or maybe repair facilities for a fighter squadron.

As Ronn slid back down the post, he had a sudden creepy thought. That long black wall to the right was where the rest of the basement would have been in relation to the real model railroad. If Uncle Jeff had really been thorough, he might have simulated a dim view of a gigantic water heater, washing machine, and dryer in the far vastness. Or a projection of a colossal version of himself standing over the layout and looking down at it like the god of a plastic world—

Ronn shook his head to clear *that* thought out of it, then went to tell Vanessa and Kiefer what he had seen.

Vanessa covered her eyes and forehead with her hand for a moment, as though trying to soothe a sudden headache. "I was married to him... I thought I knew him... And he still surprises me by doing something completely insane that I never expected..."

As an engineer, Kiefer seemed entranced by the whole thing. "I wonder if this layout *works*?" He went over to the nearest passenger car and bent down to look at the wheel assembly resting on the track below the platform.

Ronn followed him. "Like maybe there's a control panel somewhere where you could run the trains?"

"Yeah... but probably not," Kiefer decided, and pointed down at the wheels. "The trucks, the wheels in railroad talk, look like a solid unit molded as part of the car, so I don't think the wheels can even turn."

161

Ronn looked where he was pointing. The six-wheel assembly beneath the car did look solid. The wheels even seemed to fuse with the rails without a clear break where they touched.

Kiefer stood up and pointed to the door at the end of the car. "And while that may look like it's supposed to be a door, you won't be getting inside that way."

That was obvious. The door was not a separate unit set in an opening and attached by hinges, but merely indicated by a shallow groove molded into the car's outer surface, while the handle was just a rectangular lump.

"The way the replicator scan works," Kiefer continued, "you can scan the outside of something every which way, but if moving parts are involved, you have to disassemble the object and scan the individual parts, then put the copy together, or you get a solid mass of plastic like a statue. To make it run, Prescott would've had to lay metal rails, put working wheels on all the cars, and install motors in the engines. That'd really add to the amount of time and effort he'd have to spend on this project. There are limits on what one man can do even in this place, and this looks like something he probably did as an afterthought. The aliens might be able to scan complex machinery and reproduce it exactly, even down to the composition of metal alloys, so that it would function straight out of the box with discrete moving parts just like the original, but that would be an order of magnitude more complicated and I don't think that's the case here. It looks like it's all just variously colored plastic, even the supposedly metal parts."

Vanessa had moved a short distance down the platform, perhaps bored by the more technical talk, still looking around in numbed dismay. Kiefer glanced up to make sure she was out of earshot, then motioned for Ronn to step closer to him.

"So you're Prescott's nephew," he said in a low voice, more a statement of a fact he obviously already knew than a question.

Ronn nodded.

"I'm sorry, real sorry, about all this," Kiefer muttered. "But it was a job, they promised a lot of things without telling the whole story, and I didn't know what I was getting myself into. Now I'm stuck here and doing what they tell me is the only way to get back home. Same for you, it looks like—"

Vanessa turned around and came back towards them. Kiefer started talking a little more loudly, as though in the middle of explaining something to Ronn. "...There's a sort of echo-sensing in the scan that detects the size and extent of hollow spaces, so the replicator molds things like these passenger cars as shells instead of as solid masses of plastic all the way through—"

Vanessa stopped in front of Kiefer and interrupted him without a second thought, waving to take in the vast world behind her. "Is there anything we can *use* here? Alien tech, I mean?"

"I'd have to take a closer look to make sure," Kiefer replied, "but I doubt it. It's all just a lot of colored plastic. Or carbon composite or whatever the stuff is."

"*Damn* him!" Vanessa exclaimed in helpless-sounding frustration, and Ronn had no doubt whom she meant.

Now that he'd had a glimpse of the place, he wouldn't have minded spending a few hours exploring it. He was especially curious to see what the nearby town looked like up close. Unfortunately, they weren't prepared for an expedition very deep into a plastic wilderness where there wouldn't be any food or water, and there wouldn't be any point in it if they weren't likely to find some useful alien tech anyway.

Meanwhile, Vanessa had quickly lost interest. "Come on," she said abruptly, turning back towards the door in the wall. "I've got better things to do than waste any more time here."

Ronn followed her and Kiefer back into the anteroom. The engineer stayed behind to collect his equipment while Ronn and Vanessa took the elevator back up. She didn't say anything during the ride, still in a bad mood from the disappointment. He just wondered what the engineer had been so conscience-stricken about that he felt he had to apologize. Was he sorry about being a part of an operation to rob Ronn's uncle, or sorry about something worse that Ronn didn't know about yet?

On the way back through the basement, Vanessa glanced at the model railroad that had been the model of the huge layout below and shook her head in silent exasperation.

Outside, the driver was still waiting for them in the jeep in front of the house. Getting in, Vanessa told him to drive on.

To Ronn's surprise, they continued along the ring road instead of going back the way they had come.

"Aren't you taking me back to the house?" he asked.

"Not just yet," Vanessa called from the front seat. "We've got a lot more work to do today."

Somehow, Ronn suspected that *we* would mean mostly *him*.

At one point along the ring road, they had to stop to let the teddy-bear marching band go by in front of them, crossing the road from somewhere in the woods on one side to somewhere in the woods on the other. The little furballs were still loudly playing the same goofy-sounding tune as before, but now it was falling apart. The fat teddy bear with the tuba had completely lost the beat and was tooting almost at random, the bass drum player was connecting with his instrument only about half the time, and out in front of the marching column, the drum major led the way unaware that he had dropped his baton somewhere and continued the motions of twirling a non-existent object.

"Something's wrong," Vanessa said half to herself. "That marching band shouldn't be here. It wandered away from the toon zone somehow. Must be something in the perimeter codes. Oh well, it isn't my problem."

"Can't I knock a couple off?" asked the driver hopefully, fingering his sidearm as he waited.

"*No!*"

When the band had trooped past them, Vanessa motioned for the driver to continue. At the Eastgate construction site, they turned off on an intersecting road that led into the interior, heading for the Ivory Castle in the center of the crater.

The driver made a wrong turn somewhere. After Vanessa berated him for not knowing his way around, they came to a stop at an intersection. In front of them was the entrance to Clown Town, a seeming small city surrounded by a wall plastered with circus posters and heavily graffitied with spray-painted, semi-abstract clown motifs. The road led through an arched gateway that was the open grinning mouth of a huge sculpted and brightly colored clown face. Signs on either side read in ornate circus lettering:

I'D TURN BACK IF I WERE YOU
ABANDON ALL HOPE YE WHO ENTER HERE

Vanessa dubiously eyed the townscape visible through the gateway and rearing above the wall. Cockeyed buildings with architecture that seemed based on circus tents three or four stories high and leaning dangerously at odd angles, clowns chasing each other with seltzer bottles and pies, impossibly small and funny-looking cars filled with whooping clowns careening through the streets, occasional small explosions, loud circus music played on a deranged calliope somewhere... Ronn remembered the disembodied clown's head he had seen in the workshop, and guessed that it was intended for this particular set.

Clown Town was something recent enough that he was familiar with it. It had started with a vidshow called *Meet the Barnums*, about a married couple named Emmett and Kelly Barnum and their children, Jinx and Joey, an entire family of real clowns (as though clowns existed as a separate species, born looking like that instead of having to put on make-up and rubber noses) trying to live like regular people in the normal world. Occasional references to their even stranger relatives back in their old home town evolved from a running gag to a strong indication that there were many more clowns somewhere, eventually leading to *Clown Town*, a spin-off show set in the ancestral clown homeland and played with over-the-top insanity. Just to show that life usually has a joker up its sleeve, the main character was Petey Barnum, a cousin who was that rarest of all freaks in the clown world, someone born looking perfectly normal, the mirror image of the situation in the first show. Unfortunately, *Clown Town* hadn't lasted very many episodes. What was a tolerable dose of absurdity in an otherwise normal world in *Meet the Barnums* was hard on the nerves for most audiences when it was nothing *but* absurdity.

Seemingly out of nowhere, a teenage boy popped up in front of the jeep. It was Petey Barnum himself, an ordinary teenager wearing ordinary clothes.

Frantic and desperate, he exclaimed, "If you have any sense, turn back now before it's too late!"

"Why?" Vanessa asked, even though she knew as well as anyone that she was talking to a projected recording.

Petey waved towards the town behind him as though he had heard the question and was responding to it. "Because they're all *crazy* in there!" With that, he ran off, vanishing from one moment to the next.

Vanessa glanced at the driver. "Turn right. We'll go around. I don't know how long it'd take us to get through that mess up ahead or if we even can."

That urgent warning would be a good interactive gimmick for park visitors, Ronn thought, but it was also a reproduction of the actual beginning of the *Clown Town* show, in which viewer discretion was not only advised but implored.

Chapter Fourteen

They soon came out of the woods with the Ivory Castle just ahead of them, a white monolith gleaming in the daylight. When they reached the end of the bridge across the lake, Ronn was surprised to see that nothing was stirring around the front hotel entrance. No limousines were pulling up, at any rate. Perhaps that particular set-up only worked at night.

In the interior courtyard, some mercenaries were loading the flatbed truck with what seemed to be molded lumps of white plastic the size of vacuum cleaners. They were probably the external casings for some very strange machinery, though it was impossible to tell what their precise function was by just looking at them.

The driver let them out and Vanessa led Ronn across the courtyard towards the southeast corner. On the way they passed the *Moonbeamer*. Ronn was closer to it this time than he had been earlier, and it was daytime. He suddenly noticed something he had missed before. The gleaming chrome rocket had three elegantly sweeping tailfins, each ending in a torpedo-like pod. The flat bottoms of the pods were further back than the stern of the main fuselage, so with the *Moonbeamer* in an upright position, it stood on the pods with the hull somewhat elevated. Ronn remembered from the old *Starbusters* episodes he had seen that the *Moonbeamer* continuously spewed flame from a rear exhaust nozzle when in flight, never mind any considerations of fuel limitations. This version of the *Moonbeamer*, however, didn't have an exhaust nozzle.

In its place was the same sort of reflective disc and antenna affair that Ronn had seen at the rear of the *Mirage*. He could think of only one reason for it.

This thing can fly!

It wasn't just a model or a mock-up, it was a functioning spacecraft powered by alien tech. So it wasn't intended as part of some exhibit or stage set somewhere else in the crater, but why was it here, deep inside a

166

domed area without any obvious way out into space, and what was it for when Uncle Jeff had a whole fleet of several other, larger, and certainly more practical spacecraft?

It was one more mystery among all the others. Ronn gave up trying to figure it out, but decided not to mention what he had noticed to Vanessa. If she and the others hadn't realized that the *Moonbeamer* could fly yet, it would just be something else to loot when they found out, maybe even one of the most valuable artifacts in the Park for its propulsion system alone. They needed the other ships, but the *Moonbeamer* would be a spare that could be sacrificed for taking apart and analyzing.

Inside the Castle, Vanessa took Ronn along a corridor, passing closed doors. At the far end, she opened a door and had him wait outside while she went in.

From the hallway, he could see into a small, cluttered workshop where a little man in suspenders and sweat-stained shirt worked at a table filled with test equipment. The man might have been around sixty, a little paunchy with thinning gray hair since he hadn't had any anti-aging treatments. He reminded Ronn of a kindly old toymaker he had seen in an old cartoon set in the 18th or 19th Century. On the tabletop in front of the man was an empty white plastic-like casing about the size of a cereal box next to a mass of what looked like purple steel wool. It looked like the stuff spilling out of the boy Jeffbot's skull back at the old Prescott house.

"How's it going, Justin?" Vanessa asked with affected cheerness. "Got that thing figured out?"

The man looked up, startled. He lifted his magnifying visor from his eyes, and put down a tool that resembled a scalpel with tiny lights on it. "Not yet, ma'am. We don't know what it's supposed to do."

"Can't you just start it up and watch what it does?"

"Maybe, but we don't even know how to turn it on."

Vanessa suddenly lost her patience. No more good cheer, artificial or otherwise. "Look, you idiot, we need some results!"

Not "want" or "would like to see" some results, Ronn noticed, but *needed* them. *They're under pressure from somewhere.*

Justin all but shriveled in the heat of Vanessa's fury. "We're doing the best we can," he insisted, half apologetically and half defensively, "but you can't expect miracles."

With an obvious effort, Vanessa regained some of her composure, probably realizing she had an audience that should not be allowed to see her lose her self-control for a moment and reveal too much.

"With what we're paying you," she said, still sounding testy, "we ought to get at least a *few* miracles. Jeff thought that thing was important or it wouldn't have been in his office. Doesn't taking it apart tell you anything?"

"Not much." Justin gestured helplessly at the disassembled object on the table in front of him. "We could get it open, but what's inside is nothing like wires and circuit boards. It's just a mass of… *something*. I call it 'protean fuzz' because the best guess I can come up with is that it starts out undifferentiated. The aliens somehow tell it what they want the machine to do, and the stuff reconfigures itself to do it, never the same way twice. And that's just *one* form of alien tech — there are at least three others, like the one that looks like so much electronic lasagna. Just when you think you can trace a circuit, it ends up in some little ball of exotic matter we can't make on Earth or even take apart."

Vanessa frowned, expressing a distinct lack of sympathy for his excuses, but probably realizing the problem really was a lot bigger than just Justin's competence as an engineer. "All right, keep on doing what you're doing. I don't know how much more time we can spend here, but if we have to, we'll box everything up that looks promising and take it back to Earth so the big labs there can figure it out. Right now, I want you to come with me."

The toymaker sighed resignedly and pushed aside the toy that he would never be able to understand. He stood up from his bench and followed as Vanessa turned on her heel and strode out of the room.

Out in the corridor, Vanessa paused briefly to make the necessary introductions. "Ronn is Jeff's nephew," she told Justin. "He has the permissions for accessing a lot of places we can't get into otherwise. Ronn, this is Justin Hobart, one of the engineers. He'll be helping us on our next job. If he *can*," she added as a rather unkind afterthought.

As she turned away to start back down the corridor, Justin caught Ronn's eye and shrugged wearily, as though to say he was a prisoner of circumstance himself and please don't blame him for what Vanessa was making him do.

That was the second engineer who had been anxious to make it clear he wasn't really one of *them*. Unfortunately, with all those armed mercenaries in the place, the chances of the technical staff staging a revolt seemed remote.

They followed Vanessa down a narrow corridor to a door. She had no trouble opening it on her own, and as she stepped into the small room, its overhead light came on. Ronn followed Justin through the doorway — and gave a start.

The room was filled with bots. Jefferson C. Prescott bots. Bots of Uncle Jeff at various ages, several mounted upright on a wheeled rack and arranged by height in stairstep order, something like suits on a rack in a store but with people in them — or maybe like a meat rack in a horror vid slaughterhouse scene. Some were connected to test equipment by cables plugged into jacks inside their access panels, while several others sat limply on the floor in sprawling heaps like scarecrows or rag dolls. The tops of the heads of a couple of the adults had been removed, with jagged saw-cuts around the skulls and exposing masses of that purple protean fuzz. Now Ronn understood where the missing Jeffbots from the various exhibits had ended up, but *why*?

Vanessa muttered to Justin, trying not to let Ronn hear her, but he heard it anyway: "Now *there* are some bots I wouldn't mind using for target practice..."

That must have been a really bitter divorce.

Vanessa turned to Ronn and explained. "All these bots were programmed based on Jeff's mind and behavior patterns, so they should hold a lot of his memories. But when we tried to extract some information from them, they all went dead. Can you reactivate them?"

She's asking me? "How?"

"How should I know?" Vanessa demanded. "Maybe you just being here might trigger something, like some ID recognition."

Not knowing what else to do, Ronn touched the bots, put his hand on their foreheads, even took them by the shoulders and shook them. Justin helped by fiddling with the test equipment and watching the readouts on the monitors. While they were occupied with all that, Vanessa stepped out into the hallway to consult her writepad and dictate some notes into it.

Nothing happened despite Ronn's best efforts. The Jefferson bots remained inert dummies.

"How are these bots different from all the others?" Ronn asked when he had reached the limit of his ideas. "I mean, all the other bots I've seen here that were based on real people didn't seem to have copies of their minds, too." There was one big exception to that statement, but Ronn didn't want to give Bonnie away. Besides, the answer to the question might explain her as well. "Like Grandma — Uncle Jeff's mother. She just repeated the same basic behavior without any signs of remembering anything or thinking for herself."

"Some are more complex than others, but most don't have any initiative," Justin said as he checked the readouts on a monitor one more time, though without any more success than before. He seemed to be in a mood to talk, perhaps because he couldn't do anything else. "Prescott's mother was still alive when he made a bot of her, but she wouldn't have agreed to take part in anything like this, so her copy just has a standard memory and behavior module programmed to fit the set where it's placed. To the extent the bot acts and sounds like the actual woman, it's the result of programming based on old family vids. Convincing to a point, but not really complete, and the result of some guessing and approximation. But Prescott wanted his own copies to be more detailed and authentic, I guess, so he used some sort of alien equipment for making a copy of his memories and personality, which was fed into a mass of protean fuzz that had been configured for brain functions. The result was a lot more lifelike... a little *too* lifelike, actually."

"How so?" Ronn asked.

"Like I told Vanessa, protean fuzz adapts itself to perform its designated function, but sometimes the result is even better than what the original specifications called for. The Prescott bots were starting to develop fully working brains and think for themselves."

"You mean they were coming alive?"

Justin nodded. "They were getting there. When Prescott had his mind copied for all these bots, he just wanted a few memories and behaviors, whatever was appropriate for the time of his life a given bot was supposed to represent. But a lot of really deep stuff came along in the process, what you might call the brain's operating system. The best I can figure is that it gave the protean fuzz a pattern to work with, and the fuzz reconfigured itself to work like a real brain. Not just a few memories, but emotions and even independent thinking. Prescott came up here when his people on-site reported that some of his bots were apparently getting bored with what they were supposed to be doing in the various sets and wandering off. Prescott had the bots all collected here so they could be studied to see how it happened. There were a couple, though, that didn't *want* to leave where they were, like one they had to drag out of a cabin, and another was too wrapped up playing vidgames. I heard Lowther shot that one out of sheer frustration when it refused to stop playing some game, and Prescott was pretty mad about it. Before Prescott got very far with the analysis, though... other things happened—"

Vanessa came back into the room at that point, cutting Justin off. "Any results?"

Justin waved helplessly at the roomful of non-responsive Jeffersons. "Nothing. I think some self-destruct mechanism was triggered when their security was breached."

"I give up!" Vanessa fumed. "This is pointless. Come on, you two."

Actually, Ronn thought, it hadn't been pointless at all. He now knew why all the Jeffbots had been missing, and had some insight into how Bonnie came to be. Uncle Jeff hadn't been the only one whose memory had been fully copied, and that protean fuzz had done the rest. He also had the impression that Aunt Bonnie was the only other living human being besides Uncle Jeff who had undergone the complete mind copying process. Just as importantly, no one outside the guest house knew about Bonnie. The amazing thing was that when the Jeffbot at the county fair was collected, no one had noticed the Bonnie-bot was also on the way to self-awareness. Maybe she hadn't been as far along and it wasn't apparent. It was sobering to realize that Bonnie had been that close to self-destructing like the Jeffbots...

After an admonishment from Vanessa that she wanted to see results Real Soon Now, Justin went back to his workshop and probably still more futility. She then led Ronn through the staff living quarters.

They passed several of the men in the corridor, most lugging pieces of equipment Ronn recognized as advanced modeling and drafting machines from the big workroom. Devices like that probably would be the most understandable and immediately useful sort of machinery. The mercenaries barely acknowledged Vanessa and didn't seem to display very much respect for her as they went by, but she ignored them, perhaps dismissing them as the poor quality of hired help one had to put up with these days when pulling off an illegal operation with so many risks and so far from home.

There was also a woman at work, the first one Ronn had seen besides Vanessa, dressed in overalls and tapping on a writepad. She was gray-haired, middle-aged, and a bit stout, never having had body enhancement. Judging by her accent as she called out instructions to the men ("Leafe dot alone, it iss vurthless"), she was German.

"That's Kathrin Rissleben, our Marketing Analyst," Vanessa explained as they passed her. "I recruited her from New Product Development so she can tell us what's worth taking back to Earth."

Just from Kathrin's exasperation as she pointed to things ("*Nein*, dot iss no good, leafe it!"), Ronn could tell that she wasn't finding much.

He and Vanessa finished up in the deserted employee canteen, a small room with just a few tables that might have seated twenty people at most.

Vanessa motioned for him to take a seat at one of the tables. "Thirsty?" she asked.

"I wouldn't mind something," Ronn replied, surprised by her sudden consideration.

Vanessa went behind a counter at the front of the room and opened a refrigerator. "Looks like there's some Pepsi left," she said, "but that's about all. Guess it'll do."

She came to the table with a couple of drink bulbs emblazoned with the familiar red, white, and blue logo, and handed him one as she sat down across from him. Ronn tore off the tab seal, which in turn pulled out a short straw, then took a sip.

171

"Look," Vanessa began, "I know you're in a situation. You didn't ask to come here and now you're probably not sure if you're ever going to get back home. But if you play ball with us, you could come out of this pretty well."

Oh... that's what this is all about! "How so?" he asked cautiously.

Vanessa waved vaguely. "We're a little short-handed. A lot of things need to be done and we might not have much time, so we're in a hurry and we may seem a little rough at times. But once we're on Earth, having one of the heirs in our corner could help us a great deal when we start figuring out what we have, especially if we have to fight in court over patents and salvage rights. You could partner with us and lay the foundation of a very prosperous future for yourself."

I shouldn't argue with her, but... "Since I'm Jefferson Prescott's nephew, won't I get a share of his fortune sooner or later anyway?"

Vanessa shook her head. "For one thing, he isn't dead yet, so I wouldn't count on anything for possibly a very long time. The distributed profits from this enterprise could easily amount to a lot more than you'd ever get from shares of TranStella divided a dozen or more ways decades from now."

"What about Phaedra and Theo?" Ronn asked.

"If they want to participate, too," Vanessa said not very enthusiastically, "we'd certainly be glad to have them, but I didn't sense much potential cooperation from that quarter when I spoke with them. The girl is too much her mother's daughter..." She broke off, perhaps realizing that she was saying too much, and tried another tack. "So what do you say? This could be the chance of a lifetime. Do you want to spend your life on a dead-end career track in a boring job you hate in some office somewhere, or rich beyond your wildest dreams without ever having to work?"

"Can I think about it?"

Vanessa frowned, and he could guess what she was thinking. If he had been inclined to go along, he would have said so right off. Instead, he was stalling her, which meant he was tending towards no but wanted to avoid saying it outright, and she knew it. She stayed civil, however, apparently making an effort to keep the door open as long as possible.

"I'll take that as a no, but if you change your mind, let me know. Just don't take too long. We don't plan on staying here any longer than we absolutely have to."

"And another thing," Ronn said. "I want to see Uncle Jeff."

"I already told you. He's been injured."

"I could still see him, couldn't I? I just want to be sure he isn't dead."

Ronn could almost see the wheels turning in Vanessa's head as she considered the options. "Maybe tomorrow," she said after a moment, as though reluctant to concede even that much, "if we have time."

Ronn was astonished that she had agreed, if only in principle. On the other hand, she had put it off, so nothing had actually happened yet. She might have another excuse tomorrow.

She glanced at the time display on her wristcom. "Well, it's getting a little late and there are some things we need to do."

"You mean we aren't done yet?" Ronn asked.

"Not even close, so let's get back to work. There are several places I want to look at—"

And none of them panned out. Door after door led to empty rooms or corridors that went nowhere. They could find nothing that was worth looting.

One trip in a jeep had Vanessa driving because all the mercs were busy with other things, and it took them to the East docking bay. A side road at the Eastgate freight elevator led to a spiral ramp that went down level after level. Hand-scrawled signs, probably for the benefit of the mercenaries driving their truck and other vehicles, had been taped to the walls indicating each floor number and finally the level of the docking bay. Vanessa turned off there and drove for something like a mile along a wide corridor. A couple of times, they were passed by mercenaries on scooters coming the other way.

The checkpoint was more utilitarian than the North one, without any pretense of simulated airport terminals or chauffeur-driven touring cars, obviously intended for unloading freight rather than receiving distinguished guests, and much larger to allow for large and bulky items to pass through. The checkpoint had clearly suffered damage with blown-open doors and no longer functioned to restrict entry, and a couple of bullet-damaged bots in futuristic security guard uniforms lay sprawled where they had been shoved aside. As with the North bay, there was a small suite of rooms where pilots could stay while watching over the ships, but it wasn't being used now that the civilian prisoners and the mercenaries injured on the way in had been sent back to Earth on the cargo carrier.

The docking area itself was far larger than its North counterpart, with enough floor space to accommodate dozens of *Mirage*-class shuttles. Ronn saw two of the three ships in the TranStella fleet that Vanessa and Lowther had commandeered: the *Spectre*, a private shuttle identical to the *Mirage*, and the freighter that he had only heard about up to now.

The latter was a huge vessel shaped like a bulging discus and resembling a classic flying saucer to some extent. Most of it was a hold for cargo, with only a small cockpit and crew quarters at the forward edge. It lacked wings and looked as though designed for vertical takeoff and landing, and probably could have set down on the Moon. The ship's hatch doors were open and a couple of mercs were driving forklifts carrying large pieces of machinery up a ramp and into the hold.

While Vanessa spoke with the men about how to stow the loot and what they should do next, Ronn noticed several gleaming silver globes, each about eight feet in diameter, lined along one wall.

Out of curiosity, he went over to take a closer look at them. They were vehicles of some kind resting on landing skids, looking as though designed for deepsea diving with portholes and hatch-like doors, and numbered consecutively in large block-style numerals on the sides: 01, 02, etc.

Before he could make any kind of examination, Vanessa came up, irritated that he hadn't stayed where she had left him and she'd had to make the effort to haul him back.

"Come on!" she snapped at him. "We're going!"

"I was just wondering what those globe-things were."

"Never mind!"

As she led him to the jeep, Ronn's mind worked. *Escape pods! They have to be!* Some kind of last-resort, very basic emergency escape system for bailing out of Vesper. Uncle Jeff wouldn't leave his people — or himself — stranded here in case of disaster. The shuttles or other spacecraft might not always be on hand, or might have to take off before the last stragglers from remote parts of the asteroid had made their way to the docking bay. It was good to know the things were there, though Ronn wasn't sure how they might be useful to him. If the situation really did go that bad, he'd have to get back here to the East docking bay since he hadn't noticed any escape pods at the North bay. Not knowing how to launch and fly the pods, not knowing their range or where they might end up, having to get past the mercenaries who were probably always lurking around the East docking bay, this was definitely a Plan B sort of thing, if not Plan C or D when everything else had gone wrong.

Vanessa drove Ronn back to the Castle in her usual bad mood, then dragged him down into the endless corridors to look for more red panels.

As the afternoon wore on towards dinnertime, they were both getting tired, and Vanessa finally gave up for the day amid some rather salty language directed at Uncle Jeff.

Saying something about going back to her room to lie down with a cold compress on her forehead as she cursed Jeff's insanity for that enlarged model railroad, she turned Ronn over to Enzo, the Commandant's massive deputy, to run him back to the guest house. Ronn followed his escort through the big workroom, where several other mercenaries were just then stripping the place of the last of the workstations and other design and drafting equipment, and to a door off to one side. It opened onto a small garage where a jeep and several scooters were parked. The merc then took Ronn to the house in the jeep, and since Enzo's English was bad and Ronn's French was non-existent, neither said anything during the ride. Enzo dropped him off in front of the porch and drove away.

Ronn went into the house and found Phaedra lying on a couch and reading an old book in one of the front rooms. She had figured out the house's sound system and was listening to the Greatest Hits of a singer named Delilah Cantonuovo, set to a low volume. Ronn remembered hearing Delilah's songs a lot in the earliest days of his childhood but not after that. A singer who had been popular about ten or twelve years before was practically cutting edge for Uncle Jeff. It was certainly an improvement over that *Dinner Music to Put You to Sleep Before You Get to Dessert* that played as some kind of default during meals.

"Wait'll you hear what I did today!" Ronn exclaimed.

"Keep it down!" Phaedra urged him in a low voice. She pointed to the ceiling. "Danny's still sleeping! He's been through a lot."

So have we, Ronn thought, but then they hadn't been kidnapped by criminals. Kidnapped by their own government, maybe, but without the sheer terror Danny must have experienced.

"So what did she have you doing?" Phaedra asked, putting the book down and sitting upright. She waved lazily in the direction of a small lighted panel on the wall and Delilah's heartfelt trillings came to a sudden stop.

"We have to talk about the latest," Ronn replied. "Where's Theo?"

"Out back by the pool last I knew," Phaedra said. "With *her*."

"I'll go round 'em up," Ronn said, heading for the hallway. "I guess we might as well meet in the den."

Theo and Bonnie were sitting at the table under the umbrella at poolside. Both wore swimsuits but neither was damp. Theo was just then showing Bonnie something in an old book, and a stack of books was on the table next to him.

Bonnie looked up as Ronn approached. "Oh, you're back!" She seemed relieved to see him.

"Hope I'm not interrupting," Ronn said, "but I wanted to get everybody in the den for a conference. What's going on, anyway?"

"Just a little history lesson," Theo replied. "About forty years' worth, actually. She wanted to find out some more about what's been happening this century."

"A lot of things, it sounds like," Bonnie said. "I've already lost track of all the wars Theo told me about. And what's the deal with all these new states? Fifty were hard enough to remember, but *sixty*?"

Ronn tried to remember his history lessons and what he had heard on the news. "Well, California kind of fell apart and they had to split it up, and there was some reorganization after the EMP War and several other states were split—"

"Stop!" Bonnie exclaimed. "I'm lost already!"

Four decades of history all at once would be a little confusing, Ronn had to admit. He'd spent years on history in his school classes and still wasn't sure about a lot of things.

"I guess I'd better go get dressed," Bonnie then said. "See you in the den." She got up from her chair and headed towards the house, and the other two followed.

Wearing their regular clothes, Bonnie and Theo came into the den a few minutes later, joining Phaedra and Ronn. Phaedra took a seat in one of the chairs while Theo sprawled on the floor next to her, and Ronn and Bonnie sat on the couch.

"So, here's what happened after Vanessa dragged me away this afternoon—" Ronn started to say.

"Are you sure talking upstairs like this is a good idea?" Phaedra suddenly asked. "Maybe we should take this down to the garage."

Before Ronn could reply to say that it probably didn't matter *where* they talked, since if one place was bugged the whole crater was bugged, Bonnie spoke up.

"I did a little asking around with the help. Not that they're much good for conversation. They just don't *think* about anything but their jobs. As far as they know, the house isn't bugged or being monitored from the Castle. After all," she added in an exact imitation of Wilfred's well-modulated masculine tones, "one does not intrude on the privacy of one's invited guests, does one?"

Ronn was astonished. "You can *do* that?"

"Voice synthesizer," Theo explained.

"Whatever," Bonnie said with a shrug. "I don't even need to open my mouth when I talk, but it'd probably weird people out if I didn't."

"Anyway, that's one less thing to worry about it if nobody's listening in on us," Ronn went on. "We've probably spilled so much already just talking to each other that we couldn't deny anything to Vanessa if we wanted to. As short-handed and pressed for time as she claimed to be, though, it's a little hard to imagine her putting one of their goons on full-time duty doing nothing but listen to us."

"They wouldn't have to listen to *everything* we said," Theo pointed out. "They could just program the system to listen for key words like, oh, I don't know, 'escape,' or 'call Earth,' or whatever, and flag them for somebody to check out later. But it doesn't sound like they're even doing that much."

"Bigger fish to fry, I guess," Ronn said. "Kids like us probably don't count in all this. Except when they want something opened, anyway."

That was as good a lead-in as any, and he then told everyone about his day with Vanessa.

"I wish I could've seen that model train layout!" Theo exclaimed. "And *Clown Town*, too! I hope Vanessa picks *me* the next time she wants something done!"

"You *want* to help her?" Phaedra demanded.

"Actually, that did come up," Ronn said, and told them about Vanessa's attempt to lure him to the Dark Side.

"I hope you weren't the least bit tempted," Phaedra ventured.

"Not hardly," Ronn replied. "She was basically asking me to rob my own uncle, which I thought was a little much."

"I really doubt she was all that serious anyway," Phaedra said. "Maybe she was trying to split us up, get us fighting with each other so we can't put up a united front against her. Even if you did join her, they'd probably double-cross you somehow in the end anyway."

Ronn nodded. "I got that idea myself. I also think they're after something specific besides just grabbing every piece of alien tech they can get their hands on. I overheard them talking a couple of times about looking for something I'm sure they didn't want me to know about from the way they acted. I didn't hear enough to find out exactly what it was, but one of the tech guys said something about a 'grail' and Vanessa immediately made him shut up."

"Like that 'it' from this morning?" Theo asked.

"Maybe," Phaedra said, "but it doesn't really concern us. The fact is that we can't stop them from doing whatever they want, and Vanessa made it pretty clear that the less we know about what they're doing the better off we'll be. All we can do is hold out until the *Mirage* is ready, and in the meantime, we'll just have to go along with whatever they want so they don't start to suspect that we're up to something and lock us up. They *need* at least one of us to open things, and they won't be very happy if they find out we're planning to run out on them."

Ronn then explained about the Jeffbots coming to life or at least beginning to think independently.

"I kind of sensed something like that with the Jeff I was paired with at the fair," Bonnie said, "but I wasn't all that far along myself and couldn't figure out what was going on. I wish it could have gone a little farther before he was taken away so we could have talked about this instead of just saying the same things and doing the same things all the time. But you mean that's where my *me* is? Inside some purple fuzz in my head?"

"Something like that," Ronn replied. "But what have the rest of us got? A headful of jelly? You'll probably last a lot longer than we do."

"Somehow that doesn't make me feel better…"

"So that explains why all those Jeffbots were missing in places where they ought to be," Theo summed up. "And the dead one on the floor in his house. I like playing games but I don't think they're worth getting killed over, especially those old ones with really crude graphics—"

He was interrupted by the appearance of Wilfred in the doorway. "I don't wish to impose," he announced, "but dinner will be served on the veranda in ten minutes. Please dress accordingly."

"Aw, I just changed into *these* clothes!" Theo complained, but there was no appeal.

They stepped out on the veranda as the sun was setting in the west behind them. The sky in the east was darkening and the first stars were coming out. As usual, a bored-sounding orchestra played bland dinner music in the background, but Theo set the volume to a barely audible minimum.

Just as Ronn, Theo, and Phaedra sat down at the table, which had already been set and their carbonated beverages of choice poured, Danny emerged from the house and joined them. He wore a bathrobe and slippers, and looked pale and shaky.

Bonnie followed him, bringing two chairs from the dining room. Danny still wasn't sure what to make of her, but sat down on the chair she offered and scooted up to the table. Bonnie sat down in turn at an empty place.

Wilfred came out, but surprisingly did not indignantly demand that Danny go change into something more formal. Perhaps he realized that the boy was not well. Instead, he silently set a plate, silverware, and a glass on the table in front of him, then withdrew. If Wilfred ever wondered why Bonnie never required table service or even ate, he didn't say anything about it.

"How're you feeling?" Phaedra asked.

"I think I'll live," Danny replied, not sounding entirely convinced.

"How'd you get sick?" Theo wondered. "Did you catch a cold?"

Danny started to shake his head, then thought better of it. "I *wish*. It's kind of a long story." He gestured to Bonnie. "Who's she, anyway? Can I talk about things with her around?"

"It's another long story," Ronn said, "but Bonnie's on our side and you can go right ahead."

Danny then launched into his story. "So there I was, walking to school

178

and minding my own business, when this big black car pulls up beside me and two men jump out. They grab me and spray something in my face, and that's the last thing I remember until I woke up on some airplane flying out of the country. Aunt Vanessa was there, but when I tried to ask her some questions, she told me I'd find out what I needed to know when I needed to know it. In other words, shut up until I'm spoken to. So I don't know a whole lot. They didn't say much when I was around."

Wilfred came out to serve the salads. Danny looked at his without much interest, but was able to nibble on at least a leaf or two. He left off the dressing.

"They could have kidnapped any of us to get what they wanted," Phaedra said, spooning ranch dressing from a bowl onto her salad. "Why do you think they picked you in particular?"

Danny managed a shrug. "Maybe I was easiest, since I live just up the coast from L.A. Also, Mom knew Vanessa slightly, did some free-lance design work for her a few years ago, I think. So Vanessa knew my family better than she knew either of yours and had a better idea of where to find me. The reason they grabbed me, of course, was so I could open doors inside the crater for them. When we got here, Vanessa sent me through the checkpoint first and the rest were supposed to follow."

"You might get in," Ronn said, "but wouldn't the system identify the others as unauthorized?"

"Sure," Danny replied, "but they had that worked out. They had cloaking devices, something they wore over their bodies like parkas that made them invisible to the ID system."

"Why didn't our guys have something like that instead of sending us in by ourselves?" Phaedra asked.

Theo answered in the exasperatedly superior tone only a techie little brother could work up in explaining the obvious to his dim big sister. "Our guys didn't spend months planning the operation and they didn't have any inside knowledge on how the security system worked, that's why."

Danny went on. "They couldn't open the door, but I could, and I was supposed to hold it for them long enough so they could get through. I thought about going on through the doorway and then making a run for it, but where could I go? So I had to do what they said. Partway through, though, something went wrong. I think one of the men didn't realize that his cloaking device had slipped and didn't completely cover him, and the ID system noticed. All of a sudden, alarms went off and there were all these electrical fireworks. The men still in the corridor got zapped, I got caught at the edges, some bot guards showed up and started shooting what I think were tranquilizer darts... It was a mess. When it was all over, the lights were off, I wasn't in any too good a shape because I got zapped, too, they'd shot all those bot guards, but with bullets instead of darts and Vanessa was mad because the bots might have been worth something…"

"So you aren't sick?" Ronn asked. "You were, er… zapped?"

Danny nodded, then looked as though even that slight motion had come a little close to making him nauseous again. "Right. It's like being shocked. Affects your nervous system some way. I'm coming out of it now, but the other guys who got hit straight on were pretty bad off the last I saw of them."

"So that's why Vanessa had me instead of you opening doors for her," Ronn said. "You were out of action, so she yanked me into working for her as the next best thing."

"Well, that and the fact that the ID system doesn't recognize me now. All my permissions have been canceled. It was a little late since all those unauthorized people got in, but the system must have decided I was a fake or at least being used by the bad guys. That meant I wasn't any good to Vanessa and the others anymore, so they let me go, or at least turned me over to you. I guess they'd rather let you feed me."

"Did they say anything about where Uncle Jeff is?" Phaedra asked.

"Nope, not a word. I got the idea he might be a prisoner, too, and thought maybe they'd put me in with him, but I never saw him. When I asked about him, they wouldn't tell me."

He was interrupted by Wilfred rolling a cart with the main course up to the table. Danny took one look at the creamy beef stroganoff and turned even paler than he already had been.

"I think I'd better head back to bed…" he muttered and got up from the table. "See you later…"

Ronn stood on the balcony outside his room, looking out over what little he could see of the crater at night. He had been about to go to bed, but some stray thought started bothering him. The stars glittered as usual overhead, and a few scattered lights could be seen in the distance beyond the silhouettes of the nearby trees. Even though he couldn't see very much, the view seemed to suggest something to him, perhaps something important, but he couldn't put his finger on just what.

He heard someone behind him and glanced back. It was Bonnie, coming out of his room.

"Your door was open," she said as she stepped to his side at the railing, "so I came in."

"Something on your mind?" he asked.

"Yeah. I hated it when you went off like that all day with that woman. You're the only friend I have here. That girl doesn't like me and I think the boy just wants to take me apart."

"It's only a couple more days yet," he assured her, "so try to hang on. Then we can get out of here and it will all seem like just a dream."

"A really awful dream," she said. "Whatever happens on Earth, it'll have to be better than being an exhibit in a theme park. What *do* you plan on doing with me, anyway?"

"To be honest," Ronn said, "I hadn't really thought about it. Living long enough to *get* back to Earth is about as far as I've looked ahead."

Her voice turned almost shy. "If you don't mind having a new sister... maybe I could come home with you? I don't eat much. Or at all, actually."

"I'd have to run it by Mom and Dad first, but I don't see why not."

"Well, we can talk about it later," Bonnie said quickly, as though the subject was a bit sensitive and she didn't want to push it. "If nothing else, maybe I can get a job as a crash dummy." She started to turn away. "I'd better let you get some sleep. You look beat."

"It *has* been a long day," Ronn admitted.

On a sudden impulse, Bonnie turned back and hugged him briefly. "Thanks for getting me out of that place."

She went on into the house, leaving Ronn to wonder if they were ever going to get out of *this* place...

Chapter Fifteen

Tuesday, April 28

When Ronn opened his eyes and saw daylight filtering through the curtains, he had no problem remembering where he was.

Are we still here? What day is this, anyway? And how many days have we been here?

Not that many, he realized to his surprise. They had reached the guest house Friday afternoon, and it was now Tuesday morning. As he looked back, though, the days were running into each other. He was starting to feel as though they had been there forever and his life on Earth was a fading dream.

"I regret to inform you that our stock of Pepsi-Cola is beginning to show signs of depletion," Wilfred announced at breakfast.

This was discouraging news, especially for Theo, who preferred Pepsi to orange juice for breakfast and would have put it on his cereal instead of milk if he had thought of it.

"We have been anticipating an augmentation of our supplies," Wilfred added, "but the latest scheduled delivery has been unaccountably delayed."

The butler left and Theo groaned. "Well, that's just great. Why couldn't Uncle Jeff have stocked up on at least that?"

"He wasn't expecting a guest like you who would drink every last drop of it he had," Phaedra said.

"Well, you and Ronn helped drink it, too."

"It isn't just the Pepsi," Ronn said. "If something goes wrong and we're marooned here for a while, they might start running out of other things. We could be down to peanut butter and jelly sandwiches for dinner by next week."

"You're such an optimist," Phaedra grumbled. "By next week I want to be back home trying to forget this whole thing ever happened."

They hadn't much more than finished breakfast when Vanessa came riding up in a jeep out front.

Another day shot...

As Vanessa led Ronn into the office corridor of the Ivory Castle, Justin approached them. "Excuse me, ma'am," he said tentatively, projecting a schematic diagram from his wristcom, "but we're having a little problem with this..."

"Wait here," Vanessa said to Ronn, and went a few steps down the corridor with Justin to discuss the matter. "Can't you figure it out on your own? Let me look at it..."

Standing there at loose ends, Ronn noticed that a door further along the hall was ajar, and a light was on inside. Curious, he took a look.

Although the windowless little room was mostly empty without any decorations or even pictures on the walls, at first he thought it was Uncle Jeff's office. Jefferson C. Prescott himself was sitting at a horseshoe-shaped desk that was also a control panel, and several projected vidscreens floated in the air in front of him.

Is that really him? I thought he was hurt! Ronn started forward. "Uncle Jeff—?" he blurted. Then he stopped. Something didn't seem right.

Uncle Jeff glanced up, as though just now realizing someone had come in. He would have been past fifty now but looked thirtyish. He could afford the best in body enhancement, of course. There was a strong Prescott family look in his lean face and somewhat sharp nose, and Ronn had a strange feeling this was what he might look like himself in a couple of decades. If he decided to grow a mustache, anyway.

Uncle Jeff smiled, seemingly glad to see Ronn, switched off the displays, and stood up from the desk. He was close to six feet tall and still fairly slim, his clothes business casual.

"Welcome to Vesper," he said with an expansive gesture. "No doubt you've seen enough of it to wonder how it came to be, and what it may become in the future." He stepped out from behind the desk and a stylized map of the park suddenly appeared next to him. Pointing to it, he continued. "What began as a grateful friend's extravagant gift and became an overstressed executive's hobby now has the potential to be an enormous benefit for all of humanity in the years to come. My alien friends have now moved on in their exploration of the Galaxy, but with this one small asteroid they have left us what could be a giant leap for human progress. "

He's giving a speech, it struck Ronn, then he saw a slight hint of tell-tale color interference at the far edge of Uncle Jeff's suitcoat. *He doesn't know it's me. It's a recording.*

"Here on Vesper," Uncle Jeff went on, pacing the floor in front of the desk and pointing to displays as they came and went, "we have something special we've never enjoyed on Earth. That is, the advantage of size. There is enough room here to hold all the ideas and plans we can possibly imagine.

"Vesper will be a testbed for experimental concepts combining the best of state of the art human ingenuity and introduced alien technology. It will never be finished because the road to the future will never end.

"Take replicators, for instance. They have come a long way since the first 3-D printers. And they are only the beginning. I have seen huge alien facilities that employ not just carbon composite but metals, ceramics, even exotics, as well as any other desired material in any mixture or combination.

"Using programmed or remote-controlled construction machinery, an entire city could be built on Mars from local resources before anyone ever lands there, ready to move into whenever someone does. Nor is the replicator principle limited by original size. Once scanned, an object may be duplicated at any size you like. A theme park could be built on the Moon featuring a city in which people would be the relative size of ants, reliving the experience of that old film classic, *Mr. Bug Goes to Town*.

"A thoroughly ridiculous idea, you say?" He chuckled. "Well, I'll admit that a replica of the Empire State Building on that scale would be over thirty miles high, which might be a bit much even in the low gravity of the Moon. Perhaps it is a ridiculous idea, but it is merely one of many, and in space, energy and resources are immense, limited only by our imaginations.

"But the greatest role Vesper may have to play is one even I hadn't realized at first. The potential is there for encouraging the economic development of space travel. Just as trolley car companies once put parks at the ends of their lines to give their customers a place to go, Vesper may someday serve as a resort and vacation destination in space. The Moon is still a long way away and it will be a long time before it can be developed, but Vesper is already here with all its facilities in place and functioning. In the near future, I will reach out to potential business associates who might be interested in establishing hotels and restaurants here, and from this modest beginning—"

Vanessa poked her head through the doorway. "Oh, there you are. We don't have time for this! Come with me."

She all but dragged Ronn away, leaving the Jeff projection to go on expounding to an empty room.

"What was all that about, anyway?" Ronn wondered.

"Just the canned introductory lecture for first-timers to Vesper and prospective business partners, not that we ever got that far," Vanessa said. "Nothing to concern yourself with."

"Where to now?" he asked, resigned to more drudgery.

"You wanted to see your uncle? Well, you're going to see him."

From her tone, it was an unpleasant duty she wanted to get over with as quickly as possible so she could move on to what she really wanted to do. Ronn could only wonder what shape Uncle Jeff was in. She had almost made it sound as though he was stuffed and mounted, and looking at him was all Ronn *could* do.

Vanessa took him to a suite on the southeast corner. Finally, after days of looking for it in all the wrong places, Ronn had a chance to see the place where Uncle Jeff actually lived. But—

"It's just an apartment!" he exclaimed in surprise as they came into a sparsely furnished living room. Even if Uncle Jeff lived here, he apparently didn't spend much time in his private quarters, and hadn't bothered about decorating beyond some work-related charts and diagrams posted haphazardly on the walls. "I was expecting a big house."

"You'd expect that if you didn't know him," Vanessa said with a shrug that hinted she and Uncle Jeff might have had some differences of opinion about their respective lifestyles when they were trying to live together. "He was never much for luxury, always wanted to live right next to his work. Which, when I knew him, was more his hobbies than anything really productive. He did have some plans for a house on Vesper when he had the park more or less complete, but it wasn't a priority."

She led him on through the mostly barren apartment, down a short hallway, and to a back bedroom.

The room was dimly lit. Most of the illumination came from glowing red read-outs on the medical monitoring systems at both ends of a large coffin-like case on a table, connected to several tubes leading to various pieces of equipment of uncertain purpose. Ronn stepped up to it, feeling the air grow colder as he approached.

A human figure lay inside, under a transparent top covered with condensation. Ronn wiped off the chilly surface at the head end with his forearm to see better. Uncle Jeff was immersed in greenish chopped ice, with only his deathly white face exposed. His eyes were closed, his mouth was half-open, and his cheeks were sunken, as though whatever was wrong with him had eaten him out from within. Ronn felt horrified thinking of the healthy and vigorous Uncle Jeff he had just seen in the 3-D vid.

"He isn't *dead*, is he?" Ronn asked, glancing back at Vanessa.

"Not exactly," she replied almost too casually. "He's packed in respirafoam slush. It's an alien life-support system that somehow gets around the usual problems of freezing somebody. It should keep him going until we can get him back to Earth to proper treatment. All right, now you've seen him, so let's get to work."

Without giving Ronn a chance to take a closer look, she hustled him out of the room, and he still wasn't entirely sure that it really had been his uncle. The scene had *looked* real enough, but in a world of lifelike bots, it was hard to tell.

The rest of the day was a bewildering tour of Vesper's interior. As Vanessa explained it, no comprehensive maps had been found, and much was unexplored and unknown. Only the uppermost levels had been touched, and the lower levels went down for miles.

"Vesper's like a honeycomb," she warned, "so stick with me or you might get lost and starve to death wandering around."

She was probably completely correct. If she wanted to talk him out of any idea of trying to make an escape by suddenly running off, she hadn't needed to try so hard.

On the level just below the surface, they passed rooms of mysterious control panels and banks of unfathomable machinery while mercenaries rolled carts filled with boxes of who knew what along the corridors. One pair of mercenaries was tearing into a wall with a crowbar without any thought of the damage they were causing. Ronn found himself thinking it would serve them right if they accidentally bit into a live nine-billion volt power cable.

It hurt to watch. Whatever his uncle had been trying to build here, Vanessa and the others were wrecking it without a second thought.

Two more mercenaries were clumsily manhandling a large mass of mysterious but delicate-looking mechanisms packed in an open cabinet, and looked as though they were about to spill the looser parts on the ground. Vanessa stopped to lecture them about being more careful in their handling of possibly valuable loot, and they listened with distinctly sullen expressions.

Ronn noticed one of the other mercenaries taking a break. The merc had apparently been assigned to stack some crates with a forklift, but at the moment he was sitting on one of the boxes and lighting a cigarette. That in itself caught Ronn's attention. Cigarettes were a thing of the past in North America. He didn't know anyone who smoked and saw people smoking only very rarely. Watching the merc puff on his cigarette and blow a cloud of smoke was strangely fascinating, like seeing something utterly obsolete in an old movie, say, somebody slicing bread or dialing a telephone.

Ronn wasn't the only one watching him. Almost from out of nowhere,

Enzo suddenly appeared behind the merc, and without a word the brawny and brutish subcommander kicked him so hard that he went over forward and sprawled on the flooring. As the merc slowly and painfully collected himself and tried to get up again, Enzo stood over him and bellowed at him in a mix of angry French and bad, mostly obscene English. A considerably cleaned-up translation might have run along the lines of, "Get back to work, you lazy bum, or you'll get a lot worse than that!"

The mercenary did get back to work, not happily, but seemingly accepting his bruises as the price he had to pay for getting caught gold-bricking and all part of the game. There wasn't the open defiance the mercs gave Vanessa in similar circumstances. Now Ronn understood why Rafale had Enzo as his second in command. Somebody had to enforce discipline in that gang of thugs without losing their respect or loyalty.

Consulting projected diagrams on her pad as she went, Vanessa then led him through an endless series of barren white metal-walled corridors. Finally, after going down a narrow stairwell with spiraling steps that seemed proportioned for beings with somewhat longer legs than humanly usual, they came out in yet another corridor, this one dimly lit as though never adjusted for human eyes, with just a single door at the far end and yet another glowing red plastic plate in the wall next to it.

"This is something else we saw referenced in some of Jeff's notes," Vanessa said. "There seemed to be something special here, but it wasn't clear what. We think it might be an elevator shaft leading further down. There's nothing like finding out for sure, so go to it."

Repressing a sigh, Ronn put his hand to the plate. The door opened with a hiss of escaping air that had been bottled up inside.

He had to jump back as a massive tangle of branches burst out through the doorway, even before the door had completely opened. They were as thick as his arm and intertwined, and studded with slim thorns the size of screwdrivers as well as large leaves resembling dark green water bags. The branches were flexible, some combination of woody and rubbery, and surged into the corridor as though they had been pushing against the door with ever increasing pressure from behind and were now suddenly released.

With a scream, Vanessa turned and ran headlong down the corridor. Ronn was close behind while the billowing branches with their lethal-looking spikes wasted no time starting to follow. He all but leaped into the stairwell after Vanessa and slammed the door shut before any of the branches could spill in.

"What was that?" Ronn choked.

"Some alien plant, what else?" Vanessa exclaimed between gasps for breath. "Jeff must have marked the door as a warning *not* to open it!"

187

"I thought the aliens cleared all their own stuff out before they gave this place to Uncle Jeff?"

Vanessa gave him a sour *don't blame me* look. "That's what he said, but obviously they didn't get everything." She turned thoughtful and dictated a note on her pad. "I'll have to remember this door. Scientists have been anxious for years to get samples of alien life to study. I could have several universities trying to outbid each other for a few leaves and branches from that thing..."

Perhaps, Ronn thought, there had been something like atriums with live plants down below, duplicating natural settings on the aliens' own planet for the sake of decoration or a touch of home, and no one had thought to clean them out when the base was abandoned since the entire asteroid was originally intended to be destroyed. Then the plants might have grown wildly on their own without the constant pruning they probably required, fed by a continual supply of nutrients that had not been shut off, either.

Whatever the explanation and despite the prospect of an unanticipated source of possible financial gain, Vanessa had reached the end of her endurance. "I think that's enough for today," she said and wearily started back up the metal spiral stairway on the long climb to the upper levels.

Ronn followed. *I was thinking that two hours ago...*

The simulated sun was well down in the arbitrary west and shadows were long when Ronn was dropped off back at the house. While it was time for dinner, he was almost too tired to want to eat at the table. For a moment he considered going straight up to his room for a nap and having Wilfred bring him something later, but decided the others needed to hear about what he had seen and done during the day.

He told his story while everyone sat around the table and listened to him as they ate. The shock was unanimous when he told them about Uncle Jeff's current state. Bonnie, who had actually known him, was particularly upset despite the fact that this was Jeff thirty-five years later, and if she could have cried, she would have.

"What they going to do with him?" Phaedra asked, sounding stunned. "They aren't going to kill him, are they?"

"I'm sure they would have already done it if that was their idea," Ronn replied, "and it did look like they were at least *trying* to keep him alive."

"If that was him and not a bot," Theo muttered.

"All I can say is that he *looked* real enough," Ronn said, "but Vanessa didn't let me get very close. She did say they were going to take him back to Earth with them, so maybe they plan to hold him for ransom. Any other ideas?"

None were forthcoming.

After dinner, everyone scattered. Ronn headed to his room early for some needed sleep while Bonnie and Danny disappeared into their own rooms. Phaedra went into the den to practice dance moves in 80% gravity and Theo was at large somewhere.

Just as Ronn started to unbutton his shirt, an urgent male voice resounded out of nowhere:

"Emergency! Emergency! Life-threatening event in the swimming pool area!"

Theo! Ronn was out in the hall in a second or two, but Bonnie was already ahead of him, and Danny followed as fast as he could.

The pool area was deserted. If Theo wasn't anywhere around above the water, there was only one place he could possibly be. They looked down in the greenishly shimmering water, but it was hard to see anything clearly with the reflections from the bright overhead lights.

Bonnie went around towards the deep end, peering intently into the water as though she could see more than human eyes ever could. "Down there!" she suddenly exclaimed.

Ronn and Phaedra rushed over. At the bottom of the pool's murky water was a dark-colored ball large enough to contain a Theo-sized human being. A bare human leg and foot protruded from it and kicked vigorously, but the leg was tangled in a net and the ball couldn't float to the surface.

"What's that?" Phaedra managed to ask despite her fright.

"I think I know," Ronn said. "It must be like one of those inflatable bubbles Captain Rogowski told us about on the shuttle. Theo's inside and he can probably breathe okay."

Leave it to Theo to be nearly killed by a lifesaving device...

"But we can't leave him down there!" Phaedra exclaimed. "How do we—?"

Without saying a word, Bonnie suddenly turned and jumped into the pool, not even bothering to take any of her clothes off. If there were any lingering doubts about whether she was waterproof, she didn't let them slow her down. She swam to the bottom, then spent several minutes working on the netting to get Theo free. Since she didn't need to breathe, she could stay underwater indefinitely.

Finally, she got the cocoon loose and it drifted upwards. As it bobbed on the surface, resembling a giant walnut but lumpy and darkly translucent green, she helped Ronn and Phaedra haul it out of the water to the pool deck. The extended leg went on kicking, so Theo was still alive inside.

The next problem was how to get him out of the shell of hardened foam. Then Ronn remembered the tools hanging above the workbench in the garage beneath the guest house. Leaving the others to stand around the oversized cocoon, Ronn ran back to the house. A couple of minutes later, he returned to the pool with a small saw and a hammer and chisel, and started hacking into the cocoon. It took some work but he was finally able to cut through the hard crust and tear away enough of the softer foam underneath to pull the kid out.

Theo wheezed and choked, but seemed none the worse for the experience. Although he was smeared all over with green slime, Phaedra immediately hugged him in tearful relief.

He spat out a stream of frothy greenish fluid over her shoulder, then gasped, "Thank God for respirafoam!"

"Respira— wha'?" Phaedra wondered as she pulled away from him.

Theo wiped more bubbly green glop from his mouth with the back of his hand. "That stuff Captain Rogowski told us about. Some sort of oxygenated foam that hardens on the outside but lets you breathe on the inside. Same stuff Ronn told us Uncle Jeff's packed in."

"Good thing it worked," Phaedra said, then looked at Theo sternly and her tone turned from relief to scolding. "Just what did you *do*, anyway?"

Theo suddenly looked sheepish through the green stains on his face. "I just wanted to see how the automatic lifeguard worked, "so I jumped in the water and pretended to be drowning. It worked great at first. A net shot out and wrapped me up, but then something went wrong and I got tangled up in it and I couldn't get back to the surface. I thought I was going to drown until the respirafoam bubble kicked in, and all of a sudden I was inside a ball of the stuff and I could breathe just fine. I couldn't get the net untangled, though, and I'd still be down there if Bonnie hadn't gotten me loose."

"You little *idiot*..." Phaedra murmured in exasperation.

Then she turned and seemed to notice Bonnie for the first time. After a moment's hesitation, she managed a smile and hugged her, still wet though Bonnie was. Bonnie looked startled, as though she hadn't expected anything like this, then smiled and hugged back

The uncanny valley now had a bridge across it.

How much of a bridge, Ronn realized later when he went past Phaedra's room on the way to his. The door was slightly open and Ronn heard Phaedra saying something about "Aunt Jessie," his mother. That made him pause.

Then Bonnie called for him to come on in and join the party. Surprised that she had heard him standing out on the hall, he put off going to bed for a moment or two to see what his mother had to do with anything.

He sat backwards on a straightback chair that had been borrowed from the room's desk/vanity, while Phaedra and Bonnie lounged on the bed. Bonnie could have stood ramrod straight for hours in the middle of the room without tiring, but it wouldn't have seemed natural.

Through the accompanying giggling, Ronn gathered that Phaedra had invited Bonnie to her room for some girl talk. She had probably been feeling lonely as the only girl in the crew and needed someone like Bonnie just to talk to more than she realized. Now that Bonnie had proven her worth as something more than an unusually chatty bot and they were officially friends, the ice was broken. At the moment, they were comparing notes about life way back when and life right about now. In particular, Phaedra had been telling Bonnie about tattoos and how everybody had them for a while. Tattoos had gone mainstream several years after her memories stopped, and Bonnie was astonished that even middle-class high-school girls would go for something so, well, disreputable. She was familiar with body piercing from her own era, and had noticed that her new body had not duplicated the pierced ears of her old one, but *tattoos*?

Where Ronn's mother came into this… It seemed that all three of the sisters had been rather extensively tattooed in their time, but Jessie and Thalia had gone to considerable trouble and expense years later when the fancies of fashion changed yet again to have the tats removed.

"Aunt Emily didn't bother," Phaedra added. "She still has hers. Comes with being an artist, I guess. Body art, free spirit…"

"It does kind of date her," Ronn said.

"If it dates her, what about *me*?" Bonnie asked. "You're calling something old-fashioned that's after my time! Where's my rocking chair?"

By this time, Ronn was more interested in where his bed was. He told the girls good night, then left to go on to his room, deciding he needed sleep more than to listen to more juicy family gossip. He was just amazed that his own mother had once had tattoos. You could live with someone for fifteen years and still not know her as well as you thought you did…

Chapter Sixteen

Vanessa showed up even before breakfast was over, wanting to get started early on another day of opening things. Ronn just barely managed to grab a piece of toast to eat on the way out.

The first part of the morning was taken up with more doors in odd places, and as usual none led anywhere interesting. Ronn had a feeling that Vanessa was running out of doors and these were the last few. He began to hope that she wouldn't be needing his services much longer.

Towards noon, she gave up and drove back to the Ivory Castle. Once inside, she took Ronn straight to the southeast corner and several floors up.

"Where are we going?" he asked, a little out of breath as he tried to keep up with his ex-aunt striding down a corridor.

"Jeff's office, the real one," she answered with her usual impatience. "I want to check through it again. I may have missed something the first time and there's something I want you to try opening."

They came to an unmarked door at the end of the corridor. It opened at Vanessa's touch and she led Ronn inside. In contrast to the simulated office with Uncle Jeff's introductory vid, this one looked as though it was actually used by physically existing people.

On its better days, it might have been a pleasant place to spend some time, conduct business, confer with associates, and read reports, but this wasn't one of those days. The waist-high bookshelves had been pulled away from the walls, books and character merchandise and toys knocked to the floor, one of the visitors' chairs overturned, drawers pulled out of a wall cabinet, and papers scattered everywhere. A gray plush MacNabbit the Rabbit doll about three feet tall lay in a heap in a corner, grumpily muttering "Dagnab it!" in a low voice over and over again. Ronn could hardly blame him for feeling that way, though it was just an ordinary audio recording that had gotten stuck in continuous replay and not an autonomous behavior system. Somebody had been looking for something, but from what Vanessa had said, whatever it was hadn't been found yet.

Looking at the office as a whole, it seemed modest for the headquarters of a business empire. It wasn't any larger than the living room in Ronn's house, and the furniture was mainly the visitors' chairs, a couch, a small table, and the massive antique wooden desk towards the rear. The tall-backed chair behind the desk looked well padded, probably capable of instantly reshaping its configuration for maximum comfort as the occupant moved. Looming over the desk and chair were large windows looking out over misty forested scenery and the crater cliffs to the southeast. The desk stood on a low, raised circular platform that Uncle Jeff could likely turn to face out the window when the mood struck him.

The desk had probably been stacked high with paper documents not long before. Despite all the electronics and data displays, paper was one thing that stubbornly refused to go away, as Ronn had often heard his parents complain. Now sheets of paper littered the carpet around the desk. Among them were the jagged pieces of a plastic model someone had stepped on, evidently a desk display of a *Galactattack* fighter like the full-sized one Ronn had seen the other day.

On the walls were static pictures and virtual displays. One wall was dominated by a huge, somewhat impressionistic 2-D painting showing an early conception of the park as it would be when it was completed, while a smaller vid display to one side showed a real-time view of the park as it was now and seen from high overhead, apparently from a camera just under the center of the dome.

Pride of place on the other side wall had been given to a large old-fashioned oil painting in a gilt frame, a portrait of Jefferson C. Prescott himself at about age forty. Wearing a conservative dark suit and even a tie, he sat in a chair and looked out at the world with a solemn and dignified expression. That seemed normal enough, except that standing next to him was a depiction of an alien with a face something like an oversized whooping crane with huge inky black eyes. The being wore an iridescently multicolored robe made of quill-like feathers, perhaps the aliens' equivalent of formal wear, and was undoubtedly Uncle Jeff's friend and benefactor, Skhyylar.

Vanessa headed directly towards the desk, kicking some papers out of her way with the toe of her boot as she went. *"Damn them!"* she exclaimed angrily. "The idiots just tore the place apart. They could have missed all the important stuff being so stupid and sloppy!"

Ronn was about to take a closer look at the painting when Vanessa called him over to the desk.

She pointed to a bottom drawer on one side. "Try your luck on this. It's the only drawer we haven't been able to open." She pulled on the handle to demonstrate, and the drawer remained where it was as though welded to the desk. "It doesn't have an ID plate on it and at first we thought it was just locked, but there doesn't seem to be a visible lock on it. Maybe Jeff has it rigged somehow with some hidden ID sensor. We didn't want to force it in case there's a self-destruct mechanism, so I thought I'd have you give it a shot before we did anything else."

Ronn put his hand on the handle and pulled. The drawer came out easily enough. King Arthur couldn't have pulled Excalibur out of the rock more smoothly.

Vanessa exhaled exasperatedly and bent down to examine the drawer's contents. Just old-fashioned file folders, it seemed. She yanked one out and glanced through the loose papers in it.

"Old financial reports?" she exclaimed in seeming disbelief. "That's *all*?"

The drawer seemed to hold only confidential but routine company business for Uncle Jeff's various enterprises, related to things he would have to attend to even while he was on Vesper, but Vanessa started tearing through the folders to see if there was anything else that might point the way to what she was really after.

Meanwhile, Ronn went back to the painting of Uncle Jeff and Skhyylar, and noticed a gold-colored plate with small lettering on it at the bottom of the frame. He had to put his face close to it to read it.

OUR FOUNDERS

Perhaps he put his face a little *too* close to the painting.

From out of nowhere, a female voice announced:

"Identified: Ronn Evans."

Ronn jumped back, startled.

Vanessa looked up from the desk. "It's *live*?" she blurted, surprised as well and dropping the file folder she had been flipping through. She came around the desk and all but ran over to Ronn, slipping and sliding on the loose papers on the floor.

"Live?" Ronn echoed.

"A live system," Vanessa replied absently, scrutinizing the painting. "We already examined it, and thought it was just a static wall decoration... but if it recognized you at a distance..."

She pondered for a moment, then grabbed Ronn's wrist.

"Hey—" he started to protest but she ignored him and pulled his hand towards the painting, touching the tip of his index finger to the text plate.

"Identified: Ronn Evans," said the voice again, and the frame holding the painting started to swing out from the wall on invisible hinges along the left edge.

Ronn and Vanessa stepped back to give the frame clearance. As it opened, it revealed a blank wall with a red plastic plate in the center. With a closer look, the faint outline of a square around the plate could be seen as well.

"It's a wall safe!" Vanessa exclaimed in something like triumph. "Hidden behind a painting! It's the oldest cliché in the book, the most obvious place imaginable for a wall safe, the first place anybody would look, and nobody thought of it until now *because* it's such a cliché! This has *got* to be where Jeff put it!" She laughed delightedly, even a little crazily, probably relieved that she was finally on the trail of something she might be able to take home and sell for a billion or two.

"Put what?" Ronn asked.

"Never mind, just see if you can open it." Vanessa grabbed his wrist again and made him put his hand on the red plate. It glowed red under his palm.

"Identified: Ronn Evans," the voice said.

Instead of the safe opening immediately, nothing happened for a few moments.

"Come on, come on!" Vanessa exclaimed.

Then the female voice said, "Please state the password."

Password? Ronn glanced back at Vanessa.

She clearly hadn't expected this result, either. "Three-level security? A *password*? How old tech can you get? Did your uncle ever say anything to you about a password, like when they took your biometrics?"

Ronn shook his head. "They took my biometrics when I was about five. My uncle didn't say a thing to me then or ever. I didn't even know he *was* my uncle until a few days ago!"

"Please state the password," repeated the voice.

Starting to throw her hands up helplessly, Vanessa stopped in mid-motion, as though suddenly remembering something. She touched her fingertips to her forehead and closed her eyes.

"He said something once when we were first married and exchanging our vital information in case something happened to either of us. Everything went to bio-ID, so hardly anybody bothers with passwords now, but there might be a few things I'd have to get into that he still used passwords for, just for extra security. When he did use passwords, he usually opted for something personal that only he was likely to know, like something from his childhood — an old family pet's name, I think he said. What was it? Oh!"

She brightened and opened her eyes. Clearing her throat, she faced the portrait and pronounced a word as plainly as she could. *"Taffy!"* She stepped back and waited expectantly for something to happen.

When nothing happened, Vanessa nudged Ronn urgently. *"You* say it. It'll probably only respond to you anyway."

Just to get this over with, Ronn went along, feeling faintly ridiculous. "Taffy."

Instead of a door opening, the light in the red plastic plate under Ronn's hand went dark and the voice said, "Connection timed out. Access denied." With that, the frame swung back on its hinges and closed again.

Vanessa looked decidedly unhappy. "That wasn't it either, and I can't think of anything else the least bit likely. We'll have to try some other way to open this thing. I'll get the engineers on it and see if we can figure something out. That'll take until at least tomorrow..."

"Where did 'Taffy' come from?" Ronn asked.

"Don't you know your own family?" Vanessa demanded. "That was the name of his family's cat when he was a boy."

You expect me to know the name of his cat forty years ago? Ronn thought, remembering the cat he had seen on the bed in the recreation of Jeff's room.

Even with the failure of the password, Vanessa had made some progress. They now knew where some sort of vault for keeping valuables was hidden. Now they just had to figure out a way to open it.

Until that was done, there wasn't any more use for Ronn, so he was dismissed for the day even though it was barely noon. Since all of the mercenaries were too busy to drive him back to the house, Vanessa somewhat grudgingly did the honors herself.

Nobody was in the living room when he came in. Ronn took a look out back and saw the others were sitting around the swimming pool occupied with reading or, in Theo's case, playing a handheld game. Rather than bother them just yet, he ordered a cheeseburger and fries from Wilfred, then went up to his room to think things through over a quick lunch.

He remembered that something had nagged at the edges of his consciousness a couple of nights before when he stood on the balcony looking out over the crater. Some key piece of the puzzle was missing but somehow it didn't seem out of reach, if he could just think of it. He went out on the balcony again to see if he could recapture the thought while he finished off his cheeseburger.

Looking past the near treetops to the fogged distance beyond in the light of day, even knowing that out there was a whole world, vast in some terms, tiny in others, he didn't feel any wiser. Had Uncle Jeff ever stood here contemplating his domain like, say, his old neighbor standing at the controls of his model railroad and looking out over that little world?

It was a nice image, but not likely since there wasn't any sign that Uncle Jeff had ever stayed in the guest house. Which, now that Ronn thought about it, seemed odd. Why would the chauffeur in the old car deliver Uncle Jeff here if he was going to stay at the Ivory Castle over in the center? Besides, the old neighbor had stood with his eyes well above the level of his model train layout, looking down from a height. He hadn't been in with it...

Something clicked in Ronn's mind. If Uncle Jeff was brought here first thing, instead of to the Castle, but obviously didn't *stay* here... There must be something important in the immediate area, maybe the control center. Following the example of the train layout, it wouldn't be on the same level as the layout itself, but someplace where Uncle Jeff would have an elevated view.

Directly overhead, suspended from the center of the dome? Possible, Ronn thought, remembering the overhead view of the crater he had seen in Uncle Jeff's office, but a straight-down view would be too strange and unnatural. He'd want something like the old neighbor's model railroad, just a little above ground level, but from the side, looking out across the landscape...

Ronn whirled and raced through his room, into the hall, down the stairs, through the house, and out the front door. He didn't stop to take the porch steps one at a time, and hit the grass running. At the edge of the front lawn, down the slope and where the surrounding trees started, he came to a sliding stop. He turned and looked back, up past the house, toward the crater wall towering overhead in the background.

Judging by the way the simulated sky seemed to continue past the top of the cliff some hundred or more feet high, there was a ledge up there, probably a flat rim surrounding the crater, and the edge of the dome was set further back. Though it was hard to tell for sure in the hazy bright blue, there also seemed to be something *above* the cliff overlooking the guest house. It was masked by some visual field blending in with the surrounding sky but still faintly perceivable from below, more as a sense of something with some mass projecting over the edge of the cliff than anything directly visible.

That has to be it!

He went back into the house and to the elevator, taking it down to the entrance level and the Westgate Inn lobby. Outside the simulated hotel was the simulated English country road. He walked past the inn to the place where the car that had picked them up the first day had been seen to turn and disappear.

It was like passing through a curtain. Suddenly the open landscape was gone and he found himself at an intersection of dimly lit, white metal corridors. The ones to the south in front of him and to the east on his left ran straight until they were lost in the distance. The corridor on his right extended a short distance to the west, far enough that Ronn judged it went past the house above and under the crater rim. It ended in a blank wall with a door in it that resembled the elevator doors Ronn was all too familiar with from his tours of the crater with Vanessa.

Along the side wall stood the old car. The chauffeur sat unmoving at the steering wheel. He had seemed so friendly and helpful the other day, so convincingly alive that everyone had assumed at first that he was a real human being, and to see him like this was a shock. Ronn found himself all but tiptoeing past, hoping he wouldn't bother the driver by activating him unnecessarily. The chauffeur continued to stare blankly straight ahead, waiting for a call that might not come for days, weeks, months, or ever.

A scooter was parked by the elevator door. That and the fact that Ronn had to wait for the elevator to come down meant somebody was up on top just then. Who it might be, Ronn could only guess, but he'd have to be careful if it was someone who didn't want him snooping around in places where he shouldn't be.

The elevator took Ronn up several levels, higher than that of the guest house. When it stopped, the door opened and he looked around cautiously before stepping out.

The elevator door was flush with the rear dome wall. In front of it, the crater rim was a flat, rocky shelf about a hundred feet wide, extending along the base of the dome as far in either direction as far as Ronn could see and presumably completely around the crater. No human beings were in sight.

At the rear of the shelf was the smooth metal surface of the dome itself, supported by massive arching girders spaced at intervals. Beyond the level of projected backgrounds, there had been no attempt to pretty up the backstage of the theater, and swathes of thick cables were in open view along the girders. A projected blue sky with puffy clouds could still be seen overhead, extending almost to the base of the dome, but close up, the illusion was lost in the gridwork.

Looking out on the crater stretching out before him in a vast circle, it was hard to make much sense of the confusing mass of details in the center. Much of the view was obscured by masses of artificial haze, but Ronn could see a spaghetti tangle of roadways running through a dense forest past numerous clearings with structures too far away to identify. Even the Ivory Castle was lost in the fog, and if the Empire State Building and the Statue of Liberty were actually there as shown in the workroom model, they were out of sight as well.

Ronn's real interest was in what was right in front of him. A small, one-story building with long windows on the sides was perched on the edge of the crater rim, probably directly above the guest house. On its flat roof was an array of antennae like spider webs of different sizes. It not only looked like a control center, it was precisely where Ronn had guessed a control center had to be. He approached it with a growing feeling that he was finally on the right track.

A door in the back wall seemed like an invitation. It opened readily and he stepped into a small kitchen and utility room. A quick glance around showed him a refrigerator, a counter with a hotplate and a microwave, a sink, a cupboard, and a small table in the center with a couple of chairs. It looked like a break room for someone who just about lived here.

He also saw a backpack on the floor, leaning against one of the chairs, and on the table a small toolbox, several scattered tools, and the remains of a meal ration box. As he had expected since seeing the scooter down below by the elevator door, somebody else was here. Just one person, it looked like, and one of the engineers to judge by the tools.

An open doorway led straight ahead through to the front of the building. Through another open door to the side, Ronn saw a small bedroom with attached bathroom facilities, like a very basic hotel room. Someone was in there, snoring rather loudly.

Feeling it was safe to take a look, Ronn went into the bedroom. He wasn't surprised to see Justin Hobart sprawled on top of the bed. The chubby little technician looked contented as he lay there asleep.

Vanessa would have a fit.

Ronn turned to go, hoping to have a look through the rest of the control center and be gone by the time Justin woke up. No such luck. Justin heard him moving and subconsciously realized that someone else was in the room.

Justin shot upright. "I was just on my break!" he exclaimed in near-terror, still not fully awake. "I'll get right back to—" His blinking eyes cleared and he realized who it was. "Oh, er, hi, Ronn," he said nervously. "Is, uh, Vanessa with you?"

"No, it's just me," Ronn assured him.

Justin rolled out of bed and stood up. "Just don't tell her I was taking a nap, okay?" Suddenly realizing he may have said a little too much, he pulled a small black disc off his belt, held it up for a moment, then looked at a read-out on its face. "Good, nobody's listening to us. I was worried for a second. Spytech doesn't work on the crater floor, just wasn't sure about it up here."

"Don't worry," Ronn said. "I'm probably not supposed to be here, either, so it's not like I'm going to say anything."

199

Justin looked considerably relieved.

"And where *is* here, anyway?" Ronn added. "This is Uncle Jeff's control center, isn't it?"

"You haven't been up front?"

"No, I just now came in through the back door."

"Well, let me show you around the place. What's left of it, anyway."

He led Ronn out of the bedroom, through the break room, and down a short hallway. They came out in a large room—

What happened here?

The front end of the building that faced the crater bulged with an enormous transparent hemispherical extension hanging over the rim. Uncle Jeff would have sat in the chair at the end of the swiveling crane arm, in the middle of the half-bubble, with virtual displays and control panels all around him, but everything was wrecked. Not only torn apart as though in an explosion, there were charred and blackened places where there had been a fire, and here and there patches of hardened extinguisher foam. If this was the master control center, no wonder things were breaking down.

To Ronn's relief, he didn't see any burned or mangled bodies. *So maybe that really was him in the freezer back at the Castle…*

"If there's a perfect place for your uncle to have his control center," Justin said, "this is it, where he's got a bird's-eye view of the whole works. From up here, he could sit in his chair in front of an instrument and display projection panel, and control everything that happened down below. Most of the gear is alien tech. Put that helmet on his head, and he could extend his consciousness all through Vesper and control the construction equipment. It was the ultimate model railroad, and he was putting the finishing touches on it himself. "

"I've been wondering how he could build all this 60,000 miles from Earth," Ronn said, "and not only get the pieces here but assemble them while keeping it a secret without having to bring in hundreds of construction workers."

"Well, he did have some people here working on design and layout," Justin replied. "You've probably seen the workroom back at the Castle. But most of the Park's buildings and infrastructure were installed by the aliens beforehand, based on the designs Prescott gave them. So the hard part of the work was already done when he got it, and he could concentrate on the details. There *is* an area that seems to have been torn out, though, and rebuilding work begun though it's nowhere near being finished. I suspect the aliens got something wrong when they tried to follow Prescott's plans, misinterpreted something, and he's had to go in and start over. I'd be curious to see what exactly they messed up."

"But what happened up here?" Ronn asked. "Why is it wrecked?"

"Somebody realized that when Prescott was in that thing playing with his toys, he was awfully vulnerable. Pull the plug, and he can't get back to his body. Cut some cables, and he can't control anything in Vesper anymore."

"It looks more like somebody set off a bomb in here."

"They might as well have. Lowther's plan was to catch Prescott off-guard and preoccupied, and just knock him out for a while he and Vanessa looted the place clean and made their getaway. They wanted Prescott out of the way, not dead or as close to it as you can get without a coroner ruling it over the line. Prescott would come to afterwards, alive and healthy but much the poorer. It looks to me like Lowther had no idea what he was doing when he thought he was turning the system off, and he managed to blow it up instead. He was lucky he didn't kill Prescott outright, but it might have been kinder if he had."

"Then he *is* still alive? They showed him to me and at least he didn't *seem* to be a bot."

"That was him, all right. His *body* might be alive, but... How do I put this... He mostly isn't *in* it right now. Remember that his brain is where his long-term memories and all the mental support systems are. I'd guess what's hanging out in space and cut off from his body is some kind of raw consciousness without much memory of who he is. He's trapped somewhere in the system, just so many data packets zipping through the circuitry with no place to go, unable to see, hear, or do anything."

"Can they put him back?"

Justin shook his head. "I wish *I* could. It would serve that bunch down there right to have Prescott back in control again. Once he realized what they had done to him and what they were doing to his pride and joy, it'd be pure Wrath of God from on high. But I think they did too good a job of disconnecting him and he's beyond hope of ever being put right. Maybe the aliens could do it, but I certainly can't. His body is still alive but only just, and his mind is probably too far gone."

"These guys really do play for keeps..."

"It's more like they're in over their heads," Justin said. "Lowther and Vanessa just wanted to make one big play that would set them up for life, not make a career of crime. They didn't plan for things to turn out the way they did, but one thing led to another and now they're stuck in a criminal enterprise they don't really have the stomach for. After all, they did put Prescott in that tank instead of doing away with him entirely. And with him incapacitated and the controls smashed, a lot of things are going wrong — the diagnostics and self-repair systems are breaking down and he isn't there to correct them. The effects are cumulative, and in a sense Vesper is dying. But the real reason for Vanessa and Lowther's panic is that they have to load their ships with enough loot to make their foreign backers happy."

"Foreign backers... like Rafale and his crew?"

"That bunch is just here to make sure Vanessa and Lowther don't try to pull a fast one or ruin everything with some dumb mistake. That's something else our amateur pirates didn't count on. They needed foreign backing to have a place to settle down and enjoy their ill-gotten gains when this is all over, not to mention somebody to fence the loot, so to speak. Then it turned out their foreign friends wanted to make sure they'd live up to their agreements, and now they've got a troop of armed mercenaries who could turn on them at a word from their commander instead of the team of engineers and laborers they wanted. It's tense, I can tell you." Justin paused, then added sadly, "I just wish I'd known in advance what I was letting myself in for. Well, now that you've seen the worst, I guess I should fill you in on the rest of what's been going on."

They sat at the little table in the break room and Justin explained things. He seemed almost happy to have someone he could finally open up to after days of Lowther and Vanessa nagging him for results he couldn't deliver.

Ronn remembered what he had been sent to Vesper to look for in the first place. "Is this the master control center for the whole asteroid?"

"Oh, heavens, no," Justin said. "That's back at the Castle, a couple of levels down. I guess they haven't let you see it yet. Up here, it's just operation and construction of what we call 'the Park,' or what's in the crater on top of Vesper. This was probably Prescott's favorite place, since he spent most of his time here."

Bedroom, kitchen... I can see that. No wonder he was never at the guest house.

"The Park's really only a very small part of the asteroid," Justin went on. "We think it may have originally been some sort of recreation area for the aliens when this was a fleet base, maybe a simulation of their home planet's natural environment. Whatever it was, it had all been cleared out when Prescott got the asteroid."

"I saw some sort of welcome vid where he talked about making Vesper a place for tourists to go, to help develop space travel."

"That'll be years down the road... if ever. I'm not sure how much will be left after this."

Ronn shook his head. "What a wonderful place... and my ex-aunt and her buddies are wrecking it out of pure greed..."

"Not that they're going to get much out of it."

"What do you mean?"

"I mean this expedition has been a total bust so far. Oh, they've found a few gadgets that might be worth a little back on Earth as alien curiosities that can't be duplicated, but they haven't found anything big enough to justify the risks and what their backers have spent."

"I know they're having problems," Ronn said. "That's obvious just listening to them, but what's hanging them up? Why *isn't* Vesper the gold mine they thought it was?"

"What Vanessa and Lowther don't get because they don't have a tech background," Justin replied, "is that your uncle has *already* marketed all of the alien gadgets that can be readily copied at Earth's level of technology. As for things like starship engines, forget it. The aliens must have manufacturing facilities the size of small planets using the energy supplies of small stars to make things with exotic forms of matter we don't even understand theoretically, let alone will be able to make ourselves any time in the next thousand years. And here come Vanessa and Lowther with degrees in marketing, who think they can make a pile robbing the dairy without having to understand anything about cows. They thought Prescott was just holding back a lot of really wonderful products they could market, and let the engineers worry about the trivial details like how to mass-produce them. When you come down to it, your uncle's briefcase is their last hope for making anything off their little venture."

"His briefcase?"

Justin looked out the window for a long moment while he thought, then shook his head. "I really shouldn't say anything... but you'll probably find out anyway since they're having you open doors looking for it. Just don't let them know I told you." He paused again, still reluctant.

"I won't breathe a word," Ronn promised, almost a little too eagerly.

Even with that assurance, Justin was hesitant. "It's like this," he finally said. "Your uncle was known to have kept some notebooks, files, and memchips in a briefcase. They're his diary and a lot of notes and memoirs about his experiences with the aliens. Private stuff he never revealed to anyone. Vanessa knows about it because she was married to him and saw him when he was dictating some of it. It's his 'If anything happens to me, please open this' file, his legacy to Earth, though he evidently hadn't gotten around to arranging for some way for it to be found yet. He probably didn't expect something to happen to him so soon. The briefcase supposedly has things in it that will keep scientists busy for the next century. That is, really advanced tech secrets, and I mean the goodies like faster than light travel and artificial gravity. Even if we can't duplicate such wonders for centuries to come, just knowing the theoretical basis for them would be a tremendous advance for science. Not to mention astronomy from the standpoint of a civilization that actually travels to other stars instead of just looks at them. We don't know *anything* about the aliens or their civilization, and this might tell us what's going on out there in the rest of the Galaxy. What kind of life is there on other planets is the least of it. For instance, Prescott said Vesper was a decommissioned base for the aliens' space navy. That tells you something right there. A navy means defense. Who or what were they defending against? Is this something we ought to know about? What else did Prescott never bother to tell us? If Vanessa's right about what's in that briefcase, they could auction it off to universities and scientific institutions back on Earth to the highest bidder and at least get something for their trouble even if they can't make a buck off anything else they find here. But that would be chickenfeed compared to what else they're looking for."

"There's more?"

"The rumor is that there *is* something in the briefcase that alone would make the whole trip worthwhile. Vanessa isn't sure about it, but based on something Prescott said while they were married, it might be the specs for a way to defend an entire country against multiple electromagnetic pulse attacks, much more effective and comprehensive than anything used in the EMP War, and feasible with current technology. So you can see that a lot of countries would be interested and willing to pay significant fractions of their GNP to get their hands on it."

"Why hasn't Uncle Jeff marketed it already?" The EMP War had been before Ronn's memories started, but he had heard his parents and other adults tell stories of a couple of bad years in even the relatively less hard hit United States. A lot of computer and electronic-based systems no longer worked and parts of the country had been thrown back into the 19th Century for long periods until repairs and replacements could be made and electricity restored. He could understand very well why no one wanted to go through anything like that again. "It sounds like a good thing."

"Apparently it has offensive capability as well," Justin told him. "Right now, a country with this set-up could dictate terms to the rest of the world while sitting pretty behind the shield. Ten or fifteen years from now, Earth's arms tech might have advanced on its own to the point of surpassing the offensive potential in the alien specs and the defensive part could stand by itself without disrupting the international order, but not today."

Ronn had a sudden thought. Supposedly the power grid and other essential systems had been hardened so the economic disruption that followed the EMP War wouldn't happen again, and most people in the US would probably get through a second attack without too much trouble. But they were flesh and blood. What would a sudden massive voltage surge do to Bonnie's internal electronics?

It would kill her!

If Vanessa got her hands on that briefcase and turned its secrets over to her backers, Bonnie might be the only direct fatality in a second EMP War.

"But that's just rumor," Justin went on, looking off into space and not noticing Ronn's appalled expression. "We don't *know* if there's anything like that in the briefcase. Lowther and Vanessa are gambling that there is, and it's their only chance of making their scheme pay off. The problem, of course, is that no one knows where Prescott hid the briefcase."

I do! Ronn suddenly realized. *And so does Vanessa.* Except that his suspicion was that it was in the wall safe even he couldn't open, and Vanessa and her crew would probably be able to open it without him one way or another. He could only hope that the rumor of something militarily gamechanging in the briefcase was just so much vapor.

"They're tearing everything apart down there looking for it," Justin went on, "but they haven't found it yet. It certainly isn't up here."

"What I don't understand is why Vanessa and Lowther cooked up this scheme," Ronn said. "They're businesspeople, not criminals. Weren't they already making more money at TranStella than they could ever spend? Why take the risk of going to prison or even getting killed?"

"Of course they were well-paid. Probably a lot more than they were worth, but that's one of the perks of being executive level. It's just that Lowther and Vanessa saw even bigger possibilities by grabbing the still unexploited alien tech. People like them are never satisfied and they thought they could make not just millions but billions, even buy whole countries if they wanted. But they outsmarted themselves. You'd think business schools would teach the golden goose story on the first day. Vanessa certainly isn't going to get her island at this rate."

"Her island?"

"Oh, something she said. I even have a recording of it. When I saw how things were, I decided I'd better protect myself. So I started recording conversations that might interest a prosecutor. I wasn't supposed to do it and they had spytech that was supposed to detect if I did, but don't try to put something past an engineer. Let me see…"

Justin touched his wristcom, and jiggled through some menus and security walls, then a dark and somewhat unfocused image of Vanessa flared up. From her surroundings, it looked as though it had been recorded in a casual conference room setting with drinks being passed around, and she was just lubricated enough to open up to her associates.

"You want to hear my strategic vision?" she was saying. With her sales background, she was good at dramatic recitations. "Well, I'll tell you my strategic vision. In a few months, I'll be lounging on a terrace under the shade of a big umbrella and enjoying a tall, cool drink served by a handsome young waiter. In front of me will be waving palm trees, a sandy beach, and the ocean, almost blindingly blue in the bright sunlight. Behind me will be the most fabulous luxury resort hotel in the world.

"I will own that hotel.

"Around me will be an island, the most fabulous tropical paradise in the world.

"I will own that island.

"And what I'm doing now will make that possible. The bottom line is that all of you in this room can have a seat at the table when it's the end of the day and time to cut the cake, so if you're in, on board and on my team, you can have your own island or whatever it is *you* want. Our strategized synergy can move the ball down the field and score optimal added value before any other teams even show up!"

"Who were the people in the background?" Ronn asked as Justin flipped the recording off.

"Several members of TranStella's senior management to start with," Justin said. "Not all by any means, but three or four anyway, and Lowther for one. The others were just tempted by the prospect of billions, but he was frustrated because he could never advance to CEO while Prescott had that job, and he decided to cash out as best he could. I suspect there had been some resentment ever since he did those kidvid shows that made it look like he was the genius responsible for TranStella's success. Prescott was too detached from day-to-day operations at first to notice for a while, but the rumor is that the last straw was when he came across a vidcomic starring MacNabbit the Rabbit and called *Cal Lowther's Comics & Stories*. Definitely the wrong character to mess with — Prescott hit the ceiling and told Lowther in no uncertain terms to cease taking undeserved credit forthwith. I think Lowther came out of the trip to the woodshed feeling humiliated and wanting to get back at him. For her part, Vanessa had been married to Prescott and wanted more than just what her prenup and severance gave her. With what she knew from her time with Prescott, she had the keys to the magic kingdom, so joining Lowther made a coup possible. Then a few other top executives back on Earth were talked into taking part in the scheme with the promise of billions, which would turn anybody's head. And all that's why we're here today."

Justin stretched and yawned. "Guess I'd better get back to work. Not that I can really do much. I'm supposed to figure out what can be salvaged up here and if anything is worth ripping out and taking back to Earth, but it all looks pretty hopeless. Still, I have to be able to explain the problems when they ask..."

That sounded to Ronn like a strong hint that he really should be on his way, and he had probably already found out everything he could. He stood up and thanked Justin for his time, promising not to say anything to anybody about what he had been told (with a mental reservation regarding his cousins) or otherwise get him into trouble, and went back to the guest house.

Chapter Seventeen

At the house, Ronn called a meeting. When everyone had gathered in the den, he told them what Justin had said about Uncle Jeff's current state of being.

While the others were trying to absorb the shock, Ronn went on to tell them about the rest of what he had done that day, including what he had learned about the briefcase. He didn't mince words about the possibility of a second EMP war and what it might mean for Bonnie.

"I still want to go to Earth," she said firmly. "Stay here with just robots to talk to? No way. I'll take the risk of getting fried."

"And I thought Mr. Cosgrove was just trying to scare us when he said there might be war if we didn't succeed in our mission," Phaedra added somberly.

"I'm not sure what our mission even is anymore," Ronn said, "other than getting the heck out of here and back to Earth alive. I'm just about positive the briefcase has to be in the safe in Uncle Jeff's office, and if I could get it, I'd grab it and take it with us. I certainly don't want *them* to get their hands on it. Unfortunately, I can't get it because I don't know the password, so that's out."

"Gigglepuss," said Bonnie.

It was so sudden and out of left field that everyone turned and stared at her

"Er... say what?" Phaedra asked.

"Gigglepuss," Bonnie repeated. "That's probably the password."

"What makes you think that?" Ronn wondered.

"If it's something important to Jeff like a childhood pet," Bonnie said, "well, that was the name of his cat."

"But Vanessa said the family cat's name was Taffy," Ronn pointed out.

"That was the *official* name," Bonnie agreed, "but you know Jeff. He always had to put his spin on things and be funny. 'Gigglepuss' was what *he* called the cat. Vanessa probably never cared enough about Jeff to find out really cutesie and personal things like that about him."

"You know his boyhood cat's *nickname*?" Phaedra demanded.

Bonnie shrugged. "Hey, we talked. Remember, it wasn't all that long ago for me. He loved that cat. He was a little lonely, I think, and wasn't that good with people, but the cat was his friend."

"And there was a cat on the bed in his boyhood room," Theo said.

"So what do we do now?" Phaedra asked.

Ronn thought. What *he* had to do was only too obvious. "If we can be sure that's probably the password, then I have to go back to the Castle tonight and open the safe myself before they do."

"By yourself?" Phaedra asked worriedly.

"I'm going with you!" Bonnie exclaimed.

"Me too!" Theo and Danny chorused.

Ronn shook his head. "No, I have to do this on my own. I can move faster and hide better than if somebody was with me. The ID systems recognize me as one of the heirs, so I can probably go anywhere I want without setting off alarms, but an out-of-place bot might register somewhere. I especially don't want Vanessa finding out about you, either, Bonnie. A bot like you could be worth millions on Earth. Besides, even if I do get caught, they need me too much to be all that rough on me."

"Or so you *hope*," Theo said grimly. "They could just shoot you and have *me* opening doors."

"I don't plan on getting caught," Ronn told him, "so it won't be a problem."

He wished he was as confident as he tried to sound.

Dinner was another subdued affair. With any luck, it was their last night on Vesper, and a lot was riding on the success of Ronn's after-dark mission later. Bonnie was sitting in with the others as well, although she didn't have a plate or silverware.

"You know," Phaedra suddenly said, twirling her fork absently in the mashed potatoes and gravy on her plate, "I might actually miss this place a little."

That sentiment certainly caught Ronn by surprise. "Why? You've been wanting to go back to Earth ever since we got here."

"Oh, I don't know..." she replied. "Other than for having to worry about what our wicked step-aunt and her bunch are up to, it got to be kind of nice lying around the house with nothing I have to do and nowhere I have to go."

"She means she's away from Mom up here," Theo said.

"Theo! I didn't say that!"

"It's true, isn't it? Mom's got you overbooked all the time. Me, she mostly ignores no matter how good my grades are, because things like science don't count for her, but you're her favorite because you're acting and singing and modeling and doing all the things *she* never could."

Phaedra looked as though she wanted to reach across the table and throttle Theo with both hands. "Most of the time I wish she ignored me and concentrated on *you* for a while! Do you think it's *fun* having a stage mother pushing you to do those things all the time and hardly ever letting you have some time just for yourself? Breaking news, brother dear — I don't really care all that much about performing! I can do it, I can even be good at it, but do you know what I really want to do? I want to do what *Mom* does!"

"Doesn't she already have that job?"

"No, you drib — I mean I want to do what she does at the agency! Discover new talent, help it along, get people parts, find people for parts... That's the job I want, not memorizing lines and rehearsing and doing take after take!"

A pause followed with Phaedra and Theo staring daggers at each other, while Ronn and Danny went on eating as though they hadn't heard a word of an apparently long-standing family contention they would have preferred the antagonists to take outside.

"If you need a stuntgirl, let me know!" Bonnie suddenly spoke up. "I can take a licking and keep on ticking!"

That actually worked to distract Phaedra and Theo from their spat.

"Oooh-kayyy," Phaedra said slowly, trying interpret the forgotten ad slogan from long before even Bonnie's time, when mechanical time displays still ticked. "It makes some kind of sense even if it sounds a little weird. Most really dangerous stuntwork is animated now, but maybe I can talk to Mom—"

Theo interrupted. "You'd better do some tests first and see how heavy-duty you really are before you try jumping out of burning buildings and stuff. Bots might be more fragile on the inside with all their electronics than you think, and you won't heal up from damage on your own the way living bodies do. Now, if you let me have a look at you and maybe help me with my science fair project next term—"

"I don't think so," Bonnie said coolly.

Taking along a flashlight he had found in the basement workshop as well as a holstered Stinger that he hoped he wouldn't have to use, Ronn rode one of the scooters back to the Ivory Castle after dark.

After crossing the bridge, he hid the scooter in some bushes. He had planned to go around the brightly lit hotel entrance and avoid the eternal Hollywood party, keeping to the shadows as much as he could and slipping into the Castle from a side door. As he approached, however, he realized something was wrong, or at least different. The limousines were no longer pulling up in front, the doormen were gone, and there was no beautiful blonde starlet with her white dress being poofed up by a jet of air from a grating in the sidewalk.

Puzzled, Ronn decided he could risk taking a closer look, and went up to the doors. The lobby inside was still brightly lit, but it was deserted. No bots were in sight anywhere. The mercenaries had cleared them all out, leaving only a few overturned chairs.

A little depressed, Ronn headed for the shadows at the side of the building — and heard a raspy snarling in the darkness.

Suddenly, a black shape lurched out of the dark, stopping just a few feet in front of him. It was a huge dog, a St. Bernard with a red pack emblazoned with a white cross strapped to its back. Even in the dim light, Ronn recognized it as Monty, the ski rescue team's mascot on *Snow Patrol*. He had seen the dog at the party the other night — but it was now neither lovable nor lazy like the one on the show.

The dogbot was damaged. Ronn could see that somebody had shot it, whether in self-defense if the dog had resisted being removed from the premises with the rest of the bots or just out of casual vandalism. One eye was gone with some of the surrounding skull torn away, and a dim red light gleamed somewhere inside, while wires dangled from a torn, gaping wound in its chest. A third bullet had ripped into its right hip, exposing the joint of the underlying metal skeleton. Those wounds would have killed a real dog, but a bot was only slowed down, and it staggered a couple of steps towards Ronn, forcing him back. Some real dog behavior had gotten into what should have been a placidly performing replica of a dog, and as a result of the damage, like a real dog in pain and rage, it was attacking anything that moved.

Ronn was something that moved...

The dogbot opened its mouth in an attempt to bark, but all that came out was a cracked wheeze. The vocal synthesizer had taken a hit, too, which was good since no one would hear it inside the Castle. As the dog drove Ronn backwards, it was going into a crouch, as though about to leap at him.

The idea of turning around and trying to run away briefly occurred to Ronn, but even in the lower gravity he still might not be able to outrun a robot dog with three good legs.

I don't have time for this! Ronn thought as he slowly drew his Stinger, trying not to provoke the dog with a too sudden movement.

211

No use — the dog started to rear up, about to lunge at him. Praying his aim was good, Ronn pulled the Stinger's trigger. It fired with a soft *phoot* and the dart flew straight into the dogbot's eye cavity.

A flurry of crackling yellow sparks sprayed out of the wound and Ronn jumped back as the dogbot dropped in mid-leap just in front of him.

Its body jerked, its legs gave way beneath it, and it collapsed into a convulsively writhing furry brown heap on the sidewalk. Then it lay still as the sizzle of melting wiring quickly faded.

It had been just a bot, but Ronn still felt uncomfortable. This had been too much like shooting a badly injured real dog to put it out of its misery. Shaking his head, he took a moment to calm down and catch the breath that he now realized he had been unconsciously holding, then inserted a fresh dart in the Stinger and holstered it. *It was actually good for something after all…*

The sides and rear of the Castle weren't illuminated, and no one was in sight wandering around the grounds. Sixty thousand miles away from any possible enemies who couldn't have entered the crater anyway, why bother posting guards or sentries? Getting inside the building wouldn't be a problem, since there were several outer doors and a couple were in complete darkness. Once he was in, though, he would have to slip past the mercenaries who had taken over the living quarters where the design staff had stayed.

He found a door in the shadows and came into a dimly lit corridor. He heard distant voices elsewhere in the complex, where the dormitory rooms were.

Then he heard approaching voices, about to come around a corner just ahead. He ducked through the nearest door along the corridor wall. The overhead light came on, and he waved it off and shut the door behind him.

It was the room with the Jeffbots, faintly lit from the instrument panels on the banks of test equipment. The bots all stood, hung, and sat there staring blankly at him like so many dummies.

The voices in the corridor stopped just outside the door. "Do they really think they can get one to work?" one of them said in purest American. Rafale's crew did include Americans, and from what Ronn had overheard, even the foreign-origin mercenaries communicated almost entirely in English among themselves, however badly accented.

"It doesn't have to work," came the reply in some odd accent of English. "They just want to extract some information from its brain."

They're coming in here!

Ronn looked wildly around for some place to hide, then spotted a teenage Jeffbot sitting on the floor in a corner.

That's it—!

He dropped down next to the bot, sitting facing away from the door. He might pass as his uncle when he was young if they didn't look too closely.

The door opened and the light activated again. Blinking in the sudden glare, Ronn couldn't turn around to look, but he knew that two mercs had stepped into the room.

"All ages, all sizes, it looks like," said the first. "Which one would she want?"

"A young one, I think. That would be most likely to have the information she needs. Those two in the corner look about right..."

Ronn heard steps coming towards him.

Don't move! Don't move! Don't—

"This one oughtta do..."

He must mean the other one. Please let it be the other one.

A thick, heavy wave of bad breath and stale sweat hit his nostrils. An arm wrapped around his throat and started to drag him upright. Ronn choked back a gag and hoped the merc didn't hear it.

Now what do I do?

"Hey, this thing's heavy!" the first voice complained from just behind him. "Do we really need the whole bot? Can't we just cut its head off and use that?"

This just keeps getting worse... Desperately, Ronn ran through his options. Reveal who he was? Zap the man with his Stinger and give himself away, while the other man sounded the alarm? Keep up the pretense he was a bot but pretend to activate on his own—?

"Too old," said the other. "There's one over here about ten. That should have what she wants."

The merc holding him let him drop and he flopped limply to the floor, trying to hold in his sigh of relief.

The mercs then took a boy-Jeffbot out of the room, perhaps the one missing from the Geography class, and closed the door behind them.

Ronn lay there for a while to let his nerves recover. When he decided that enough time had passed that the mercs would be out of sight, he stood up and slipped out the door back into the now empty corridor.

Their expressions utterly empty, the Jeffbots behind watched him go without blinking.

"Information she needs..." And a young Jeffbot would have it? Ronn guessed it was the password since Vanessa had reasoned that it was something important to Uncle Jeff as a boy. It didn't sound as though she had been having any luck so far in getting information out of the other Jeffbots, so this was probably just a shot in the dark that wouldn't amount to anything. He would have to hurry, though, so he could get out of there before he was caught where he shouldn't be, especially now that he knew what the password likely was and they could squeeze it out of *him*.

He saw lights down at the end of the hallway, where the canteen was, and heard voices from that direction. A meeting of some kind, it sounded like. He probably should have gone well around it, since somebody might spot him if there were people in the area, but he was too curious about what Vanessa & Co. were up to. It might be something he should know about if it affected his chances of making an escape with his cousins the next day.

Hiding in the shadows in the corridor just outside the brightly lit canteen, he could see and hear everything. The leaders of the raiding expedition were in conference. The Commandant had the floor and he was obviously not happy, striding back and forth in front of Vanessa and Lowther, who sat at a table looking like schoolkids being scolded by the principal. Enzo and one of the other mercenaries stood by, impassive and waiting for any orders.

From what was said, Ronn gathered he had come in late and missed the preliminary explanations that might have helped him understand exactly what was going on, but it did sound as though Commandant Rafale was confronting Vanessa and Lowther over their lack of success in finding much that was useful.

"We're working on it!" he heard Lowther protest. "I've got the tech guys trying to extract the info from one of the Prescott bots."

"Maybe those children know something more than they are telling?" Rafale replied with a sneer, and Ronn suddenly felt very cold inside.

"They're just scared kids!" Vanessa exclaimed. "They don't know anything!"

"What about that boy you take around?" Rafale demanded and Ronn felt *really* cold. "He cannot be so stupid that he does not notice things!"

"Hardly," Vanessa replied. "He's actually the dumbest of the three. That's why I'm using him and not the others."

Ouch!

Vanessa went on. "The girl is lippy and too independent, too much like her mother, and her brother is some kind of boy tech genius. They might figure things out and get in the way, so I decided to keep them isolated in the house and get some mileage out of their clueless cousin. He's always asking the stupidest questions, so it's obvious he has no idea what's really going on."

Guess I won't ask her *for a recommendation when I apply for college...*

Rafale looked doubtful. "Whatever you may think, they all must know too much by now in any case. We should have locked them up days ago!

In fact, we should make sure they can never talk when we leave."

"That's crazy!" Lowther choked, and for once Ronn agreed with him. "We'll be in enough trouble with what happened to Prescott if things go bad. I don't want to add outright murder to it!"

"As you wish," Rafale said, more to drop an inconvenient subject for the moment than to indicate that the matter was closed. "I am only offering my professional opinion. But if it comes to ensuring our safety and leaving here with something sufficient to satisfy your backers... all options are open. And we need to finish this enterprise and leave while we still can. So far, however, we have little more than nothing—"

That got them back to what they had been arguing about before, and Ronn decided he had heard enough. If anything was clear, besides what Vanessa really thought of him, it was that he had to finish his own enterprise before the meeting broke up. The fact that the leaders were occupied in the canteen meant no one was likely to walk in on him in Uncle Jeff's office very soon, but he couldn't waste any more time.

He trotted lightly through the corridors, keeping an eye out for stray mercenaries, ran up the stairs, and reached the office moments later.

Opening the door, he waved the light off as he stepped inside, not wanting to attract attention if anyone happened to be outside and noticed a lighted window where nobody was supposed to be.

He froze for a moment when he heard a muttering in the blackness:

"...Dagnab it! Dagnab it! Dagnab it..."

Ronn exhaled in relief. It was the MacNabbit plush toy he had seen earlier, still rather understandably complaining about an irritating world that just wouldn't leave him alone to hoe his carrot patch in peace.

Ronn shut the door behind him and turned on the flashlight. The office looked the same as when he had last seen it.

He stood in front of the portrait of Uncle Jeff and his alien partner. *Here goes, guys*, he thought and touched the tip of his index finger to the text plate.

"Identified: Ronn Evans," the female voice said and the picture frame swung open.

He winced. The voice wasn't even all that loud, but in the silence with hostile forces all around, it had sounded loud enough to him to be heard all over the Castle.

"Please state the password," added the voice.

Ronn took a deep breath and murmured:

"Gigglepuss."

The safe opened. Inside was a small compartment with shelves filled with various odds and ends. Just at a glance Ronn saw a stack of gold bars, a couple of oversized diamonds, some jewelry that may not have originated on Earth and glistening in strange colors, several old books that may have been the rarest of collectors' items... even a sheaf of old letters in envelopes tied with a ribbon. Ronn wondered if the last were love letters from the real Bonnie. They looked about that old, and it'd be a sweet, sentimental touch for the old boy, but he resisted the temptation to take a closer look. There wasn't time and the briefcase was front and center.

Hoping it wouldn't be fried by some laser barrier, Ronn inserted his hand. Red rays played over it, tickling and prickling but not obviously harmful.

"So it's you, Ronn," said his uncle's simulated voice as the light display faded. "Since I have no children of my own, I've sometimes wondered who I'm doing all this for, besides myself. My business associates, my partners and employees, even my wives, never shared my enthusiasm for my work on Vesper. My sisters have lives of their own and would have no interest. So I turned to the next generation, you and your cousins, as both the family I never had and my heirs. If something happened to me and I was unable to complete my work, perhaps one or more of you might pick up from where I left off. Such was my hope, anyway, and I planned to discuss it with you and the others when the project was further along and you were older. In the meantime, I arranged for you and your cousins to have permanent access to Vesper so that you could come inside if the need arose, as a last resort in case others had failed or betrayed me. Although I never had much personal contact with any of you, I've always felt that you were the ones I could trust since you were, after all, family. I'm sorry I'm not here to talk to you in person, but if you've reached this point, something really must have happened to me. Make the best use of what you find here. It's your world now. Good luck."

Realizing that was the last he'd hear from his uncle, Ronn pulled the briefcase out. *Is it going to be as easy as that?* Well, he wasn't home yet...

He closed the safe and the picture frame returned to its shut position. As far as he could tell, there was no sign he had ever been there. Taking the briefcase with him, he slipped out of the office into the corridor, and keeping to the shadows, he made his way out of the Castle. No one popped up unexpectedly to challenge him. He found his scooter and headed back to the house.

The others were waiting for Ronn, relieved to see he had made it without being nabbed. He held up the briefcase in triumph as everyone clapped and gave him high fives, and Bonnie hugged him.

They gathered in the den again and watched as Ronn went through the briefcase. It was stuffed with papers and files that would take too long to read, and they looked hopelessly cryptic anyway with mathematical formulas and technical jargon. The most important item was a small leather wallet that held memory chips with labels like **DIARY** and **OBSERVATIONS**. Unfortunately, there weren't any chip readers in the house. Lots of antiques but not what they really needed, so there was no way to find out if there really was some ultra-high tech plan for defense against electromagnetic pulse attacks. If there was, and if the United States could do something with it… he might have just extended Bonnie's warranty by a few decades. Getting anything out of the chips and papers was a job for experts, however. All they could do was take the briefcase to Earth and let Mr. Cosgrove deliver it where it would do the most good. Keeping it out of Lowther and Vanessa's hands was the main thing.

Ronn also told Bonnie and his cousins about the last message from Uncle Jeff.

"Does that mean *we* get this place?" Theo wondered. "Wow — a moon of our own!"

"Why would you want it?" Phaedra asked in sheer disbelief. "A half-finished theme park way out in space where nobody can get to it?"

Theo shrugged. "Oh, I don't know. I was just thinking, that's all. It beats having a treehouse in the back yard."

Ronn had been doing some thinking of his own. *I could have a lot of fun with a whole theme park to play with… Finish it up if Uncle Jeff can't, maybe add a few of my own ideas…* Then he shook his head. It was 60,000 miles from Earth, and if things were starting to break down… He'd be better off going back home and checking the Net for college course catalogs for something practical like Architecture programs, assuming people could still find jobs in even practical fields by the time he graduated. Unless either of his parents could use an extra hand, he might have to team up with Aunt Emily selling artwork at those weekend craft fairs.

After that, they sat staring at the artificial fireplace. Nobody felt much like doing anything.

"I guess we might as well hit the sack," Ronn finally said. "Big day tomorrow, and we'd better be out of here before the bad guys know we're gone."

Before going to bed, Ronn put the briefcase on the floor by the dresser so he wouldn't forget it in the morning.

Another lurch woke him up during the night, and it wasn't over in an instant. A series of lesser aftershocks followed, only slowly dying away. Despite Vanessa's assurances that the occasional Vesperquakes were nothing to worry to about, and they hadn't seemed strong enough to cause any noticeable damage around the crater, Ronn had his doubts that she had been exactly forthright and honest. As he drifted back to sleep, he mainly felt glad that they would be leaving tomorrow. Of course, if it really was the beginning of the asteroid's plunge to Earth, getting home in time to watch the world be destroyed was hardly an improvement.

Part Four

Diamond Fire

Santa Barbara

Chapter Eighteen

Thursday, April 30

At first, Ronn thought it was part of a dream. Wilfred's muffled voice protesting, "Yes, this is Ronn's room, but you can't just—"

Then, as he started to wake up, he heard the door open, and when somebody grabbed his shoulders and started shaking him, he realized it wasn't a dream at all, but only too real.

"Wake up! We think we've found a way to open the safe!"

Oh no! Ronn thought blearily, realizing that it was Vanessa who had barged into his room. The plan to clear out of the house an hour or so before she usually showed up had just gone down in flames.

"Move it!" Vanessa added without any pretense of politeness, yanking his covers off. She was looking distinctly unkempt and un-Marketing-like by this time after several days in the field far from Earth, not even trying to dress for success with her hair askew, no make-up, and her clothes dingy.

As she waited impatiently out in the hall, Ronn threw his clothes on. This could be for the best, he told himself, since it would keep Vanessa occupied while the others made their escape. Even if it meant days or weeks on his own in the place waiting for help to arrive, it would be fun having time to explore the Park along with lots of books to read and vids to watch.

The amazing thing was that the briefcase was all but in plain sight on the bedroom floor by the dresser, but Vanessa hadn't noticed it. She hadn't been looking for it, of course, and the bed had blocked it from her view while she was in the room.

Something seemed odd about the daylight behind the curtains, as though it wasn't as bright as it usually was, but he didn't have time to investigate further.

When he came out of his room, he saw Phaedra in her robe down the hall, looking frantic. She could do the math as well as he could.

If Vanessa had Ronn open the safe, the briefcase would not be inside. She would realize that if it had ever been there, somebody had gotten to it first, and only one of the cousins could have done it. She hadn't been easy to convince that Ronn didn't know the password, after all. Vanessa and her troopers would be back in an hour or less, ready to tear the guest house apart looking for the briefcase.

"You took long enough," Vanessa complained. "Let's *go!*" As usual, she grabbed Ronn by the wrist and pulled him behind her. Much more of this and he'd go back to Earth with most of the joints in his arm dislocated.

Ronn's eyes met Phaedra's as he passed her but he couldn't tell her what she had to do. Not without Vanessa overhearing, anyway. *I've got to get a message to her — but how?*

As they went past the door to Bonnie's room, he saw that it was open a crack, but she couldn't step outside and let Vanessa see her.

Then he remembered something. The night when they first saw Lowther and Vanessa, Bonnie had shown that she had considerably better hearing than normal for humans. So just maybe...

"Uh... Vanessa? Can you hold on for a second? I think I'd better... well, one for the road, just to be safe."

Vanessa stopped and turned to look at him even more sourly than usual. "Oh, all right — but hurry it up!"

Ronn went back to his room, stepped just inside the doorway and out of sight from the hall, and spoke in a low voice barely above a whisper.

"Bonnie? Can you hear me? Knock on the wall if you can. Lightly, though, so Auntie doesn't catch on."

A moment later, he heard a slight knock down the hall.

Relieved, Ronn went on. "Tell Phaedra to take off without me. I can hold out for a while, but the rest of you have got to get out of here right now. The briefcase is in my room by the dresser — whatever you do, don't forget it! Once you're on Earth, Phaedra can help you get hold of my mother, and you can tell Mom I want her to look out for you. Got all that? Knock if you did."

Another barely audible knock followed.

"Okay, signing off. See you back on Earth!"

I hope. And aren't Mom and Dad in for a surprise when she shows up on their doorstep...

Ronn went into the bathroom, flushed, and ran the sink faucet to make it sound convincing to anyone down the hall.

As he came out of his room again, Vanessa waved for him to follow. "Come *on!*"

Danny and Theo stood in their pajamas by the stairs, their expressions worried. To keep Vanessa from suspecting that the kids were about to run off, Danny managed a hopeful-sounding "See you at dinner, Ronn!"

Vanessa pushed past them, ready to shove them down the stairs if they blocked her directly. "Get out of my way!" she barked, no longer even trying to put up a front of being their kindly aunt with their best interests at heart.

Going down the stairs after her, Ronn half-turned to wave at the now very horrified-looking Phaedra and the others. He wished he could have said goodbye to everybody, but with any luck he'd see them all again sooner or later. If Vanessa didn't shoot him on the spot out of rage when he opened the safe and she saw it was empty, anyway.

Outside, Ronn was startled to see that the sky was overcast, even murky. While the bright blue sky continued to be projected far above, large masses of gray mist drifted just overhead, and he felt an occasional raindrop on his face. He wondered if this was normal — did Uncle Jeff have occasional drizzles scheduled to water the plants and wash off accumulated dust from everything? Or was this an unplanned result of some problem with the ventilation system, since the area under the dome was probably large enough to have its own weather if left to itself? Vanessa was clearly preoccupied and not in a mood to talk as she drove the jeep towards the Castle, so he wouldn't be getting any answers from her, either.

Ronn realized something really was terribly wrong when they came into the courtyard. The *Moonbeamer* still stood tall, towering overhead, while beneath it, half-panicked mercenaries were frantically loading crates and everything else loose they could find on the waiting truck.

"What's going on?" Ronn asked Vanessa as they got out of the jeep.

"Never mind. Just come with me."

She took him inside the building, which was normal enough, but surprised him by leading him to a stairwell that went downwards instead of up to Uncle Jeff's office.

They came into the one place that Ronn had known must exist somewhere but had never seen before: the control room, the command center for the entire asteroid. It wasn't much larger than a classroom at school. Narrow aisles ran between banks of control panels, and the walls were filled with data and vid displays. Multi-colored lights blinked or shone steadily, and images of graphs, meters, and columns of glowing symbols formed and dissolved in mid-air. Suspended in the center of the room was a projected 3-D image of Vesper floating in space, like the one Mr. Cosgrove had shown back at Edwards but even larger.

Lowther and Rafale stood at the central control console, watching intently over the shoulders of the two seated engineers. Justin and Kiefer were desperately manipulating the physical and projected controls, input-ting commands while scanning the data display images flickering in the air in front of them. They didn't look exactly comfortable, as though the proportions of the seats and the countertop were designed for beings with longer than human legs that didn't bend in quite the same places.

"Any luck?" Vanessa asked as she came in.

Kiefer looked up at her hopelessly. "No, we can't override it this time. It won't let us cancel the program or even accept anything we input now. Unless we can think of something, we have—" he glanced at a time display floating near his face— "an hour and forty-seven minutes until Vesper shifts its orbit."

Shifts its orbit? It sounded ominous the way Kiefer said it, but hadn't Vesper already been doing that? Or was it a lot more serious this time, like the head-on collision with Earth that Mr. Cosgrove had talked about? Whatever was meant, it couldn't be good. Maybe Ronn didn't have the option of a few quiet and relaxing days on his own waiting for rescue after all...

"But you were always able to abort the procedure before—" Vanessa began.

Kiefer shook his head. "Just barely and it got harder every time. I think the system learned from experience and now it's smarter than we are."

Vanessa scowled. "Well, I hope you can figure it out fast or we're all going to be stuck here."

"Not all of us," Lowther spoke up. "At least Enzo caught an early flight home."

"What? How?"

Rafale answered with pure contempt dripping from every syllable. "You think you are so clever to chase the Americans out, but you do not follow up when they leave something valuable behind. Just yesterday one of my men discovered an entire shuttle that you overlooked! There are so few spacecraft with such capabilities, it is worth a billion in itself."

"We knew the shuttle was there," Lowther protested. "We just didn't need it. Besides, it would have to be recharged after a couple of flights and only TranStella has the facilities. We didn't think anyone would buy it."

Rafale snorted. "TranStella itself would! What they would pay to have it back! And you would have left it there!"

"I never thought of ransoming a shuttle..." Lowther said weakly.

"You are such fools! It may bring us the most money of anything in this failure of an enterprise, and you didn't realize it! So I sent my loyal associate, who is an expert pilot despite his perhaps rough appearance, to take the shuttle back to Earth. He has most certainly taken off by now, and we had best follow him before much longer."

Ronn had listened in growing horror. It would be a race between Enzo and his cousins to get to the *Mirage* first, and Phaedra and the others might end up marooned on Vesper right along with him. At least he'd have some company... Then he noticed Rafale was looking at him, and not at all fondly.

"I see your wonder boy is with you," Rafale remarked to Vanessa with a sneer. "Why not let him try something?"

"But I don't know anything about—!" Ronn started to protest, then caught Rafale's sudden glare and Vanessa shot him a warning look. At least pretending to be useful might increase his chances of living through this. "All right," he said quickly, "what can I do to help?"

Justin stood up from his seat. "You're one of the heirs, so maybe you can get in where we can't. Sit down and give it a shot."

For the next several minutes, Ronn tried to input what Kiefer and Justin dictated, both orally and manually, but nothing worked. The system just wouldn't accept any new commands, even from him.

"This is useless," Rafale finally said. "All we are doing is wasting time! Let us get the briefcase and go!"

Vanessa pulled Ronn out of the chair. "He's right. Come on. You too, Justin." To Kiefer she added, "Keep working on it as long as you can. Try to think of *something*."

As they raced back up the stairs to the upper level, Ronn asked, "What was that about Vesper shifting its orbit, anyway?"

Vanessa was angry, exasperated, impatient, in a rush, close to panic, but she did answer him between gasps. "There's a last-ditch defense system—

"It's left over from when the aliens used the asteroid as a military base, which is why it's out of our control Too alien, too built-in—

"Vesper has its own propulsion system and it can move under its own power—

"When security is completely compromised, like when intruders like us break all the way in—

"Or like when Jeff had his accident—"

"It triggers an automatic process that will move the asteroid *somewhere else*. That's what those lurches you felt were, the asteroid starting to move—

"Lowther and the engineers were able to stop it before this, before the program could get very far each time it tried, but it kept trying and now it's unstoppable—"

"Where will Vesper go?" Ronn asked as they reached the top of the stairs.

Vanessa started down the corridor at a trot. "We don't know, but it's probably a long way away. Now come on! We don't have much time!"

As he ran behind her, Ronn realized there never had been any danger of Vesper falling to Earth, but this was another can of fancy grade nightcrawlers entirely.

I really can't stay here!

If the asteroid moved somewhere else in the Solar System and out of the TranStella ships' range, he couldn't hope for rescue. Even if he scrounged what was left at the Castle and the docking bay crew quarters after supplies at the guest house ran out, was there enough food stored on Vesper to last him for years? And would the life support systems work for much longer if everything else was breaking down? Or if Vesper was transported to the other side of the Galaxy, would the aliens find him and send him home? Or put him in a zoo instead?

None of the possibilities sounded even close to good. He really would have to depend on Vanessa for a ride home, although he'd have to be a prisoner or a hostage for a while. That meant playing along as best he could. He was starting to feel sorry he had taken the briefcase, since with it everyone would be leaving Vesper in a happier frame of mind than they actually would be in a few minutes.

They had all gathered in Uncle Jeff's office. In the corner, MacNabbit was still muttering "Dagnab it!" Vanessa had used Ronn to make the Uncle Jeff portrait swing out and Justin was examining the safe door with electronic devices. Behind them, Lowther was looking over their shoulders. Rafale stood in the back, glowering.

Whatever Justin was trying to do with his instruments, he had failed to open the safe. The door remained just so much wall.

"Enough of this!" Vanessa burst out. "Let me do it my way!"

"Are you out of your mind?" Lowther demanded. "If you blow up a secured lock, you'll set off every alarm in the place and trigger another lockdown! If that happens, we never will get off this rock in time!"

"Nothing as crude as a bomb," Vanessa said evenly. "We have something better."

As though they had been waiting for their cue, two mercenaries came into the office, carrying one of the adult Jeffbots between them. It depicted Uncle Jeff as he was when he was about forty and wearing a suit and tie, and had been pulled out of some display Ronn hadn't seen yet, perhaps one dramatizing his appearance at the astronomers' conference. Had they already fried the brain of the young Jeffbot he had seen them take away the night before? They laid it on the floor in front of the safe and Justin knelt at its side. He pulled up its shirt and coat, opened its access panel, inserted a couple of cables connected to his laptop, then called up a pro-jected keyboard display and typed a few commands.

The bot stirred, opening its eyes. Its mouth moved with a slight flutter of its lips.

"It's working," Justin said. "We finally figured out a way to override the shutdown and reactivate it. Okay, let's see what it knows…" He typed some more, then addressed the bot. "What is the password for the office safe?"

The bot writhed helplessly. Lights flashed on the display.

"It's fighting me," Justin muttered. "Even so, this is the furthest we've gotten. Every other bot we tried, the brain self-destructed automatically when its security was breached… let me try this bypass…"

The bot jerked. Almost as though it hated doing it but couldn't help itself, it choked out a single slurred word from its voice processor.

"Giggapuuuss."

It suddenly stiffened for a moment, then went limp and lay still on the floor. A smell of burnt-out wiring wafted from somewhere inside its head.

Justin groaned and looked up at Vanessa. "I'm afraid that's all we're going to get out of this one. Should I have your men get us another bot?"

Vanessa ignored him. "Giggapooze?" she repeated. "That doesn't even make any sense!" She thought a moment, then grabbed Ronn by his shoulders and pushed him in front of the safe. "Say it!" she exclaimed.

Knowing better than to try to correct the mispronunciation, since he wasn't supposed to know the password, Ronn merely repeated the slurred word as instructed. "Giggapooze."

Unfortunately… "Identified: Ronn Evans. Password within acceptable parameters. Access authorized."

And the safe door opened.

So much for that…

The interior of the safe loomed darkly. Rafale stepped forward, shoved Ronn away, and pointed a pocket light inside.

As Ronn knew it would be, the safe was empty, at least of any brief-cases.

Slipping back into his native language, Rafale angrily spat the "m" word.

"But it *has* to be here!" Vanessa exclaimed, completely baffled. "Did Jeff move it somewhere else?"

Lowther exhaled in exasperation. "That safe was the last likely place he would have hidden his secrets. Now the files could be anywhere on this rock and it would take years to search it at all thoroughly—"

He broke off as a burly figure staggered into the office.

"*Chef!*" Enzo choked, sickly pale and out of breath. "*Ces putain de mômes... la mallette—*!" The massive lump of muscle was actually shivering and twitching.

Rafale looked at him questioningly and Enzo replied in halting, gagging French. Even without understanding a word, Ronn had a very uneasy feeling that he knew what was meant. Then Enzo leaned against the wall and threw up.

Rafale's face darkened and he muttered some French obscenities. "I *knew* we should have locked away those interfering children!"

"What's wrong?" Lowther demanded.

"Enzo went to the docking bay to fly the *Mirage* home," Rafale replied, his voice cold and deadly. "He encountered the children, who were just then about to take off themselves — with the famous briefcase! He attempted to stop them, but when he was not looking, a girl shot him with a Stinger! He is a big man and could laugh at one such shot, but one of the boys shot him, too. Two shots were too much for him, and the children made their escape!" He gave the miserable looking Enzo a withering, scornful look.

Phaedra and Theo had actually gotten the better of Enzo? Ronn could hardly believe it. For all that Stingers were supposed to be a weapon of last resort that probably still wouldn't do any good, they had proved their worth once again. He was glad that Bonnie and his cousins had managed to get away after all, but he had his own problems now.

Vanessa was ready to spit fire. She whirled and glared at Ronn, looking as though only sheer force of will was stopping her from grabbing his throat in both hands. "*You* did this! I don't know how but you did this!"

Ronn didn't — couldn't — say anything. Enzo's story had made it impossible to play dumb or innocent.

"It is too late for that," Rafale said crisply. "The valise is gone, and this boy is no longer of use to us." He reached for the sidearm in the holster on his belt.

Ronn went cold.

"Wait!" Vanessa held up her hand. "He's one of Jeff's heirs. We can still get a ransom out of him!"

Rafale paused, considering, then took his hand off the pistol butt. "Very well, as you wish."

It was all Ronn could to do to keep from sagging in relief.

Vanessa glanced at Enzo and said something in French. The man-mountain gulped and gathered his remaining strength with a visible effort, then suddenly grabbed Ronn with a painful grip by the arm that almost pulled it out of its socket, and hauled him out into the corridor.

Vanessa came alongside and muttered in Ronn's ear. "I saved your life just now. Don't make me regret it."

Enzo yanked Ronn down the hallway to the nearest door, jerked it open, and shoved him inside. The room was small, with a bed and a desk with a chair, perhaps for naps when Uncle Jeff had long work sessions, but to all appearances never used.

"I'll deal with you later!" Vanessa all but shouted at Ronn from the doorway, the angriest he had ever heard her. "Stay here until I get back. If they see you outside, they'll shoot you on sight and I won't stop them this time!" She slammed the door and Ronn heard her stalking off down the hall.

Although sneaking out wasn't possible, the room wasn't the worst place to be confined, with a soft bed to lie on while his heartbeat dropped back to normal after the sudden prospect Rafale might shoot him. But even if he ended up a hostage they'd hold for ransom, at least he would be going back to Earth.

While he waited for Vanessa to show up again and drag him out of the room, Ronn heard noises outside, running feet up and down the hall, shouts in French and English, some thumps of large objects. Then, muffled and indistinct, some way down the hall, he heard Vanessa's voice.

"But what about the boy?"

Ronn could just barely hear Rafale's cold reply. "Forget him. I would just shoot him if I saw him again. He is useless, not worth the trouble, not even for any ransom. We have better if we act quickly."

We have better what? Well, never mind. Maybe things were looking up after all, not that they thought they were really doing him any favors. He could just wait until they were gone, then he would be free to move. One option immediately occurred to him: the escape pods in the East docking bay. If he could get there in time, he might be able to go home after all. It was certainly worth a try.

Before long, the noises and voices out in the hall all faded out. Maybe everyone really had gone away and left him.

Rubbing his sore arm and shoulder, Ronn stood up and looked out the window that faced the inner courtyard. Some of the mercenaries heaved a last few crates on the now overloaded truck, then climbed on top of them. It looked like the last train out.

Just as the truck started to roll, the two engineers and Kathrin came running out of the building and up to the truck. From Kiefer's panicked rush, it was clear he hadn't been able to stop the countdown and prevent Vesper from shifting to parts unknown. They were desperate to get on board the slowly moving truck, but a couple of mercenaries held them off. It looked bad for the three for a few moments, then somebody relented. An officer yelled something to the driver and the truck stopped. The three were allowed to climb on, then the truck started off again and headed out of the courtyard.

Thinking the coast should be clear by now, Ronn opened the door and looked up and down the now deserted hallway. Everything was quiet. Vanessa, Lowther, Rafale, and Enzo were most likely on their way to the docking bay in one of the jeeps.

Just as he decided it was time to leave the room, he heard a gunshot far away, faint through the intervening walls and with distance, but clear enough in the overall silence.

Maybe I'd better stay put a while longer.

He waited a few more minutes. Without a wristcom, he couldn't tell how much time had passed, but he suspected it hadn't been nearly as much as it had seemed. Finally, more just tired of waiting than entirely certain it was safe, he ventured out into the hall.

Trying to reach the East docking bay two miles away and several levels down in however much time remained would be hopeless on foot, but if he could find a scooter, it ought to be doable. Also, everybody else in the scurvy crew should have had enough of a head start that they would have taken off in the freighter and the second shuttle by the time he got there, though he had to be careful that he didn't accidentally run into them if they had been a little slow. He would still have to figure out how the escape pod worked, but if it was meant for use by untrained personnel in emergencies, it probably wasn't very hard.

He remembered the scooters he had seen in the Castle garage, just off the big workroom, and started down the corridor. For the first time in a while, he was feeling almost cheerful. Earth now seemed closer than ever.

He came out of the office and dormitory block and into the huge, dimly lit workroom with the tables and gigantic model in the center. Most of the tables had been looted of the drafting and design equipment he had seen the other day.

Then, in a pool of light from an overhead spot, Ronn found a body.

It was Lowther, lying crumpled on the floor in a large, redly shimmering puddle of blood.

The shot he heard... There must have been a double-cross. Whether Lowther had fallen out with Vanessa or Rafale, Ronn didn't know, but the little man who had wanted to be a big man had paid the price for his ambition.

Even if Lowther had been a louse, it was a jolt to see him like this. Violent death was something Ronn had never seen in reality before, and it was somebody he had known at least slightly. This was nothing like the sanitary sort of death of fictional characters that was considered exciting entertainment in games and vids...

You can be sick later, he told himself. *You can't help him and you've got to get out of here!*

Somewhere behind him, a male voice like that of a goofy toon character muttered, "Too bad, so sad."

Ronn looked back, but nobody was in sight in the gloom.

"At least it isn't *my* funeral," the voice added.

Now Ronn saw who — or what — was speaking. It was the clown's head he had seen before, still on top of one of the cabinets. The mercs evidently hadn't considered it worth stealing. This wasn't the time to be concerned with technical matters, but Ronn guessed that the head could talk without lungs to provide air because like Bonnie it had some sort of electronic speech synthesizer in its throat.

"Did you see what happened or who did it?" Ronn asked. He was talking to a disembodied clown's head and expecting an intelligent reply, but by this time he was getting used to how things went here.

"Not my circus, not my monkeys," said the clown.

"Just what I need," Ronn muttered. "A crazy clown..."

"I'm not all there because I'm not all here," the clown added not very helpfully.

Sitting there day after day in the dark, with nothing to do and nothing to see, even a robot clown head might go insane. Ronn wouldn't be getting anything useful from it and turned to go.

Lowther stirred and moaned softly. So he *wasn't* dead. Even so, he was in a bad way from a bullet in his chest, and he soon would be dead if he didn't get help.

Ronn paused. Should he help him? *Could* he help him? He didn't have any first-aid training and there was no one on Vesper to call on. He didn't want to just walk on by and leave Lowther there to die, even if it could be argued that the man had it coming, but did he have a choice?

It was a long shot, but... Ronn looked back at the clown head.

"He's still alive! Is there a first-aid kit around here? You've got to help!"

"Laugh and the world laughs with you," mused the clown. "Cry and the world laughs *at* you. Yuk! Yuk!"

I should have known. It looked as though Lowther was finished...

Then, sounding almost serious, the clown said, "Say the magic woid."

"Please?"

"Bingo!" The clown raised its voice: "Is there a doctor in the house?"

Like that will help?

Ronn could only assume that the clown was just being crazy some more... until he heard a beeping behind him.

He turned and saw a cart with flashing blue and red lights approaching from somewhere in the vast workroom's shadowy corners. It resembled a motorized gurney, but on top of it was an open, coffin-like case. Some sensor had picked up the clown's call for help. As Ronn watched, the cart pulled up to Lowther's body, then extended long, supple arms or tentacles. They slipped underneath Lowther, lifted him, and gently placed him inside the tank on top of the cart.

Ronn stepped to the side of the tank and looked inside. Manipulator arms were cleaning Lowther's wound and applying some sort of seal to stop the bleeding. Meanwhile, the tank was filling with a cold and thick, greenish slush that was probably the same semi-frozen form of respira-foam, that Ronn had seen in Uncle Jeff's tank. If Lowther couldn't be nursed back to health by the automatic facilities, at least he'd be preserved until somebody who could do something showed up. Then the tank's lid slid into place and the cart rolled away, taking Lowther somewhere to wait for who knew how long. It was the same fate he had arranged for Uncle Jeff.

With a clear conscience and a muttered thank you to the clown, Ronn trotted towards the door to the garage.

"Come back when you can't stay as long," called the clown after him.

The jeeps were gone but Ronn found a scooter. Once outside, he rode as fast as he could along the road leading to the Eastgate entrance. If anything, the overhanging clouds were thicker than before. On the way, he passed several bots wandering aimlessly, far from the sets where they belonged. A masked member of the Gopher Gang, a lost-looking Squirrel Scout still carrying boxes of cookies, a few civilians from the Salisbury set, a couple of confused clowns from Clown Town… One of the clowns was headless and perhaps the missing body for the head back in the Castle. Something had gone wrong somewhere, and the bots just walked along the road following some path of least resistance, no longer doing what they were supposed to be doing.

At Eastgate, Ronn found the ramp that spiraled down into the Vesperian underground and followed the signs to the level with the corridor that led to the East docking bay. A couple of jeeps and the flatbed truck, now unloaded, stood haphazardly parked at the end of the corridor by the docking bay entrance. He kept an eye open for any mercenaries who might not have left yet, but it looked as though everyone really had cleared out.

The docking bay was cluttered with crates and miscellaneous pieces of machinery strewn at random near the entrance, as though time had run out before the last of the loot could be loaded, and both the freighter and the shuttle were gone.

Ronn approached the escape pods and saw that 01's hatch was open. Cautiously, he looked inside. The pod was partitioned so that up to three people had their own separate if cramped and narrow minicabins, and at the moment the pilot's section was unoccupied, with just a padded seat, dangling shoulder and lap straps, and some rudimentary controls with glowing readouts. Spending a couple of days in such confined quarters would definitely not be fun.

Had someone been about to use the escape pod, only to decide otherwise?

Ronn heard a gasp behind him and turned. It was Vanessa, as surprised to see him as he was her. She was carrying an armload of food packets looted from the docking bay's crew quarters.

Can't I ever get away from her? Going by the look on her face, the feeling was mutual.

"I thought you were going with Rafale in the other shuttle!" Ronn exclaimed.

"I thought I was, too," Vanessa replied, "but there was a change of plan."

She still didn't sound as though she was any too pleased with Ronn, but her outright anger towards him seemed to have faded. Perhaps it was because things had happened since that made him seem less important in the scheme of things, and she was now more inclined to be relatively civil to him.

Vanessa then tossed her armload of food packets into the escape pod, more to get rid of them than to stow them properly. Two of the packets fell short and dropped to the floor. "You know, this could be a bit of luck for both of us."

"I don't see how," Ronn muttered. Recalling that he had missed breakfast, he bent down and picked up food packets Vanessa had dropped, then stood up again. A ham and cheese sandwich and an apple turnover wouldn't be the heartiest of meals but they would have to do for who knew how long.

"Do you want to be home in a few hours," Vanessa said, "or do you want to be crammed into one of these pods for days? There's a better way, believe me. But you don't know about it without me, and I can't use it without you. So it's win-win for both of us. Come on, we're running out of time."

Leaving the escape pod behind them, Vanessa led him to one of the parked jeeps outside the docking bay and they took off down the corridor.

"I saw Mr. Lowther in the workroom," Ronn said between bites of his sandwich as she drove. "Did Rafale double-cross you somehow?"

"Not exactly," Vanessa answered, staring grimly ahead down the barren corridor. "Cal and Rafale got into an argument about whether it was a good idea to go after your cousins in the *Spectre*. Cal thought it would just lead to more problems and complications, and the briefcase wasn't worth the chance there might be something useful in it. Rafale then told him that the briefcase was the only thing our backers really wanted, and we couldn't go home without it. And I've never been 100% positive the briefcase contains what it's supposed to — it's just a suspicion based on something Jefferson once said. Cal and I may have oversold that particular talking point a little when we presented our business plan to our backers...

"Cal held out for heading straight for our base anyway, arguing that we were bringing back enough random alien tech in the freighter to satisfy our backers even without the briefcase, but Rafale then informed Cal that he wasn't running the show. That was the one thing you don't tell Cal. It was something of a sore spot for him. He popped an artery and tried to take a swing at Rafale — and Enzo shot him, like the obedient dog protecting his master that he is.

"Seeing my partner murdered right in front of me made me realize I could be next, and for all I knew, Rafale might have had orders to do away with Cal and me all along so our backers wouldn't have to share any of the proceeds with us. It seemed as though the time had come to dissolve the partnership, and I made a discreet exit in the confusion. By the time I got down here, the freighter had already left, so my options were limited."

"Actually, Enzo didn't murder Mr. Lowther," Ronn said. "He was still barely alive when I found him. Some kind of medical bot picked him up and put him in a freezer case like the one Uncle Jeff is in."

Vanessa looked relieved. A little, anyway. "That's nice to know even if it doesn't change things. Rafale wants that briefcase for his employers, and he's going after your cousins to make them land where he wants them to. Then he'll have both the briefcase and some hostages for bargaining chips if he needs them. Otherwise, he'll shoot them down to make sure *nobody* gets the briefcase. I definitely didn't want to be part of that. I can tell you don't exactly care for me or my methods, but give me credit for at least that much."

"Can he *do* that?" Ronn asked, horrified.

"He can if he catches up with them," Vanessa answered. "The *Mirage* isn't armed, but the *Spectre* is."

"With *what*? I thought Uncle Jeff said the aliens wouldn't give him offensive weapons."

"Oh, it's nothing like photon torpedoes or atomic death rays or whatever you're thinking of, though we did have some hope that he might actually have things like that secretly tucked away on Vesper. We should have known better... Your uncle thought he might have to fight a small-scale space war at one point, but he wanted something mainly for warning shots and not all that lethal. Killing people isn't good for the corporate image, after all. The aliens gave him something along the lines of a short-range plasma cannon. It might not cause a lot of physical damage even with a direct hit but it will mess up the target's electronics, which could be bad enough. Rafale will have to get close to use it, though. Since the *Mirage* got a head start, it all depends on how well Rafale can fly."

That meant there was some chance that Phaedra might get to Earth before Rafale could catch up with her. Ronn hoped she was a fast learner when it came to piloting a shuttle.

"So what's your better way out of here?" he then asked.

"The *Moonbeamer*, the display rocket in the Castle courtyard. It's actually Jefferson's personal escape rocket."

"I could tell the *Moonbeamer* could fly," Ronn said, "but I didn't realize that was what it was for."

"You figured out more than Rafale did, I'll give you that," Vanessa conceded. "Maybe you aren't as dumb as I thought after all."

Well, thanks for that much!

"I knew about it all along," she went on, "but never said anything because I thought I might need an ace in the hole. The docking bays are a long way from the Castle and down several levels. If there was a disaster and everything was breaking down, it might be hard to reach a docked shuttle. So your uncle kept an emergency ride home right inside the Castle, charged and ready to launch at a moment's notice. It has just enough charge for one flight to Earth, maybe with a little margin. The hitch is the usual red plate next to the cockpit, since the rocket was reserved for Jefferson's own use, so I need you to open it for me. Don't worry — there should be enough room in the cockpit for two people."

Ronn had to ask about the one obvious problem. "How does it get through the dome?"

Vanessa's impatience was starting to show, but she did answer the question. "There's some sort of portal directly overhead that will open up automatically when the *Moonbeamer* takes off. At least it's supposed to."

"What about Uncle Jeff? It doesn't look like you're taking him to Earth after all. What'll happen to him?"

"Would you stop pestering me with all these dumb questions? That freezer tank he's in has its own power supply, so he should be good for a couple of centuries at least. That'll be plenty of time for somebody to figure out what to do with him."

They came out of the ramp well and onto the main level, and Vanessa drove as fast as she could down the road. The clouds overhead were thicker now and the occasional raindrop had turned into a damp mist. There were also more wandering bots than ever, many Ronn didn't recognize and probably from sets and exhibits he hadn't seen, and Vanessa was constantly swerving to dodge them.

"Damn!" she exclaimed as an Uncle Sam bot with legs at least ten feet long suddenly stepped out in front of her. Ronn guessed the long legs were an effort to simulate stilts under the red and white striped pants, and it was perhaps a refugee from a Fourth of July parade set somewhere. Vanessa veered to avoid it, but still clipped one of the legs. Uncle Sam went down as she sped onwards.

The starred and striped top hat landed in Ronn's lap. Not needing a souvenir of this trip, he tossed it out of the jeep as he turned and looked back. Uncle Sam was lying in the road and flailing, Ronn had no idea how the bot could get back up again even if its leg was undamaged. Feeling bothered about it even though it was just a bot, he thought that if he had been on his own time, without a nasty ex-aunt driving and without the world he was currently on about to shift to somewhere halfway across the universe in not too many minutes, he would have stopped to help just on general principles. Vanessa, of course, had no such scruples.

"Things really are falling apart!" she muttered half to herself. "Good thing I'm getting out of here!"

It was not lost on Ronn that she hadn't mentioned him among those getting out.

Chapter Nineteen

The mist had turned into a drizzle under a solid gray sky by the time Vanessa braked the jeep to a sudden stop in the Castle courtyard. She hopped out and urged Ronn towards the *Moonbeamer*.

They climbed the wet and slick gantry steps and came out on the small platform at the top, on a level with the ship's cockpit and about six feet below of the tip of its nose. A bridge-like walkway led the several feet from the gantry platform to the ship itself. They were well above the courtyard wall and should have had a good view of the surrounding landscape, but a thick limited visibility to just the immediate area.

"Put your hand there and open it up," Vanessa said, pointing to the red plastic plate under the rocket's cockpit canopy.

Ronn stepped to the hull and pressed his palm against the wet plate. It lit and the canopy slid back, revealing the open cockpit with room only for the pilot. Behind the upwards-facing seat was some space, perhaps intended for luggage, that a human being could just barely fit into, but it would mean spending several hours impossibly doubled over. It was clear that only one of them would be leaving by this route

While Ronn took that in, Vanessa stepped forward to climb into the cockpit. Her hand rested on her pistol grip to discourage him from any thought of trying to push her aside. Then, perhaps out of some slight touch of remaining decency buried deep down, or to soothe some last remnant of a conscience, she paused to add, "If you hurry, you might be able to make it back to the East bay in time to use one of the escape pods."

"Do you ever tell the truth about *anything*?" Ronn asked, thoroughly exasperated. He was probably most dismayed by the idea of having to make that trip to the East bay all over again, and now with hardly any time left and no scooter.

Vanessa was impatient to be off, but still felt a need to justify herself. "I thought there *was* room for two. Too bad I was wrong, but those are the breaks. Now if you'll excuse me, I'll be going."

So it would have to be an escape pod after all. Ronn stood back to let her climb into the *Moonbeamer*, then started to head down the gantry steps, wondering how long it would take him to reach the East bay—

Vanessa screamed as a loud electric discharge crackled in the air. Ronn turned and saw her knocked away from the ship, nearly falling to the platform floor.

"I should've known..." she choked, gasping and white-faced, clutching the railing for support. "Even though you got the cockpit open, it won't accept me as a pilot."

"Maybe I can fly it and you can squeeze in back of the seat...?" Ronn offered.

"Not hardly. There's about enough room there for a suitcase. Or for a briefcase that for some reason I don't seem to have with me. I just hope there's enough time left to get back to the East bay."

"Well, good luck," Ronn said. "Then I can use the *Moonbeamer*—"

"I don't think so. You're coming with me."

So much for optimism. "But what do you need me for? I didn't see any red plates on the pods."

"The pods are set to home on in the TranStella landing field at Santa Barbara. If word of my role in all this has leaked and the feds are waiting for me, I'll need something to facilitate negotiations."

"You want me for a hostage?"

"Certainly not for your charming conversation on a long flight. Now move!"

He was about to do just that — when something dark and hairy rose above the edge of the platform.

A very large gorilla's head.

While not nearly the size of the one in the movie, the ape was a respectable twelve or so feet tall. (Was there really a replica of the Empire State Building somewhere in the Park interior like on the workroom model?) And riding on the giant gorilla's shoulder was—

"Bonnie?" Ronn exclaimed. "Why didn't you go with the others?"

"I didn't want to leave with you still here," Bonnie replied simply, "so I told them to take off without me."

Her appearance complicated things just when it was down to him and Vanessa and a race to the East docking bay, but Ronn was somehow glad to see her just the same. Meanwhile, Vanessa stood open-mouthed, trying to take in the new development.

Bonnie hopped off the ape's shoulder to the gantry floor. "Take a break, Jocko." She waved and the ape climbed back down and out of sight.

"I was looking all over for you and I happened to come across the big guy," she added almost conversationally, turning towards Ronn and ignoring the still dumbfounded Vanessa. "Just walking around like a lot of the other bots. Nothing like a big monkey when a girl needs a lift, I always say. I figured you'd most likely be around the Castle, so I came over here and—"

"Who the *hell* are you?" Vanessa suddenly demanded.

Bonnie seemed to notice her for the first time. "The best thing that ever happened to Jeff, probably. I still can't believe he took up with you unless you drugged his drink or something."

Something like a light went on inside Vanessa's mind. "*Bonnie...*? But *how*...? So *young*...!" She turned a little purple, then stepped forward and slapped Bonnie. A bot's reactions should have been fast enough to dodge, but she just wasn't expecting it.

It sounded wrong. Instead of a clean thwack, it was more of a rubbery plop.

It also pulled Bonnie's face to one side. Her lips were somewhat over her cheek instead of her mouth and her nose had been moved grotesquely off-center.

Vanessa dropped back a couple of steps in horror. No human being could possibly look like that.

Recovering fast from her initial astonishment, Bonnie sensed that her features were askew. She twisted her lips, scrunched her nose, and worked her face back into place with whatever corresponded to muscles under the skin. There was no redness on her cheek where Vanessa had struck her.

Now the ghastly truth dawned on Vanessa. "You're a *bot!*"

"And one of the better ones, too," Bonnie said.

"I've been talking to you like you're a human being!"

"I'm more human than *you'll* ever be."

"Why, you—!" Vanessa shrieked and lifted her pistol.

Before she could aim and fire, before Ronn could even move, Bonnie was suddenly in front of her and easily swatted the pistol aside.

"You know, you're really getting to be annoying."

In a quick blur of motion, Bonnie ducked and slipped her arms under Vanessa's back and legs. She was a slim simulated sixteen and Vanessa was a grown woman a little taller and heavier — but Bonnie lifted her off her feet like so much foam rubber.

"Wait—!" Ronn blurted as Vanessa screamed, suddenly realizing what Bonnie was about to do.

Ignoring both Ronn's exclamation and Vanessa's shrieking, not to mention her kicking and squirming, Bonnie casually stepped up to the railing with her load and called down, "Catch, Jocko!"

Then she dumped Vanessa over the side. The scream went with her —

and suddenly choked off.

"Okay," Bonnie added, looking over the railing, "put her down. Gently—! Oh well, I guess that won't hurt her *too* much. Now get lost, lady!"

Ronn looked over the side. Down below, Vanessa seemed to be taking the hint, hobbling stiffly to the waiting jeep. Without even bothering to look back at the giant ape or up at the kids on top of the gantry, she clambered into the jeep, started it, and set out with a jerk and a little too fast. She sideswiped a stack of crates, knocking them over, and sped through the open gateway, scraping the side, and out of the courtyard. She knew only too well how little time she had left to get back to Eastgate.

Ronn wondered if she would make it. He hoped she would, since starving to death when the last of the food supplies ran out wasn't a fate he would wish on anyone, but it was another problem that was out of his hands. His problem now was escaping in time himself, and taking Bonnie with him. Vanessa's precipitous departure had solved that, he hoped.

"Thanks for your help, Jocko," Bonnie called down, "but you'll have to find somebody else to play with!"

The ape rumbled something in reply. Then it turned and ambled over to the courtyard wall, climbed over it, and headed off into the mists and the uncharted territory to the south.

"You can control it?" Ronn asked.

"Not exactly," Bonnie replied. "It's more like I can make him understand what I want and he goes along with it."

"I see..." Ronn said, not sure of the distinction. "Anyway, I don't know how much you heard, but this rocket is our ride out of here. If I can make it work for me, anyway—"

He broke off as he heard music down below. It was the teddy bear marching band, trooping into the courtyard. The bears came to a stop at the foot of the gantry and continued playing. They seemed to have gotten their groove back and whatever tune they were playing, they were playing it about as well as they ever played anything. The drum major was still tossing a long-missing baton, though.

"Aw, that's cute!" Bonnie exclaimed. "They came to see us off!"

"But how could they know—? Oh, never mind." Just one more mystery of the place. "I wonder what they're playing?"

"Who can tell, the way they—"

She broke off in mid-sentence. The bears down below broke off in mid-song. After a moment of statue-like rigidity, the bears started moving again, not playing or marching in formation but shambling silently towards the open entrance to the courtyard

"What's that all about?" Ronn asked, but Bonnie didn't answer.

He turned to look at her. She had also frozen where she stood, her face expressionless, as though the light inside had gone out. Then she began to walk towards the stairs, one slow, stiff step following another.

"Bonnie! What's wrong?"

Did she reset again? Even all this way from the county fair scene?

Somehow, painfully and tortuously, she managed a strangled reply, without moving her mouth or lips. "I must return... to where I belong..."

With all those aimlessly wandering bots, something must have finally registered somewhere and corrective measures instituted, resulting in a Park-wide bot recall.

Time winding down to zero, the asteroid about to relocate... He could have just taken off without her. It would have been the smartest thing to do. She was a bot, after all, designed and built for that county fair set where he had found her. Did it make any sense to risk his future, even his life, for a manufactured thing?

Maybe not, but she had been a friend, even family, maybe even more. He didn't even bother to debate the pros and cons.

"Bonnie, no! Fight it! You're coming to Earth with me!"

"I must return... to where I belong..."

Was that even Bonnie talking anymore, or just the recall program?

Ronn grabbed her from behind, tried to wrap his arms around her waist.

She shrugged him off like *he* was so much foam rubber, and he landed on his back on the gantry platform floor as she reached the top of the steps.

It's hopeless... He really would have to leave her behind—

When the gantry shook with a sudden jolt from the ground below, more powerful than any before. Bonnie lost her balance and fell backwards, all but on top of him. In the courtyard below, a few crates on top of the stacks toppled to the ground.

Bonnie started to stand up again, to follow her irresistible urge to go back to her appointed place in eternal theme-park hell. Ronn scrambled to his knees and reached out for her, one last futile effort to hold her back, and she simply waved him off as she got to her feet — when she suddenly went limp and fell back into his lap.

Her eyes were wide open and unseeing, and she seemed to have gone completely dead. Or temporarily offline or something. All Ronn could figure was that the quake had interrupted the recall signal, and he could only hope she would start up again on her own sooner or later. Worst case, the people at TranStella could probably give her a jump-start if he could just get her back to Earth.

This was the moment, while she was still out of action. Ronn pulled her along with him as he stood up, lifted her limp body with an effort — even in 80% gravity, she was probably still heavier than a biological girl of her size — and shoved her into the space behind the cockpit seat.

No living human being could have tolerated her bent-over position for very long, let alone for hours on end, but fortunately she was unable to feel discomfort. Vanessa certainly never could have lasted in there for the whole trip.

Then Ronn climbed into the seat, on his back, and the canopy automatically closed over him. The ship had accepted him. He put on the helmet that he found in the cockpit, strapped himself in, and slipped his hands and arms into virtual control sleeves and gauntlets. The fit wasn't perfect since they were sized for hands with two thumbs each. He would probably come out of this with nearly sprained little fingers from having to spread them too far.

Virtual displays lit up in front of his eyes, information flowed directly into his mind. The outside of the *Moonbeamer* may have been of satiric human design, but the inner workings were borrowed alien tech, most of it a mystery. One thing was certain, however. An emergency escape rocket was meant to protect the occupant.

The imagery that filled Ronn's mind was strange, not human. The AI was designed in terms of very deep, very ancient alien psychology. Protecting helpless chicks, defending the nest. Much about the aliens was harsh, perhaps even cruel by human standards. The reason Uncle Jeff's alien friend had been placed on Earth to begin with was a coming of age rite of passage symbolizing leaving the nest and learning to survive or giving up and dying. But on protecting the young and helpless, humans and aliens could agree.

The AI sensed Ronn's youth, his need and desperation, and... *understood*.

Ronn felt a shudder in the ship, coming from outside. It reminded him that Vesper could shift at any moment. There was no more time left.

"Okay!" he exclaimed. "Let's go!"

That was all it took, without even a button to push, and the *Moonbeamer* started to rise. It was slow at first, and Ronn could sense the tall, spindle-shaped craft balancing itself to keep from toppling over as it climbed, pushed upwards from the bottom.

As the ship rose, the clouds above broke and warm golden sunshine poured down. Then Ronn caught a glimpse of something out the canopy to the west. A vast ghostly figure loomed over the far edge of the crater. It was almost too transparent to make out very clearly in the misty distance, but Ronn could tell that it was Uncle Jeff, seen from the waist up and his image magnified enormously. Jefferson C. Prescott looked out across his domain like a model railroader over his layout as his hands rested on the controls.

Was it really *him*, the data packets that constituted his shattered identity finally coming together at the very last second before the asteroid shifted, making him whole and conscious again even if disembodied — or just some recording accidentally activated and projected as the last few still intact systems broke down in the wrecked control center on the crater rim?

Ronn had no idea which explanation was correct, just that it was awe-inspiring to see and even unsettling. The vision of Uncle Jeff as a god-like colossus looking out over his creation was Ronn's last view of the park.

As it ascended, the ship started picking up speed. Above, Ronn saw only bright blue sky, and somewhere beyond that was the inner surface of the overarching dome. Vanessa had said some sort of portal would open up automatically, but after what had happened with the swimming pool rescue system, his confidence was not quite 100%.

Please, Uncle Jeff! Let it be the one thing that still works!

A small black disc suddenly appeared ahead, increasing in size, and revealed blackness and stars beyond. The *Moonbeamer* shot through the hole with barely enough room to clear on either side, then they were in space. Vesper rapidly shrank behind them.

The ship around him turned invisible, as though he was flying on his own, with just his body hurtling through the void. The *Moonbeamer* was still there, of course, responding to his control as though it was part of him, and he sensed the instrument readings with an awareness beyond anything he had ever felt before. He remembered what Captain Rogowski had said about being the ship, and it really was as though he felt the wind in his feathers

More than that... He had once seen an astronomy vid about the con-stellations with an animated depiction of the Greek gods placing the hero Orion in the sky, *among* the stars. He now knew how Orion would have felt (except that he seemed to recall Orion was dead by that point in the story, but never mind).

The *Moonbeamer* had an automatic course setting for Earth that could have taken a sick, injured, or even unconscious Uncle Jeff straight to the landing field by his corporate headquarters in Santa Barbara without his active control. For the moment, Ronn could relax and let the ship do the work. As the ship accelerated, he noticed variations in the brightness of the torch behind him, increasing as more energy was poured into the sys-tem. A sudden burst of acceleration would be blinding if someone were looking at it at close range, not that it would be a good idea for someone to be anywhere near it, as Captain Rogowski had mentioned several days and what seemed like a lifetime before.

The *Moonbeamer* then began a long slow turn to line itself up with Earth. It came back around Vesper, passing close to the gray, meteor-blasted surface. It was much the same view Ronn had seen several days before, approaching a tiny, rocky world of craters and rugged hills, but the feeling was different since this time he was leaving it. He felt some regret mixed in with his relief. It would be fun to come back sometime, to explore it without a cranky, pistol-packing ex-aunt dragging him around.

Past the curve of Vesper's jagged edge, the Earth appeared, a huge, brightly shining blue-white crescent, far larger than Ronn had ever seen the Moon from back home, almost close enough to touch in cosmic terms, still several hours away by every measurement that mattered to human beings.

Then Ronn noticed that Vesper was shimmering behind him as the *Moonbeamer* headed out on its course towards Earth, shot through with color flashes like prismatic reflections.

Suddenly — a flash, a brilliant flash of rainbow color — and Vesper was gone. Where it had been, only distant stars shone in the blackness.

Ronn realized with a chilly feeling how narrow the escape had been. He wondered if Vanessa had been able to reach an escape pod in time.

"Er... Ronn?" It was Bonnie, just behind him.

"Oh good, you're back. I was worried for a while."

"Sorry I went a little weird for a moment there. Something got into my mind and I couldn't fight it. I'm all right now, I think. Did we make it? I can't remember anything after I started thinking I had to go back where I belonged."

"Yep, we got away just in time. You shouldn't have any problems now that Vesper's gone. It's probably a good thing that we never went back to that county fair scene."

"Right, or I'd be waiting for Jeff again and wondering where the teddy bear came from."

Then Ronn filled Bonnie in on what had happened since he left the house that morning. In turn, she told him how she had decided not to leave with the others, instead going out to find him. It might not have been the smartest idea she'd ever had, but he could hardly argue with the results.

Meanwhile, as the *Moonbeamer* accelerated, Ronn checked over the controls and the information flooding the sensors. The ship's — and his — awareness extended, feeling through the depths of space in front of him. Somewhere far ahead were two objects that were probably the *Mirage* and the *Spectre*. The torches of both were out and they were coasting towards Earth, but the nearer one, which had to be the *Spectre*, was moving faster than the *Mirage* further ahead. A third ship that had to be the freighter was out there, too, but off to the side and not moving as fast as the other two ships.

Looking at the numbers projected on the display panel, Ronn suspected that Phaedra hadn't taken off immediately, perhaps needing time to familiarize herself with the *Mirage*, and she hadn't reached its maximum speed before cutting the engine. That might have been automatic, anyway, to save wear and tear and conserve charge, and she was letting the ship's AI do the flying. As an experienced pilot, Rafale had probably taken over the controls and accelerated all out to boost the *Spectre* to whatever speed he needed to overtake the *Mirage* somewhere close to Earth two or more hours from now, when he would make his move to force her to land where he wanted. Phaedra might not have even realized he was behind her and gradually catching up, or if she did, that he had hostile intent, so she wasn't increasing her own speed.

With a sinking feeling, Ronn realized that he was the only one who had some slight chance of stopping Rafale.

Since the *Moonbeamer* wasn't armed, he had no idea what he should do or even could do— but whatever it was, he would first have to catch up with the other two ships. That meant a high-G acceleration to a speed even faster than the *Spectre* at the risk of burning out the engine and using up the energy charge at a dangerous rate, making landing difficult if not impossible. It seemed like a risk worth taking, though — and he didn't have many other options. The AI seemed reluctant when he made his intentions clear, but went along. Then he settled in for about ten minutes of 3-G acceleration.

The *Moonbeamer* was a one-shot, never intended to fly more than once, and it lacked the shuttles' safeguards for minimizing wear on its systems. He could push it to its arbitrarily set limits and beyond, and fly somewhat faster than the shuttles were allowed. With the AI's help and judicious applications of thrust from the torch, he set a course and speed that would bring him close to the *Spectre* in about two hours.

When the ship reached its maximum velocity, the engine shut down so it could coast the rest of the way to Earth. Now that the ship was no longer accelerating, there were no more G-forces. The torch went dark as well.

The cabin didn't have artificial gravity, probably because there was no point in installing such a complex system in a ship that would only fly once and only for a few hours. Ronn felt weightless, but he was too strapped in to float freely and enjoy it. Whether he would have enjoyed it was another matter. He had a queasy feeling in his stomach at first, and a light-headed dizziness that might have been the result of disorientation from no longer being able to sense the difference between up and down. His perceptions soon righted themselves, and the discomfort passed.

After everything that had happened that morning and over the past few days, it was good to relax for a while. He suddenly felt exhausted, and he needed some time to catch his breath.

It then occurred to Ronn that if he could sense the other ships, they could sense him. Not letting Rafale know he was somewhere behind him seemed like an excellent idea. His perception of the *Moonbeamer's* controls and systems told him that a cloaking field was available for whatever contingency, and he activated it. If Rafale had been aware of him, he had suddenly disappeared from the board. Since Rafale hadn't known about the *Moonbeamer's* capabilities, he wouldn't know what that stray signal had even been, and with any luck would dismiss it as an escape pod, perhaps with Vanessa inside.

Speaking of whom... there was a faint blip somewhere behind the *Moonbeamer*, moving very slowly compared to the other ships. That was probably Vanessa with a long flight ahead of her. While Ronn had fairly little sympathy for her, he was glad that she had been able to make her escape after all.

He still had no idea what he would do when he caught up with the other ships. Uncle Jeff had considered the possibility of hostile spacecraft out in space where international law was unenforceable, so the *Spectre* was lightly armed, but he hadn't allowed for one of his own ships being hijacked and used against another. As basically a lifeboat, the *Moonbeamer* wasn't armed at all. If Ronn had to do something to save Phaedra, Theo, and Danny in the *Mirage*, what *could* he do? Ram the *Spectre*? At these speeds and with on-board power sources that probably equaled small atomic bombs, there wouldn't even be vapor left of either ship. There definitely wouldn't be enough left of Ronn for the gods to make a halfway decent constellation out of him.

He hoped he could think of *something* by the time the *Moonbeamer* caught up with the Spectre.

Five thousand miles ahead, the vast blue and white globe of the Earth took up nearly half the sky. In a few minutes, Ronn would have to turn the ship around to face backwards, relight the torch to use it as a brake, and start decelerating. Diving into the atmosphere at his current speed would end up in a spectacular fireball.

The other ships would have to decelerate, too, and he soon saw the torches of both the *Spectre* and the *Mirage* light up again — but both ships were actually increasing their speed. Rafale was in hot pursuit of Phaedra and she now knew it. While she was trying to maintain her lead, he was now just a few hundred miles behind her and closing.

Now Ronn realized what Rafale's strategy was. Phaedra couldn't continue accelerating much longer. She would have to start braking soon so she wouldn't hit the atmosphere at full speed. He would let her brake first, and then he'd be right behind her, just a little faster. It was a game of cosmic chicken.

Ahead Ronn could see the brilliant white torch of the *Spectre* and beyond it the somewhat less bright light of the *Mirage*, like stars against the vast blackness of Earth's night side, and slowly moving across his field of vision. "Diamond fire," Captain Rogowski had called it back in the hangar at Edwards...

That exhaust must be really bright to shine like that at this distance, Ronn thought, then realized letting his mind wander like that wasn't helping.

Wait a second...

The *Moonbeamer* used the same propulsion system.

What would diamond fire be like seen up close, say, through a cockpit windshield?

It would be close, insanely close at these speeds, clearing another ship with maybe a hundred feet to spare at seven miles per second. Even if he could keep the *Moonbeamer* under tight control, the slightest lurch of the *Spectre* might smash the two ships together. On the other hand, they would be traveling at nearly the same speed, with the *Moonbeamer* a little faster to overtake the *Spectre*, so the *Spectre* would be effectively standing still. The down side was that accelerating enough to shoot past the *Spectre* would eat up so much of the *Moonbeamer*'s charge that being able to land safely would be questionable.

"Can I do this?" he murmured to himself. It wasn't just his life he was risking. The lives of Phaedra, Theo, and Danny were depending on him, as well as the existence of Bonnie. He suddenly felt thoroughly inadequate, not up to the job at all...

"Sure you can," Bonnie suddenly said. Of course — with that ultra-sensitive hearing of hers, she had heard him muttering.

Heartened by her encouragement, he realized there was no backing out now.

"Plot an intercept course to the *Spectre* and calculate a speed to overtake it," Ronn ordered the AI.

"What exactly are you up to?" Bonnie asked.

He felt a little guilty for not consulting her first. He was risking her life as much as his, and he used the word "life" in his mind without the least trace of irony.

"We're going to come in over the *Spectre* and then drop down just in front of it," he explained. "As bright as the torch is, it can't be much fun shining through the windshield. At the least, it should distract Rafale and maybe give Phaedra a chance to escape."

"It sounds dangerous," she said, not frightened but merely stating a fact.

"I won't lie to you. We'll be cutting it crazy close. The least little miscalculation with the last-second push and we'll be getting fitted for wings and halos."

Her voice was suddenly very low. "Do you think I could go to Heaven?"

Ronn had no idea how to answer that, but Bonnie was as human as he was where it counted. That seemed to lead to some kind of optimistic conclusion.

"Don't see why not," he said. "Let's just hope we don't have to worry about it for a few decades. Anyway, what I'm doing is a risky move but it's the only way to do it I can see. Unless you have a better idea—"

"No, go ahead."

The shining blue and white crescent of the Earth ahead grew ever larger, filling out to a half-circle. Ronn and Bonnie talked a little, but there didn't seem to be much to say. The situation was just too serious for small talk.

"Two minutes from intercept," Ronn announced at length. "It'll all be over then." *One way or another*, he added a little grimly to himself.

"I don't really have any regrets," Bonnie said. "It's been nice to finally be awake and alive these past few days, and to meet you."

Ronn was about to reply when he suddenly heard voices. Perhaps voice-activated, perhaps the result of coming within some specified distance of another spacecraft, the radio had come on automatically. As part of the same fleet, the three ships must have used the same radio frequencies, and he could overhear the exchange between Phaedra and the Commandant.

"Change your course to follow me!" Rafale ordered. "I will show you where to land!"

"Go away and leave me alone!" Phaedra exclaimed.

Ronn saw what happened next as abstract schematics. The *Spectre* fired a plasma burst at the *Mirage*, a shooting star that blazed through space. Fortunately, the shot missed, flashing past the *Mirage* to one side and disappearing into the distance. While it had apparently been just a warning shot, the next one wouldn't be. From what Vanessa had said, the plasma might not cause much physical damage, but it would wreak havoc with the *Mirage*'s electronics and probably leave it an uncontrollable derelict about to burn up in the atmosphere.

"That wasn't funny!" Phaedra yelled.

"This is not a game and I am not a child like you!" Rafale snapped. "I am giving you one last chance! If you do not change direction at once, I will fire again! This time it will strike you directly. I will not let you land in America with what you are carrying!"

The torch of the *Spectre* blazed brilliantly just ahead of Ronn. The minute, the second, to act had come — and he wasn't sure he could pull this off. But he didn't have a choice. He lit the *Moonbeamer*'s torch and accelerated, dropping the shields for still more power.

For a moment he was afraid he wouldn't be in time to beat Rafale's trigger finger, but the *Moonbeamer* responded to his emotional state. Just when he thought he had boosted it to the maximum, when all hope was lost and the worst was only too horribly inevitable, there was still something left in it.

Phaedra replied with something on the order of "Bite me!" Only squared.

Rafale snarled French that sounded even more obscene. "*Then die!*"

Now was the time—

Like a silver arrow, the *Moonbeamer* shot straight at the ship ahead. At the last split-second, Ronn came in over the *Spectre* and a little ahead, dropping down in front of it and accelerating, channeling the full load of stored energy into the propulsion unit.

The torch at the rear of the *Moonbeamer* exploded in a blast of brilliant white light, and for a split-second until the canopy automatically darkened in response, the cockpit was flooded with its glare, almost blinding even nearly fifty feet away from the source and facing away. Behind the ship, the incandescent exhaust blazed straight into the *Spectre's* windshield.

Diamond fire!

At best, Ronn had hoped it would be a distraction, allowing Phaedra to get clear, and with luck maybe damage some of the *Spectre*'s optical sensors, even if its windshield also darkened as a reaction to the sudden light.

Ronn had underestimated the effect — the damage was much worse. Rafale's scream stung his eardrums.

Then the *Moonbeamer* was clear, leaving the *Spectre* behind him. As he blinked away the afterimages and started to see again, all that was visible in the rear view was its torch, a brilliant star diminishing with distance and headed off in a direction at a right angle to its original path. Just ahead was the torch of the *Mirage*.

I'm still alive! Ronn thought in amazement.

"Did we do it?" Bonnie asked.

"I actually think we did," Ronn said, hardly daring to believe it himself. "I liked the sound of his scream, anyway."

"I'm just glad *that's* over with…" Bonnie said simply, and he agreed.

"What just happened?" Phaedra asked baffledly over the radio.

"Score one for the *Moonbeamer*!" Ronn exclaimed exultantly.

"Ronn?" Phaedra gasped. "But how — and with *what*?"

"The rocket in the courtyard was Uncle Jeff's emergency escape rocket!" Ronn explained, almost laughing in the relief of finding himself and Phaedra still alive and their ships intact. "After Rafale took off after you, I thought you could use a hand."

"Thanks..." Phaedra said weakly. "I thought I was going to die..." Then she thought to ask, "Did Bonnie ever find you?"

"I'm right here!" Bonnie called cheerfully.

"See you in Santa Barbara!" Ronn added.

"I don't think so," Phaedra replied as the distant star of the *Mirage* far ahead began to turn away. "In all this scrambling around, I missed the window for landing in California. Now the automatic landing procedure for some other airport kicked in."

"Where are you headed?"

"Let's just say I'll wave to your mom when I fly over your house."

Then the two ships went their separate ways, and the *Mirage* was soon lost in the distance.

With the crisis behind him, Ronn suddenly realized how close the Earth was now, a vast globe of shining blue streaked with white clouds. He couldn't take too much time to appreciate the splendor — the *Moonbeamer*'s speed was dangerously high and it was about to run into the atmosphere. There were limits to how much the ship could withstand even with alien-tech anti-friction glazing on the hull. Despite being a Hollywood attempt at something that looked cool in a retro sort of way rather than a scientifically sound airfoil design, the *Moonbeamer*'s short, stubby wings might be aerodynamic enough that it would just graze the atmosphere if it came in too fast, and go sailing on past the Earth. Already he could feel the resistance of even the few stray molecules in the outermost layers of the atmosphere, what his science teacher would have still considered a respectable vacuum in a bell jar, and things were starting to heat up outside.

But the AI had been programmed for this. Ronn let it take over and the *Moonbeamer* flipped from front to back in a sudden, stomach-turning lurch, its rear thrust now directed forward to cut its speed. Its trajectory flattened, taking advantage of the Earth's atmosphere to skip over the outer edges several times, cutting speed still further with each skip, before diving into the denser lower layers. After about three minutes, the torch went out, the ship righted itself with the bow facing forward once more, and it began its dive.

The black of space was lightened by a faint hint of pink. Pink turned to orange, then to red at the center of a tunnel of rainbow colors. Even at the now much reduced speed, the ship was engulfed in an inferno, like flying through a mass of flame although Ronn sensed the heat only as data from the ship's sensors instead as anything physical. All he could see around him was a torrent of almost blindingly glowing, superheated gases. They had lost the radio and heard only static.

For as spectacularly frightening as the light show was, the sensors told Ronn he was well within the margin of safety and the shockwave in front was taking the brunt of the heat and air resistance.

As the *Moonbeamer* slowed still further, the blaze enveloping it gradually died away. The livid red outside faded to orange, orange to pink — and then to blue. Now they were gliding through the sunlit lower atmosphere over puffy white clouds. The ocean was a glistening blue mass below, the sun shone brightly in the blue sky above. From a display showing the Earth beneath him as an abstract 3-D graphic, he saw that they were coming in over the Pacific, heading east.

As they approached the southern California coast, the automatic landing program kicked in and the *Moonbeamer* began a wide turn towards the north. When the radio came back on, Ronn could tell from the chatter he overheard on a number of stations that the fireball of his reentry had been seen by people on ships across the Pacific, but the *Moonbeamer* itself had been lost from view after it had slowed enough that the flame trail died out. While Vandenberg AFB was fairly close by, apparently the *Moonbeamer* had still not been noticed. With the torch out and gliding at a subsonic speed, its stealth protection made it invisible.

In front of them were several large islands in a line with only narrow gaps between them. The *Moonbeamer* streaked over the rugged mountains of Santa Cruz Island and then the gently rolling blue water of the Santa Barbara Channel lay beneath them. Ahead was a stretch of Old California shoreline that actually ran east to west, with mountains in the distance. A virtual map display identified the city sprawling along the coast as Santa Barbara.

Ronn knew that the *Moonbeamer* was programmed to head for Tran-Stella's headquarters. If the ship had still had the anticipated amount of stored energy at this point in the flight, it would have landed at the company's small airport somewhere inland, but the effort to overtake the *Spectre* and the sudden acceleration at the end had left its power cells all but depleted.

As the ship dropped in its unpowered glide, Ronn realized that it wouldn't make it quite that far. He saw the whitecaps of the waves below, coming up fast—

The *Moonbeamer* slammed into the water with a colossal splash, practically cracking Ronn's bones and rattling his teeth in their sockets, and continued on, skimming the surface with a huge spray of water and foam trailing behind it.

I just hope there aren't any boats in front of us…

As far as he could tell from the forward scan, everything was clear all the way.

No, wait… something large was moving into their path just ahead, a cruise ship. The projected course of both the *Moonbeamer* and the other ship showed an inevitable collision somewhere about amidships.

With the torch out and the *Moonbeamer* plowing straight ahead by sheer momentum, Ronn couldn't control it. It looked like there was no way to avoid the smash-up—

But there was still a little juice in the power cells and there were steering thrusters. The AI realized the situation, and squeezed what little it had left into the system. The *Moonbeamer* turned slightly at the last second, and slid by the passing ship just clear of the stern, probably drenching any people on deck with its backwash.

The darker line of the shoreline was now just ahead, but the *Moonbeamer* was slowing as it sliced through the water, just barely dodging a couple of sailboats along the way with the very last dregs of its steering thrusters.

Then it hit the beach, plowing into the sand, scraping the bottom of the hull, crumpling the landing struts — and came to a stop partway, the forward half on dry ground and the stern still in the water.

Everything went silent. They were down. On the ground. Back on Earth. Ronn was his normal self again, no longer a seemingly free body flying through space but sitting in a very cramped cockpit with an ordinary control panel and windshield in front of him.

The ship was shutting down. One after another, Ronn sensed the various ship's systems going off-line, something like lights winking out. There was no charge left. The *Moonbeamer* had given everything it had and burned itself out. It would not be taking off again.

Not even sure who he was talking to, Ronn murmured, "Thank you."

For a moment or two, he sat there, too exhausted to do more than enjoy the moment and take in the sheer bliss of the fact that they were down and on the ground in one piece and the trip was over. Whatever happened after this, at least they were on Earth where there was plenty of air to breathe and solid rock eight thousand miles thick under them.

Then the canopy sprang open. It was perhaps a strong hint that the wisest course of action would be to abandon ship. He heard a loud hiss behind him and looked back. A cloud of hot, damp, white steam was rising. The propulsion dish was lying in the water and it must have been extremely hot.

He unstrapped himself from the seat and started to clamber out of the cockpit.

"Bonnie? Can you get out of there?"

"I think so. You first so I can unpretzel myself. I'm not complaining, but your baggage-stowing technique could use some improvement…"

Chapter Twenty

With the *Moonbeamer* lying horizontally half in the water and half on the beach, the sand was just a short drop.

Several hours crammed into the cockpit had left Ronn a little stiff. He stretched and tried walking. It took some adjustment since he had gotten used to the 80% gravity on Vesper, and now he was back on Earth where it was full strength.

Bonnie looked curiously around at the beach, the palm trees at the edge, the street beyond, and the line of mountains in the distance. "I've always wanted to take a trip to California," she said. "This wasn't exactly how I imagined I'd get there, though."

"You're about to see a lot more of California," Ronn replied. "We can't stay here."

Out on the street, cars were stopping and people were getting out to gawk at the spaceship on the beach. No one had worked up the nerve to come down and take a closer look, but it was only a matter of time.

As the billowing clouds of hot steam rolled in, Ronn realized he would be cooked if he stayed any longer. He and Bonnie took advantage of the cover to leave the *Moonbeamer* behind and make a dash to a nearby boathouse. Going around the building, they made their way to the street and joined the growing crowd on the sidewalk. No one connected the two casually dressed teenagers with the mysterious spaceship and they walked on.

The street was Cabrillo Boulevard, to go by the signs, a four-lane highway lined with towering palm trees. On one side were rows of white apartment buildings with reddish tile roofs, and on the other were the beach and the ocean.

"Where to now?" Bonnie asked.

"I guess downtown is that way," Ronn replied, looking west. "First thing we need is a phone. I'm starting to think there's one person we should talk to before we do anything else."

"Who? Do you know somebody here?"

"I mean *you*. The Bonnie you were copied from, anyway. Aunt Thalia said she lives in Santa Barbara. She should be able to tell us what's what."

Bonnie seemed a little perturbed by the idea. "I guess that makes sense, but... I can see it now. 'Hi, me! You're fine, how am I?'"

"You're not bothered by it, are you? We don't have a whole lot of choices here. I don't want to approach the people at TranStella because we don't know who was in on the mutiny. At least you should be on your side."

"I guess I can handle it, and if I can, she ought to."

Occasional cars passed them on the street, fast and silent. They had changed a great deal since the point where Bonnie's memories stopped.

"The cars all look like bugs!" she exclaimed. "Or bubbles! Buggy-bubbles!" She laughed at her little wordplay.

It sounded like something a four-year-old would come up with. Ronn hoped she hadn't fried a circuit, but with their huge, dark, polarized windshields and almost globular shape, they did have an insect-like appearance that hadn't occurred to him before because he had grown up with cars looking like that.

A pair of police buggy-bubbles raced by with flashing lights. Somebody must have called in with the news that a rocket ship had crashed on the beach. Ronn was relieved that they had gotten away and wouldn't have to answer a lot of questions just yet.

They came to a bus stop. He checked the posted schedule flimmering in the air in front of the shelter and saw that the next Waterfront Shuttle would be along in a few minutes.

When it arrived, Bonnie remarked that buses looked like Oscar Mayer Wienermobiles now, but Ronn had no idea what she meant. A bus was just a bus. They got on and he flashed his cash card in the general direction of the front.

"Where's the driver?" Bonnie asked.

"Isn't one," Ronn said. "It's all automatic."

"Is it safe?"

"Supposedly more so than with a human driver. Besides, didn't you want to be a crash dummy? I'm the one who has to worry."

"I *used* to be human, you know. Old habits stick."

Once they were downtown, they got off the bus. The generally white buildings were mostly one or two stories high, and the streets were thickly lined with trees along the curbs. Passing in front of the stores, which tended to trendy boutiques, Bonnie marveled at the 3-D advertising displays. There had been nothing like them in her time. She paid particular attention to the clothes, since she would sooner or later have to get something besides her shorts and blouse.

"Berets are big this year?" she murmured.

Ronn just felt annoyed by an especially obnoxious display that tried to get him to buy athletic bootlets by showing him a projected image of himself wearing the product.

Thank you for making this possible, Uncle Jeff!

They stood on the curb as traffic passed in front of them and Ronn looked up and down the street. "Now to buy a phone…"

"Can't you just find a pay phone?" Bonnie asked.

"Maybe about thirty years ago," Ronn said. "Everybody has their own phone now."

He spotted a nearby convenience store and they went in. Bonnie was astonished that there was no sign of any human staff in the store and Ronn paid by simply holding up his cash card as they left.

Back out on the street, Ronn opened the shrink wrap, took the phone bud out, and tucked it in his ear. Just hearing the slight dataline hum when he activated it gave him a sense of relief at being back in touch with the world for the first time in days. He called his mother and she answered at once.

Mrs. Evans was already at home, having been released from protective custody some time before. She sounded extremely happy to find out that Ronn was safe and back on Earth after days with no word.

"I just heard on the news that your cousins landed all right near Chicago, but nobody said anything about you, so I was getting worried. Where *are* you, anyway?"

"California, in Santa Barbara. I came on a different ship. Do you happen to know Aunt Bonnie's current home address?"

"Aunt Bonnie? You mean Bonnie Hutchinson, Jeff's ex? Not offhand but I can look it up. She remarried and I think she goes by MacMillan now. Just a sec—" Mrs. Evans gave Ronn a street address, then asked, "When will you be home?"

"I'll call you later about that. There's something I have to do first."

Ronn rang off after exchanging goodbyes. "Now we need a cab—"

"Shouldn't we call first?" Bonnie asked worriedly. "Is it really a good idea to just drop in on her out of the blue like this?"

"You tell me," Ronn said. "What would *you* think if somebody called you asking if they could bring a robot double of yourself over? And this *is* you we're talking about, sort of."

Bonnie winced. "I could have done without the 'sort of,' but I see what you mean. Knowing me, we'd better just show up with the proof and not even try explaining it first."

Ronn found a taxi stand nearby and an available taxi. As they got in, Bonnie noticed there was no driver here, either.

"Now I even get to ride in a buggy-bubble," she remarked, "but not having a driver still seems like an awful idea to me."

"We're used to it," Ronn said.

The cab dropped them off at a security checkpoint by the entrance to a gated community of some very upscale mansions. After they went through an ID scan in which Bonnie didn't register at all, Ronn called ahead. Bonnie stayed discreetly out of camera view, while it was voice only from the other end. Not surprisingly, Mrs. MacMillan sounded like an older version of Bonnie, and at first seemed puzzled that a former nephew she had never seen before had shown up out of the blue. She had some idea of what had been happening with Uncle Jeff's disappearance and the Vesper crisis, however, so she wasn't caught completely unaware. She gave him the authorization to come on in, and he and Bonnie walked through the gate and into the enclosed neighborhood.

Mrs. MacMillan lived in a large, white stucco Spanish-style house with a tile roof, set back on an expansive grassy lawn with palm trees out front. Flower beds and planters lined the sidewalk that led to a round, turret-like extension of the house that enclosed the front porch.

"Fancy place," Bonnie said. "I wouldn't mind living here myself. But I guess I kind of *do*..."

They went up to the front door. A voice much like Bonnie's announced from somewhere: "Welcome, Ronn." After a few moments, they heard approaching steps inside, then the door opened.

A woman stood there, wearing white shorts and blouse as though she had been caught just as she was about to go out and play tennis. She would have been just past fifty, with styled, sun-bleached short hair that still had most of its original light brunette color, tanned and mature but only lightly touched by time. She was Bonnie thirty-five years later.

"You must be Ronn, then," she said in her older Bonnie's voice, smiling warmly. "I'm Bonnie MacMillan. I was your Aunt Bonnie for a while, though we never met while I was married to your uncle. But what's this all—?"

Then she had a good look at the girl on her porch, and her hand went to her mouth.

"If you've been on Vesper," she said to Ronn, her smile fading, "I think I know what this is. But why bring it back here? It's just a bot, even if it was modeled after me. It wasn't one of my or Jeff's better ideas and I'd just as soon not see it again."

Bonnie-bot looked stricken. Dealing with, say, Phaedra's prejudices against her had been one thing, but rejection by her own older self was

256

rejection about as ultimate as it got. Then her eyes narrowed and her mouth tightened. She stepped forward and just about touched noses with Mrs. MacMillan — Aunt Bonnie — who fell back a step, startled. The body language, even to the play of expressions on both their faces, was identical.

"Look," Bonnie snapped, "I don't know if you're my mother, my twin sister, or just plain me with wrinkles, but you *made* me, so how about showing some consideration here?"

"*Wrinkles?*" Aunt Bonnie choked. "I had those done *years* ago—"

Then she realized what she was doing.

Arguing with a bot.

"Oh my God!" She stared at Ronn in horror. "You mean she's... she's... *awake?*"

It's as good a word as any. "Yes."

Aunt Bonnie looked as though she was only barely resisting the temptation to scream. "I think you'd better come inside," she finally said after a few moments, forcing herself to calm down. "We need to talk."

She led them into the simple but elegant living room that looked like something Ronn's mother might have designed for a client more concerned about taste than expense. A live vid newscast was on with the sound turned down, covering the mysterious appearance of a rocket on the beach.

"Your doing, I take it?" Aunt Bonnie asked.

Ronn nodded. "Afraid so. It was the only way off Vesper."

Aunt Bonnie considered the projected image taken from a helicopter hovering above the silver rocket, a white cloud of steam still roiling up from the stern. "Jeff's emergency escape rocket... I guess it belongs to TranStella and somebody will have to claim it. Why didn't you wait for the police when you got to the beach?"

"I thought we'd better come straight here and see you before we did anything else," Ronn said. "I wasn't sure what people would do with Bonnie when they found out what she is. I saw what happened when somebody tried to get information out of the Jeffbots."

Aunt Bonnie smiled a little wryly. "I don't think there's much risk of anyone taking her apart to see what makes her go. Her plans are already on file. You were probably right, though. Depending on the kindness of strangers might not be exactly wise in a situation like this. But about her..."

First, she needed to assure herself beyond the slightest doubt that this was not actually some elaborate scam involving a made-up or even surgically altered real girl posing as a Bonnie-bot. The side access panel would be hard to fake, however, not to mention the mouth that was closed in back and didn't lead to a throat. The case was clinched by a few whispered personal questions out of Ronn's hearing that showed Bonnie knew things from Aunt Bonnie's childhood that no one but a duplicate of herself could possibly know. Whatever those things were, they had both Bonnies giggling. Ronn did catch something about a first crush named Leonardo DiCaprio, a name he actually recognized from somewhere as a veteran vidstar. It was hard to believe that an old guy like him had once warmed the hearts of tweenage girls. That seemed to break the ice and Aunt Bonnie no longer regarded Bonnie as a terrible mistake that had come back to haunt her. In the end, they hugged each other — but whether as sisters or mother and daughter, Ronn wasn't sure.

They broke off when the newsvid changed to a live scene of the *Mirage* standing on the tarmac at an airport, and Aunt Bonnie waved for the sound to come up.

"...To recap, an unexpected arrival from space landed at the DuPage County Airport near Chicago earlier today. The shuttlecraft *Mirage*, owned by the TranStella Company and piloted by Phaedra Knuppel, seventeen-year-old niece of Jefferson Prescott, reportedly made the 60,000 mile journey from Vesper."

Ronn knew exactly what was meant. It was a large community airport just outside of Chicago and not all that far from his home town of Maple Heights. The only thing he could figure was that when Uncle Jeff's business took him to Chicago, he landed at DuPage to avoid the congestion at O'Hare, and the next available programmed landing procedure had been activated when the *Mirage* missed the opening for Santa Barbara.

While Ronn was relieved to see that his cousins had arrived safely back on Earth, it did occur to him that it might have saved some trouble all around if he and Phaedra had been able to swap landing places. As it was, the *Moonbeamer* had been programmed only for California, and just barely made that.

A subsequent shot showed Phaedra standing in front of the *Mirage* with Danny to one side and looking a little lost, while Theo posed grinning with a pretty flight attendant. Even as grimly serious as the situation had been, he must have activated the Ashley-bot in the closet while Phaedra was too busy in the cockpit to stop him.

That was followed by the national news going back to the beach with more shots of the abandoned *Moonbeamer* enveloped in steam.

"The rocket-like object that came down on the West Coast has been identified as a second TranStella spacecraft, a replica of the *Moonbeamer* from the classic science-fiction vidshow, *Starbusters*. Though reported to have been piloted by Jefferson Prescott's fifteen-year-old nephew Ronn Evans, rescue workers found the cockpit empty. A search is now underway for the young man who is thought to have flown the ship all the way from Vesper."

Being talked about on the news was definitely a new experience for Ronn, and he found it more than a little disconcerting. He wondered if Travis back home was seeing all this.

The news cut to another breaking story, the disappearance of Vesper itself. Aunt Bonnie was shocked, since it had once been a major part of her life. After she waved the sound down, Ronn briefly explained and she shook her head.

"Jeff mentioned something like that as the Final Option if his enemies ever got too close, but he never said *where* Vesper would go. I was there several times, when it was still his great dream, and I remember all the plans and enthusiasm he had for it. Even after we went our separate ways, I always liked seeing Vesper in the night sky as a bright star reminding me of old dreams and memories. It's sad to think it's gone now.

"But," she went on, her tone turning more matter of fact, "things change, and then they change again. Now that you're here, we have to decide what to do next."

"I already talked to Mom so she knows I'm okay," Ronn replied, "but I guess I'd better call somebody so they can stop looking for me. There's a government official named Mr. Cosgrove I should probably get hold of, too, and let him know what happened, but I'd really like it if nobody else knows where I am just yet."

"Good idea," Aunt Bonnie said. "From the sound of it, you just made yourself famous, and you won't get any peace once the media catch up with you. As for who to call first, I'd suggest your Mr. Cosgrove. Him I know because he was here last week grilling me about everything I know about what's been happening at TranStella, not that anybody ever tells me anything anymore. Besides, I had a non-disclosure block put on me so I couldn't even tell him what I did know about Vesper."

"You seem to be doing fine with me," Ronn pointed out.

"The hypnotic block dissolves when there isn't any more need for it. Now I could probably sing like a canary if he came back. I have his contact number if you need it."

Ronn called the number, Mr. Cosgrove answered, and he explained what was going on.

"So you're at Bonnie MacMillan's house?" Mr. Cosgrove said briskly, skipping over the part about how happy he was that Ronn had made it back alive. "That saves us having to send a rescue mission. Stay where you are. I'll be there shortly. Meanwhile, I'll inform the Santa Barbara authorities of the situation. Since that's a gated community, that should make it easier to set up a perimeter and keep the media at bay if someone catches wind of your location."

With that arranged, Aunt Bonnie wanted to hear what had happened on Vesper. Ronn and the Bonnies then sat down in the living room and he launched into his story.

When he told his uncle's third wife about what the fourth had been up to, she reacted disgustedly to the mention of Vanessa.

"I knew she was rotten, but I didn't know she was *that* rotten! I thought what Jeff was doing on Vesper was magnificent, at least at the start. He had a way of drawing you into his enthusiasms that made you excited about them, too—"

"That's what I told Ronn!" Bonnie exclaimed. "In just about those same words, too."

"And why not?" Aunt Bonnie asked. "It's the same person talking about the same person! Vesper did get a little out of hand as one man's obsession, but it was his crowning achievement just the same, and for Vanessa to ruin it like that…" She shook her head.

The description of Uncle Jeff's present state of being left Aunt Bonnie looking both sad and thoughtful. "He hasn't been part of my life in years and we've both moved on, but I'm sorry to hear this. From what you say, I just don't know how he could come back from something like that, even if somebody can get to him."

Then Ronn came to how he found Bonnie.

"The recreation of our first date at the fair was my idea," Aunt Bonnie said. "Jeff had his moments of being distant and I thought working together on something that reminded us of a romantic moment could bring us closer. He had already made several bot copies of himself at various ages, so making one of me should have been cut and dried. The result, we thought, would be a very limited copy that wouldn't be self-aware. You probably saw bots on Vesper like that."

"Just about all of them," Ronn replied. "But one of the engineers told me the Jeffbots were different because they used some kind of purple fuzz for brains."

"Purple fuzz?" Aunt Bonnie echoed with a raised eyebrow. "Is that what they're calling it? The term we used at the plant was S2CS, for Self-Configuring Component Substance. The aliens used it in a lot of devices, which made them impossible to mass-produce because we'd been given only a limited amount and we couldn't make any more of it ourselves. We could analyze it and get some idea of what it was made of, but the internal programming that made it capable of reconfiguring itself to accomplish a given task was beyond us. In some ways it was like an artificial brain, and Jeff realized it could be used as one. We used most of the S2CS we had for bots based on him as well as the one based on me because he thought it might make the bots better at duplicating the behavior of specific people than the usual standard memory and behavior modules. We were at the extreme edge of something we didn't understand all that well, using equipment and materials we definitely didn't understand, originally designed for minds that weren't quite like ours. The idea was just to copy a few scraps of memory here and there so that there would be an essence of me, enabling it to talk and behave like me only as much as was necessary. Something like that was done with some of the bots you met, like Wilfred, who was based on a real butler, but only up to a point and with just the butler parts left in and exaggerated a bit."

"I kinda got that," Bonnie said. "I tried talking to him, but it was like butling was all he ever thought about. Except for his job, there just wasn't anything *there*."

Aunt Bonnie nodded. "Exactly. That was how it was supposed to work for me. They could even program the copying machine so it wouldn't register anything in my mind from after I was sixteen. Maybe I just stayed under the hood too long. Instead of taking a simple snapshot of me at sixteen, it must have copied *everything* in my head that I experienced before I turned seventeen.

"Not only that... there's a lot in your mind that's below the surface. All the deep structure in my subconscious must have been copied, too. I've heard human consciousness compared to a tiny, tightly focused spot of light on the surface of a deep, dark ocean. Down in the depths are memories, emotions, instincts, habits, learned responses, a whole lot of things that add up to making us human. We aren't just the sum of our memories.

"With me, we didn't intend it, we didn't even realize at the time that we had done it, but we must have made a complete copy of my mind. It was like a blueprint of the brain it had come from, which the S2CS seems to have reconfigured itself to match so my copy could have emotions. With the result we have here in my living room.

"This was never supposed to happen," Aunt Bonnie summed up. "We didn't even think it *could* happen. But somehow my memories and all the support structure integrated into a whole personality. Human consciousness is a very complex thing."

"So now what?" Ronn asked.

"This is getting way beyond anything I know much about," Aunt Bonnie replied, "and we'll have to be very careful about any decisions we make. I'm going to call my lawyer and get some advice about our rights and obligations."

She made the call and without saying what it was all about, asked the lawyer to come to her house at once.

While waiting for him, Aunt Bonnie took Ronn and Bonnie on a tour of the house. Bonnie was impressed that her older self would live in such a nice home. Then Aunt Bonnie gave Ronn a quick lunch, which he appreciated considering how long it had been since he'd had that ham sandwich and apple turnover for breakfast.

Bonnie sat at the table and watched him tear into some leftover cold chicken. "I remember eating…" she murmured ruefully.

Just as Ronn finished, the lawyer was at the door. Mr. Webber was a tall, thin man leaving middle age behind, and seemed mildly put out.

"We couldn't take care of this matter over the phone?" he asked Aunt Bonnie as everyone sat down in the living room.

"No, I think you had to see this for yourself. I'd like to introduce you to Bonnie."

"Hi!"

Still not sure where this was going, Mr. Webber scrutinized the girl. "There is definitely a strong family resemblance. Your niece, perhaps?"

"Why don't you talk to her yourself and find out?"

Still irritated by the interruption of his meticulously organized schedule for the day and even less pleased by having to play a game imposed on him by the whim of a client too rich to argue with, Mr. Webber asked Bonnie a few polite questions. Very quickly, the name, age, and birthdate she gave added up to a disturbing picture.

He turned to Aunt Bonnie in alarm. "You didn't *clone* yourself, did you? That's illegal, and I can't be a part of anything involving—"

Bonnie rolled her eyes. "Oh, enough with the drama already!" She stood up, lifted her blouse to expose her lower abdomen, and opened the access panel in her side.

Now Mr. Webber saw where this was going and his alarm turned to astonishment. "She's a *bot*? I've never seen one so… aware."

"Oh, I'm aware all right," Bonnie said. "I'm supposed to be a copy of the old lady here when she was sixteen."

"*Old lady*?" Aunt Bonnie exclaimed indignantly, then shook her head. "Now I'm suddenly feeling a lot of sympathy for my poor mother for having to put up with me…"

"Is Mom still around?" Bonnie suddenly asked.

"Sure. She isn't even eighty yet. She and Dad still live in our old house in Salisbury."

Bonnie simulated a sigh of relief. "I'm glad to hear it. I was getting worried that everybody I ever knew would be gone after all these years."

"I'm just wondering how I'm going to break *this* news to her…" Aunt Bonnie murmured.

Bonnie thought of something. "Say, if you're Bonnie MacMillan, is there a Mr. MacMillan somewhere?"

Aunt Bonnie paused as though trying to think of a delicate way to put it. "I'm afraid Mr. MacMillan is no longer with us."

"We just can't seem to hold on to husbands, can we?"

The lawyer sat there in wide-eyed amazement as he listened to the exchange between older and younger versions of the same person. "Would you mind explaining to me what's going on here?"

Aunt Bonnie gave the lawyer a quick summary of what had been happening, with Bonnie tossing in some smart remarks and Ronn adding background information as needed.

"So what is her status?" Aunt Bonnie asked. "Legally, I mean?"

Mr. Webber thought for a few moments. "I've heard of religious groups trying to baptize bots because they believe they might have souls. If they had met Bonnie here, they wouldn't have any doubts. A good case could be made for her being your daughter. She may have started out as a copy of you, but she seems to have acquired an independent existence. I'd say she's entitled to recognition as a legal person with civil rights. And you were married to Mr. Prescott at the time of her creation?"

"Yes."

"Did the two of you collaborate on Bonnie's creation? Was Mr. Prescott directly involved?"

"Certainly. It couldn't have been done without his active assistance."

"Then a case can also be made that he's legally her father, even if not biologically, since he was partly responsible for her coming into being. That would make her his daughter as well, his only child, and his heir. You've just opened Pandora's cargo container."

Bonnie saw the implications at once. "Ew! You just made the guy who would have been my boyfriend and husband into my father!"

"Only technically for paying the bills, dear," said Aunt Bonnie. "Besides, all that never happened for you."

"I've been wondering why Uncle Jeff never had any kids of his own," Ronn said. "It wasn't like he couldn't have afforded a few dozen."

"You'll have to ask his second wife about that," Aunt Bonnie replied. "She was married to him when he was still young enough to start a family."

"I remember her," Mr. Webber put in. "She had worked for TranStella's animation and cartoon division before they were married. After the divorce, she wasn't satisfied with the settlement, so she sued him claiming that she was the co-creator and designer of just about every character the company owned. She didn't have a leg to stand on, but the case could have dragged on in court for years. He ended up paying her a great deal of money to go away."

"I came later," Aunt Bonnie added, "a childhood sweetheart Jeff had never forgotten. We had known each other since we were teenagers, so he knew me well enough to have some confidence that I wouldn't turn on him the way someone he had met recently might — a lesson he forgot when that gold-digger from Marketing started batting her eyelashes at him. Also, I could be useful to him for his more personal projects like Vesper since I'd had an art and design career of my own. I was getting to the end of my childbearing years and already had two children from my first marriage, but we might have managed something."

Bonnie's eyes went wide. "We're a mommy now?"

"Well, I am. A granny, too. Anyway, Jeff always seemed too busy with his work and projects to give having a family much thought. And as you saw on Vesper, he seemed to be working out a few issues left over from his *own* childhood. At the same time, we weren't trying *not* to have any children... After a while, we realized something might be wrong. We had tests done, and it turned out that there wasn't anything wrong with me. Jeff, though... he'd spent all that time in space with the aliens and hadn't even considered the risks of exposure to radiation. Bottom line, he was sterile. There might be ways to repair the damage now, but we were just at the beginning of that kind of thing then. We even thought about cloning Jeff and mixing my DNA with his, but human cloning was illegal and too many people would have had to be in on it to do it anyway. So we let things rest where they were. The marriage ran into trouble later for other reasons, and we never pursued the idea of having a baby any further."

Cloning? Ronn had a sudden thought. "Could we give Bonnie a human body if we can somehow get around the legal problems?" he asked the lawyer. "Clone Aunt Bonnie, say, to give her a body identical to the one she used to have, and accelerate the growth? I know Uncle Jeff was doing it with extinct prehistoric animals. Then Bonnie's mind could be transferred to the clone's brain, maybe..."

Bonnie lit up. "You mean that's possible? I was starting to get used to this robot thing, but being human sounds wonderful!" Then she glanced at Aunt Bonnie. "Except then I'll get old and stuff..."

Her older self frowned. "If you weren't me, I'd slap you harder than Vanessa did. I may just yet... If it could be done, a human body might be better in the long run than your bot body. You've got parts that will wear out, after all. Some can be replaced, but we don't know how long that alien fuzz stuffing your head is good for and it's irreplaceable. And the way things are going with medical science, perpetual youth might be possible by the time you're my age."

"Great!" Bonnie exclaimed. "Sign me up for a body!"

"Not so fast," the lawyer broke in, shaking his head. "I don't know much about the technical possibilities, but I do know that human cloning is illegal due to the ethical problems that have arisen over the years. I'm sorry."

Bonnie's face fell. "I should have known it was too good to be true…"

"There are foreign labs that will do human cloning," Aunt Bonnie said, "though I've heard the quality control is poor and there have been some horrible results. They also don't have the alien equipment TranStella does to do the mind transfer, or the accelerated growth. I don't think you'd want to wait sixteen years for your new body to catch up with your mind. Maybe the scientists up at TranStella can figure something out if cloning people is ever legalized."

"If there was ever a case when it should be," Mr. Webber said, "this is it."

Aunt Bonnie started to say something, but broke off. She touched her ear and said, "This is Bonnie MacMillan," then grimaced as she heard who was calling. "Yes, he's here. Come on in." She tapped her ear again and glanced at Ronn. "That was your good friend and mine, Mr. Cosgrove. He's at the front gate."

Barely a couple of minutes later, Mr. Cosgrove breezed into the house with a pair of black-suited and visored security agents in his wake.

"You sure didn't take long to get here," Ronn said in some exasperated amazement.

"I was already on my way to Santa Barbara when you called," Mr. Cosgrove replied. "Landing a space ship on the beach here gave me a clue as to where I might find you."

He didn't waste any more time on pleasantries. He wanted Ronn to spill everything he knew right now, and set him up in the living room with one of the bodyguards recording him. Aunt Bonnie insisted on the lawyer being present to make sure all the legal niceties were observed, and Mr. Cosgrove had no objection to him or even the Bonnies listening to the debriefing.

"Secrecy will be a moot point anyway," he said. "To begin with, Ronn, we intercepted your radio transmissions earlier, and we know from a voice ID that you were in some sort of conflict with a wanted terrorist known to intelligence services around the world as Commandant Rafale. Believe me, we never anticipated that matters would escalate to that level, and allow me to apologize for involving you and your cousins."

A little late…

"Not only that," Mr. Cosgrove continued, "Vesper itself seems to have vanished entirely. While it no longer presents a danger to Earth, which is a relief, the disappearance of an object of that size would seem to require some explanation. Can you give me your high-level takeaway on what happened up there?"

So Ronn told him. He had hardly begun when the first revelation hit Mr. Cosgrove like a thunderbolt.

"*Lowther* was in on this? We never suspected!"

Aunt Thalia did...

Mr. Cosgrove went to his phone, ordering some minion or other to have Mrs. Lowther brought in for additional questioning.

There's somebody who's in for some bad news... If she really had put her husband "up to it," it had backfired horribly on her.

Then Ronn was allowed to go on with his story, winding up with why Vesper had disappeared and how there had never been any serious danger of it crashing into the Earth after all.

"You've had quite an adventure, young man," Mr. Cosgrove said, glancing at the time display in his opticom. "We have to get you to Washington right away so you can tell this to the FBI, the CIA, the FTC, the SEC—"

All of a sudden, everything from the past few days hit Ronn hard. "I don't care about all that!" he exclaimed. "I just want to go *home!*"

Sleep in his own bed, in his own room, wake up without having to be somewhere or do something for somebody...

Mr. Cosgrove looked a little startled, even annoyed, but didn't argue. "We can always vidconference, I suppose. If this reaches the point of Congressional hearings, though, we will want you there in person. Very well, you are free to go for the time being. I have to fly back to Los Angeles so I can debrief your cousins when they arrive, and we can take you with us down to LAX and put you on a commercial flight. Give me a few minutes—"

Bonnie had a sudden woebegone look of *What about me?* Aunt Bonnie motioned for her and Ronn to follow her into the kitchen. Meanwhile, it sounded as though Mr. Cosgrove was calling the first on his list of important people who needed to know right away, to pass on what Ronn had told him. At least Ronn overheard him say, "That's correct, Madam President."

"What were you planning on doing with Bonnie?" Aunt Bonnie asked Ronn as she shut the kitchen door behind her.

He shrugged. "Take her home with me, I guess. She did ask me if I'd like a new sister, and Mom shouldn't mind too much—"

Aunt Bonnie shook her head. "That may not be a good idea."

"Why not?" Bonnie demanded, definitely not liking the possible change of plans.

"Hold your horses and listen to me." Aunt Bonnie turned to Ronn. "Bonnie is basically a machine and she will need occasional maintenance. She should be checked out over at TranStella and maybe recharged fairly soon. She won't be able to get that in downstate Illinois."

"I guess a really long extension cord won't help?" Bonnie asked.

Aunt Bonnie ignored the remark. "There also may be questions about whether TranStella legally owns her and what her rights are, and it might wind up in court. I have the money to fight that battle, and your parents don't even if they wanted to."

"So you think Bonnie should stay with you?" Ronn summed up.

"Like she said," Aunt Bonnie replied with a smile, "I made her, so I'm practically her mother. Who better?"

"I'm still not calling you Mom," Bonnie said.

So it was decided. While Bonnie had been set on going home with Ronn, she reluctantly agreed that it would be best after all to stay with her older self. After giving it some further thought, Ronn realized his mother would not be entirely pleased if he showed up at home with a robot girl-friend. Mrs. Evans would fight tooth and claw for her own family, but to take on possibly expensive obligations for a complete stranger with dubious legal status... Bonnie would probably end up back on Aunt Bonnie's front porch and peeling off the address label and postage chip as she rang the bell.

"I'd better go see if our friends out front are ready to leave yet," Aunt Bonnie then said, and stepped out of the kitchen. Since she was basically the same person as Bonnie, she may have known what would happen next and had the compassion and discretion to remove herself from the scene so it could happen.

Bonnie threw her arms around Ronn and pressed her lips against his. It was his first kiss, and he was too astonished to react for a moment. Then he realized something wasn't quite right. Her lips felt warm but that was all.

"Uhm..." she said, able to talk even with her mouth otherwise occupied, "you might have to work with me on this. I don't have any power in my pucker."

Right... since she didn't breathe, she couldn't produce any suction. So he kissed her, and did the work for both of them.

"I'll miss you," she said when they came apart.

He'd miss her, too, but it wasn't like they'd never see each other again or lose all contact. Not in this century. "I'll still be as close as a vidcall," he assured her.

"That's not exactly close."

"You don't know modern tech yet. They could advertise, 'just like being there but without the body odor.' They'd be working on that, too, if there was a demand for it."

"I don't have a sense of smell, so you can be as stinky as you like."

"All right, you two," said Aunt Bonnie from the doorway. "That has to be the worst exchange of endearments I've ever accidentally overheard without meaning to. Your ride is about to pull out, Ronn, so exchange addresses and com numbers and come on back into the living room."

There was another parting at the front door. As Aunt Bonnie hugged Ronn, she bent her head to his ear and murmured:

"Bonnie has a heart even if it doesn't show in her blueprints. Please be careful with it."

Startled by how suddenly *serious* she sounded, all Ronn could think to mumble back was, "Er...okay, I will."

Bonnie could hug if nothing else, and may have left a few bruises. Ronn promised to call, then Mr. Cosgrove, who seemed to have less sympathy than ever for sentimental scenes of farewell, all but dragged him to the rental car in the driveway. Ronn's last glimpse of Bonnie was out the back window, as she stood waving.

Epilogue

Late That Summer

After Grandma Prescott died, no one expected another family reunion. The sisters were too scattered and too much at odds with each other for any one of them to replace Grandma as the central rallying point.

Who knew the family had one last reunion to go — and that it would be held in the White House Rose Garden?

Officially, it was an awards ceremony for Ronn and Phaedra, unofficially (as Ronn's mother cynically thought) perhaps an attempt to make up for the poor political impression left by sending kids into space on a dangerous mission. As Ronn looked around that hot, sultry August afternoon, he saw his entire extended family milling around and chatting before sitting down in the rows of folding chairs that had been set up on the patch of lawn. The seats faced the West Wing and the Oval Office, while to the right was the roofed walkway known as the West Colonnade.

Aunt Emily was there in a sleeveless outfit that was about as formal as she ever got, not caring who saw all the tattoos on her arms, and with her were Danny and his sister Julia. Aunt Thalia stood somewhat aloof next to Phaedra and Theo, trying her best to ignore Ronn's mother along with his father and younger brother and sister. After the temporary truce and even though Ronn had saved Phaedra and Theo's lives, and now that there was nothing actually important to worry about, the family feud seemed to be on again. Even Aunt Bonnie was on hand, part of the Prescott clan once more. With her were her two grown children and a couple of small grandchildren. It would have been interesting to be a fly on the wall when they were told about Bonnie. Captains Rogowski and Saha, were also in the crowd as guests. Mr. Cosgrove floated between people like a bee from flower to flower, shaking hands and making small talk, and looking rather hot in that suit.

Naturally, Bonnie was there, too, the first time Ronn had seen her in the flesh, if that was the word, since the last Congressional hearing. At first, he had kept in touch with her with almost nightly vidcalls. He had been her go-to source for answers to questions about the strange new world she was now living in, but before long she was busy, too. As the first bot known to have become aware, Bonnie had been a media sensation in her own right as well as a subject of scientific study. She was soon tired of the notoriety, and at last report Aunt Bonnie was trying to put a limit on some of the more excessive demands for interviews and media appearances.

Bonnie was dressed for the occasion. Instead of the shorts and blouse she had lived in back on Vesper, she wore a slacks, jacket, and high-collared vest combo with a stylish beret. On anyone else, it would have looked overly warm for such a hot day, but she could have worn a fur coat in the Sahara without overheating her circuits. She also carried a ventriloquist's dummy on one arm, a caricature of a bratty little girl in the Sunday best of circa 1900. It was as though a Victorian Age collector doll had come to life with an attitude.

"Who's your friend?" Ronn had to ask after a bone-crunching hug with her free arm. Since they hadn't had a chance to do much vidchatting lately, the dummy was something new.

"Ronn, meet Emmeline," Bonnie said. "Say hello to Ronn, Emmeline!'"

"Hello to Ronn, Emmeline!" said the dummy in a squeaky cartoon voice completely different from Bonnie's own. It moved its mouth but Bonnie didn't move hers. For a moment, the impression that the dummy might be doing its own talking was completely convincing.

"It was Phaedra's idea, actually," Bonnie explained. "Since I'm pretty famous now, I've been getting requests for personal appearances at places like hospitals and summer schools and camps where there are a lot of kids. So what am I supposed to do? Come out on stage and just have people look at me? If I really want to give 'em a thrill, open up my access hatch? Which sounds kinda gross, actually. So we came up with a little act I can do, and the kids love it. Especially since I'm a doll making a doll talk."

"Oh, the irony...!" said Emmeline.

"There was one little girl I met in a hospital," Bonnie went on, seemingly trying to ignore the smart-aleck doll she was holding. "She'd lost her arm in an accident, so she was being fitted with a prosthetic arm that she could use until her new arm grows out. She was kind of depressed about the whole thing, even though she'd have a whole new arm in a year or so. Back in my day, that arm would have been *gone*. So I told her, 'Hey, look on the bright side! So you've got a prosthetic arm — I'm *all* prosthetic!'"

"Did that cheer her up?" Ronn asked.

Bonnie shrugged. "Well, at least she laughed. That was the main thing. It depressed *me* a little when I thought about it, though."

"So how are you holding up?"

"Pretty well. I got checked out at the robot factory, power cells recharged and stuff like that. Then they asked me how my body was working out for me and what I thought could be improved, and gave me a questionnaire. They said it was probably the first product evaluation form ever filled out by the product itself."

"Sounds like fun."

"It was until somebody started asking who exactly *owns* me and am I some piece of TranStella property that somehow wandered off on its own. I think some of the engineers really *would* have liked to take me apart to see what changes the purple fuzz has been making to the original design. Aunt Bonnie got me out of there quick when the conversation started heading in that direction, but she says there may be a custody battle unless somebody does something."

"Like what?"

She smiled. "You'll see. It's partly why I'm here."

Mysterious, isn't she? But besides that...

"*Aunt* Bonnie?"

"I have to call her *something*. I still think of my mother in Salisbury as Mom, we have the same first names, Bonnie-*senpai* sounded a little odd, and Bonnie Senior would make me Bonnie Junior and I didn't much like that."

Phaedra joined them at that point. "This circus doesn't stop, does it?" she said, looking around at the crowd. "I almost wish I was back on Vesper, with nothing to do all day but lie around the house and read or watch vids. But leave it to Mom to figure out an angle after all the publicity..."

Ronn nodded, trying to think. "Oh, right. I saw a clip on the news about you being signed for a vid series... what was it? *Honey* something?"

"*Honey Hughes*."

Now he remembered. She had been cast as the lead in a period piece set a century before in 1938 and featuring the adventures of Howard Hughes' teenage niece as a daredevil racing pilot and amateur detective getting into adventurous scrapes. The fact that Phaedra really was a billionaire's niece and she really had flown an aircraft of some sort in a real-life perilous situation made her a natural for the part. The fact that the real Howard Hughes had been an only child and so couldn't have had a niece... well, after a hundred years, who would look into it that closely?

"I'm going to be in it, too!" Bonnie added.

"She'll be my stunt double for some scenes," Phaedra explained. "The writers pitched a couple of plots to make use of her special talents, like hunting for sunken treasure and a hydroplane crash. Shooting underwater's a lot easier when the actor doesn't have to come up for air."

"Are you Bonnie's agent?" Ronn asked. "I remember you saying you'd rather do what your Mom does than act yourself..."

"Well," Phaedra replied, "as far as *Honey Hughes* goes, Mom finally came up with something I can have fun with, so I don't mind. It's like everything changed at home after Vesper and I have a lot more say about my career now. As for being Bonnie's agent, it's still Mom's agency and I'm not old enough to sign things yet, but if I come up with something, she'll at least listen and maybe let me go ahead. I tried getting Bonnie and Emmeline into one of the comedy clubs in L.A., but we ran into problems like how old is she really and is she of legal drinking age. It's all ridiculous since she *can't* drink, but they said they had to obey the law."

"And after all that," Bonnie said mournfully, "the Brew Haha finally let me try out, and they bounced me anyway. I'd just be a novelty act good for about the first two minutes, they said, and after that my jokes are too clean or too old-fashioned or something for their audience. Guess I'll have to stick with wowing kids in hospitals."

"Yeah," piped up Emmeline, "where the audience can't get up and leave!"

"Stop that, Emmeline!"

Mr. Cosgrove came by just then, and Phaedra buttonholed him to complain about something involving her hotel accommodations. They moved some distance away and as soon as Phaedra was out of earshot, Bonnie turned to Ronn.

"She's been coming up with all kinds of ideas for how to take advantage of my fame as a living doll," she said in a low voice. "The latest was a product endorsement for the WD-40 people. Sometimes she's so pushy I almost think I liked it better when she hated me. I guess she learned all the wrong lessons from having a stage mother."

"Which were...?" Ronn prompted.

"How to *be* one," squeaked Emmeline.

Vid crews had set up just beyond a barrier, under a flock of hovering dronecams, and Ronn wondered if Travis would see a clip of the ceremony on the news. Not that it probably mattered now...

He had seen Travis just once after getting back. It was clear that the guy he had considered his best friend was reluctant to talk and dodging his calls, but they finally agreed to meet in a diner to chat over cheeseburgers and fries.

As far as Ronn was concerned, nothing should have changed between him and Travis. He was the same Ronn Evans, he would have thought, even after a few days in space, but Travis couldn't get past his being an heir to the Prescott fortune, assuming Uncle Jeff ever reached a state legally recognized as death. Then it finally came out:

"I'm just a kid in high school in some dink small town, and you're... you're *famous!*"

Ronn assured him that it was more luck than anything he'd actually done, and he wanted to be just good old Ronn and Travis again, Friday night vid parties with pizza and Coke, but he could see that it could never again be like it used to be. They shook hands and mumbled something about getting together again sometime, though it would probably never happen.

He'd had some other friends, if not as close as Travis had been, and they seemed even more daunted by a few billion dollars that he was still a long way from collecting. And it wasn't like he hadn't had to work for his inheritance...

On the other hand, he could have made some new friends. He was getting calls from girls who had never paid any attention to him before. If they had shown that kind of interest a few months earlier, he would have been delighted, but he had a feeling that being famous and a billionaire's nephew had more to do with it than his wit and charm. It was a busy summer and he let his sudden bevy of admirers slide. Besides, he would be going to a private school somewhere out East that fall, and any friends and acquaintances he made in Maple Heights would just fall by the wayside before very long.

His social life was mainly confined to vidchats with Bonnie and sometimes Theo and Danny. The last two had their limits, since Theo complained a lot about being his mother's new hobby now that Phaedra was becoming more independent, and Danny had his own resentments about Ronn and Phaedra getting all the attention even after what he had been through. But they were family and had been on Vesper with him, so they *understood* what no one else did, and he put up with them.

After all that he had been through, Ronn had been looking forward to some quiet time at home just to relax and decompress, despite the occasional bad dream where Vanessa was dragging him by the arm through a maze of metal-walled corridors, or Rafale was about to shoot him. He had hardly stepped in the door at home for a warm welcome from his relieved parents and little brother and sister, however, when Mr. Cosgrove called him and his cousins to Washington for endless rounds of debriefings, hearings, and conferences with various officials and office-holders about what had happened on Vesper. Sometimes he thought he'd rather be back there.

There wasn't a prayer of keeping anything secret, and the Vesper affair was the summer's big media story. With so much public interest, Uncle

Jeff could have sold a lot of tickets to people wanting to see Vesper — if they had been able to get there, and if anyone knew where it was now. Ronn had to deal with the consequences of suddenly being famous as the boy pilot who brought the *Moonbeamer* home and defeated a world-class terrorist on the way, and he was in demand for his own rounds of interviews and media appearances. Having to spend so much time in Washington shielded him from the worst of it, but living a normal life at home was impossible for a while when he couldn't even go downtown without people staring and pointing at him or being cornered by reporters and followed by paparazzi. He was startled the first time he saw a dronecam outside his bedroom window, and his father had to get a court injunction to keep the media at a distance. Ronn was mainly relieved when the attention finally began to let up.

A rather testy message came from Ms. Crowley about ignoring her assignments, but by that time it was too late to finish out the spring term anyway and he ignored it. His classes had marched on without him and he'd have to catch up in summer school. Ms. Crowley was not heard from again, probably writing him off as a hopelessly lazy lout destined for a bad end...

After Mr. Cosgrove had talked Phaedra into being less unhappy, he came by and shook Ronn's hand.

"How are things coming along with the stuff that was in the briefcase?" Ronn asked. "I haven't heard a word about it since it was turned over to your people."

Mr. Cosgrove smiled mysteriously. "All I can tell you is that it's now out of my hands, but the last I heard, it was still being sorted out. I'm sure the contents will be made public at the proper time, of course."

Whenever that is...

Then it was time to sit down. Everyone took their seats in front of the lectern with the Presidential Seal on it, which had been placed on the steps leading up to the West Wing doors. Ronn was ushered to a seat in the front row with Phaedra on one side of him and Bonnie on the other. Several rows behind them, some projections suddenly flared up, and Captain Ramirez as well as Dr. Kininger and the rest of the science crew that had been on Vesper appeared, although they were physically in different places around the country.

A recording of "Hail to the Chief" played from somewhere and everyone stood up again as President Sylvia Mao came out of the White House. She was a small figure almost lost next to the beefy dark-suited and visored Secret Service agents on either side of her. At one time, when China was led by a dictator named Chairman Mao and tensions with the United States

274

were high, it might have astonished people to hear that America itself would someday have a President named Mao — but memories fade over the decades and historical ironies are lost on later generations. When she had taken her place at the lectern, everyone sat back down and settled in for some indefinite period of prepared remarks to solemnize the occasion.

Ronn half-dozed in the warm sunlight. His mind drifted amid all the high-flown flattery about these fine young people who had answered when their country called (*Dragged kicking and screaming is more like it...*), and he thought back to what had brought him here today, and to some of the loose ends that were still dangling...

One was the final fate of the *Spectre*. The scientists were saying that the super-bright flash of the *Moonbeamer*'s torch shouldn't have caused much or any damage to the *Spectre*, and the automatically darkened windshield would have protected Rafale and anyone else in the cockpit from the worst of the glare. Apparently, though, Rafale had fired the plasma cannon just as the *Moonbeamer* dropped down in front of him. How the torch worked to propel a ship was a mystery, but the glowing field had to be some kind of repulsive force. The plasma burst had struck it directly and was reflected back, and the *Spectre* had been enveloped in a plasma cloud that must have wreaked havoc with the ship's electronics. What Ronn had only hoped would distract Rafale had been far more effective than anything he could have deliberately planned.

No one was certain whether some hardened automatic pilot had taken over or if Rafale had been able to regain control of the crippled shuttle despite the damage done to it, but it came down in a rough but survivable landing somewhere in western Asia. No sign of Rafale, Enzo, or any other occupants was found, dead or alive, and it was thought they had jumped out and taken off running just as soon as the ship stopped rolling. A local military commander was claiming the wreck as salvage and offering to sell it to the highest bidder. The next question was whether the new owners could get anything useful out of the alien systems on board, like the artificial gravity and the propulsion unit, or if they would just blow up half a city when they breached the power core.

Ronn wondered a little worriedly if Rafale was the type to hold grudges, but someone on the run on the other side of the planet probably had more things on his mind than petty revenge.

Phaedra's colorfully expressed defiance of Rafale's orders to change her course to land at some out of the way airport in eastern Europe had been overheard on the ground, and it had given her some considerable fame as a gutsy heroine who wouldn't let even an international terrorist for hire bully her. Aunt Thalia had been worried at first that the not very ladylike language might be bad for her image, but if anything it had enhanced it.

Phaedra did admit privately to Ronn later that if she'd been thinking straight at the time, she would have realized that Rafale had her right in the crosshairs and she couldn't dodge, and maybe she should have followed his orders. But — "He just made me mad," and so she made her own bit of history. Ronn wondered if she even could have landed where Rafale wanted her to anyway, since she would have had to override the *Mirage*'s preset landing procedures for just a few designated airports, but fortunately they hadn't had to find out.

Meanwhile, Vanessa's escape pod had turned up in South America. Although it was supposed to go to Santa Barbara, either it had malfunctioned or she had found a way en route to divert it to some remote valley in the Peruvian Andes. By the time it was found, it was long empty and Vanessa had disappeared. Maybe she'd had the foresight to arrange beforehand for a secret bank account and a place to hide just in case things went bad, and she was even now sitting on some tropical island she didn't own and glumly nipping at her drink on the veranda of a hotel she didn't own, either... well, in any case, *Good riddance*, Ronn thought.

The TranStella employees who had been held hostage on Vesper and then confined in an undisclosed location on Earth were released not too much the worse for wear. If some rumors were to be believed, that had been the result of behind the scenes negotiations with a certain unfriendly foreign government suspected of being Lowther and Vanessa's secret backer, with threats of military action that could easily topple an already shaky ruling party. Less definite rumors asserted that a substantial ransom was finally paid just to get the people back and put an end to the dispute. Cargo ship 02 was also returned in the same deal, since it wasn't of any use without access to TranStella's recharging facilities.

The freighter with the mercenaries, the TranStella engineers, and a cargo of looted alien tech landed at some secret base in the Balkans, the only part of the operation that had been remotely successful. Bots resembling Hollywood celebrities soon appeared in odd places, like a carnival in Singapore that had several and a seedy waterfront wax museum in Australia that had a few more, so some of the loot had been fenced, though evidently at desperately low prices to get rid of it. Almost all of the outright alien tech was incomprehensible, and difficult to sell on the open market. The low-level mercenaries had little or no idea of what they even had, and were unable to profit very much, or at least not as much as they had hoped. An American special ops team was sent to recover the abandoned freighter and fly it back to California, but the engineers were still missing. Ronn hoped Justin and Kiefer were alive and safe somewhere, since they had been decent sorts.

TranStella itself was in chaos with several high-level executives facing indictments. Meanwhile Jefferson C. Prescott's current state of limbo, not exactly dead but certainly sidelined, further confused the issue of who was running the company. An interim board of directors had elected a provisional CEO, but this kind of turmoil in a company that directly or indirectly controlled a huge portion of the world economy was not good for the markets. Stocks plunged and there were calls to break up TranStella if not nationalize it outright.

The *Moonbeamer* was transported to TranStella's headquarters. After an examination, it was determined that it would never fly again. It had burned itself out and could not be recharged. That didn't mean there was no longer any use for it or that no one wanted it.

In the final episode of the *Starbusters* series, the decommissioned fictional *Moonbeamer* spent its last days as a rusting backwoods tourist attraction for gum-chewing yokels to gawk at until it was finally cut up for scrap, and its cockpit section found its final resting place as a chicken coop on some farm. In the real world, the *Moonbeamer* would stand for centuries to come in the Smithsonian. It was a vidshow icon that had actually flown in space and, some historians were saying, had fought and won the first single ship action in the history of human spaceflight. What had been intended to mock and sneer had found glory.

As for Vesper, it had vanished completely. Space is a big place, and no one knew where to even start looking for a single tiny asteroid. With its disappearance, the Earth was back to having just one moon, no doubt irking the people who had to update the reference works yet again...

Phaedra had to nudge Ronn awake. "Hey!" she whispered. "It's our cue!"

With a start, he realized that the President had finished speaking and she was looking straight at him and smiling expectantly. Meanwhile, Captains Rogowski and Saha were coming up the aisle.

Ronn and Phaedra were then presented with honorary civilian astronauts' wings. That was something Ronn could appreciate even if flying the *Moonbeamer* had been so easy with the help of the onboard AI that he wasn't convinced he had really earned the award.

Captain Rogowski, looking uncomfortable in a blue dress uniform even with the usual shades, did the honors of pinning the wings to Ronn's chest.

"You did good, kid, even if that landing was a little rough," he said in a low voice, "but I gotta tell you, if you ever want a job as a pilot, you're *still* gonna have to go through training at the Academy. Rules are rules, you know."

After Captain Saha had pinned Phaedra's wings and everybody had taken their seats again, the President gave Theo and Danny some appreciation, though Danny later griped that it was just an award for participation instead of a cool medal. Then she continued:

"Because there has been some doubt about the legal status of Bonnie Prescott and even a threat of 'repossession' by certain parties although she has demonstrated in every possible way that she is not a mere thing, I have resolved to remove all doubt and declare her a person with full civil rights that may not be violated." When the clapping died down, the President added, "Bonnie, would you come up here, please?"

As Bonnie stood up, she reached past Ronn and shoved Emmeline into the startled Phaedra's lap. "Hold her for a moment—"

"Impulsive girl, isn't she?" Ronn remarked to Phaedra after Bonnie had squeezed by them to reach the aisle.

"You don't know the half of it," said Emmeline.

For a moment, Ronn had the alarming thought that the doll really could talk on its own, but no, he had seen Phaedra's lips move slightly.

Bonnie went up to the lectern, where she took the oath of allegiance. Then she was sworn in as an American citizen by no less than the President herself. Since Bonnie was legally both a continuation of Aunt Bonnie and the daughter of natural-born American citizens, the ceremony was probably unnecessary even if there was some technicality about whether she had been "born" on foreign soil by becoming aware on Vesper. Still, it did make it harder for some bean counter at TranStella to reclaim her as lost property.

Afterwards, the President had Ronn and Phaedra brought into the Oval Office for a private talk. She took her seat behind the desk and the cousins sat down on chairs in front of it. Having a personal conversation with the President would have been pretty colossal not too many months before, but after everything that had happened, it was just one more thing for Ronn to take in stride.

"This country owes you an immense debt of gratitude that it can never fully repay," the President began, glancing at some of the news and information displays floating around the desk to make sure no breaking crises required her attention at the moment. "Just that briefcase you brought back contains scientific riches beyond imagining, if some of the things I've been hearing are correct. Asking you to do what you did at such personal risk was an enormous imposition, of course, but you came through magnificently. Sometimes we underestimate what the young people of this nation are capable of accomplishing when put to the test. If there are any small services or favors you might like as a token of our grateful appreciation, we can certainly consider them."

"You could mention in your State of the Union speech how much you like my new show," Phaedra suggested.

The President frowned. "Don't push it."

"Kidding!" Phaedra said quickly, though Ronn wasn't convinced she had been. "I'm pretty well set, actually, and don't really need anything."

The President looked at Ronn. "What about you?"

It was almost unsettlingly quiet in the national nerve center as he tried to think of something.

Then he remembered what Bonnie had said earlier about feeling a little depressed when she realized she was "*all* prosthetic." Being a robot hadn't bothered her before and she had been able to laugh it off with jokes like getting a job as a crash dummy, but perhaps as she became more human, deeper feelings were coming to the surface. And for this one moment, he had the attention of someone who could do something about it...

"I was told there's a law against cloning people," he said.

The President nodded. "Yes, I believe that is the case."

"So I'm wondering if you could have an exception made," Ronn went on. "Bonnie was really helpful and we couldn't have done it without her. She's practically human already, but I don't think it's enough. Uncle Jeff's people have the facilities to clone the real Bonnie MacMillan and put Bonnie's mind into the new body, and I think she deserves it."

Out the corner of his eye, Ronn saw a surprised look on Phaedra's face, followed by a knowing grin. Well, yeah. Bonnie was a friend, and perhaps more than a friend. Making her human would be a way to find out how much more. But he was fifteen and she was nominally sixteen, and they had years yet to see how things worked out.

The President smiled. "I understand. I'm not a dictator and I'm just as much subject to the rule of law as anyone else, but I'll have it looked into."

"Don't do it *too* soon," Phaedra spoke up. "I'll need her as a bot for a while for my show." Again Ronn wasn't sure if she was joking or not.

The President's smile turned a little crooked, then she looked back at Ronn. "But isn't there anything you might want for yourself?"

"Well, there's one little favor I'd like..."

"Yes?"

"How about no homework for the rest of my time in school?"

The President shook her head. "My powers may be considerable, but that's one thing I can't do for you. Homework is somewhere right up there with death and taxes."

It had been worth a shot, but Ronn had expected about as much and wasn't terribly disappointed.

279

Along about September, a faint audio transmission was picked up by sensitive receivers on Earth, a snatch of music and a few scraps of a chorus singing "Dagnab it!" Somebody somewhere out in space was broadcasting MacNabbit the Rabbit cartoons. The source was quickly traced to the asteroid belt, and from there to the neighborhood of Ceres, the largest asteroid. All indications were that Vesper was now in orbit around Ceres, in effect a tiny Cererian moon. There was no response to radioed inquiries, and the assumption was that the MacNabbit broadcasts were simply the accidental result of some system going haywire in the midst of Vesper's overall breakdown. Some TranStella people familiar with Vesper thought it might actually be a sign of just the opposite — that the Park's diagnostic and self-repair systems had come back online, and with the invaders and destroyers gone, Vesper was instead in the process of healing.

No one would be going back to Vesper any time soon to find out, and whose moon it now was didn't matter. Ceres lay far beyond Mars, and even when it was favorably situated relative to Earth, a journey would take the better part of a year each way in one of the TranStella ships. It might have been possible to fit out the hold of the freighter for more comfortable crew quarters for such a mission, but at the moment there wasn't any very urgent reason to do it.

It was enough to know that some vast distance out in the cold and dark of space, far beyond human reach, there was a little oasis of warmth and light where MacNabbit the Rabbit would always be hoeing his carrot garden.

Also Available

Novels & Short Stories
by Dwight R. Decker

Pleistocene Junior High
An entire middle school full of kids winds up 30,000 years in the past, but nothing in the wilds of prehistoric Ohio threatens the students and teachers more than themselves. Meanwhile, one boy holds the key to their return in the palm of his hand. Literally.

The Napoleon of Time
In a near-infinity of alternate worlds, two college instructors from different centuries find each other in 1912 Poughkeepsie — and in her rush to join him, she *would* have to book passage on the most famous doomed ship of all time.
Coming soon.

Dancing with the Squirrels: Tales from Comics Fandom and Beyond
New and old stories featuring the misadventures of comic-book fans. In the title story, destiny strikes like lightning at a comics convention — but its aim is a little off. In the other tales, teenage comics fans hunt for rare and valuable old comic books in unlikely places while trying to live down the damage done to their reputations by the *Batman* TV show, the mystery of the most unreadable fantasy novel ever written is solved, and a comics fan visiting California finds himself entangled in Hollywood history gone wrong.

The fictional locales range from a small town in Illinois to Los Angeles and even England, but the strangest story of all is set in Cincinnati… and happens to be perfectly true! (And led directly to the publication of *The Crackpot* — see next page.)

Collections & Translations
Edited by DRD

The Crackpot and other twisted tales of greedy fans and collectors
by John E. Stockman

Between 1962 and 1979, the reclusive Mr. Stockman wrote some of the wackiest stories ever, recounting the strange antics of deranged comic-book collectors and obsessed fans of the author Edgar Rice Burroughs.

Eight of his best stories have been rescued from the crumbling mimeographed pages of the legendary (and only too aptly named) fanzine *Tales of Torment,* including many of Stockman's own illustrations. With historical notes and commentary, published by Ramble House.

Flying Fish "Prometheus"
by Vilhelm Bergsøe

Jules Verne-style science fiction first published in Denmark in 1870 and now translated into English. A journey from Denmark to Central America by airship in the far future year of 1969 goes terribly wrong. With translation notes, maps, vintage illustration, and historical background.

The Speedy Journey
by Eberhard Christian Kindermann

Published in German in 1744 and never before translated, the first fictional account of a trip to Mars (or at least somewhere close by). Historical and literary detective work puts together a background story that has mostly been missed until now. With notes, new and vintage illustrations, and historical essays.

Available from the usual on-line sources. For the thrifty fan reluctant to pay for ink, glue, and paper, several of the books can be had in the form of their pure spiritual essence as Kindle e-book editions. Check book listings for availability.

About the Author

Dwight R. Decker was born in Ohio and is currently hiding out somewhere in the Chicago area until the heat is off. A longtime science-fiction and comics fan, he worked as a technical writer in the telecommunications field with a sideline translating several languages, and now devotes full time to fiction. *A Moon of Their Own* is his second novel, combining childhood obsessions with adult enthusiasms.

CPSIA information can be obtained
at www.ICGtesting.com
Printed in the USA
FSHW011346190719
60194FS